The Polarian-Denebian War
War
(Volume 2)

The Polarian-Denebian War

(Volume 2)

Space Commandos
Our Ancestors from the Future
Prisoners of the Past

by
Jimmy Guieu

translated by
Michael Shreve

A Black Coat Press Book

Visit our website at www.blackcoatpress.com

ISBN 978-1-61227-555-0. First Printing. September 2016. Published by Black Coat Press, an imprint of Hollywood Comics.com, LLC, P.O. Box 17270, Encino, CA 91416. All rights reserved. Except for review purposes, no part of this book may be reproduced or transmitted in any form or by any means, electronic or mechanical, including photocopying, recording, or by any information storage and retrieval system, without permission in writing from the publisher. The stories and characters depicted in this novel are entirely fictional. Printed in the United States of America.

TABLE OF CONTENTS

1975 comics adaptation of Space Commandos
Art: R. & R. Giordan

Introduction

Of all the authors published by Fleuve Noir's *Anticipation* imprint, Jimmy Guieu(1926-2000) was, without a doubt, the one who achieved the most surprising commercial success. His first novel, *Le Pionnier de l'Atome* [The Pioneer of the Atom] (No. 5; 1952), dealt with the classic theme of a journey into the microcosmos and used the already old-fashioned concept of using a Hindu mage's psychic powers in order to travel to  Subatomica. The book introduced the character of Jean Kariven, a French anthropoarcheologist.

With his second novel, *Au-delà de l'Infini* [Beyond Infinity] (No. 8; 1952), Guieu used a new protagonist, American biologist Jerry Barclay and reversed the theme of his previous book. This time, it was our universe that was a microcosmos contained within the knee of a beautiful woman from a macrocosmos. Guieu continued the Barclay series for three more books, usually teaming Jerry up with good aliens in order to defeat evil aliens, and returning him to the macrocosmos for further adventures: *L'Invasion de la Terre* [The Invasion of Earth] (No. 13, 1952), *Hantise sur le Monde* [Fear over the World] (No. 18, 1953) and *L'Univers Vivant* [The Living Universe] (No. 22, 1953).

Kariven returned in Guieu's third novel, *La Dimension X* [Dimension X] (No. 27; 1953) and *Nous les Martiens* [We Martians] (No. 31; 1954), in which the hero discovers that, in the far distant past, Martians had emigrated to Earth. The

Kariven series enabled Guieu to explore his favorite themes such as UFOs, secret alien encounters, Von Daniken-like theories of ancient astronauts, secret societies, etc. He began sprinkling his novels with footnotes claiming that the various facts upon which he was basing his tales were indeed "authentic."

Nine more Kariven novels followed, often dealing with time travel, lost civilizations, and a vast space war between the good Polarians and the evil Denebians, with Earth secretly caught in the middle: *La Spirale du Temps* [Time's Spiral] (No. 36, 1954), *Le Monde Oublié* [The Forgotten World] (No. 41, 1955), *L'Homme de l'Espace* [The Man From Outer Space] (No. 45, 1955), *Opération Aphrodite* (No. 47, 1955), *Commandos de l'Espace* [Space Commandos] (No. 51, 1955), *L'Agonie du Verre* [The Death of Glass] (No. 54, 1955), *Univers Parallèles* [Parallel Universes] (No. 58, 1955), *Nos Ancêtres de l'Avenir* [Our Ancestors from the Future] (No. 62, 1956) and *Prisonniers du Passé* [Prisoners of the Past] (No. 72, 1956). *Univers Parallèles* featured a cross-over with Jerry Barclay, said to live in a parallel universe.

Guieu continued to exploit the UFO vein with increasing success, becoming a major French figure in UFO circles. After Kariven, he penned a number of mostly non-connected novels. Two featured a team of American investigative reporters, Ericksson and Wendell: *Les Monstres du Néant* [The Void Monsters] (No. 70, 1956) and *Les Êtres de Feu* [The Fire Creatures] (No. 80, 1956). He portrayed the near-death of Mankind, caused by the increase in ambient radioactivity in the atmosphere, and its rebirth in a trilogy: *La Mort de la Vie* [The Death of Life] (No. 87, 1957), *Le Règne des Mutants* [The Reign of Mutants] (No. 91, 1957) and *Cité Noë No. 2* [Noah City No. 2] (No. 100, 1957). Guieu later revisited the same theme in *Demain l'Apocalypse* [Tomorrow the Apocalypse] (No. 402, 1969) and its sequel, *L'Arche du Temps* [The Ark of Time] (No. 407, 1970).

In *Expédition Cosmique* [Cosmic Expedition] (No. 134, 1959) and its sequel, *Les Cristaux de Capella* [The Crystals from Capella] (No.140, 1959), Guieu tackled space opera introducing a new hero, Claude Rousseau, a scientist aboard the *Fulgurant*, the first European interstellar exploration ship. But looking for a more flexible format, he soon switched to chronicling the exploits of two daring space traders of the future, Ronny Blade and Will Baker. The series began with *Piège dans l'Espace* [Space Trap] (No. 145, 1959) and continued in *Le Secret des Tshengz* [The Secret of the Tshengz] (No. 199, 1962), *Les Forbans de l'Espace* [The Space Pirates] (No. 224, 1963), *Les Destructeurs* [The Destroyers] (No. 237, 1963), etc. A listing of all the Blade & Baker adventures is provided at the end of this introduction.

Another notable work of the period is *Opération Ozma* (No. 203, 1962) and its sequel *L'Âge Noir de la Terre* [The Dark Age of the Earth] (No. 212, 1962) in which the hero, Ned Gowland, discovers that Project Ozma, a pioneering SETI experiment, is being used by aliens to invade Earth.

In 1967, with *Le Retour des Dieux* [The Return of the Gods] (No. 337), Guieu revamped the Kariven character into that of journalist Gilles Novak. Unlike Kariven, Novak is Guieu's alter ego and lives the kind of life that the author would have liked to live. Indeed, most of the supporting cast are thinly-disguised portrayals of Guieu's own friends. Like Kariven, Novak dealt with all kinds of X-files phenomena, but unlike the dashing archeologist of the 1950s, he was helped in his battles by Michael Merkavim, the head of a new, powerful Templar Order, the *Chevaliers de Lumière* [Shining Knights] equipped with a variety of futuristic weapons, including flying saucers, and based in a parallel dimension. Merkavim was introduced in *Les Sept Sceaux du Cosmos* [The Seven Seals of the Cosmos] (No. 343; 1968) and *L'Ordre Vert* [The Green Order] (No. 384; 1969) the latter a cult favorite.

Due to the phenomenal growth in popularity of his novels, Guieu was granted his own imprint in 1979. At first, it reprinted updated versions of his original novels, then it began publishing a series of share-cropping novels written by other writers. A separate spin-off series devoted to the Shining

Knights was also published from 1987 to 1989. In the 1990s, Guieu became a trademarked phenomenon, unique in the annals of French science fiction. His tremendous success was attributable to a clever mix of occult facts, mild eroticism, ultra-conservative bigoted politics and a forceful, if simple, story-telling style, successfully imitated by his successors. Most of his loyal readers were drawn from the general public rather than the science fiction market and were not science fiction fans *per se,* but only Jimmy Guieu fans.

With Guieu's death in 2000 and the changing tastes of the public, this publishing phenomenon did not long outlive its creator and the imprint was cancelled in 2003.

Jean-Marc Lofficier

Blade et Baker:

Fleuve Noir Anticipation:

Piège dans l'Espace [Space Trap] (No. 145, 1959)
Le Secret des Tshengz [The Secret of the Tshengz] (No. 199, 1962)
Les Forbans de l'Espace [The Space Pirates] (No. 224, 1963)
Les Destructeurs [The Destroyers] (No. 237, 1963)
Joklun-N'Ghar la Maudite [Joklun-N'Ghar the Accursed] (No. 352, 1968)
Traquenard sur Kenndor [Ambush on Kenndor] (No. 395, 1969)
Les Orgues de Satan [Satan's Organ] (No. 447, 1971)
Le Grand Mythe [The Great

Myth] (No. 470, 1971)

Les Maîtres de la Galaxie [The Galaxy Masters] (No. 504, 1972)

Les Rescapés du Néant [Survivors of the Void] (No. 521, 1972)

L'Exilé de Xantar [The Exile from Xantar] (No. 618, 1974)

Les Pièges de Koondra [The Traps of Koondra] (No. 662, 197)

Les Fugitifs de Zwolna [The Fugitives of Zwolna] (No. 674, 1975)

Le Bouclier de Boongoha [The Shield of Boongoha] (No. 707, 1975)

La Colonie Perdue [The Lost Colony] (No. 730, 1976)

Les Légions de Bartzouk [The Legions of Bartzouk] (No. 802, 1977)

Traffic Interstellaire Interstellar Trafic] (published under the nom-de-plume of Claude Vauzière at Marabout, Junior imprint No. 167, 1960)

Captifs de la Main Rouge [Prisoners of the Red Hand] (published under the nom-de-plume of Claude Vauzière at Marabout, Junior imprint in 1963)

Share-cropping novels:
FE: Frank Essem; NG: Nicolas Gauthier; CM: Chris Maya; PR: Philippe Randa; RCW: Roland C. Wagner; FW: Frank Walhart

Vaugirard/Vauvenargues:

Les Rebelles de N'Harangho [The Rebels of N'Harangho] (PR) (VG 88, 1992)

Le Serpent-Dieu de Joklun N'Ghar [The Serpent God o Joklun N'Ghar] (RCW) (VG 89, 1992)

Le Poison de Thogar'Min [The Poison of Thogar'Min] (LG) (VG 90, 1993)

Les Maudits d'Hertzvane [The Accursed of Hetzvane] (PR/NG) (VG 91, 1993)

Les Albinos de Sulifuss [The Albinos of Sulifuss] (RCW) (VG 92, 1993)

Les Naufragés du Temps [Castaways in Time] (PR/NG) (VG 93, 1993)

Echec au Destin [Fate in Check] (RCW) (VG 95,1994)

Les Magiciens des Mondes Oubliés [The Magicians of the Forgotten Worlds] (RCW) (VG 97, 1994)

L'Ombre du Dragon Rouge [The Red Dragon's Shadow] (RCW) (VG 99, 1994)

Le Maître de la Main Rouge [The Master of the Red Hand] (RCW) (VG 100, 1995)

Les Brumes de Joklun N'Ghar [The Mists of Joklun N'Ghar] (RCW) (VG 102, 1995)

Les Voleurs de Dieux [The God Stealers] (CM) (VG 103, 1995)

Flammes sur Batoog [Flames over Batoog] (RCW) (VG 105, 1995)

Au Coeur de Kenndor [The Heart of Kenndor] (RCW) (VG 106, 1996)

La Fin de Gondwana [Gondwana's End] (RCW) (VG 108, 1996)

Embuscade sur Eileena [Ambush on Eileena] (RCW) (VG 110, 1996)

L'Offensive des Frotegs [The Frotegs Attack] (RCW) (VG 111, 1996)

L'Alliance des Invincibles [The Invincible Alliance] (RCW) (VG 113, 1997)

La Planète sans Nom [The Nameless Planet] (RCW) (VG 115, 1997)

Panique sur Wondlak [Panic over Wondlak] (RCW) (VG 117, 1998)

Les Prisonniers de Bangor [The Prisoners of Bangor] (RCW) (VG 119, 1998)

Conjuration sur Joklun N'Ghar [The Joklun N'Ghar conjuration] (RCW) (VG 121, 1998)

L'Étoile aux cent planètes [The Sun of a Hundred Worlds] (RCW) (VG 123, 1998)

Sur l'Aile du Dragon [On the Dragon's Wing] (RCW) (VG 125, 1999)

Les Mousquetaires de Terniog 2 [The Musketeers of Terniog 2] (FW/RCW) (VG 127, 1999)

Les Templiers des Étoiles [The Cosmic Templars] (FW/RCW) (VG 129, 2000)

Les Ravisseurs de Ktan [The Kidnappers of Ktan] (FW/RCW) (VG 130, 2000)

La Fugitive de Z'Lanna [The Fugitive of Z'Lanna] (FW/RCW) (VG 132, 2000)

La Guerre des Épices [The Spice War] (FW/RCW) (VG 134, 2000)

La Planète Bérézina [Planet Berezina] (FW) (VG 136, 2001)

Les Zhelfes de Thanos [The zelfs of Thanos] (FW/RCW/FE) (VG 138, 2001)

Les Banquets de Gh'urrmandhia [The Feasts of Gh'urrmandhia] (FW/RCW/FE) (VG 140, 2001)

Les Marchands d'Esclaves de Brusshnaï [The Slave Traders of Brusshnai] (FW/FE) (VG 142, 2001)

Les Maîtres-Sculpteurs de Kündest [The Master-Sculptors of Kundest] (FW/FE) (VG 144, 2002)

Le Satellite des Olympiades [The Olympic Satellite] (FW/FE) (VG 146, 2002)

La Jonque Céleste de Pa'Kang [The Celestial Junk of Pa'Kang] (FW/FE) (VG 148, 2003)

L'Athanor général de Zodiann [The General Athanor of Zodiann] (FW/FE) (VG 150,2003)

Compétition autour de Zandharr [Competition over Zandharr] (FW) (VG 152, 2003)

Gilles Novak / The Shining Knights:

Fleuve Noir Anticipation:

La Force sans Visage [The Face-less Force] (No. 118, 1958) [this novel does not feature Gilles Novak, but only its future arch-enemy, the evil organization Narkoum]
Le Retour des Dieux [The Return of the Gods] (No. 337, 1967)
Les Sept Sceaux du Cosmos [The Seven Seals of the Cosmos] (No. 343, 1968)
La Terreur Invisible [The Invisible Terror] (No. 360, 1968)
L'Ordre Vert [The Green Order] (No. 384, 1969)
Le Triangle de la Mort [The Triangle of Death] (No. 425, 1970)
Plan Catapulte [Plan Catapult] (No. 439, 1970)
La Voix Qui Venait d'Ailleurs [The Voice From Beyond] (No. 459, 1971)
La Charnière du Temps [The Time Hinges] (No. 480, 1971)
Enjeu Cosmique [Cosmic Stakes] (No. 496, 1972)
La Mission Effacée [The Erased Mission] (No. 547, 1973)
Opération Neptune (No. 568, 1973)
Les Germes du Chaos [The Germs of Chaos] (No. 578, 1973)
Les Veilleurs de Poseidon [The Poseidon Watchers] (No. 602, 1974)
Le Maître du Temps [The Time Master] (No. 630, 1974)
Manipulations Psi [Psi Manipulations] (No. 647, 1974)
Les Krolls de Vorlna [The Krolls of Vorlna] (No. 688, 1975)
La Stase Achronique [The Achronic Stasis] (No. 718, 1975)
La Lumière de Thot [The Light of Thot] (No. 779, 1977)
Les Yeux de l'Epouvante [The Eyes of Terror] (No. 851, 1978)

Hieroush, la Planète Promise [Hieroush, Promised Planet] (No. 941, 1979)
La Clé du Mandala [The Mandala Key] (No. 982, 1980)
Les Fils du Serpent [The Sons of the Serpent] (No. 1273, 1984)

Spoutnik VII a disparu [Sputnik VII Has Disappeared] (this novel does not feature Gilles Novak but only the Shining Knights; it was initially published under the nom-de-plume of Claude Vauzière at Marabout, Junior imprint No. 197, 1961)

Shining Knights:

La Force Noire [The Black Force] (No. 1, 1987)
Le Pacte de Kannlor [The Pact of Kannlor] (No. 2, 1987)
La Terreur Venue du Néant [The Terror That Came From The Void] (No. 3, 1988)
Narkoum: Finances Rouges [Narkum: Red Finances] (No. 4, 1988)
Plan d'Extermination [Extermination Plan] (No. 5, 1988)
Réseau Alpha [Alpha Network] (No. 6, 1989)
L'Héritage de Noé [The Noah Inheritance] (No. 7, 1989)
Les Sentiers Invisibles [The Invisible Paths] (No. 8, 1989)
L'Empire des Ténèbres [The Empire of Darkness] (No. 9, 1989)
Le Piège du Val Maudit [The Trap of the Accursed Valley] (No. 10, 1989)

Share-cropping novels:
AD: Arnaud Dalrune; PR: Philippe Randa; FW: Frank Walhart

Vaugirard/Vauvenargues:

Magie Rouge [Red Magic] (PR) (VG 87, 1992)
Les Brumes de l'Effroi [Mists of Terror] (AD) (VG 118, 1998)

Ankou, La Vengeance d'Ys [Ankou : Ys'Revenge] (AD) (VG 120, 1998)

Enez Bel, Le réveil de Gradlon [Enez Bel : Gradlon Awakens] (AD) (VG 122, 1998)

Les Revenants de l'Aube Dorée [The Revenants of the Golden Dawn](AD) (VG 124, 1999)

Rosslynn, La Crypte des Templiers [Rosslyn : The Templars' Crypt] (AD) (VG 126, 1999)

Les Visiteurs du Suaire [The Shroud Visitors] (AD) (VG 128, 1999)

La Mort d'un Maître [The Death of a Master] (AD) (VG 131, 2000)

Le Vol AF54679 ne répond plus [Flight AF54679 Does Not Answer] (AD) (VG 133, 2000)

Novak contre Novak [Novak vs Novak] (AD) (VG 135, 2001)

Les Légions du Père Noël [The Legions of Santa Claus](AD) (VG 137, 2001)

Les Héros de la Toison d'or [The Heroes of the Golden Fleece] (AD) (VG 139, 2001

Le Sacrifice du Grand Cerf [The Sacrifice of the Buck] (AD) (VG 141, 2001)

Le Jeu de la Mort [The Game of Death] (FW) (VG 143, 2002

Arcana Arcanorum (AD) (VG 145, 2002)

Ecce Homo (AD) (VG 147, 2003)

Les Frères Rouges de Mortemer [The Red Brothers of Mortemer] (AD) (VG 149, 2003)

Cauchemar aux Seychelles [Nightmare ion the Seychelles] (AD) (VG 151, 2003)

Commandos
DE
l'Espace

JIMMY
GUIEU

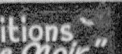

★ ANTICIPATION ★

Editions
"Fleuve Noir"

SPACE COMMANDOS

In the present state of our Human Sciences, it is pretty certain that no country has suddenly discovered the secret of a power source that would explain how "Flying Saucers" could accomplish their extraordinary feats... It comes down, therefore, to an extra-terrestrial origin, to that famous ESMA[1] that are increasing their observation flights because the Earthlings have discovered the secret of the atom and appear able to become a danger to other worlds.

-- General L. M. Chassin, Commander on Chief of the French Air Force and Air Defense Coordinator

---

[1] *Escadrille de Surveillance des Mondes Attardés*, i.e.: Surveillance Squadrons of Backward Worlds.

CHAPTER ONE

For a long time Hogounn watched the blurry spot form on the triangular screen of his space teleradar and start to come into focus. Sitting in front of his tilted control panel he skillfully maneuvered a kind of hexagonal dial, slipped in two cream-colored strips that touched two contacts and when all this was done he put his hands flat on the blue metal panel and sighed.

Injya, sitting next to him, was piloting the spaceship. She pulled down three small levers, slowly turned an oval wheel with an off-center axis and leaning back in her strange, bowl-shaped chair, left everything to the guidance system of the electro-magnetic radar-pilotage.

She looked over at her companion with a smile and said, "You're funny, Hogounn. Every time we approach planet T27 you sigh the same way and do the same thing. Even if I don't see you I'm sure that after sighing you're going to put your hands flat on the instrument panel and look up at the ceiling, exasperated."

Hogounn smiled back at the ironic remark and shrugged his shoulders, replying, "I don't know if you're having fun but these observation trips are awfully monotonous to me. Since we've been studying the pseudo-civilization of these natives on T27, I've ended up wondering if we'll ever get the go ahead to contact them."

"Our leaders are full of wisdom, Hogounn. From time immemorial they've studied the galactic races who are still in their 'infancy' and they know perfectly well that any premature contact could have negative consequences for our projects. You purposely forget that we're dealing with primitives."

"And what primitives!" Hogounn added. "They are as big as they are stupid. A *decan* hasn't gone by without one of their nations attacking another or some bloody civil war destroying their people."

"They're barbarians, I agree, but they're crossing an evolutionary stage that we crossed before. In time and thanks to our future intervention they'll get the wisdom they're lacking. We have to be patient. Besides, luckily for our future relations with these beings, there are a few among them who have a quotient of perception and knowledge clearly higher than most of their brothers."

"How lucky!" Hogounn grumbled. "If the order to land and show ourselves to these primitives doesn't come soon I think I'll ask for a transfer to a commando unit operating in some other solar system."

Injya cast a furtive glance at her companion who saw the disappointment in her eyes and in her fleeting frown. He regretted his words because he was pretty sure that Injya felt more than just friendship for him. To transfer to a commando unit was a pure and simple desertion of the girl whom he hoped to get up enough courage to confess his feelings for some day.

He was shaken out of his thoughts when a bank of lights on the triangular teleradar started blinking. On the frosted glass was the surface of a continent, growing bigger very quickly, looking like it was coming straight at them. Under the spaceship, which had just entered the atmosphere of T27, and on the hemisphere plunged in darkness, some lighter spots sprinkled with luminous dots marked the location of the cities being flown over at 3000 miles an hour.

Injya hovered over the urban area for 20 seconds and zigzagged down for several miles before heading toward a kind of narrow path on which ran two metal rails crossed by countless strips of wood.

The spaceship set down smoothly at the same time as six telescopic legs emerged from its underside. Without a bump and in perfect silence the ship landed.

Injya and Hogounn opened a narrow recess across from the cockpit and took out two heavy spacesuits so they could make a brief outing on this world whose atmosphere they could not breathe.

Hogounn courteously helped Injya put her spacesuit on, seal the huge, metal helmet with a rectangular opening at eye level make of transparent *xoning* and checked her reserves of artificial air built into the stocky "chest" of the protective suit.

When he, too, was stuffed in his clumsy metal outfit whose legs were the only jointed parts, he went to activate the long-distance security system. The controls inside the space-suit could also work the system no matter where they were. The robotic device could "cover" them, if need be, if they were far from the ship.

A rectangular hatch opened in the side of the ship and the two astronauts jumped to the ground. A polygravity belt automatically corrected their weight to the same as their home planet, allowing them to walk without any trouble. Their metal outfits, however, sometimes made them waddle in a strange way.

Hogounn, followed by Injya, walked down the path between the two metal rails, jumping from one cross beam to the next. Their upper limbs were imprisoned in the cylindrical chest where it was easy for them to work the controls of their various devices: weight corrector, podogyroscope (so they would not fall), feeder valves (for the artificial air), weapons and remote control for the long-distance security set up around the spaceship.

On the edge of the path cut by the two rails stood one of those odd, rectangular houses with a roof slanting on two sides away from each other.

Hogounn stopped, as did Injya.

"My *Onka* ray detector is reacting," he spoke into his transmitter. "A living being is not far from us."

"I've got it too," Injya said. "It's a little thing because our projection beams stop detecting it at thigh-level."

"Exactly. The tingle from the reflecting waves stop a little higher than my knees."

"Intelligence quotient 0.13," Injya announced, "warm blooded. It's a creature much more primitive than most of the natives on this planet."

Looking toward the gray building on the side of the iron-lined path, they noticed a rectangular opening up above casting a pool of light on the ground. In the sky the only satellite of the T27 planet colored the landscape with a whitish-blue light. Some clouds, a mixture of oxygen and hydrogen, sometimes veiled the glow of the satellite, which lacked an atmosphere.

Hogounn increased the power of his Onka ray detector. Thanks to the sensory scale affixed directly to his skin he controlled the magnitude of the reactions on a small screen that was clearly visible in the bottom of his helmet.

"There are two natives in that building, maybe three. I detected a double intelligence quotient varying from 65 to 77. The third barely reaches 29."

"I think it's a non-adult native," Injya guessed, "because its heartbeats is around 105 as opposed to the 70/75 of the two others nearby. They are normal beats and not sped up by an emotional disorder."

A long, faint rumbling that soon turned into shrill, clipped cries screamed through the silent night. Hogounn and Injya stopped and went on the defensive.

"It's that small creature," Hogounn said. "Sneaking around in the shadow of that wall. It's found us out."

"Doesn't matter. We can still go a little farther to test the natives reactions… if they decide to leave their shelter."

The two astronauts waddled along the crossties and metal bars. They stopped a second time on alert.

A big rectangle opened in a wall of the cubic building. A bright light poured out. In the rectangle of light the outline of a creature appeared with two arms and two legs and a head covered with black hair on top. In its general shape it resembled the two observers but it was twice as big.

"An inhabitant of planet T27," Injya whispered as she watched with curiosity.

"You can speak louder," her partner said. "It can't hear us in our helmets."

The native pronounced some garbled words, apparently talking to someone much, much smaller than itself and also pointing to something in the dark. In fact, it was speaking to a small, hairy creature with four short legs. An extremely mobile appendage came out of its body above its rear legs. When the primitive stopped talking, the hair system of the small creature bristled, its eyes turned shifty, its rear appendage curved between its legs and it started grunting and growling. The giant bent down and with one of its long upper limbs it tapped the head of the scared thing, whispering to it.

Hogounn turned up his phonic recorder to capture the sound emissions of these strange beings.

The small creature continued growling and casting frightened glances in the night. The giant stood up straight and lifted up a cylindrical object. The instrument threw a beam of light toward the place where its four-legged friend was looking.

The giant jumped and cried out. It looked disturbed at the sight of this weird "thing" (it obviously did not know what a spaceship was!) that sat so close to its box dwelling. It must have wondered how this amber object could have arrived so secretly. Was it an airplane? If so, it was very different from what it was used to.

All of a sudden the small, four-legged creature started barking furiously. Then it crouched down on its belly and slunk behind the giant, yelping and whining. The native, stupefied and terrorized and not believing its rudimentary senses, finally saw the cause of its dwarf friend's fright.

There, close by, in the shadows that its light tube was now chasing away, two creatures, like cylindrical mannequins, were standing there on two legs (skinny compared to its own) and staring through the transparent part of their helmets.

Hogounn and Injya enjoyed the terror that they struck in this inhabitant of planet T27.

"I think that's enough," Hogounn counseled. "Let's activate the security and get back to our ship."

Lowering a tiny lever inside his spacesuit he turned it on.
A short distance away, an opening in their ship parked on the
path shot out a green ray and swept across the countryside
until it rested in the giant, who stumbled back in fear. It was
instantly paralyzed while its four-legged friend, because of its
size, escaped the emerald green light beam and scurried into
the boxy house where the other two natives remained.

Hogounn and Injya headed for their spaceship, passing
close by the giant who could not move, frozen with a look of
utter confusion.

The two astronauts jumped onto the ramp leading into
the ventral hatch. Very soon, sitting at their command posts,
they stopped the green paralyzing ray and started up the
gravito-magnetic thrusters. When the ray was gone the giant
could move. In a daze and pale with fear it dropped its portable light and backed away. Its big, frightened eyes watched the
mysterious machine rise up with its two weird "creatures" that
came straight out of a nightmare.

In a few seconds the spaceship reached a very high altitude and shot off toward the second observation astrobase that
had been orbiting around planet T27 for a little while. Out of
their spacesuits now Hogounn and Injya looked at each other
and broke out laughing.

"I'm a little ashamed of playing tricks like that on these
primitives," Injya confessed.

"Nah, it's necessary… and it confirms our opinion of
them. With a few rare exceptions their reactions are always the
same. When they see us either they run away as fast as their
long limbs can carry them or they fall to the ground. We make
them so scared every time."

"When the giant saw us our Onka detector showed its
heart rate jump from 75 to 95, then to 100 instantly!"

"Put yourself in their place. Seeing an inexplicable and
frightening 'vision'—like our appearance—is a rude awakening. We can't lose sight of the fact that these beings are like

giants to us, so we must look like dwarves to them. When they see us, many of them are first wondering if they can believe their eyes. And then when they tell their 'unbelievable' stories to the other natives, they're considered crazy or frauds. Since they can't travel in space from one solar system to another they don't know about or refuse to accept the existence of other beings living on countless planets in the galaxy. It's hard for them to imagine that they're not the only intelligent beings in the cosmos. So, the creature we just scared and paralyzed will have a lot of trouble convincing others of the truth about the adventure. Only a few inhabitants on T27 with a more evolved mind will admit that he really did experience this 'strange encounter'. For the others, the vast majority unfortunately, he'll be out of his mind or playing a bad joke."

Injya shook her head and sighed. "These Earthlings are really a stupid and backward race!"

The spaceship of Hogounn and Injya slowed down. On the black background speckled with bright stars, far beyond the atmosphere, it took two hours for the huge astrobase to make the complete orbit of planet T27, the galactic name for planet.Earth.

The disc-shaped reconnaissance ship approached the base—an extraordinary spherical ship over a mile and a half in diameter—and slowly entered the huge hatch that was 165 feet wide and long and closing up behind it.

The spaceship (20 feet in diameter and 5 feet high on its axis), a tiny orange chip compared to the formidable observation base, landed on its round platform at the end of the first row of other similar machines. In the huge "garage" of the artificial satellite, in tight rows were lined up almost 500 *Fimn'has*, the disc-shaped reconnaissance ships that the inhabitants of T27 persisted in calling "Flying Saucers."

Around every ten minutes one or more of these Fimn'has took off for Earth. Others, at pretty much the same rhythm, came back to the base after a mission to film the cities and industrial centers or perhaps a "quick experiment of contact with the natives."

Hogounn and Injya sat in a kind of metal cube that started sliding over the shiny floor then gradually rose up to around eight inches off the ground. The cube went around the impressive squad of spaceships, climbed up a ramp and jumped into a circular opening, a kind of well with bright walls where it sped up. Over a mile up the cube entered one of the many openings along the tube that linked the two "poles" and moved down a 12-foot wide, 20-foot high corridor that wound around the axis of the artificial satellite.

The space station had 117 floors that included the air-conditioned living spaces, various laboratories, observatories, stock rooms and numerous centers of scientific research. Four special sections, two at the top and two at the bottom, served as astrodromes able to hold up to 500 spaceships depending on their size and function.

Every floor, with pressure and air system adapted to the physiological requirements of the occupants, had several corridors in addition to one big, inner corridor that had no atmosphere where the different types of living beings on the base had to move about in the spacesuits fitting their biological category.

The inhabitants of the astrobase, to get from one floor or section to another, could use either the gravito-magnetic tubes and corridors or simply the two- and four-seater cubes. These vehicles, by varying (sometimes totally eliminating) the strength of the artificial gravity of the satellite, moved every which way with extraordinary ease thanks to their electromagnetic propulsive field.

The cube in which Hogounn and Injya were sitting stopped in front of a big hatch. The two astronauts jumped onto the metal floor and straightway the strange, wheel-less vehicle rose up to the ceiling and sped off in the opposite direction.

The hatch opened and the two "visitors" entered a huge, triangular room in the middle of which, sitting behind a kind of desk, waited someone quite different from the two astronauts. The latter were around three feet tall, their skin orange and their delicate hands each had six fingers, but the being awaiting them, on the contrary, was taller at almost four feet and its skinny arms ended in a kind of hand with four opposable fingers. In his black face were huge, oval, extremely movable eyes that jutted out rather creepily. On his cheeks and chin clumps of long hair grew straight and rigid, very thick, all the way down to his bare chest that was covered with long, blackish fuzz.

His nose was stuck in a capsule with two flexible tubes that hooked up to an air tank strapped to his back. Just as the regulations of the base demanded, although the chief of the base belonged to a different race than his visitors and therefore did not breathe the same air, he had to adapt his inhaler. After emptying the air from his office and replacing it with an artificial atmosphere fitting for his visitors, they could then be welcomed and make their report without needing to wear their bulky spacesuits.

Hogounn and Injya bowed to Fohag, the base chief, and rattled off their identities, "Hogounn and Injya, numbers AL-279 and AL-3017, originally from the planet Alkar in the Valnyk solar system," Hogounn said. "Hello, Fohag!"

Fohag spun his bulging pink eyes in their sockets to glance at them as he watched the spaceships moving on a video wall map. Then in a familiar gesture he raised the four fingers of his left hand to his right shoulder and broke the silence by using the universal language of the Federated Worlds.

"Hello, Centaurians."

Fohag paused and his pink eyes turned blue, which on his planet meant he was smiling.

"I call you Centaurians because that's how the Earthlings would call you if they knew about your existence. Valnyk, your sun, is for them the star Alpha in the constellation Centaurus. I make this brief digression because I know that after your mission you're going to ask again to teach you one or more languages spoken on T27. Right now I can only give you a few words, like the Earth name for Valnyk, for example."

One of his big eyes stared at the animated star chart while the other concentrated his attention on his two visitors.

"I'm listening, Centaurians."

When they had told him of their expedition down to the slightest detail, Fohag declared, "You were careless in landing your Fimn'has on what you figured was an unused road. We haven't been exploring this planet from the air for eight years just so you could take a stroll. Hundreds of thousands of films have been taken on all the continents. Today we have a topographical map of this world more precise than its own inhabitants possess. These maps are at your disposal. If you'd carefully studied the map of the region you were in, you would have seen that what you took for a path was, in fact, what the Earthlings call a 'railroad'."

"Railroad?" Hogounn and Injya echoed, embarrassed for committing a tactical error.

"It means a special road with twin metal runners sticking up that guide a heavy steam engine, sometimes electric, to transport natives, animals and all kinds of material. If such a vehicle had hit you during your landing, despite the ship's unbelievable strength in Earthling terms, vital elements could have been damaged. Staying faithful to our principles of non-violence when violence is not an issue, you would not have been punished. However, from now on I insist that you follow the rules of landing to the letter."

"We will follow them, Fohag, and thank you for your leniency," Hogounn promised, disturbed by this incident.

Any witness to this interview would be surprised by the logic and ethics that was so different, if not paradoxical to the human mind.

Hogounn handed the Chief a kind of pyramid with notched edges. Through the notches was wound a magnetic thread on which the different sounds they heard during their mission were recorded.

Fohag took the pyramidal spool in his three long fingers and slipped it pointing downward into a rectangular opening on his half-moon desk. He pressed the bottom of the small spool and they heard a click. The magnetic thread was starting to feed into the "reading head" of the machine that was built into the strange metal furniture with levers, buttons, dials and screens all over its top.

Hogounn and Injya listened carefully. Over the background speakers came the thousands of sounds that they had heard during their visit to T27. First there was the muffled stomp of their boots on the railroad ties, the rustling of the wind in the vegetation along the path and then the first growls of the small, four-legged creature that was soon barking furiously. After a silence, disturbed only by the yelping of the scared dog, the barking started up again, sometimes cut with oddly pitched howls. Finally came the entrance of the primitive "giant", the Earthling, intrigued by the unusual behavior of his dog.

Hogounn and Injya paid close attention to the polyphonic jumble that they did not understand. Only Fohag, being Chief of the base, had received instruction in the main terrestrial languages and could understand the meaning of this weird recording.

The ambient stereo produced the clear and distinct voice of the Earthling speaking to his dog: *Come on, Kiki, be quiet!* Here the sound of his hand petting the dog affectionately. *What's going on?* Yapping followed by howling, then fading away. *Holy shit!* Barking that faded and scratching on the pavement when it scampered away while its master stood paralyzed.

The two Centaurian astronauts were amused to relive the episode of their routine landing on planet Earth.

"Is the recording... interesting?" Injya was still hoping that the Chief would decide one of these days to give them a few translations of their many recordings.

"Well... yes, interesting enough. When the Earthling saw your Fimn'has so close to his habitation he said something

31

that I don't understand... I'm going to make a semantic analysis immediately with the help of the comparative-translator to get the exact meaning of the word. You can go now, Centaurians. Even though your missions seem boring and eternally repetitive to you, they are nonetheless very useful because they bring us some new knowledge every time. Go, brother Centaurians. You have ten *sfang* of rest. Spend the time however you want and come back when it's over."

When the two Centaurian troopers of the Space Commandos assigned to this solar system had walked out to enjoy their "leave", Fohag got to work on searching for the meaning of the new word. For this he isolated the word in question and ran it several times through the "reader". He listened carefully until it became monotonous and then passed it into the electronic comparative-translator.

With his long fingers bent back, which neither the Centaurians nor humans could do, Fohag reflected on the weird sound of the incomprehensible word while waiting for the machine to give him a translation.

After a relatively short time he heard a click and in the galactic language of the Federated Worlds the speaker pronounced in a monotone the various comparative ideas that the word evoked under its multiple forms in the seven primary languages spoken on T27.

After listening to the voice of the electronic brain that controlled the translator, Fohag shivered. His eyes went from pink to green, thus betraying his outrage and confusion caused by the translation of this... "perfectly English" word!

"Really, these Earthlings are not only primitive but very crude!" the Chief of the astrobase concluded.

His Wolfian sensibility (for, he was originally from the planet Mongan in the Wolf 359 solar system according to Earth's astronomical nomenclature) was deeply shocked.

CHAPTER II

A period equal to four earth days went by during which the disc-shaped Fimn'has made many observations on planet T27.

Fohag, Chief of the astrobase, had just summoned the members of the Space Commandos to a meeting. In the huge room, a kind of amphitheater shaped to the outer curve of the satellite, were gathered 300 astronauts mostly belonging to the Centaurian race from the planet Alkar. On the hollow seats arranged in a semi-circle there were also some Wolfians, bigger than the Centaurians and covered in their strange, black fur. Their big, round eyes were in constant motion.

On a gray metal stage, behind a kind of long, slanted desk with a chrome top covered with switches and buttons and dials with as many blinking lights, sat Fohag, the section chiefs and the officers of the astrobase. To an Earthling this assembly would have looked like a "Freak Show" or better like a vision out some hideous nightmare. In fact, on the stage with the section chiefs, besides Fohag there were two, 3-foot tall Centaurians wearing transparent spacesuits that revealed their almost human morphology, in spite of their small stature, orange skin and six fingers. Then came the two Wolfians, four feet high, wearing like Fohag a dark blue metal spacesuit with a round helmet fitted with a rectangular opening in transparent *xoning*. To Fohag's right, finally, were three Polarians, also in spacesuits that hugged their powerful muscles. These three, for sure, would have astonished an unwitting Earthling witness to this meeting because they were identical to "primitive" humans on the planet Earth. The only difference between them was in the fact that besides their extraordinary scientific knowledge (inherent to their supra-evolved civilization) they had four extra senses: telepathy, paroptic vision, polyperception or the ability to follow different currents of thoughts simultaneously and finally the ability to paralyze or even kill at a distance by the simple projection of an electro-cuting current somewhat like the gymnotus[2].

These *Homo Superior*, through the spectacular antiquity of their race and the no less spectacular technical abilities, had peacefully colonized countless solar systems spread through-out the Galaxy. Called "Grand Instructors," boundlessly good and understanding for the under-evolved or primitive races that they had educated and protected against all attempts at brutal colonization—in fact, against the slavery to which cer-tain warlike civilizations had tried to subject them—the Polarians were particularly beloved masters of no matter who they were protecting. However, their kindness and wisdom did not keep them from acting with merciless strictness against the races who remained hostile or deaf to their peaceful missions. There exist in the galaxy beings with visions of power trying to enslave the planets of certain solar systems that have not yet reached the evolutionary stage to defend themselves with equal arms against such tyranny.

The interstellar wars and the unbelievable disasters that followed were things that an Earthling could not even imag-ine. His reason would systematically refuse to consider for one second what he considered "a figment of the imagination", even a delusional fantasy worthy of some scatterbrained sci-ence fiction story!

The truth, however, was there only 400 and 600 miles away, the distance separating the two astrobases of planet Earth. These two artificial satellites were the "outposts" of the Space Commandos sent to this solar system by the Galactic Federation of the United Worlds. The goal of these "beings from space" was to study the Earthlings in detail before mak-ing official contact with them. For, official contact was soon going to be necessary because the Space Commandos had

---

[2] Gymnotus: fish of the order Gymnotiformes, a kind of eel living mostly in the rivers of Central and South America. Its strong electrical discharge—that it controls at will—is capable of stunning a man or killing certain fish.

more than once spotted and intercepted reconnaissance patrols launched by the Denebians, the green, scaly-skinned monsters from the solar system Deneb in the constellation Cygnus. These pirates of the Galaxy and their allies from Procyon, driven by their desire for conquest, were seeking planets to colonize.

Twice already the Polarians had driven the Denebians away when they tried to set up a base in a deserted region on Earth and on its moon.[3]

In astrobase 2 orbiting 600 miles from Earth, the meeting of the various representatives of the Federated Worlds had two goals: to inform the participants about the latest observation missions on the ground and to decide on the nature of future peaceful forays.

Fohag stood up and in a position familiar to the Wolfians he curved back his arms so that his four long fingers touched his shoulders. Then, using the universal language of the Galactic Federation he said:

"Eight years ago, according to the measure of time used on T27, when our space exploration squads were drawn by the first atomic explosions that occurred on Earth, we were pleased at first. We're well familiar with this old planet that we visited at the dawn of its civilization when it was only inhabited by beings still close to their animal nature. Over the course of many millennia we followed the development of the different civilizations that succeeded one another.[4] We abandoned it to its fate when the inhabitants, still hardly evolved, were searching for their way, groping along paths of knowledge, a little before the arrival of the one the Earthlings call the Son of God, the greatest Initiate that the planet Earth ever saw. After this coming, which shook up the peoples of this world, we were happy just watching from afar the first stages of the reborn civilization. Because after the cosmic cataclysm that buried Atlantis—the last supra-evolved civiliza-

_____

[3] See Volume 1.

[4] See Volume 1.

35

tion to receive the teaching of the human-like Polarians—Knowledge had been almost completely lost.

"Now, therefore, when our space squads saw their hypersensitive detectors recorded an atomic explosion on T27, the Polarian officers felt great joy. In their great wisdom they thought that the Earthlings had finally discovered the *primordial energy* and after domesticating it were using it for industrial purposes, like razing land, drilling the ground to build giant reservoirs, breaking up mountain chains to modify the climate or other profitable uses.

"Alas, although men had discovered the power of nuclear fission, they did not use it for a beneficial end. No. They had domesticated the primordial energy in order to build a powerful weapon: the atomic bomb! Here we don't have to know the reasons that pushed one side to bomb the other. Moreover, staying faithful to our politics of non-intervention in the internal affairs of an under-evolved world when the safety of its civilizations is not at stake, we couldn't intervene. So far such was the case with the wars that have been waged between men. These wars, in any case, had not destroyed Life on Earth. However, with nuclear energy it was no longer the slaughter of hundreds of thousands of men we feared but the extinction of Life on this planet. For, from the atomic bomb to the hydrogen bomb was a small step that the Earthlings took in only a few years. The H-bomb is more powerful than its younger sister and more dangerous with its fallout. From the hydrogen bomb to the cobalt bomb is only one more step… relatively easy to take. If men take this unfortunate step and start a war in which one side or the other uses cobalt bombs, it'll be the end of Life on Earth. Its atmosphere will be completely polluted by the radioactive gas and destroy everything up to the tiniest spores and microorganisms. Human civilization will survive only as ruins that will quickly crumble into radioactive dust.

"We don't want a genocide and especially such carnage to strike Life itself. Our duty, therefore, is clear: to keep the Earthlings from committing the collective suicide that their scientists refuse to believe in. We've got a little time since they haven't yet developed the C-bomb and also because they're not at war right now… at least not yet. Besides, there's a good chance that a new threat coming from outer space will hit their planet: I'm referring to the Denebians and Procyonians. But how can we contact the humans without causing general panic? How, first of all, to make them see that we're their friends, their protectors? With their minds still clouded by primitive feelings, many of them will see us as conquerors, monstrous warriors trying to take over the Earth. Even our brother Polarians, who look like humans, will have serious trouble convincing them.

"There's an important reason for this: the inhabitants of T27 consider themselves the Kings of the Universe. Most of them anyway. In their pride they refuse to imagine that there *might* be other worlds with beings superior to them, smarter and especially wiser. This thought shocks them and wounds their foolish vanity. If only the common people had this ego-centric idea we could figure on contacting its leaders, scientists and scholars. But alas even the 'doctors' and leaders, with rare exceptions, stubbornly refuse to admit *the hypothesis of intelligent life capable of sending representatives to their planet.*

"We have decided, therefore, based on this information furnished by our mechano-psychic detection devices, to make frequent observation flights at low altitude, figuring that if the Earthlings see a lot of disc-shaped flying objects they'll end up facing the fact that these machines, whose characteristics and abilities are so superior to their own, can lead to only one possible conclusion: if thousands of Earthlings attest to seeing 'flying saucers' and other cigar-shaped objects it's only because strangers to their planet are watching them.

"Once again we were sorely deceived. We had made the mistake of believing that we were dealing with (relatively speaking) intelligent beings able to use their heads and humbly recognize that such machines could not possibly be the work of their fellow humans. In fact, although men are thinking beings, their intelligence quotient is, nine times out of ten, obliterated by hallowed doctrines, chauvinism and, I have to say, by their excessive pride.

"Our countless 'demonstration' flights over the United States and other countries changed nothing in the thoughts of men, so we decided to fly over France. It did nothing. In spite of tens of thousands of trustworthy people confirming that they had seen with their own eyes the 'flying saucers', the stubborn Earthlings continued to deny the existence of our Fimn'has. We had to make brief landings in remote areas so as not to cause panic or at least on the outskirts of small towns. Our Polarian, Centaurian or Wolfian pilots showed themselves fleetingly to the few Earthlings they came across. The Polarian did not need spacesuits since they can breathe freely in the T27 atmosphere, but the Centaurians and Wolfians put on their suits. In most cases the sight of us scared the humans and they ran away. Some, however, had the courage to wait on pins and needles. Several of you, my brothers, took the opportunity to approach them briefly. And on several occasions the Polarians even made physical contact with the Earthlings who look like them.

"Well, something unthinkable happened: despite all our demonstrations, all our landings, all our brief but repeated contacts, most Earthlings still deny our existence! To convince these primitives beings do we have to land thousands of spaceships in a big city… and unleash panic among them, not to mention all the accidents and mishaps that would happen? Moreover, we know that out of stupidity these natives could very well attack us… not knowing that a force field protects us individually during our visits. Remember when one of these ridiculous primitives fired a gun—that obsolete weapon—at one of his fellow men, thinking it was a Martian, which our viewers showed us in their newspapers.[5]

"Naturally, it would be easy for us to convince the Earthlings once and for all by leaving an unknown object on Earth

---

[5] Absolutely true. (Author's Note)

after a landing, something that mystifies their physical laws and that will force them to admit our presence. But we won't do this because in order for the Earthlings to open their minds to other, less conventional knowledge, they have to analyze the facts calmly and use their own logical reasoning to conclude that we exist."

Fohag interrupted his harsh criticism of the stupid blindness of the inhabitants of T27, then after pushing in a pearl-colored strip and lowering a lever he continued.

"Hogounn and Injya, two Centaurian pilots, have recently made a routine visit to Earth that made a little splash among men. The commentaries on the witness of their appearance are outrageous and more proof, if need be, of the incredible stupidity of this Homo called Sapiens, meaning 'Wise Man' in a dead Earth language, a title that these creatures willingly and very modestly give themselves! Just look at the translation of the news published this morning on the bright side of the planet in a big newspaper."

The curved wall of the room seemed to fade away and be replaced by a kind of stereoscopic diorama of a wide Parisian street (Boulevard des Italiens) at rush hour. It looked like a colored, 3-D view taken from the top floor of a building near the Opéra. The ground came closer. An Earthling reading a newspaper was framed in the middle of the screen and as the view zoomed in part of the paper became visible. The headline and subheading became legible. The man seemed to have stopped moving, like in movie special effects when a scene turns into a photograph. The image moved away from part of the screen where two hands were holding a newspaper but opened up to page 7 on which the information was the headline.

"Here, then," Fohag explained, "is one of the many articles describing the 'adventure' of an Earthling who claims to have seen two Martians. Because for these primitives who like to mock their fellowmen, the flying saucers are piloted by Martians! If only they knew what Martians really looked like, they would never talk about us Wolfians and Centaurians as

39

monstrous gnomes but rather as Apollo, an ancient civilization's God of Beauty!"

The screen with the frozen image of the article blurred
and the two hands holding the paper disappeared. In their
place came a text in the universal language of the Federated
Worlds whose characters, lit up in relief with a slightly green
tint, looked like they were floating in mid-air.

In Quarouble, in Nord, France, a rough translation of
this weird group of signs unknown to Earthlings read, *Marius
Dewilde, a steelworker, claims to have seen two "Martians"
in a flying saucer and he has told us his strange story. They
were two beings around three feet high, extremely wide at the
shoulders and a huge head.*

After the headline and subheading written to lure in an
Earthling "bored" with all this "nonsense" about "so-called"
flying saucers and their "imaginary" occupants, the details
followed:

Lille, September 13, 1954, (by tel.)[6]

*Martians land on Earth... That was the rumor spreading
around Quarouble yesterday. A rumor that we cannot relate
without a great measure of skepticism: the "Martians", if they
were Martians, left no tangible trace of their visit to Earth.
But one man claims to have seen them and he described them
so precisely, so sincerely that the most cynical are starting to
believe his story. This man is a steelworker, 34 years old,
named Marius Dewilde.*

*He is a serious man. At the steel works in Blanc-
Misseron where he works, he has a reputation for being level-
headed and down-to-earth. There is apparently no reason for
him to pull off such a huge prank. And yet he insists on this
incredible thing: he saw, from his backyard, next to a mysterious, oblong machine, two human-like beings wearing spacesuits—two "Martians".*

---

[6] This article appeared in *France-Soir* on September 14, 1954.
(Author's Note)

40

It was Friday evening, September 10, 1954. The clock in the kitchen said 10:30 pm. Mrs. Dewilde and her son had just gone to bed. Mr. Dewilde was sitting in the kitchen, reading. In the yard "Kiki" his dog started barking so loudly that his master grabbed a flashlight and went outside.

From the yard, he tells, I saw a dark mass on the railroad a little ways to my left. I was thinking: it's a farmer who unhooked his cart. Tomorrow morning I'll have to tell the station agents to come and get it. Right after I thought this I heard like footsteps to my right on the other side of the fence, on the "Smuggler's Path". That was the direction my dog was looking and still barking at. I turned on my flashlight. Then I saw the two beings. They were 10 or 12 feet from me, separated by the fence. They were walking one in front of the other toward the dark mass that I'd seen on the tracks. The one in front turned to me. My light flashed on its face and it glittered like metal. I had the distinct impression that it was wearing a helmet and a spacesuit. Plus, the two beings were dressed alike. They were small, no more than three feet tall, but extremely broad-shouldered and the helmet protecting their heads looked huge. I saw their legs, which were proportionate to their size. But I didn't see any arms. I don't know if they had any.

When the initial surprise had passed I ran toward the backdoor in order to cut them off. Just then, in the big thing sitting on the tracks, a square window opened. A projector was pointed at me. This projector shined a bright light with greenish tints. Its beam paralyzed me. I wanted to cry out but I couldn't. I wanted to keep moving but my legs wouldn't obey me. Then like in a dream, a few feet away from, I heard the sound of footsteps on the cement porch in front of my backdoor. It was the two beings heading for the tracks.

At last the projector turned off. I could control my body. I went to the train tracks but the dark mass was already rising off the ground. It swayed a little going up, like a helicopter, with no sound but the whistling from a thick black smoke that it threw in my face. The machine rose straight up to around

100 feet then headed west, still gaining altitude. It was the shape of a cheese cover, around ten feet high and 15 to 20 feet in diameter. At a certain distance it turned a glowing red. Within a minute it had disappeared.

In the huge meeting room Centaurians, Polarians and Wolfians, each in its own way, felt what the humans call "a laugh coming on". When the big, bulging eyes of Fohag (who had just turned purple with red flushes) resumed their usual color, he brought up the translation of a following article on the 3D screen.

The "Martians" of Quarouble landed on the train tracks[7]. The Air Marshals found traces of landing gear on the railroad.

Three Air Marshals came to Quarouble (in Nord) yesterday to hear Mr. Marius Dewilde, the man who "saw" two Martians at his backdoor. They left the town convinced that on Friday night a mysterious flying machine really did land, as Mr. Dewilde claims, on the Saint-Amand-Blanc-Misseron railroad tracks: near the number 79 crossing...

...One of the crossties showed traces that could have been made by a machine during landing. In five places the wood was indented around 1.5 inches square. These marks are all identical: they are in a straight line and the three middle ones are 15 inches apart. The two outer ones are 25 inches from the last. A machine landing on a stand and not on wheels like our airplanes would leave the same marks, declared one of the Air Marshals.

The story that Mr. Dewilde told is also confirmed by several other witnesses in the region. At Onnaing, a young man, Mr. Edmond Auverlot, and a retired man, Mr. Hubbard, saw a red light moving across the sky around 10:30 pm, the time indicated by Mr. Dewilde. The same light was seen in Vicq by three young people coming out of a dance.

Fohag interrupted the characters rolling out on the stereoscopic screen and with a hint of cynicism said, "And now I

---

[7] See *France-Soir*, September 15, 1954. (Author's Note)

want you to pay particular attention to the conclusion of this article."

All these witnesses and facts give some credibility to Mr. Dewilde's story. However, many people remain skeptical. Mr. Dewilde is without doubt sincere. But one year ago he suffered a serious accident at work, brain trauma, after which he exhibited some neurological problems. Could he also have been the victim of a "waking hallucination," a well known phenomenon among doctors.

"There we have it!" Fohag exclaimed, holding in his anger and indignation that his eyes betrayed, turning from pink to brownish purple. "This sincere Earthling, reporting what happened when Hogounn and Injya landed near his home in their Fimn'has, is treated like a madman and accused of hallucinating by those whose closed minds refuse to believe in our existence. The marks from the landing gear on the railroad, the witnesses who saw the spaceship after taking off, everything is the result of 'brain trauma'!"

Addressing Hogounn and Injya in particular Fohag added:

"This Earthling you scared and who could tell only what he actually saw is going to be the butt of endless, imbecile jokes! For some he'll be crazy... until the day we make official contact with the governments of Earth and our mass landing in the major cities on T27 will astonish the skeptics and deniers but will delight those who saw us during our brief visits. Our arrival will exonerate them somewhat in the eyes of the primitives and the ignorant who are a little too quick to call them hoaxers or lunatics!"

Fohag sat down and a Polarian in a gray spacesuit stood up. He was tall, at least 6'2", twice the size of the Centaurians and one third taller than the Wolfians. Through his round, transparent helmet could be seen his clearly human features. With copper skin, black eyes and a prominent chin he could easily pass for an athlete on Earth who spent a lot of time in the sun.

"The detailed report that Chief Fohag just gave us," he began, "does not say much for the natives of planet T27. Most of them are still very primitive since they won't accept the multitude of witnesses who have seen our spaceships or pilots. Although the time to make contact is approaching, it is not any time very soon. Therefore, we have to continue visiting Earth, appearing on the different continents every day until the natives are equally divided into two clearly distinguished clans: those who openly admit being convinced about the extra-terrestrial origin of 'flying saucers' and those who are too blind, stubborn and proud and will publicly maintain their futile assertions calling our spaceships weather balloons, hallucinations and other ridiculous things.

"When the time comes, in all likelihood, a government on Earth will have the courage to side with the extra-terrestrial origin and reveal what it knows and *what it is hiding from the public*. On that day, then, we will land on the planet, confident that part of the human race knows that our coming was inevitable. Furthermore, we are already being helped in this by various private groups who insist on investigating our flights over their territories and who regularly publish the results of their research... in order to educate their fellowmen and prepare them for our coming[8]. At the right time they will become our friends and help us to prove our good intentions to their backward brothers.

"Moreover, preliminary contact has been made by us Polarians with certain of these more evolved humans. A most satisfying contact, I have to admit. Besides, the only government on T27 that may be convinced—without admitting it openly—about the extra-terrestrial origin of 'flying saucers' is the USA, a country that has reached a more developed stage

---

[8] In France the Commission Internationale d'Enquête Ouranos, Rue Etienne-Dollet, Bondy (Seine) publishes the journal *Ouranos*. In the USA, Flying Saucer International, in particular, publishes *Saucers*. In England the Flying Saucer Club publishes *Flying Saucer News*. (Author's Note)

than the other peoples. It is, therefore, likely that we will make our first official contact with the leaders of this country. This is not to say, however, that the said leaders will publish the details of this meeting that is *currently under consideration*."

The Polarian paused, seemed to listen to something. He kept silent for half a minute before continuing.

"Metna, the Centaurian radar controller on astrobase 1 has just sent me a psychic message. The space radar has detected a terrestrial rocket coming toward us at 5,000 miles an hour."

CHAPTER III

On the huge wall screen appeared an experimental super-rocket whose pieces had just detached. Lightened by dropping the tailpiece, which had exhausted its fuel reserve, the two last pieces of the multi-stage rocket sped out of the ionosphere. Remote-controlled from its launch pad at White Sands in New Mexico, the machine turned slightly off course and made a rectilinear ascension, heading for the first space satellite that orbited around 400 miles from Earth under astrobase 2.

The next-to-last conic piece detached and soon fell toward the ground while the "nose" of the rocket containing the research and observation equipment shot straight up. It reached the peak of its trajectory at a point seven and a half miles from the astrobase, continued its course, slowed down gradually, turned vertically and fell back down at high speed. Watched by the cameras on the two astrobases that kept it in constant focus during its fall, the guided missile remained the same size on the screens.

The Polarians, Wolfians and Centaurians saw it approach the ground and at 25 miles altitude they observed the ejection of a huge, metallic plastic parachute. Thus slowed in its fall the super V2 landed with less shock, which allowed the Rock-eteers[9] to pick up the observation equipment in relatively good shape. It was, in fact, important to get the data intact that recorded the different measurements as well as the photographs. When the rocket had touched down Fohag turned two black knobs that controlled a spinning drum with the signs of the universal characters and then he pressed two white buttons on a control panel in front of him.

"We're going to capture the radio messages sent by the White Sands base to the technicians in their mobile observation posts whose mission is to pick up the rocket. You'll first

---

[9] Technicians specializing in rockets. (Author's Note)

hear the voices of the Earthlings speaking in their own language and after lowering the volume you'll get the instant translation out of the electronic translator. Listen."

The assembly heard the voice of an American technician coming from above:

White Sands Headquarters to all tracking stations... White Sands Headquarters to all tracking stations... The rocket is fallen 32 miles east of Caballo and 47 miles north of Tularosa near point 75 B 7.

The Earthling's voice faded into an indistinct murmur under the monotone voice of the electronic translator changing the message into the universal language of the Federated Worlds.

"Join up at point 75 B 7. A helicopter has already taken off and is heading out there. Meet up with it. The helicopter will give you the exact coordinates of the landing. Over and out."

Fohag stood up and commented on the event.

"This is the third guided missile sent by the Earthlings to the zone around our astrobase 1. When they discovered the presence of our two space bases the General Staff of the Earth race called 'American' felt quite a fright[10]. The superior officers immediately thought that the astronomers had not spotted two meteors but two artificial satellites launched by the Earthling Russians, with whom they do not have friendly relations. The first observation rocket that they sent reached only 350 miles altitude. That was not enough for them to film our astrobase 1, which orbits at over 400 miles from the surface of the planet. Moreover, an error in calculation apparently ruined the test and instead of passing under the orbit where our base should have been the rocket was 70 miles off. The test, therefore, was a failure.

---

[10] True; two unknown satellites described as being "meteors" were discovered by American astronomers in 1954 (See *Ouranos*, n.12, November 1954). These objects are, according to official sources, *artificial* satellites. (Author's Note)

"However, the second one was not. This time the rocket ascended to almost 400 miles and was within five or six miles of our base. The photos it brought back must have stupefied whoever studied them. We examined them ourselves on our viewer. Even though blurry they still showed a perfectly round mass with a light source on top: the directional beam that keeps astrobase 1 in contact with us here. Despite these photos certain members of the General Staff remained doubtful. But what this latest rocket brings back should be able to convince them. In fact, this missile reached over 400 miles altitude and was only three miles from the base."

After a pause Fohag concluded, "Now, every team should go to their operational HQ. Orders are awaiting you to continue the observation exercises and the brief landings on the planet."

The Polarian chief who had already spoken stood up and said, "Over the coming *K'bogs*, Wolfians, Centaurians and Polarians from this section will be operating simultaneously on T27. At the end of this period of joint operations we'll meet again to compare our results."

In another section of astrobase 2, teams made up of all three races from the Space Commandos got ready to leave the sphere and accomplish their separate missions. A first group of 80 Fimn'has—or Flying Saucers—left the huge interior astrodromes to scatter into space. These orange spaceships, because of their small size (20 feet in diameter), were occupied by Centaurians, the small, human-shaped beings barely three feet tall. As they gradually separated from one another the Fimn'has headed for the various regions on earth that they would fly over. Some shot across the skies of France like a meteor; others flew over Belgium, England, Switzerland, Spain or Italy. Some landed in one country or another, unleashing terror among the "primitives" who saw them.

A second squadron of 80 ships came out of the wide-open hatch in the side of the fourth upper section of the astrobase. These discs were going to fly over the lesser known regions of Africa, Asia and the poles. This mission fell upon the Wolfians in their 25-foot ships.

A third and final squadron made up of both types of ships as well as even bigger ones up to 50 feet in diameter because piloted by almost human Polarians, left the mid-section of the base for interplanetary zones. With 50 ships this Space Commando was going to make an inspection of the permanent bases set up on ST28, ST26 and ST29, conventional galactic names representing Earth's satellite, the Moon, and the planets Venus and Mars.

Flying in triangular formation the Fimn'has aimed the directional magnetic beams in their cones at ST28, the Moon. At the head of the triangle was the spaceship piloted by Zimko, Chief of the Space Commandos, a well-built Polarian, very tan, with short, black, wavy hair and one loose lock curled stubbornly on his forehead. His upper lip bore a little black moustache, well-groomed, that would have made him the envy of a Terrestrial native like Robert Taylor or Errol Flynn.[11]

A sapphire blue bodysuit hugged his muscular chest and athletic legs. Over his tight black shorts he wore a huge belt that looked like it was made of gold leather and accentuated his "V-shaped" figure. Two big disintegrator pistols hung at his sides, swinging on his hips. On his belly was a diamond-shaped device about the size of a pack of cigarettes that contained a tiny but powerful two-way radio. This device turned on automatically to send an SOS if he were wounded and unable to use his telepathic abilities to communicate with his own or with his Wolfian and Centaurian allies. On his left wrist, finally, he wore a big watch with three screens that doubled as a radiation detector. The three screens told him: the time on the main planet of the solar system where the Commando was operating; the Universal Time on the astrobases of said solar system; and the time in the capital of the "mother planet" of the Polarians.

---

[11] See Volume 1.

In the cockpit was another "Man from Outer Space," Oïpku, Chief of the Lunar base who was going back to his post.

The incredible distance separating astrobase 2 from the Moon (240,000 miles on average) was covered in ten minutes by the mixed squadron that was now flying over the bright side of the Earth's satellite. Slowing down to a cruising speed of 1,200 mph, three minutes later the 50 spaceships, propelled by the energy of sub-cosmic rays to create a powerful magnetic field, came to a halt 60 miles above the Aristarchus crater.

As far as the eye could see the chalky white lunar ground looked pocked by countless craters of different sizes, scarred with sharp cracks, and fenced in here and there by jagged rocky chains standing out against the inky black of space. The squadron dropped straight down into the Aristarchus crater in the middle of which stood a gigantic, transparent dome almost half a mile high and over one mile wide that sheltered the lunar base, a fantastic city with emerald green buildings sparkling with the rays of the sun through the artificial atmosphere. The buildings, arranged in tiers, formed a giant pyramid whose "steps" were flat roofs used as aero-garages or decorated with magnificent hanging gardens. Strange flowers, as high as trees on Earth, swayed their colorful corollas in the warm breeze produced by the blowers built halfway up around the protective dome.

A bright beam of purple light coming from an airtight turret at the top of the transparent dome swept across the black sky. It soon caught the descending squadron, shined a weird light under the spaceships, then went off to probe outer space over the base. The 50 Fimn'has landed gently on the astrodrome encircling the dome. From the first ship Zimko and the Chief of the lunar base stepped out. Walking effortlessly despite their cumbersome spacesuits the two Polarians headed for one of the many decompression chambers giving access to the base.

Since Zimko could not stay more than an hour (T27 time) on the Moon the rest of his squadron did not leave their ships.

When they came into the dome the two spacemen quickly took off their helmets, tilting them back so they could breath the artificial atmosphere full of herbal scents. They took a raised path equipped with a moving gravito-magnetic field that brought them rapidly, at 1,300 feet off the ground, to the Technical Service for the Solar Observation Center on Mercury.

Everything in this building as well as the others was bright, awash in sunlight. They could breathe a restorative atmosphere, faintly light green and scented with an unidentifiable perfume. In a rectangular room (whose transparent wall let in the sunrays filtered by the dome) a beautiful Polarian woman welcomed them. She graced her visitors with a gorgeous smile and raised her right hand, palm open, to her shoulder, the traditional universal greeting known on all the planets in the Galactic Confederation.

The two spacemen answered her with the same gesture and Zimko asked, "What's in the last message sent by the robot-station on Mercury?"

The young woman typed a series of signs on an electronic wall keyboard and a monotone voice rang out, the "voice" of an electronic brain:

"The curve of magnetic variations of the 'solar field' will be at its lowest in one lunar month and 17 days. The activity of the solar prominences and other coronal phenomenon linked to sunspots will reach its maximum starting at the end of this time."

The voice went silent and the young woman went to where a cabinet had just opened in the wall and she took a bluish metallo-plastex sheet on which was inscribed various graphs for the Fimn'has crews to illustrate the variations in the solar magnetic field. This information was terribly important for all the spaceships in a solar system. In fact, an abrupt "maximum boost" in the intensity of the magnetic field could be fatal to one or more spaceships caught in its impact zone. They had already mourned the loss of seven Fimn'has disintegrated by these swirling electrons spit out by the sun and crashing through the driving and lifting magnetic field of the flying discs.

Zimko and Chief of the lunar base leaned over and examined the graphs. They frowned.

"In around a month and a half, T27 time, we'll have to be very cautious around Venus and even the Earth," Zimko observed. "Like in the past we'll have to interrupt our space operations from Mercury's orbit up to Mars' for a period of one Earth year. Only a few sporadic, very prudent flights will be made in this trouble zone... as few as possible."

"These magnetic storms that happen pretty regularly are obviously a serious handicap for our ships," Chief Oïpko commented.

The young technician smiled, "The cyclical reappearance of the Fimn'has flying over the Earth every two years should make the inhabitants pretty curious."

"Not only curious but some of them, in forming hypotheses, are wondering if the 'flying saucers' don't come from Mars because the planet reaches its perigee almost every two years. These Earthlings think that the 'Martians' wait for their planet to be close enough to Earth so the shorter distance between the two planets can be crossed more easily."

The young woman and the two men laughed at this joke but Zimko calmed them down to say, "Let's not laugh too much at the simple minds of the Earthlings. Everyone isn't as primitive as you might think. And even if their hypotheses about us and are origins are wrong, some of them at least have the virtue of admitting not only the existence of flying saucers but also their extraterrestrial existence. Of course, these who are right are called dreamers or lunatics!"

Zimko took off from the Aristarchus crater at the head of the squadron followed by the 49 lenticular ships heading for Venus.

After setting his controls and letting the automatic astronavigator pilot the ship, he settled back comfortably in his soft chair to study the inspection report that Oïpko, the lunar base chief, had given him. Everything was in order. The laboratories and research centers studying the Earth's satellite were carrying on their work, accumulating an impressive amount of scientific data of all kinds. Two other bases of research and observation were being built: one on the dark side and the other at the bottom of a big crevasse more than half a mile deep.

Some "archeological" digs had been undertaken in the Plato crater to get rid of the powdery matter piled up for millennia and uncover the ruins of the first Polarian base set up on the Moon at a time when the civilization of Atlantis (now buried) flourished on T27. In a brief account the report said that exploratory space squadrons had, over the past centuries, done some digging in this crater and on the surface of the satellite. It was specified parenthetically that the removal of dust had changed the floor of the crater and some Earth astronomers had been intrigued by the slight modifications, especially by the weird flashes of light—the giant spotlights—that showed up once in a while in this crater[12].

Zimko smiled thinking about the faces of the terrestrial astronomers when they would learn one day, from the very mouths of the men from space, that these craters sheltered observations bases and these "lights" and other strange signs had really seen by many of their fellows... quickly put down to optical illusions and hallucinations.

The Polarian turned on his space viewer and walked up to the visual transmitter—a tiny blue lens—blinking over the control panel at eye level. On the tilted screen appeared the blackish, hairy face of a Wolfian with pink, oval eyes. Lit up

---

[12] We have, in fact, observed over the past centuries weird flashes and points of light on the Moon that are not sufficiently explained away as "optical illusions." (author's Note)

by the lens of his own transmitter the long, stiff whiskers that grew on its chin and cheeks look like blue steel spikes.

"Greetings, Tim'hu," the Man from Outer Space raised his right hand.

The Wolfian's big eyes turned a little green, sunk into their sockets, then slowly came back to their normal place, popping out, and turned pink. "Peace to you, Zimko," he spoke in the universal language.

"I'd like to refer to your vast, historical knowledge, Tim'hu," Zimko began. "And not only your learning but also your deep wisdom."

"Speak, brother. Tim'hu will be happy to help with his modest knowledge."

"When the Polarians discovered the planet Mongan tens of thousands of years ago in the solar system that the Earthlings call Wolf 359, what were the reactions of the ancient Wolfians? This episode in Galactic History could tell me what the future reactions of Earth inhabitants might be. Aren't they at the same 'historical' stage as you Wolfians were when our exploration squads entered your world?"

"Your question is relevant, Zimko. But you are forgetting that we Wolfians have a mental formation, a psyche and an intelligence fundamentally different from the Earthlings who have the same shape as you. Although the reactions of our ancestors were the same as the first astonished reactions of the Earthlings when they saw strange 'flying machines' appear in the sky, it wasn't the same afterward. The Wolfians were unable to imagine that different beings could exist outside their planet Mongan. Our ancestors had reached a high level of civilization, spiritual development and I'd even say technology, relatively speaking. They had big cities, buildings perfectly organized for their mode of existence... almost contemplative and they lived very happily. However, they lacked one important things that gives a very particular orientation to the minds of other races in the galaxy. I'm talking about stars, the incommensurable sprinkling of suns that eyes contemplating the sky can see on those clear nights during what the Earth-lings call summer.

"*Because our ancestors were unaware of stars.* It was impossible for them to imagine that other Mongans existed tens, hundreds or thousands of light years away. And this strange shortcoming in their minds is understandable when you know that Mongan is perpetually clouded by a thick atmosphere filled with nitrogen, carbon dioxide, methane and ammonia gas. This opaque cloak barely lets the rays of our own sun through, giving us a feeble heat. Our ancestors lived in a kind of milky fog and their organs were adapted to very particular physical conditions.

"When your first spaceships crossed the higher strata of our atmosphere and came into the less dense biosphere of Mongan, we wondered what the mysterious, disc-shaped flying creatures could be. Were they hitherto unknown birds? Were they sent by K'tang, the Fire Spirit in the Sky, which is what we called the atmospheric lightning? Or were they visions caused by using too much *Pzond*, a wild vine that grows in our gardens and whose heady perfume often causes vivid hallucinations?

"Our ancestors could never have imagined that beings from another planet were watching them. Unable to understand what the flying discs were, we ended up accepting them as real and as an impenetrable mystery of what you Polarians or the Earthlings would call Destiny or the Unknowable.

"For years your spaceships flew over our lands, gathering evidence, probing our atmosphere and thanks to your detection devices and your paroptic vision studying the forms of Wolfian life and social, economic and spiritual organization. Convinced that we were peaceful, gentle and wise your ancestors, Zimko, dared to land near a small town. A few Polarians in spacesuits left their Fimn'has and cautiously approached two Wolfians. Naturally, they were afraid and ran away to watch the 'monsters' from farther away as they came out of the famous, mysterious objects that had been haunting their air for years. Seeing that the Polarians were not chasing them but on the contrary stood still, holding out their arms, they ended up coming back. Timidly at first, then more boldly they came within a few feet of your ancestors.

"Using their audiophones they spoke two or three words that they obviously didn't understand, but softly so as not to scare them, then they went back into their Fimn'has and took off, leaving the Wolfians stupefied. They ran back to their town, told their adventure and soon were summoned by the Kn'ag, the Chief of the place. And here is where the Wolfians' reaction will be fundamentally different from the Earthlings'.

"When the Kn'ag heard the story of the two villagers, he thanked them and right away send his report to the Grand Master of Mongan, the Supreme Sovereign. Not for one instant, Zimko, did my ancestors doubt the word of the witnesses and their strange encounter. Since lying is an abominable act for Wolfians, akin to a crime, no one thought that the story could have been made up. For our ancestors, just like for us today, the word of a Wolfian is sacred. What is said, *is*. Our legendary sincerity, of course, is known throughout the Federated Worlds in that old saying, *Honest as a Monganian!*

"So, we waited patiently for another meeting and welcomed your ancestors with joy… even though we were totally ignorant of who they were, where they came from and how."

Zimko thought about this for a long time before responding with a smile, "My ancestors quickly made contact with yours because they knew they were dealing with peaceful beings, fundamentally good. I understand now the difference that you explained between your people and those of T27. The Wolfians were, and still are, sensible whereas the Earthlings, despite their technical development, are still violent barbarians. Lying holds sway among them. Deceit and vileness are masters. Not everyone is like that, fortunately, but the human mind is so full of these traces of dark paganism that it's perpetually on the defensive. Everything extraordinary and wondrous is doubted. Everything that seems to partake of the supernatural—at least the idea that the Earthlings have of it—is right away called hallucinations, hoaxes… or head injury, to use the term a newspaper there used to explain the so-called 'vision' of the man who saw two Centaurians and their Fimn'has land on the train tracks."

The Wolfian historian rolled around his pink eyes in his hairy face and with great wisdom concluded, "The inhabitants of T27, Zimko, are at a turning point in their evolution. They are anxious and fearful of another war far more devastating than what they seen before. They refuse to believe in what they call 'flying saucers'... *but they're scared of them*, perhaps subconsciously. The day will come, however, when they'll have to recognize their mistake. This will be the day when they'll understand that in spite of their racial and religious differences all men are brothers. It will be harder for them to admit that Centaurians and we Wolfians are also brothers, but that too will come in time... when the threat of the Denebians and Procyonians looming over the galaxy is finally cut off."

CHAPTER IV

The space squadron commanded by Zimko split into two groups of 25 ships each. One of the groups led by Ruanoor, Chief of the Wolfian section, headed toward Mars. The second squadron, under Zimko's command, flew off into the star-studded space toward Venus.

In his cockpit Ruanoor, with his four long, six-knuckled fingers resting on a star chart, was studying the cosmographic coordinates and the tables showing the shaded zones disrupted by the sun's electrical storms. Next to him a Wolfian woman, Woodna, sat at the space radar carefully watching the three triangular screens of her detector.

Ruanoor put away his charts, adjusted some controls, tuned the electromagnetic cone of the detection beams to the polarity of Mars and leaned back, satisfied, in his bucket seat.

The luminous spiral that ran around the cockpit emanated a pinkish light, almost the same color as the Wolfian eyes when they feel no emotion. Because the color of their eyes changed according to their mood.

Faint traces of methane and ammonia gas produced by the air conditioning units appropriate for their race floated around the smooth chrome walls of the round room from time to time. Quickly dissipated by the combining with the nitrogen and carbon dioxide, these traces sometimes shined with a pink fluorescence when drifting in front of the spiral of the lighted rail.

The Wolfian watched the slow movement of a liquid metal "ball", like purple mercury, that rolled in a clear, calibrated tube in the shape of a horizontal circle. His right oval eye popped out of its socket every once in a while and rolled over to see Woodna leaning over her screens. He watched her—with what the humans would call "love"—who had been his crew mate for many K'bogs. The Wolfian leaders, being good psychologists, from the start of their space treks, had understood very well the use and need of mixed crews. Far from their home planet the Wolfians who were temporarily exiled in space or on foreign planets could not live without the presence of the opposite sex. Wolfian women quickly proved themselves excellent radar operators. Moreover, because of their ethics and great wisdom Wolfians could live with these operators without succumbing to arousing passions—if their feelings were not mutual—that might cause emotional conflict.

Gentle and lacking the "tactical" tricks so frequent among Earthling women, and being aware of their two-fold mission as aides and Muses, by the very presence of a little poetry in the hearts of their companions, Wolfian women were proud of the role they played in this grand space age of their people.

Woodna was thinking about all this while the mental waves sent out from Ruanoor slowly entered her. The silky black down on her face bristled and quivered as if being petted when her mind caught the psychic thoughts and send their vibrating effects through her body. With taking her right eye off the three radar screens she popped out her left and turned it, with no pretended confusion, toward the pink eye that had been watching her longingly for a moment.

Ruanoor's right eye and Woodna's left eye abruptly turned emerald green, a sign of affection. In a perfect coordinated movement their arms reached out for each other and their long fingers caressed the part of their head that served as a neck, the seat of an erogenous zone. This weird "finger kiss" was abruptly interrupted. With their senses heightened, on alert, the two Wolfians seemed to be listening hard to an almost inaudible sound.

On the three radar screens a kind of shadow sometimes come out to cover the spiral of blinking light that served as a tracer.

"That's weird," Woodna said. "It's like something just entered the detection field. According to the tracer it's pretty big but it's blurry... it even disappears sometimes. I can't really say if it's solid… or gas. There's no echo to speak of being sent back by it but a kind of hazy interference."

Ruanoor consulted a device under a vacuum jar in which a small bright sphere was emitting a violet light.

"I'm getting no magnetic disturbance that would explain the reactions of the radarscope… as far as these mysterious, ghostly shadows appearing very hazily off and on your screens can be called 'echo reactions'."

Turning on his viewer he tuned into the general communication wavelength to send a message to the whole squadron:

"Ruanoor to the teams of Commando MT3. Are you getting anything strange on your radar screens?"

The answers came back one by one following the customary order in communicating with the chief of the Commandos.

"In fact, we were about to contact you about the presence of an inexplicable 'shadow' on our space radar."

"Since we don't know the origin or nature of this 'moving shadow', stay on your guard and be ready to move at the first signal. Spread out to 100 diameters. That way, whatever happens, our squadron will be a lot less vulnerable to a would-be attacker. However, I don't think it's a real threat. If an enemy ship were operating in our zone it would have certainly been detected already. This mysterious shadow isn't precise enough to call it a material body. Maybe it's a cloud of cosmic dust composed of pyrite or some other magnetic material."

The 25 spaceships spread out, still keeping a triangular formation but putting 600 yards between each other. Ruanoor and Woodna kept one eye on the three triangular screens while lost in thought about the cause and origin of this shadow detected by all the ships.

They both felt a peculiar sensation. It was not awkwardness, at most a discomfort, a kind of odd unrest that was slowly wiping out their ability to think straight. The flight controls seemed to stretch away from them only to shoot back to their normal place before the cycle started up again: slowly stretch away and suddenly shoot back. But every time the commands came back into clear view a little more slowly. Finally their vision fogged over and they saw nothing but a hazy, impalpable mist that drowned everything in the moving shadow of "something" present and yet unseen.

"Woodna! Woodna!" Ruanoor struggled to call out.

"Your voice is… so far away," the Wolfian girl managed to sigh out before being frozen in her chair with her head thrown back.

In a last effort of will Ruanoor flipped on the general alarm, instantly putting him in contact with the rest of the commando.

"We're suffering… some… psycho-physical malaise," he murmured. "Take… our ship… under control… of your…"

He could not finish as he completely stopped thinking. Stiff, staring at the controls and obeying an unknown mental order, he slowly turned a small sphere that opened the ventral hatch of his spaceship. After a minute the small sphere returned to its normal position, thus showing that the exterior hatch had been closed by someone *from the inside!*

Protected by a screen that absorbed almost all detecting rays emitted by the 25 Fimn'has, which it had been following for almost an hour, a giant, disc-shaped Denebian vessel was fearlessly navigating the velvety darkness of space. Its impressive size would only appear as a vague shadow on the Wolfian radar. And the dwarfish crew would be unable to discover the origin of this weird "ghost" in the middle of their triangular screens.

Now, in a 600-mile radius, the enemy ship was sending out beams of hypnotic waves to annihilate the wills of the astronauts piloting the Fimn'has.

After sending psychic orders to the Wolfians to open the hatch of all their ships, M'nag, the Denebian Chief of the huge, lenticular ship with a dome on top, ordered the boarding while P'tonk, his second-in-command, took the helm.

The giant spaceship had just synchronized its speed with the 25 Fimn'has and was keeping at least 1,000 yards over the tight formation. Under its belly a long, reinforced door panel opened where 50 Denebians were standing in transparent spacesuits that revealed their repulsive, scaly green, humanoid bodies. Their green heads were encased in rectangular helmets. Their bumpy skulls were topped by a blood-red, fleshy growth. Their beady eyes, always moving, were orange with vertical black stripes. Inside their spacesuits all they wore was a yellow-orange jacket and black bodysuit with a belt from which hung a long tube that shot thermal rays.

With a bending at the knees the 50 Denebians leaped into space, turning on their jet packs in order to escape the pull of their giant spaceship and especially so as not to drift off into outer space. Like birds of prey they spread out in pairs and slowed down when they finally had to grab onto the open bellies of the Fimn'has with their magnetic grappling gloves. With short bursts of their jet packs, using their hands and feet, they slipped in through the narrow hatches of the flying saucers before closing them up behind them.

When all of them had disappeared inside the Wolfian and Centaurian discs, the giant spaceship shot off at incredible speed to the swarm of asteroids (between the orbits of Mars and Jupiter), one of which contained their base.

M'nag, the Denebian Chief of the spaceship and P'tonk, his second-in-command, a specialist in attacking the Space Commandos of the Federated Worlds in this solar system, opened the interior hatch of the Wolfian ship where they had entered. Bent over in the narrow cabin of the Fimn'has—made for Wolfians only four feet tall and not these six and half feet tall hideous monsters—they struggled out of their spacesuits.

Being sympodic creatures able to adapt to all environments and thus breathing the methane and ammoniac air as easily as their own full of cyanogen, they could, therefore, take off their suits to have more freedom of movement.

Both of them folded up their spacesuits, put them to the side and sat on the floor, their backs against the chrome metal wall of the cockpit. Then they slowly ran their horny fingers over a small machine with different colored "bumps" that was installed in their belts. And they waited.

Ruanoor and Woodna, the one slumped over the control panel and the other leaning back in the pilot's seat, started moving. They shook themselves, their big eyes fluttering in their sockets and their shiny black fur bristling. With their backs to the Denebians they were not yet aware of their presence.

"What made us pass out?" Ruanoor mumbled as he examined the instruments.

"I feel like I'm waking up from a very long sleep," Woodna confessed. "The astronavigator says that we're at least six million miles from Mars. It read 15 million just before we were knocked out by… the loss of consciousness. We couldn't have been out for more than ten minutes."

"In seven minutes T27 time we'll reach Mars and get in touch right away with our home planet to tell the cosmobiologists about the symptoms of this weird psychic-physical attack."

"You'll say nothing of the kind."

At these words the two Wolfians jumped in surprise and turned around. M'nag, who had just spoken, was pointing his thermal ray tube at them. His sidekick was also gripping his menacing weapon in his claws.

"You're at our mercy," M'nag's guttural voice said in the universal language. "In all of your ships there are two of us. The slightest false movement or any attempt to escape or alert your planetary base will get you fried. Keep heading toward Mars. At the appropriate time we will give you specific orders."

Zimko's squadron descended slowly through the thick atmosphere of Venus, guided only by radar. Piloting was always done like this on Venus where there was no visibility until 10,000 feet altitude. Above this a dense cushion of atmosphere, ten and a half miles thick, barred all normal, sight-based flight. On Venus no eye could contemplate the stars.

The rays of the sun, in spite of the relative proximity[13], barely reached the surface. If "evolved" Venusians did exist, they would have been incapable (like the first Wolfians) of imagining the presence of other worlds in outer space.

Zimko veered off course slightly. His viewing radar was showing a tall chain of mountains. The ship gained altitude, flew over the rocky range and came back down into a wide valley where the permanent base stood.

Under the thick, cloudy layer of cottony fog rose up the Polarian city's dull dome, not sparkling in the sunlight filtered by the Venusian gas. It was the middle of the day on this hemisphere but it was nothing like a sunny day on Earth. Stifling heat lay outside the dome that sheltered a pyramidal city that looked exactly like the one on the Moon. Strange plants and enormous trees, flowers like huge umbrellas, vines as thick as tree trunks and hundreds of feet long, all tangled in the tropical atmosphere that was saturated with carbon dioxide. Ironically, although this gas made up a large part of Venus' atmosphere, it became much rarer under 10,000 feet down to the surface, in spite of the density that normally should have trapped it on the ground, especially in the valleys.

This particularity had allowed a kind of life to adapt to these physical conditions. Although unbreathable for Polarians and humans, the air on Venus maintained the life of a category of rudimentary thinking beings. Anthropologists and paleontologists on Earth would have called them "pre-hominid" or maybe even "hominid"—"spiritually" speaking—in the first stage of mental evolution. But all comparison would stop there. The morphology of the Venusians was radically different from Polarians and their human characteristics.

For millennia the so-called "Men from Outer Space" had tried to educate this race of half-insect, half-biped creatures with their gangly bodies like a praying mantis, three pairs of "arms" and two long legs with yellow thighs protected by ser-

---

[13] 67 million miles whereas Earth is 93 million miles from the Sun. (Author's Note)

rated spikes. They had gotten satisfactory results after a few generations but, alas, as soon as their influence stopped the Venusians left to themselves returned to their natural state and forgot all the teaching. Therefore, they had to live in permanent contact with the Polarians.

For 15 years, starting from the reestablishment of a fixed base, many Venusians had started "to think" intelligently again with more or less success.

The 25 flying saucers landed gently not far from the dome and the mixed crews—Polarians, Wolfians and Centaurians—came out in their spacesuits.

"It's weird," Zimko said to his friend Tim'hu, a wise old Wolfian. "I don't see any life in the city."

Standing absolutely still he concentrated and used his paroptic vision. All of a sudden his face tensed and he clenched his jaw.

"The people on the base are unconscious and most of them are probably dead! The ones still alive are unable to think. Their psyches are slowed down to the utmost limit of perception. It's impossible to tell what happened to them. Let's go. I don't see any foreign presence under the…"

He broke off, then cried out, "I just saw a series of huge cracks in the protective dome. The artificial air has escaped and been replaced by the Venusian gas… That explains why everyone is either dead or in a coma."

He sent out orders: three groups of Wolfians and Centaurians would put on their spacesuits to bring out various strange instruments that acted as both metal tanks of compressed air and submachine guns.

As fast as their freezing legs allowed they would all run to one of the three cracks indicated by Zimko. The first crack they came across measured at least three feet wide and 20 feet long. In the blink of an eye the "dwarves" put their material on the ground, took out a long flexible tube that they changed into an instrument resembling a submachine gun and they pointed the "barrel" at one end of the giant crack.

A strong jet of fluid spread over the angular crack that puffed and swelled noticeably. On the other side of the crack another team of small creatures in spacesuits did the same thing. The liquid jet spread quickly from one end to the other of the break changed into an opaque, bulbous material that swelled and hardened almost instantly. In less than three minutes the two "lips" of the crack closed up and bonded tightly. The Wolfians and Centaurians sprayed their quick-set "mending" with one last air-tight layer and hurried back to their spaceships where they put away their tools.

While the cracks were being sealed, Zimko along with three Polarians, four Wolfians and two Centaurians ran through the eerily silent city. The Polarians, being faster than their dwarfish companions, were the first to reach a 30-foot square, super-metal building. The Chief of the Space Commandos halted, surprised that the armored door of the "block" was open.

His paroptic vision assured him that no hostile presence was inside. He and his team entered the cube with lighted walls and immediately turned on six huge wall switches while the two Wolfians, crouching on their short legs, turned a big, calibrated wheel. At their feet, in front of the controls that they had just worked, lay a Polarian with his chest and head burned.

"The Denebians wrapped up their crimes!" Zimko growled. "After cutting the three cracks in the dome in order to empty the city of its air, some of the green monsters came into the base, killed the technician at the supply source and then shut off all the distribution valves and ventilation ducts."

On saying this he increased the flow of oxygen and turned up full blast the air-purification control. A low hum rose in the city, echoing ominously under the transparent dome made of xoning.

"Three minutes from now," Zimko announced, "all the carbon dioxide under the dome will be sucked up and spit outside. The over-oxidation will help us revive those who can still be saved."

The crew went back to work as pretty much everywhere on the Venusian base the Wolfian, Centaurian and Polarian Space Commandos struggled to revive the suffocated by shooting them with a drug that would shorten the usual time needed to practice artificial respiration.

Gradually as Zimko and his friends approached the center of the base the number of corpses lying on the metal ground grew. All of them were stretched out in the direction of the central building.

"From the looks of the bodies," Tim'hu remarked, "and the fact that we saw no corpses on the outskirts of the base it seems like the automatic alarm was sounded when the three cracks were opened."

"Indeed," Zimko agreed. "If the inhabitants had been knocked out right away we would have found the bodies all over the dome. But we didn't. The Polarians, therefore, were warned of the disaster and everyone ran to the heart of the city where there was the airtight building that could hold everyone. When the automatic alarm closed the doors and windows, it's likely that some survivors were still at home, unless they took the private evacuation tubes that end up in the central building. The unfortunate people in the streets, far from any shelter, were struck down. Maybe we can revive some of them if the blood vessels in their brains are not totally deprived of oxygen."

Zimko went up to a panel that slid into the metal wall of a building and he consulted the three luminous screens on the back wall. "The barometers are showing normal air pressure coming back," he spoke into his audiophone. "There's only trace amounts of carbon dioxide and the flow of artificial air is back to normal. The indicators are positive. We can take off our helmets but keep your spacesuits on."

The return to normal conditions made the doors and windows open after being closed by the automatic security system. Many Polarians, both men and women, came leaning out the windows or filling up the entrances. Their faces betrayed their intense emotions. Shaken up, they all joined the members of the Space Commandos to revive those who had not found shelter and were suffocated by Venus' toxic atmosphere.

Two hours later Boïdo, the chief of the Venus base, broadcast a message calling on everyone to "check off" their presence so they could count the survivors.

In every house and every lab or research facility, the Polarian men and women entered their identification on the keyboard of the *multiplex* and sent them to the Demographic Counter. After ten minutes the central electronic brain had collated and classified all the numbers and with the total had calculated the number of missing. The results came up in the indicator that had just lit up in front of the Base Chief standing next to Zimko and his Space Commandos.

"1735 casualties out of a population of 7000 people!" Boïdo stormed. "That's the first time in this solar system that we've seen such a massacre by the Denebians!"

"But didn't your radar spot the approach of the enemy spaceships?" Zimko questioned.

"I checked all the observation posts. The radars were clear: nothing was spotted. No foreign ship entered the beam of detector waves. All they registered on the screens, and only right before the attack came, was a faint, blurry shadow, but it couldn't have been the echo of a material object. It was obviously thought to be a magnetic perturbation, a pretty frequent phenomenon on Venus due to its relative nearness to the sun."

Zimko shook his head, skeptical. "It had to be the Denebians—or the Procyonians. They must have developed a system like ours that makes them invisible to our screens. A device that absorbs radar waves instead of bouncing them back to their source. Even if their ships weren't invisible—unlike our Fimn'has that can become so whenever they want—they could, thanks to this hypothetical absorption system, pass undetected in the upper atmosphere of Venus.

"Protected like this the Denebians could come out and with their jet packs it'd be easy for 10 or 15 of them to land in the forest around the base. Divided into three groups, shooting cracks in the dome was child's play for them, no problem at all with their thermal rays. Once their sabotage was done, taking advantage of the confusion caused by the alarm, they sneaked into the dome, killed the technician in charge of the air circulation and blocked all the controls, which stopped the air purification but also shut down the supply of artificial air.

"Then they could leave calmly and use their jet packs to shoot back up to their ships, which flew back, without being spotted, to their astrobase somewhere in the solar system."

Boïdo, thinking long and hard, completely agreed. "It could've happened like that. But in any case, we have to immediately reorganize our defenses throughout the solar system and revise our detection systems, which have just proved to be inadequate."

"That's the gist of the psycho-message I just sent to all the Chiefs of bases and commandos in this galactic zone," Zimko said, gifted as he was with the strange psychic power of instant communication with anyone of his race and anywhere in the galaxy.

CHAPTER V

The 25 Fimn'has of Ruanoor—under the control of the Denebians—had just entered the orbits of Phobos and Deimos, the two tiny moons of Mars, and were slowing down as they neared the ground.

The surface of the planet came in view, rather flat with occasional vast red plains, the dominant color of the Martian crust due to a high level of iron oxide. Areas tending to light green with yellow halftones became clear just south of the northern polar cap that spread its whitish blue crown over a fairly large zone.

At 12 miles altitude the squadron veered off to the northwest, toward the Hellas Desert in the middle of which was a lighter area called Zea Locus by the T27 astronomers. Little by little as the spaceships got closer, this zone, located at the junction of four groups of huge, paired canals protected by tunnels of transparent matter, revealed its true nature: a gigantic base under a dome like those built on Venus and the Moon by the Polarians.

Huge terraced buildings forming a pyramid city were fitted with big windows twice as wide and tall as the other bases because of the weak sunlight on the planet Mars.

While the 25 spaceships dropped straight down, the rectangular panel of a giant access hatch opened on the ground in the dome. The Fimn'has closed ranks, leaving barely three feet of space between them, and formed two rows under the huge decompression hatch. The transparent, super-metal door closed behind them. Then the opposite door opened and the formation of "flying saucers" rolled on their landing gear made of three balls for 50 yards to come out under the dome on the airstrips surrounding the city.

The 50 Wolfians and Centaurians left their Fimn'has and crossed the astrodrome. In their squat, bulky spacesuits with cylindrical torsos and round helmets the small beings came hopping from right to left. The lookouts perched on top of the four control towers watched this weird hopping due to the weak gravity on the planet, which the Space Commandos were not used to. They must have forgotten to turn on the gravity control system and were playing around with their lightness. They never could have suspected that the crew was feeling the effect of the psychic annihilators controlled by the Denebians hiding in the Fimn'has.

Thanks to their clever attack the green monsters had succeeded in this amazing exploit: to overcome the crew of the Space Commandos and without facing any opposition entering the heart of one of the planetary bases of the Federated Worlds! Not only had the first phase of their plan worked but they could make the Centaurians and Wolfians under their control do whatever they wanted. Without leaving their hiding place in the spaceships on the edge of the city they would be able to manipulate the actions of those whose wills they had destroyed.

The 50 Wolfians and Centaurians took the central pathway of Rynka, the Martian Base, and after around 700 yards they entered the imposing building in the center of the city with a metal tower that rose up through the dome and was crowned with a transmitter that flashed a light at regular intervals. Taking a wide platform that worked by a gravito-magnetic field, the 50 astronauts were soon on the 237th floor.

Hudako, the Polarian Chief of the Rynka Base, welcomed them but with a wrinkled brow. "Greetings, Ruanoor. I'm happy to see you and your crew. To what do I owe this honor?"

Ruanoor stepped forward and bowed slightly. "We figured we should come out here and tell you about a recent disaster on Venus."

"Zimko just sent me a psychic message, so I know all about it."

Ruanoor stayed silent for a moment, apparently searching for what to say. Intrigued by this attitude and by this unusual visit, Hudako used his telepathic sense and searched the minds of all the Wolfians and Centaurians there in his control tower.

Surprisingly he ran up against a psychic resistance, a kind of unbreakable barrier obliterating their consciousness. Knowing full well that these creatures were incapable of putting up barriers to the mental probes of the Polarians, he sensed something wrong and without being able to explain this resistance he started sending out a psychic message to the surveillance posts. He did not have time to finish.

Ruanoor, acting on the orders of the Denebians, abruptly fired a paralyzing ray at him and his assistant.

M'nag, the Denebian Chief hiding in Ruanoor's spaceship, watched the operation on a viewer. He immediately adjusted the controls on a small mechano-psychic transmitter and took control of Hudako and his assistant. The two Polarians were suddenly awake but under the influence of the green monsters.

Looking normal, Hudako sat before a big screen and pressed some buttons. The screen lit up. A circular control room appeared, the walls full of screens and dials, chrome levers and various colored buttons, where three Polarians, two Wolfians and five Centaurians were busy working in spacesuits.

"Call for a general assembly," Hudako ordered. "Everyone on the base has to meet in the west zone of the astrodrome immediately. Evacuation drill. Inform me when everyone's there and then you, too, leave your posts to join them. The electronic robots will replace you. Immediate orders. Over and out."

In Ruanoor's 25 spaceships the Denebians got busy. They readied their tiny mind annihilator devices and adjusted their mechano-psychic transmitters before putting the entire population under their mental control.

After half an hour the Polarians, Centaurians and Wolfians living on the Rynka Base started lining up in closed ranks on the astrodrome ring, less than 200 yards from the 25

Fimn'has where the green monsters were about to secretly bend them to their will.

In less than an hour the 9,000 members of the Martian base were gathered together by their chief, Hudako. Everyone had put on their spacesuits, including the Polarians who, however, were living in air adapted to their physiological functions.

Since evacuation drills were common in Rynka just like in the other bases of the solar system this call was not terribly surprising. But although the tedious exercise was no fun for anyone, it was enjoyable to the young Polarian boys and girls, as well as their Wolfian and Centaurian friends, because they all got along well with each other; the weird little hairy creatures just over one foot tall but endowed with incredible agility and the "giants" who were the children of spacemen to them. From the youngest age they were used to living together and despite their physical differences the three types of "thinking beings" formed a perfectly united "racial partnership".

While the adults waited patiently for the orders from Chief Hudako—who was really making them wait, some of them thought—the children of the three races, instead of staying in obedient lines like their parents, were playing with each other, breaking ranks, switching lines and bumping into the adults who scolded them for their misbehavior knowing that when the chiefs arrived the excited little kids would calm down.

The last members of the population arrived and joined the others. The Denebians in the spaceships were only waiting for the technicians from the control tower to come to the astrodrome to act. Two groups of 20 and 25 Polarians, Centaurians and Wolfians children were huddled together a little behind the back row and holding a mysterious council—whispering even though using their microphones! Speaking aloud, of course, would have made no difference but it was much more fun to play the conspirators.

They cast frequent, sly glances at their parents who were lined up dutifully. Having agreed to play "Space Conquerors" they stole away from the adults, who were starting to get impatient, and one by one snuck over to a big transport ship parked at the end of the line of adults. Hiding behind the ship they whispered together again (through their mics again) and then ran as fast as they could to the deserted city. They imagined they were attacking the palace of the tyrant who lorded over this recently discovered planet. To reach it they would have to cross unknown, hostile regions.

For them the huge, empty streets were wild canyons inhabited by bloodthirsty monsters. The fragrant gardens and their tall plants swaying gently in the perfumed breeze were impenetrable, putrid jungles.

The pounding boots of a group of adults in spacesuits echoed in their helmet earphones. The technicians from the control tower, the last to evacuate the base, were joining the others in the astrodrome. The little rascals and their Wolfian and Centaurian friends dove into a bed of Tr'link, the tall, red plants with black flowers, carnivorous plants that "gobbled up" a huge amount tiny, harmless insects. Their big, velvety black petals would make a perfect screen for them.

The technicians ran by less than ten yards from the Tr'link but they did not see anything. The sound of their boots pounding the metal street faded away.

The "conquerors" in the grass came out of the "jungle" and all together they ran toward the Nuclear Center, a huge building with thick lead walls.

"Let's attack the tyrant's palace," a young. 12-year old Polarian shouted, pointing his thumb at the formidable building protecting the atomic generators.

He grabbed the wrist of a tiny Centaurian, lifted her up and stuck her on his shoulders while yelling out a war cry that led the gang to attack the palace. Being much more agile than the Polarians, the Wolfians and Centaurians got ahead and reached the lead wall first. A few seconds later the Polarian kids caught up, everyone out of breath from their mad dash.

"Take a rest, Tink," the tiny Centaurian girl patted the round helmet of her friend.

Tink did so, taking the girl in his big gloves and setting her on the ground.

"What are we going to do?" B'tna, the young Centaurian, asked.

"We're going to have a war council before attacking the palace," Tink pointed, still with his thumb, at the atomic factory.

The rascals sat in a circle around their "chief" and planned the second part of their game... without realizing that inside the thick iron walls, *they would escape the annihilating rays shot at their parents and all over the base by the hideous green creatures from Deneb!*

From astrobase 2 orbiting 600 miles off Earth, a squadron of Fimn'has came out of the middle section and shot off into space. The ten ships quickly veered off in different directions.

One of them, piloted by Hogounn and Injya, headed for France, which it flew over at high speed and no less than 6,500 feet altitude. It stopped over the Drôme department and came down diagonally after hovering over Chabeuil, a town southeast of Valence. The spaceship slowed down and landed very gently on the edge of a cornfield after snapping off a branch of an acacia tree. The sun was still shining high in the sky and flooding the countryside with its rays.

Injya stayed in the cockpit of the ship while her companion, Hogounn, left through the hatch. His transparent spacesuit hid nothing of his "human" features or of the light blue Space Commando uniform.

With his small size Hogounn easily hid behind the trunk of the acacia and watched the Earthling who was walking up from 500 yards away. Apparently he had not seen the Fimn'has land. A few feet in front of the Earthling was scampering one of the four-legged creatures that Fohag had called "Dog."

Hogounn watched the primitive walking toward him for a long time and noticed that he was wearing a loose, brightly colored garment, very different from the tight-fitting clothes that hugged the legs of the Earthling he had seen in the north of this country during a previous mission. Then the Centaurian remembered the televised stereofilms and the comments of the instructor describing the fashions on T27. No, the being approaching him was not a primitive man but a primitive *woman* and her loose garment was called a "tress" or maybe "dress."

The small spaceman backed away. While the Earthling, with her back turned, was examining some vegetation he went to stand in the middle of the cornfield and watch her. The four-legged creature spotted him and started screaming—the instructor had said "parking" or "barking"—a few feet away from him. It bared its fangs menacingly.

Hogounn turned on his sound sensor and waited.

The Earthling woman turned around, looked at the Centaurian and shrugged her shoulders, saying something to her four-legged companion.

Her unexpected behavior was completely astonishing to the dwarf. It was the first time that a primitive, on seeing him, showed no signs of fear.

All of a sudden the Earthling stopped talking to her dog and looked more closely at Hogounn, squinting her eyes. Then her eyes suddenly popped wide open. Her pink face turned red, then white and she shrieked before running away as fast as she could. She reached a patch of vegetation and dove in, lying flat on the ground and screaming even louder.

"You hear that, Injya?" Hogounn asked in his mic as he strode calmly back to the ship. "Doesn't it sound like the cry of a Z'nog being hit by a stream of energy during a hunt on the planet Myln'dha?"

"Yes," Injya smiled in agreement. "It really does sound like a Z'nog. That's funny."

While a tragedy with serious implications was being played out on Mars and while Zimko and his squadron were preparing to take off from Venus, the "flying saucers" on Earth were carrying on their business, submitting the primitives to tests in order to study their reactions to the presence of "Martians."

With a Polarian at the controls a single-seater Fimn'has landed in a rather remote area on French soil. Night was falling. Hidden by a hedge the small ship, around 15 feet in diameter, could not be seen from the bend in the road at this spot.

Through the bushes the Polarian watched the Earthling coming in his direction. When he was only a few yards away he stepped out. The Earthling, surprised at seeing a man dressed in a mechanic's uniform with a motorcycle helmet come out of the bushes, stopped short. On the defensive the primitive swung out a long, wooden instrument ending in four, slightly curved, metal spikes.

This movement surprised the Polarian. He had thought the instrument could only be something to help the Earthling walk. Waved in front of him like this the long, wooden pole with a split end became a dangerous weapon. The Polarian decided to smile and holding out his hands he approached the Earthling and said something that the Earthling could obviously not understand.

The human hesitated a moment and ended up lowering his instrument. The Man from Outer Space stepped closer and in a friendly manner took the primitive's hands in his, squeezing them fraternally. The Earthling, standing agape, let him do it, thinking he was dealing with some harmless lunatic escaped from a foreign asylum, since the lunatic did not speak his language.

The Polarian dropped the human's hands and jumped through the bushes and back into his Fimn'has. Then he took off, glad to have made friendly contact with a primitive of T27[14].

---

[14] This encounter actually took place on September 10, 1954 on the Plateau de Millevaches (Corrèze). The farmer, Antoine Mazaud, saw a "spaceman" who shook his hands before getting back into his spaceship, but did not hug him as some

Tired of playing now the Polarian, Wolfian and Centaurian children, after miraculously escaping the effect of the Denebian annihilating rays, were getting ready to go back to the astrodrome and join their parents. Since the entire population was busy they were pretty sure that their escapade would go unnoticed.

But when they were on the way back they saw the first adults returning to the city. In fear of being scolded the kids hid in a big, perfumed flowerbed and waited for life to get back to normal on the base before sneaking back to their houses. They would come up with a good excuse for their absence and tell their parents that they were at the end of the row when Chief Hudako started the evacuation drill.

Therefore, peaking through a bush the three different races of children watched the "big people" marching by. Tink, the group's leader, opened his helmet, as did his Polarian friends. The Wolfians and Centaurians did not breathe the same air so they kept theirs on. B'tna crawled over to Tink and with her little, six-fingered hand tugged at the thick spacesuit to get his attention.

"What is it, B'tna?" the boy asked, putting his hand on the tiny creature's helmet.

"Look, Tink," she pointed at a group of Wolfian adults passing by a few feet away.

The Wolfian children stopped whispering together. They were stunned seeing the adults wandering back to the center of the base.

"Did you see that, Tink?" the Wolfian girl asked.

"See what?"

"Their eyes, come on!"

"Oh, yeah!" Tink blurted out. "That's funny…"

---

newspapers claimed. (Investigative Report of the Ouranos Commission) (Author's Note)

In fact the big Wolfian eyes were unusual. All of them, without exception, were not only motionless but even the same yellow color.

"Yeah, that's funny," G'bho, one of the young Wolfians, said. "You know, Tink, our eyes never stay the same color for long?"

"Of course," Tink affirmed. "Wolfian eyes change color depending on their mood or in reaction to their environment," he repeated from a textbook on basic cosmobiology.

"By Kosmos!" he cried out. "Why are they all the same color? Could they all be thinking about the same thing and reacting in the same way to their thoughts?"

"That's impossible," G'bho said, his own eyes popping out of their sockets. Fidgeting his four fingers in his bulky spacesuit, a sign of deep worry, he grumbled, "My brothers are different somehow."

Watching the Polarians carefully Tink noticed that they were all walking alike, staring straight in front of them. Nobody was talking.

Tink was disturbed by this. He felt vaguely like some extraordinary event had taken place, an unimaginable event that kept the "big people" from acting normally.

A group of young Polarians Wolfians and Centaurians was walking past Tink and his friends. Not a one of them was talking. They were not playing either, just keeping that weird blank expression on their faces, staring ahead, inexplicably. They looked normal but were not acting like they usually did.

Tink yelled and jumped out of his hiding place in front of a young Polarian couple: his parents. They looked down and stared at him blankly. A shadow of a smile crossed their faces and without saying a word they continued on their way, leaving the boy dumbfounded.

Panting and crying Tink was about to run after them but B'tna held him back, grabbing the leg of his spacesuit. Her little voice begged through the microphone, "Don't go, Tink! Stay with us. Something happened when we were playing.

Something we don't understand. Did you see all my brothers and sisters?"

Tink sniffled and nodded his head.

"They're as weird as your parents and brothers. I think that we're the only ones in Rynka who stayed normal."

"We have to do something, Tink!" G'bho cried, grabbing the young Polarian's arm.

The other voices called out to him, begging, demanding that they do something. In other circumstances Tink would have felt a certain pride in this unanimous trust in his capacities as leader, but today, faced with this incomprehensible stupor that struck the inhabitants of Rynka, he felt very uncomfortable. A knot formed in his throat. He wiped away a tear and plopped down in the high grass.

B'tna climbed up his knees and rubbed her six-fingered hand over his tear-soaked face. "Oh, Tink, do something! Do something!"

The shadow of a huge flying object passed over the group of desperate children. Tink looked up and through his tears saw a gray spaceship flying over the transparent dome. He wiped his eyes, blinked and stopped crying. Then he jumped up. "Look! That's not one of our ships!"

In the purple sky where the thin atmosphere let a few stars shined at the same time as the small, bright sun, a huge spaceship was coming down.

"It looks like it's going to land…"

"Right… It's coming down on the outside astrodrome."

"Let's go see!"

"Okay but be careful and try to see without being seen," Tink advised.

The gang ran down the streets past the adults who were acting so strangely. No one paid any attention to them.

Soon they slowed down and walked along a green metal wall. They slipped into a building and stormed into the gravito-magnetic elevators. A minute later they were floating in all positions over the pipe leading to the flat roof of the building. An agile leap carried them out of the repellent field and they all landed on the edge of the vertical well, waving their arms to keep their balance like tightrope walkers on a high wire.

They hurried to the west edge of the roof and threw themselves on their bellies. Cautiously lifting their heads to look over the low metal wall they all cried out in surprise. High over the city they could see the part of the astrodrome stretching out to the west of the base. Beyond the dome surrounding Rynka a huge spaceship had landed on the ocher sand of the Martian desert. A long, rectangular hatch was open in its belly.

"Oh, look at…"

The words got caught in Tink's throat. His trembling hand pointed at the 25 Fimn'has that made up the Commando Unit of Ruanoor and Woodna. The decompression chambers in the ships had just opened and from each of them came out two green monsters, roughly human in form but covered with scales from head to toe.

"De… Denebians… here in Rynka," G'bho stuttered in astonishment.

The 50 scaly green creatures activated the opening of the exit hatch and went through the dome's thick wall. After closing the hatch behind them they walked into the Martian air, their spacesuits under their arms.

"They… they can breathe *outside*? A young Wolfian was surprised.

"They're sympodic beings," Tink explained distractedly, fascinated by what he was seeing. "These monsters can adapt to almost all physical conditions and I think they can even survive for a time in outer space."

The 50 Denebians strode toward the spaceship. They looked satisfied. The trap they had set for Zimko should succeed. Thanks to a tiny adjustment of all the mechano-psychic relays left working in the 25 Fimn'has, the population of the base was completely under the control of an electronic super-brain in which the Denebians had put tens of thousands of very precise instructions. These instructions would allow the fantastic instrument to make the inhabitants of the base act intelligently in a number of unimaginable situations. Naturally every action thus programmed would preserve or further the interests of the Denebians.

This huge, intricate plot was supposed to end up, sooner or later, in capturing Zimko alive. The Space Commando Chief would fall into the hands of the Denebians and they would just have to annihilate his will. Under their control Zimko would then give orders to his squadrons to bring them into the carefully prepared trap. After that the conquest of the solar system would be just a little interplanetary war, a series of sporadic battles that would all end up in the surrender or extermination pure and simple of the inhabitants of the bases set up in this galactic zone by the Federated Worlds.

The giant spaceship—a disc 1,300 feet in diameter with a phosphorescent dome on top—rose into the purple sky where the stars were shining faintly. Shooting off into space it went 30,000 miles from Mars surrounded by a force field that absorbed all detector waves and waited patiently for the arrival of the Space Commando squadron led by Zimko.

Trying to capture him in flight by doing the same thing they had done to the Wolfians and Centaurians to enter Rynka was not reliable enough. The Denebians, as hardened warriors, did not underestimate the strength or insight of their enemies. However, they were sure that their plot was foolproof. Everything would work like a fine-tuned machine impervious to outside influences.

What they apparently did not know was that an inside influence was in serious danger of messing up their plans.

CHAPTER VI

"What are we going to do?" Zendka sobbed, a ten-year old girl with very curly blonde hair.

"Well, stop crying, all of you!" Tink got angry at his comrade and the two young Wolfians whining at his feet, their hair standing on end and their big eyes vibrating in fear. He regretted his outburst right away and patted their helmets while running his hand through Zendka's blonde locks. "Don't get upset with me, friends. I'm… as scared as you are and I don't really see what we can do."

He looked toward the horizon where the disc of the sun was slowly going down and absent-mindedly he watched the two small Martian moons—Phobos and Deimos—pursuing their orbits in opposite directions, Phobos following a retrograde movement.

"I think we should go back home," he ended up saying. "Don't be surprised to find your parents acting weird like we saw. Let's watch them and tomorrow morning at dawn we'll meet in the central park near the *Knoktbanss*. I don't think our parents will try to stop us leaving so early… They probably won't even know we're gone," he said sadly, dreading to return home.

In groups of three or four the young Polarians, Centaurians and Wolfians reached Central Park. The lighted walls of the buildings cast a gentle glow over the wide, deserted paths. The sky above the dome was soot black; the stars were twinkling dimly in the rarified atmosphere of the planet Mars. The sun would soon appear on the horizon as its light was just starting to seep into the background.

When the young survivors of the Rynka base were all together—there were about 40 of them—they sat in a circle around Tink. Over their heads the hooped flowers of the

Knoktbanss, the weird plants in the shape of concentric circles like giant cacti crossed with magnolias.

"I tried to talk with my parents," Tink began. "They paid no attention to me."

The boy tried not to let his emotions get the best of him and went on, showing his friends a big belt with a black, triangular holster hanging from it.

"My father even let me take his disintegrator when he usually won't even show it to me up close."

They took turns telling what their night had been like in the crazy environment around their parents who seemed sunk in a perpetual daydream.

"Does anyone know how to fly a Fimn'has?" Zendka, the blonde girl, asked.

Tink shrugged his shoulders, "But even if one of us can, where would we go? Flying is one thing but space cruisers are something else altogether. We'd have to be able to read the galactic coordinates on star charts, translate the astronavigator readouts and especially know how to spot the electron currents being spit out by the sun... Getting a Fimn'has caught in a flow of whirling electrons would be certain death if we couldn't get around it."

"So, what do we do?" a Centaurian girl asked, her head barely higher than Tink's knee.

"Since our parents are still out of it, I figure we should send an alarm to astrobase 2 and explain what's happening."

"You know how to work a space viewer?"

"Yes. One day my father showed me how to put a selector unit on whatever wavelength you want."

B'tna, the little Centaurian girl, grabbed his boot and said, "You think the Denebians did 'this' to our parents just to mess with them? They must be preparing something that needs everyone in Rynka sleepy... I'm sure they're watching the base from their spaceships parked off in space..."

"And if they're watching the base, they're also watching over any possible communications!" Tink finished her thought.

He looked at her with obvious admiration. This frail creature was really sharp. If it was not for her, he would have made a serious mistake.

"You're right, B'tna, so now we're back in the same place. We know that something serious is happening but we can't ask for help from the other bases in the system. If there were one adult among us he could at least send a psychic message into outer space... but we're just kids! Our mental waves can't even get beyond the orbit of Deimos."

Nervous and angry at feeling helpless Tink paced back and forth inside the circle of his comrades. After a few minutes of deep thought he stopped suddenly, his face beaming with joy.

"I think I've found a way to communicate with the astrobases or a squadron in this zone of space. What we have to do is make the Polarians on the bases or the Fimn'has understand that we need to get in touch with them. Even though we can't sent a long range psychic message, the adults can receive our thoughts with no problem. So, we have to get their attention without the Denebians suspecting that there are minds in Rynka that aren't under their control."

"And you think it's possible?" G'bho asked, very excited by the prospect, which made his big oval eyes quiver in their orbits.

"It's simple. We'll get into the Space Transmission Center and while you're keeping an eye on the technicians I'll get the attention of the Space Commandos. Come on!"

Without trying to hide the 40 survivors hurried after Tink down the streets of Rynka. The city was starting to wake up with the purple dawn typical Mars. The Polarian men and women were coming out of the buildings and heading for their various posts. The Wolfians in their metallic spacesuits and the Centaurians wearing their opaque or transparent spacesuits were also on their way to the research centers or science sections. But everyone, no matter what race they belonged to, looked like they were sleepwalking.

Just as the survivors had expected no one paid any attention to them. They marched into the lobby of the Space
Transmission Center without a single guard trying to stop
them. It was the same for getting into the huge, round room in
the middle of which were six big three-dimensional screens,
each hooked up to a semi-circular control panel on a chrome
stand.

Tink's father, the chief engineer of the tele-transmissions
was standing before one of these machines. Five other operators were at the other commands. When the face of a Polarian,
Wolfian or Centaurian—a spaceship pilot or base technician—
appeared on the screen a strange transformation took hold of
these previously passive tele-transmitters. Their faces became
normal, their eyes lit up and calmly, perfectly naturally, they
answered the questions of their distant collaborators.

"Hey, did you see that?" B'tna whispered to Tink.

"Yeah. Now I understand. The evil green monsters are
controlling our parents' thoughts. When they don't have to
deal with someone off Rynka they're acting like on automatic
control. But when they have to communicate with the outside
the Denebians make them act naturally so they don't raise any
suspicions with their blank expressions and droning voices.
They say what they're told by whoever's holding the keys to
their brains.

"I think I saw once in some school session that an
omniorama has these very effects. So, our fierce enemies can
destroy the will and then control their subjects who are completely at their will and can commit the worst crimes without
even realizing it. Like we just saw with the viewers. When
they have to the Denebians can twist our parents' minds to
make them look normal while still keeping them under their
mental control."

"That's awful!" Zendka sniveled.

Tink gave two or three orders to his comrades standing
around him, hoping they would have the courage to act if an
adult tried to stop the young Polarian from using the space
transmitter.

Tink sidled up next to his father—oblivious to his presence—and boldly started pushing, off and on, a red button in the middle of the slanted panel. With a wave of his hand he made his friends squat down so that they would not be in the field of vision. Tink repeated the operation making sure that he stayed out of the picture as well.

B'tna scurried up to him and whispered, "What are you doing?"

"This button, with three different clicks, changes the wavelengths for the emergency channel of the Space Commandos. When it's pressed down completely the wavelength goes from one size to another but it has to be done at a specific moment of Universal Time used in this solar system and in very specific conditions that the Commandos know about. Now, by pressing it down not completely but a bunch of times in a row and not at the good time, I'm messing with all the Space Commando communications, even if they're not in contact with us. There's got to be a technician on a ship who'll get annoyed and use his paroptic vision to find the source of these variations in Gossenka waves, as they're called."

The doll-like face of B'tna lit up with a big smile and Tink, smiling back, read the admiration in her little eyes.

All of a sudden Tink froze. A psychic image had just flashed through his mind. He felt like he had "seen" mentally the face of a Polarian but the fleeting vision had disappeared. After a few seconds another face appeared, along with a few scraps of thought. Concentrating with all his (still young) psychic might, he sent out a mental call:

"Alert for all Space Commandos. Alert for all Space Commandos. Message for Zimko. Message for Zimko."

A psychic image burned into his mind. At first a little hazy it quickly took shape and was accompanied with this thought: *What is going on?*

The words now rang clearly in his brain's receptive zones.

"I'm calling Zimko, Chief of the Space Commandos. Don't use the tele-transmitter. Answer by psychic message."

The Polarian on a reconnaissance flight outside Jupiter's orbit had been intrigued by the purple flashes on his screen. Where were these Gossenka wave variations coming from? As Tink had hoped, his plan was working.

The Polarian pilot, puzzled by the constant disturbance, used his paroptic vision and probed the different transmission centers in the solar system. A few minutes later he focused his vision on Rynka, the Martian base, where the disturbances originated. Now he was "seeing" clearly the 12- or 13-year old boy, his hand pressing the red button and obviously trying to stay out of sight of the viewer.

He also noticed the presence of a group of young Centaurians and Wolfians along with boys and girls of his race. What were they doing in the Space Communications Center where access was forbidden to anyone outside this service?

A deeper psychic probe into each of them told him the frightening truth. All the mental images—all the same—perceived at the same time assured him of the accuracy of his perceptions: except for these 40 young kids the population of Rynka was under the psychic control of the Denebians! Without understanding how they alone had escaped, he had to give in to the evidence.

I'm going to alert Zimko immediately, Tink, he sent into his mind. *You and your comrades must be very careful. Hide somewhere or else imitate your parents. Pretend to be totally passive. Copy all the others who are acting under orders from the Denebians. Don't worry, Zimko will know what to do to free your parents and friends from the psychic control over them.*

The image of his face and the echo of his thoughts faded out of the young Polarian's mind.

With tears of joy trickling down his cheeks Tink whispered, "I did it... A reconnaissance pilot captured my mental call, as weak as it was. Without saying a single word into the space viewer our message was heard. Zimko will hear about it and come save us with the Space Commandos."

An armored door suddenly opened and made them jump. In the frame of the metal panel that had just slid open stood six Denebians, disgusting green creatures with reptile skin.

Tink and his friends felt their legs wobble. A horrible feeling of panic seized them as they choked up, as if their throats were caught in a vice.

"We didn't catch your mental message but we quickly spotted the source of the Gossenka wave disturbances," one of the Denebians snapped, walking up to a terrorized Tink. "Your little call for help is going to get Zimko here double quick. *And that's exactly what we want!*"

On astrobase 2 Fohag, the Wolfian Chief, was presiding over another assembly of almost 400 Polarians, Wolfians and Centaurians.

"First of all," he began, "as you will be able to see for yourselves once again the inhabitants of T27 are not yet ready to receive us intelligently. I'll show you translations of the news being broadcast today in the Earthling press about the latest missions carried out by our 'Probe Commandos' with the goal of studying the reactions of the primitives who meet us unexpectedly. First here's the translation of an article reporting in its way about a test by a Polarian pilot on a native of T27."

The big 3-D screen turned on. As if suspended in a bottomless pit the fluorescent characters started scrolling by, faithfully translating (in the universal language of the Federated Worlds) the newspaper article:

The pilot of a flying cigar hugged me and spoke to me, a farmer confirmed.
Limoges, September 14, 1954[15] *A farmer in the town of Mouniéras, in the commune Bugeat (Corrèze), on the Plateau of Millevaches, Mr. Antoine Mazaud on September 10 had an*

---

[15] As reported in *France-Soir*, September 15, 1954. (Author's Note)

89

extraordinary encounter that we never would have known about if it was not for his wife, who told the following story about her husband's adventure.

That night Mr. Antoine Mazaud was coming back from work in the fields. It was 8:30 pm and the night was falling in the countryside. The farmer took the sunken lane on which the thick bushes bordering it made the twilight even darker.

All of a sudden he found himself face to face with a stranger of medium height, wearing a motorcycle helmet. Both of them were very surprised. When Mr. Mazaud made a defensive movement with his pitchfork, which he was carrying on his shoulder, the other came up to him quickly, holding out his hands, no doubt to assure his peaceful intentions.

Fearing that he might not be understood he approached the farmer and while saying something incomprehensible he hugged him. Then, before Mazaud could get over his surprise he hopped over the hedge and sat inside a weird, cigar-shaped machine, 10 or 12 feet long. The machine, which was not lit up, shot straight up as quiet as a buzzing bee and disappeared to the west.

When Mr. Mazaud returned home, about a mile away, his wife noticed how pale and strange he looked. He told her about his bizarre encounter but asked her not to tell anyone. "They'll make fun of us," he said.

But the temptation was too strong and Mrs. Mazaud could not resist telling her neighbor, in strict secrecy of course. Her neighbor then told a travelling salesman who spread it around until... the whole country know about it. The police, the last to hear, only found out about it yesterday.

Mr. Mazaud was questioned by the lieutenant in Ussel and repeated what he had told his wife. Unfortunately it was not possible to find any traces where the machine had landed. Mazaud, who has a spotless reputation, does not suffer from hallucinations.

"This, then, is the first report by one of those brief contacts that have now become classic," Fohag said. "According to what the newspapers on T27 report we can easily see that nine times out of ten the primitives who encounter our ships and their occupants say nothing about it. Most of the time it takes some slip-up to make them talk. If all the witnesses of our incursions told their stories, the papers wouldn't have enough space to print any other news[16]."

"I don't think their readers would lose anything if that happened," a Polarian commented, not trying to funny. "Crimes, robberies, murders, attacks, the fall of governments, revolutions, wars, all kinds of abuse. That's the daily news in the Earth's press. Of course a primitive could answer us that we, too, in spite of our extraordinary degree of evolution, are at war pretty often with the Denebians and the Procyonians. That's right but these conflicts will end very soon. We've seen a period of total peace throughout our Federated Worlds over tens of millennia. It's only the last few years that the Denebians and Procyonians, still refusing to join our Galactic Federation, decided to extend their zone of influence and try to annex the planets rich in natural resources but poor in evolved beings. We have always stopped them and the primitive races we saved from their slavery are eternally grateful. All we want, as far as we can, is to stop our enemies from harming the worlds they desire and this in not using radically destructive methods. However, if our enemies should present a serious threat to all the worlds, federated or not, we will be forced to use... the most formidable, frightening weapons unlike anything we've used so far. And we won't hesitate to use them some day if the security of the Galaxy is at stake."

The Polarian bowed before Fohag in thanks for letting him interrupt and then sat back down.

---

[16] The International Investigative Commission *Ouranos* has countless, credible testimonies that were not published in newspapers as the witnesses feared the mockery of narrow minds and of those who stubbornly refuse to honestly accept the evidence and the reality of the facts. (Author's Note)

The Chief of the base took up where he had left off on the "psychological tests" that a good number of Earthlings had undergone unknowingly.

"Here now is an article reporting the incursion of our pilots Hogounn and Injya, specialists who have already carried out 15 missions in a T27 country called France. Zimko, the leader of us all, to whom I sent these various translations along with the original texts, assured me that the article you are about to see is very funny. The incursion, such as it is described by the eyewitness, seems very amusing to the natives of T27. Zimko, as you know, lived incognito for a time on this planet so he's very familiar with their reactions and outmoded customs.[17] So, I believe him when he says that in the eyes of the Earthlings this adventure in question is funny. For my part, I don't get it all. But here's the translation."

The screen lit up slowly and the weird scroll of fluorescent characters appeared in the velvety abyss, a kind of indescribable void but with words.

A lot of flying saucers in our region:
" On Sunday in Chabeuil just like I'm seeing you I saw the pilot of a mysterious machine," Mme. Leboeuf of Valence confirmed[18].
Chabeuil, September 28, 1954.
"Don't think I'm crazy. I'm not off my rocker."
Our witness, Mme. Leboeuf of Valence, who asked us for an interview about this "serious affair" and who, by way of introduction, swore to us she was perfectly rational, fiddled with her handbag and gloves in her weak fingers while glancing worriedly from right to left. She opened her mouth, closed it, cleared her throat, swallowed hard and finally, leaning forward, spit this out:

---

[17] See Volume 1.
[18] As reported in *The Progès de Lyon*, Sep. 29, 1954. (Author's Note)

"I saw the man from the flying saucer like I'm seeing you here."

Mme. Leboeuf chattered on, talking about her fear, her personal skepticism before this event, then describing the man and the saucer taking off, etc. Here is her account:

"It was Sunday afternoon. I had gone to Chabeuil to spend the day with my parents-in-law. After lunch I went to the cemetery to put flowers on the family vault and from there I went to the woods to pick some mushrooms. I'm very familiar with the area. It was around 2:30 pm. The road went along an alfalfa field whose last 10 yards are planted with corn. I was busy picking blackberries when my dog started barking behind me. But I had never heard him bark like that. He was next to the cornfield, standing in front of what I first took for a scarecrow and he was trembling, his fur standing on end as if an electric current was shooting through his body. Do you have to be so stupid, poor dog, I was thinking, to be scared of a scarecrow?

"I walked over to my dog and that was when I saw the scarecrow moving toward me. It was a man-shaped creature but very small. Must have been around three and half feet tall. It looked to me like a boy stuck in a cellophane bag. I screamed, ran as fast as I could and dove headfirst into the blackberry bush where I stayed down.

"How long did I stay there? I don't know. I didn't see anyone in front of the field but I did see the flying saucer rise up out of the corn. It took off sideways. It was as quiet as a big spinning top, purring, with a soft whistle. It didn't go too fast. At the end of the field it wobble a little and then vroom... it shot straight up.

"I tried to stay still in the bush. Three farmers passed by. I wanted to call out to them but I couldn't utter a sound. They saw me and my face and must have figured that something crazy had happened. So, the first thing they did was to take me to their farm and give me a big glass of rum. I told them the best I could about what I'd seen. They went back to the corn-

*field with me and we found where the flying saucer had land-
ed."*

*We went to the locale after hearing this astonishing sto-
ry. The cornfield, which has ten rows, is bordered on one side
by an alfalfa field and on the other by a row of acacias. That
was where we did indeed find a round space around ten feet in
diameter. Seven stalks of corn in the first row were lying flat,
the grass separating the corn from the acacias was pressed
down, some hawthorn twigs were broken and acacia branches
snapped off—toward the top of the trees the branches were
stripped of their leaves...*

The last fluorescent characters faded away into the
depths of the 3-D screen.

Fohag, sitting with the Polarian and Centaurian section
chiefs, stood up. "The translation that I gave you is one of the
clearest and most courageous accounts published about this
mission of Hogounn and Injya. Many newspapers purely and
simply mocked the Earthling woman and took wicked pleas-
ure in describing her as certainly out of her mind.

"This proves to us that the majority of T27 inhabitants
are not only primitive but also proudly stupid and ignorant.
Unable to imagine that beings from another planet could have
reached a level of civilization clearly superior to theirs, they
fiercely deny their existence and make fun of their brothers
who admit, in all honesty, having seen such beings come out
of a flying saucer.

"Wisdom advises us to carry on. A day will come when
the pile of testimony will erase all doubt. Then the Earthlings
will know for certain that other beings are watching them and
they will be totally prepared to accept us without panicking.
Their governments, moreover, will be prudent enough to give
strict orders to stay calm and peaceful in the face of events
that only a few initiated Earthlings are expecting impatiently."

A shrill alarm rang out in the huge room with metallic
walls. The intrigued audience looked toward the 3-D screen

where the face of Boïdno, Chief of the Venus Base, popped up.

"The entire population of Rynka, the Mars Base, has fallen under the psychic control of the Denebians!" he announced in a shaky voice. "After Venus, Mars. The green monsters seem to be gathering their 'space guerillas' in this solar system. Other similar attacks are, therefore, to be feared. We're making all necessary preparations to counter it... but the Denebians have perfected a 'scrambler' that jams our radars and our mechano-psychic field protectors.

"Zimko is finishing up the final preparations for battle and is ready to send his own commando team to help Rynka. Stay in constant contact and alert all the Fimn'has squadrons on observation flights. All ships should be ready to go back to their base at the first signal. Over and out."

CHAPTER VII

The Space Commando led by Zimko flew through interplanetary space toward Mars. Made up of 50 Fimn'has it had Centaurian and Wolfian ships of 20 and 25 feet in diameter as well as Polarian "flying saucers" twice as big. The combat squad, equipped with disintegrator cannons and tetanizing ray guns, entered Earth's orbit like lightning.

After receiving the psychic message explaining the events at Rynka, Zimko had immediately devised a masterful plan of action. One detail had struck him right away: if the Denebians were taking all this trouble to submit the entire population of the Martian base to their control—and without occupying the city—this obviously meant that taking over Rynka was not their main goal. It was one step of a much bigger operation.

Zimko knew that the Denebians and the awful creatures from Procyon had put a price on his head. As Chief of the Space Commandos his elite squadrons had foiled all tricks by these monsters to take over the solar system. He also knew that his enemies used force only as a last resort and this because terribly destructive weapons would come into play, weapons prone to massacre both attackers and attacked alike.

Zimko was sure that in attacking Rynka the Denebians wished to set a trap for him. Paradoxically, he had also decided to fulfill their wishes.

"But that's crazy!" cried Honky, Chief of the Information Service of the Federated Worlds, who had known Zimko for a long time. "Going to Rynka is throwing yourself into the claws of the Denebians who are trying to capture you in any way they can."

Zimko winked and smiled mischievously. "Don't worry, Honky, I've got a plan. Let's look at it. If the Denebians capture me, what are they going to do next?"

Without giving him time to answer he went on.

"They'll be in a hurry to take me far away from the solar system… to make me talk or to plunder my mind. And these monsters know very well that my brain contains secrets of the utmost importance to the future of the civilizations of this galactic zone. If they can find out what we're preparing, if they can know our plans, it would be very easy for them to anticipate us or to attack our weak points."

Honky looked at him, surprised, honestly wondering if his old friend had lost his mind. "Listen, Zimko…"

The other laughed, "We're on duty, Honky, don't forget formalities. Do you really doubt my sanity? No, I'm telling you, I'm perfectly sound in body and mind when I say I've decided to go to Rynka and fall into the hands of our old Denebian pals. Don't worry. Zimko knows what he's doing and will pull through just fine. Besides, while the damned reptiles are running away with their prize, we can strengthen our bases calmly and set up a real defense barrier around the planets of this system."

"Hoping you can escape after your capture, Zimko, is a grave error that surprises. You must know that the Denebians will take extraordinary precautions to cut off any chance for you to escape when they have you at their mercy."

Zimko replied, making his old friend more surprised than ever, "I've thought of all that and I'm sure that being captured by these monsters will mean certain death. That's why, in pretending to fall into their trap, I'll have a big surprise for them."

Honky looked infuriated. Taking on a more formal attitude he said, "If you deem my post of Chief of the Information Service as unworthy of knowing the details of your plan, which sounds to me rather obscure to say the least, then I must…"

Zimko laughed again, interrupting him. "Save your resignation for another time. Anyway, you've threatened me with quitting at least ten times already whenever I try your patience. Did you think I was going to undertake such a thing without giving your service the details?"

He stood up, walked to an armored door that was lined with magnetic locks and announced, "I'm going to present to you the crew, the very special crew that will participate in my… suicide."

Honky looked aghast. "It's here in the bio-genetic lab? In the hibernation chamber?"

Smiling enigmatically Zimko joked, "My men are pretty tough, you know!"

Zimko's space squadron had just entered the orbit of Deimos, Mars' farthest moon. The surface of the planet was now in their field of vision. The green and ocher zones of the deserts and areas covered with the sparse Martian vegetation formed the puzzle whose huge irrigation canals separated into pieces.

The red splash of the Hellas Desert with the Zea Locus at the center came speeding up until the Fimn'has, adjusting the strength of their gravito-magnetic fields, slowed down to descend vertically on Rynka, the Martian base of the Federated Worlds. Its transparent, airtight dome gave off only a dim light due to the weak sunlight. On a planet like Earth a dome of this kind would reflect a blinding light.

Hovering at a fixed point the space squadron stopped 30 miles above the base. Zimko turned on his viewer and called the chief of the base, who popped up immediately on the screen. He showed no exterior signs of the psychic control he was under, like all the inhabitants of the city.

"Welcome to Rynka, Zimko," he raised his right hand. "I'll take care of you from here. You can land."

A long beam of purple light from the tower on top of the protective dome swept over the star-studded sky. It reached the squadron, which started descending, and kept it in its cone of purple light until it was on the ground. The "control" beam had detected nothing unusual in the Fimn'has cargo.

The 50 flying saucers landed gently on the outside astrodrome and all the crew, dressed in spacesuits, came out.

With Zimko at their head the group of 35 Polarians, 40 Wolfians and 40 Centaurians headed for the decompression chamber at the base of the dome. The Man from Outer Space knew that somewhere in a building in the city—or in an invisible ship hovering in space—the Denebians were watching his strange group. In fact, the beings from Deneb must surely be observing every gesture of the three groups of "weird creatures", as monstrous to them as they were to the inhabitants of the Federated Worlds.

The 35 Polarians in light gray spacesuits and round, transparent helmets formed the head of the group with an average height of six and a half feet. Then came the Wolfians with their big, metal suits that made them look stocky at four feet, four and a half tall maximum. The Centaurians were last, small, human-shaped creatures with orange skin. In their spacesuits, some transparent, others soft metal with cylindrical chests they could have passed for children wearing "Martian" costumes, the tallest of them barely three feet tall.

At their approach the rectangular access hatch of the base opened. They entered the decompression chamber in groups of 20 and waited in the interior astrodrome where 100 Fimn'has of all kinds were lined up.

The newcomers crossed the runway and took a large avenue that led straight to the central square containing the huge building in the shape of a tower housing the control center and the main technical services.

While walking, Zimko and his companions kept a discreet eye on the inhabitants of the base. To an unsuspecting eye they looked normal, a little too serious in their expressions, perhaps, but nothing showing that they were no longer "thinking". Nobody would have suspected that behind these cold faces was hiding a foreign will controlling their actions at a distance for more than two Martian days already.

On Zimko's orders, as he kept only five Polarians, one Wolfian and one Centaurian with him, the other members of his space crew went to their assigned duties around the central square. Armed with disintegrating pistols and paralyzing tubes each of them had a mission to defend the access of the Command Tower in case of a ground attack.

In the meantime, outside the base, four teams made up of a Wolfian and a Polarian went to the observation posts along the exterior astrodrome, which had long-range disintegrator cannons.

Zimko and his seven companions jumped into the gravito-magnetic elevators that took ten seconds to bring them to the 217th floor of the tower, the seat of the Command Post. Hudako, Chief of the Rynka base, welcomed them smiling.

It must have been hard for the Denebian brains controlling his actions to act as naturally as possible. And the visitors noted, they did not quite pull it off. In fact, although it was relatively easy to make a group of beings act under mental control in circumstances not requiring a great deal of "style", like walking, eating, drinking and sleeping, it was something entirely when it came to putting on a sincere smile, for example, when meeting a friend.

Hudako, without question, was smiling. But an unusual crease for a friendly smile furrowed the corner of his lips. Some of his facial muscles looked painfully tense. In spite of all their efforts the Denebians could only "live in another's shoes" clumsily. Their way of thinking and their ideas of everyday things were fundamentally different from Polarian concepts and prevented them from perfecting their imitations.

Cool and collected, showing no sign of noticing the strange behavior Zimko played his role. "A psychic message from a pilot flying in your zone, Hudako, alerted us that something strange was happening here."

"Indeed, we found and chased away a corps of Denebian saboteurs that obviously came to capture some of Rynka's leaders," the base chief lied under psychic command of the masters of his brain. "But everything is back to normal. We even took some prisoners. Would you like me to take you to where we're holding them? Since we don't have special cells for that we had to shut them up in big room with strongly guarded doors."

"I'd love to see them, Hudako. Lead away…"

Meanwhile, on the exterior astrodrome, the Polarians and Wolfian on the watch by the disintegrator cannons were ready to aim their rays at any enemy ship that might get in their crosshairs.

They looked casually at the Fimn'has—unmistakable—that were taking off or landing on one of the astrodromes around the huge dome protecting the city. However, it was one of these disc-shaped ships, so familiar *but piloted by a Denebian*, that had flown over them and landed on the runway after spraying its will-destroying rays.

The same maneuver was repeated at every post equipped with a disintegrator cannon. The exterior defense ring fell into the hands of the Denebians.

Lying low in the rich vegetation of the many gardens and decorative flowerbeds placed around the central square, the Denebians were spying on the groups of Polarians, Wolfians and Centaurians that Zimko had posted around the Control Tower. With weapons in hand they formed a circle around the gigantic building. 200 yards farther out the Denebians encircled the tower in secret and with their will-destroying rays at the ready.

After a meticulous adjustment the green monsters squatting in the tall flowers and leafy bushes figured the moment had come to turn on their portable devices. A faint hum broken by vibrations and light crackling—like a spark plug—could be heard. But before this barely audible noise had crossed the distance separating the Denebians from their victims they had already fallen under the power of the will-destroying rays.

The Polarians, Wolfians and Centaurians making their rounds went from normal beings to creatures being "controlled" without any visible transition. They barely even slowed down before resuming their now useless patrols. Hiding motionless behind the screen of plants the Denebians were rejoicing in their success.

In Rynka only Zimko and his seven companions were still in possession of their mental faculties. Guided by Hudako they had just arrived before a big, ribbed door at the end of a hall with fluorescent walls. The Chief of the base went first, placing his hand flat against a pink wall plate, which opened it. The metal door slid silently into a vertical slit and revealed a huge rectangular room with bare walls.

In the back of this room eight Denebians without space-suits, wearing a short orange jacket and black bodysuit, stand-ing with their backs to the wall, looked at them. They were holding out a kind of black metal cube covered with shiny rods that vibrated fast while emitting a weird crackling sound that echoed through the empty room.

Zimko and his team, for a brief moment, felt a gentle warmth envelop them from head to toe. They stopped in the middle of the room, staring blankly, unblinking, calm and submissive.

Then the eight Denebians stopped sending out the rays and highly satisfied with the complete success of their trap, they all started adjusting the controls of the complicated de-vice strapped to their bellies with a big red belt. Amplified by a special helmet on their heads—from forehead to neck pass-ing over their temples—their psychic orders would infiltrate the minds of their eight captives, who quietly turned around and went back the way they came.

One of the Denebians turned on his radio and announced the good news to his accomplices outside. In the beautiful gardens around the control tower the long leaves and tall flowers started shaking as if a storm was blowing through. 100 green scaly monsters came out of the plants and swaggered toward the huge lobby of the central building.

Followed by the rulers of their brains Zimko and his team went down the ramp along the main street that brought them quickly into the interior astrodrome at the exit hatch. The 100 or so Polarians, Wolfians and Centaurians posted at dif-ferent points on the base also started their mentally-controlled march to follow their chief to the astrodrome.

The captives checked that their spacesuits were airtight and in groups of 20—accompanied by five Denebians—they entered the big decompression chamber opening the tunnel into the base of the thick dome protecting Rynka.

The strong airlocks automatically closed the reinforced panels behind them while the opposite hatch slowly opened onto the ochre Martian sand. The air imprisoned in the hatch blew out and kicked up a cloud of rust-colored dust that swirled for a few seconds before drizzling back down more slowly than would happen on T27 with its strong gravity.

Zimko and his team, controlled by the Denebian brains, headed toward an empty space that extended for several miles between two transparent tunnels that covered secondary canals bordered by vegetation. The only exterior vegetation that grew on the surface of this planet was puny and drab, pale green tending to dirty gray, a kind of lichen growing in patches around one and a half feet tall on the vast plains. They were mostly found in the zones around the canals whose water, coming from the polar caps, slowly sifted through the underlying layers of Martian soil.

The column of prisoners marched for hours across the gloomy land of the red planet, easily climbing up the low slope forming the side of a hill to the rounded summit and coming back down the other side to cross another red plain scattered with a purple shrubs and their sparse, soot-brown, foul smelling flowers like wide bowls that constituted the main species of flora on this world headed for extinction.

At the top of one of these low hills the prisoners and their guards, whose sympodic nature required no spacesuits, found a strange landscape different from the desert airs that they had just crossed.

At the intersection of two canals protected by a tunnel stood the spectacular ruins of an ancient Martian city. Big walls with incomprehensible sculptures, but whose fine workmanship proved a deep sense of artistry, were still standing. Traces of raised roadways remained—crumbling sections hanging in the air with only one pillar to support them—and by their sturdy conception bore witness to the high degree of civilization that had once built this powerful city.

The presence of these ruins, just a few hundred yards from the branching of two covered canals, was shocking at first sight. One wondered why the canals, which were not the work of the Federated Worlds, had stood up while the Martian city was nothing but ruins. The Polarian archeologists, anthropologists and ethnographers, on their arrival on this planet, took little time to find an explanation. The Martians, around 300,000 years ago, following a cosmic cataclysm, must have left their planet to emigrate in the solar system in search of a suitable world for its physical and climatic conditions[19].

Unfortunately, everyone could not emigrate and most of the population was destroyed. The survivors, once the cataclysm had passed, found themselves on a blasted world, the air thinned, the cities razed to the ground. Only the canals had stood for the most part because they were built with almost indestructible materials. The survivors repaired the tunnels protecting the canals as best they could in order to have that water that was indispensable to life and later they started rebuilding the cities.

Unluckily for them, before they could repair the entire irrigation network, the harsh physical conditions in the aftermath of the cataclysm had devastated their ranks. On Mars there was only a small number of particularly strong survivors left and it was very hard to adapt. From one generation to another they gradually lost their scientific knowledge and they fell back into almost animal nature. Their race mutated little by little to survive in the dying planet's climate and slowly evolved anew. However, all the physical changes and modifications that followed led the last Martian race into an ethic and social organization that was very far from their ancestors.

As the physical conditions on the surface of the planet became harsher and harsher over the course of millennia, the

---

[19] Guieu is referencing here events described in his earlier novel *Nous, les Martians*.

"natives" noticed that birth rates declined and more monsters and abnormal babies were being born. It did not take pong for them to realize that their time was coming to an end. With the fear of a quick, unavoidable extinction at hand, the sight of their monstrous offspring awoke in them the old secular superstitions that had been latent in their subconscious. They fell further into anarchy and ended up separating into clans that kept harassing each other.

In the Martian hills they found weird tunnels cluttered with even weirder machines that belonged to their long-lost ancestors. They hid inside and led the gloomy life of troglodytes. What they did not know was that these countless tunnels were in an area full of radioactive minerals. Victims, no doubt, (and unable to imagine the problem), of a constant bombardment of radioactivity, the Martians soon suffered strange mutations in their organism and morphology. Birth rates rose again but, alas, produced creatures so monstrous that their own parents first blamed it on demons living in the bowels of the planet, which, considering their total ignorance, was not so wrong since these weird genetic mutations were due to radioactive elements in the ground.

In the mines of the old city, at the foot of the tunnel-ridden hills, phosphorescent eyes in the form of a triangle fearfully watched the approach of the "Sky Gods"—the Denebians and their prisoners—who were skirting around the relics of their hunting ground: those strange walls and crumbling buildings in which tiny animals crawled, resembling cockroaches, hard-shelled worms, a kind of big centipede and a multitude of insects similar to the parasites on T27.

From time to time a gruesome shadow jumped over a pile of rocks and slipped one of its hairy arms between the cracks in the walls to grab some of these tasty bugs, which would someday replace the degenerate and primitive race on Mars that was rushing to its own extinction unawares.

When Zimko and his companions, deprived of their wills, surrounded by the Denebians, walked along the ruins of the city, 30 grisly creatures rushed at them and, stopping at a

105

respectable distance, they crouched down on the ground as a sign of superstitious veneration.

The "Sky Gods" with green scaly skin looked scornfully at these dregs of thinking beings before continuing on their way. The other "Gods," who also came out of the sky (to their primitive minds), did not even glance at them. This indifference threw the Martians into a gulf of sorrow. If these three very different types of "Gods," who had always been good to them, did not even bother to look at them, it was because they were angry with them! But what could they have done to cause such anger and deserve their scorn?

The Martians, creatures around three feet tall with a flat little head sitting on a huge torso—"all lungs" the Polarian anthropologists had joked—with their four greenish tentacles ending in suction cups and their two skinny legs, lay prostrate in the dust emitting a tuneful whistle barely audible in the thin air of the planet.

The three, green, phosphorescent eyes set triangularly in their flat skull blinked to express their distress at seeing the "Sky Gods" who had passed by them without giving them that sweet sensation that usually marks friendly physical contact. The "Gods without shells" (the Denebians without spacesuits) on every other occasion had never acted kindly to them but the "Gods" of three different sizes who lived in the North, in a weird, domed city, had never spurned them like today.

And the degenerate Martians wept, their faces in the sand, their four arms trembling, watching the scornful Gods as they stopped in the middle of flat, barren plain, far from their domed city.

Obviously they did not know that the good Gods whom they loved ever since they came down from the sky were the prisoners of the other Gods, without shells, who also came from the sky but with a goal of conquest and domination.

CHAPTER VIII

The giant Denebian spaceship—disc-shaped, around 350 yards in diameter and topped by a dome fitted with windows—seemed to appear out of nowhere at only 1,500 feet altitude above the captives and their guards. Faintly haloed in blue it came down slowly and landed on the sandy ground, crushing hundreds of bunches of "umbrella moss" on their stems.

A big rectangular hatch opened in the vertical base of the cylindrical dome at the same time as a kind of ringed, metallic corridor—like a snake—came slowly down to the ground, swinging a little.

The prisoners, under the psychic order of their masters, entered this "sleeve" and were soon in a hold with a lot of square blocks, airtight crates containing food and supplies.

A new mental order led them to an inner walkway before bringing them to the section housing the Superior Council of the Forces of Space Liberation, a name the Denebians gave themselves hypocritically.

When the captives were about to meet the Commander in Chief of the Freedom Forces, the giant spaceship took off and protected by an invisibility field it flew diagonally toward Rynka, which it reached a few minutes later. While flying over the base the ship stopped all the will-destroying devices on Rynka, then with an extraordinary leap it went from observation flight to actual space flight and disappeared into outer space 100 times faster than the speed of light[20]. Still, the speed of a cruiser was infinitely greater than even this unthinkable speed!

---

[20] 300,000 km/sec.—which physics, until otherwise proved, asserts to be the limit of speed, wherein it will one day be wrong! (Author's Note)

In the big cockpit more than one technician leaning over his controls was thinking of the narrow-minded primitives on T27 who could not imagine such fantastic speeds and denied the possible existence of those who, in the near future, were going to enslave them in a mass landing on their planet, which they arrogantly consider to the only seat of Intelligence in the Universe.

In Rynka the Polarians, Wolfians and Centaurians were abruptly freed of their psychic chains. There was a brief moment of confusion that they blamed on a temporary dizzy spell. None of them realized that for three days they had been puppets being manipulated by their implacable enemies. In their minds, returned to normal, no memory of their mental enslavement remained.

Those who would later reveal this incredible episode of their life would have a lot of trouble making them believe it. Remembering only their habitual actions—being carried out in spite of everything under the control of the Denebians—they would have a "hole" in their memories and keep in mind the details of their daily lives. Therefore, there would not even be a time difference in the passage of days since they would have lived out the three days in their routines.

In the Denebian spaceship speeding off to the sun Deneb in the Cygnus constellation, according to the terminology in use among the primitives of T27, Zimko and his mixed team stood motionless in a huge circular room around 200 feet in diameter.

Lined up in four rows, their eyes blank, deprived of their wills, they seemed to be staring (without seeing) at the Commander in Chief of the Denebian forces and the 17 members of his general staff. Like generals reviewing an army corps they were pacing a few feet away from their captives and examining them closely.

They stopped in front of Zimko, calm and mindless, to scrutinize him even more closely. S'bilk, the Commander in Chief, a seven-foot tall green giant with big scales, stared at him arrogantly:

"So this is Zimko, Chief of the Space Commandos in this solar system that we're going to conquer! This is the one who caused all our defeats, the one who made us abandon our first attempt at infiltrating the third planet[21]. He's also the one who stopped us from capturing the first inhabitants of the planet who reached their moon[22]. He's a devil! I'd like to kill him with my own hands but we need him alive. Besides, we can't deal with him like we do with his accomplices. They are of no importance because they are, despite their rank, just pawns. We can easily suck out of their brains the essence of what they know. After turning them into empty rags from the treatment we'll take them to our cosmobiology labs to use them as test subjects."

The Denebian Chief, trembling with rage, looked at Zimko and slapped him hard with the backside of his claws. The Man from Outer Space wobbled from right to left but did not fall. He stood calmly, feeling the pain but unable to react.

"This evil creature," S'bilk erupted, "will escape the fate of his partners. We'll use him at the right time to fight against his brothers after he's told us the details of their defense plan among other things we need to know."

"Do you think he'll talk willingly because we'll have to keep his brain intact?" a Denebian officer asked timidly.

S'bilk narrowed his red, yellow-striped eyes. The green scales on his bulging forehead raised slightly and in a hoarse voice he barked, "We'll torture him until he talks!"

The Denebian spaceship, after crossing a 400 light year gulf of space in less than 24 hours (T27 time) started slowing down at the approach of the sun Omink, or Deneb, in the Cygnus constellation. This fantastic sun, more blinding than so

---

[21] See Volume 1.
[22] See Volume 1.

many other stars in the galaxy[23], had a train of seven planets, three of which contained life.

The planet Ptopa, the home of the race of green scaly beings, the Ptopans or Denebians, is a globe 18,000 miles in diameter with two moons. It appeared now like a green balloon with a bluish halo—the atmosphere—ionized by the powerful rays of Omink/Deneb.

Gradually its roundness seemed to grow in volume as the giant spaceship transporting its captives approached. Grayish yellow or brown continents with marbled zones and multi-colored seas, but mostly purple, became clearer through the thick atmosphere of Ptopa.

High mountains with summits rounded by erosion were crowned with green and purple clouds. In the deep valleys where wild torrents foamed yellow other clouds, pink or blue, spread out like shreds of cotton, composed of methane and cyanogen oddly tinted by the rays of Omink.

On a plain through which wound a river bordered by low bushes with branches fatter than the trunk of an oak tree, twisted and with black leaves veined with red, stood Lucknah, the capital of the planet. Its building, mostly hexagonal, with concave roofs topped with strange masts full of thin, shiny, metal crossbeams, were covered from top to bottom with anti-corrosive panels, yellow and crossed sideways with black bands.

The common decoration, unexpected to say the least, gave the city a look of asymmetrical construction—and this because the buildings were not the same size—that disturbed the mind. It looked like a jumble of discordant geometric forms or maybe a weird three-dimensional, painting created by a genius on the verge of insanity.

The ship landed on the astrodrome, also with black bands on a yellow background, not far from the gigantic space base,

---

[23] Deneb, Alpha of Cygnus, is 4,800 times brighter than our sun, a rather medium-sized star in the galaxy. (Author's Note)

totally round, over half a mile in diameter and surrounded by hundreds of green, scaly technicians working busily.

Controlled by mental orders, the captives in their space-suits left the ship and flanked by their masters crossed the astrodrome to go to the palace of K'wyil, the Emperor of the Denebians.

The heavy gravity on Ptopa, three times greater than on the home planet of the Polarians, made it hard to walk. Every movement was in slow motion and required painful effort. In their round helmets they panted and their faces ran with sweat. If it was hard for the Polarians to walk, for the Wolfians and even more so for the Centaurians it was nearly impossible. After a few minutes the poor, tiny creatures collapsed, crushed by the terrible gravity, seven and nine times greater than their worlds.

Deprived of their own will none of the prisoners could turn on the compensating device that each suit was fitted with. But on seeing their captives collapse and unable to move the Denebians realized their mistake. They immediately ordered the Wolfians, Centaurians and Polarians to turn on their gravity compensators, putting them back into their usual condition.

With effort the "dwarves" lifted their arms, managed to press the two correct buttons among the multiple controls in the small round plate fixed to their belt. Back on their feet in no time they resumed their march into the center of the city.

The Emperor's palace raised its hexagonal mass, yellow striped with black, in the middle of Lucknah, the strange Denebian capital.

On orders from their guards the prisoners got on a kind of moving walkway that brought them through a maze of bright corridors, from one floor to another, halfway up the palace, over 600 feet off the ground and on the axis of the building, which had no pictorial decorations, at least in the sense that the Polarians understood it. In the speedily crossed hall they barely saw even the mishmash of geometric motifs in relief.

The Wolfians and Centaurians received orders to stand still in a kind of circular vault with gray metal walls while the Polarians, except for Zimko, were inexplicably sent down into a similar vault located 600 feet under the palace.

Only Zimko was led into a semi-circular room in the middle of which, on a seat of black metal in the shape of a splayed cube, sat an enormous creature, vaguely human, with skin made of hexagonal, green scales: K'wyil, Emperor of Ptopa, Supreme Chief of the Denebian race that ruled over seven solar systems conquered by violence over the past centuries.

His head, a wide oval, was protected by a black helmet that only revealed his face with smaller, softer, light green scales. His slanted eyes, with puffy lids, were crimson red and striped vertically with gold. His short, bony nose and turned-down, lipless mouth made him look like a turtle.

At his sides sat three other Denebians on cubes that were not so high. S'bilk, the Commander in Chief of the Freedom Forces, very proud of his capture, bowed low and joined the four dignitaries.

Four guards ordered Zimko to raise his arms, which he did calmly. Shiny cables ending in soft but extremely strong straps came down from the ceiling and grabbed his wrists. His feet were shackled to the concrete floor with chains. Thus immobilized it was impossible for him to make the slightest movement.

Emperor K'wyil made a sign to one of the guards who aimed his device full of vibrating spikes at the prisoner. After a quick adjustment of the controls on the side of the will-destroyer, the humming spikes stopped moving and Zimko, as if by magic, was back to himself.

He looked around in astonishment and suddenly realized that he was in the presence of Denebians. He wanted to protect himself but with the solid bracelets and chains he could only wiggle ridiculously. A glint of rage flashed across his face. The muscles under his round helmet contracted into an expression of savage hatred.

One of the guards came up to him, unhooked the airtight seal of his helmet and yanked it off the head of the prisoner. Instinctively he held his breath.

K'wyil sneered at him. "You're not going to die today, Zimko. You can breathe. This room is sealed, air conditioned, pressurized and has an atmosphere identical to your planet. We've copied the physical conditions of your home planet here, so you can breathe normally without your spacesuit... which will soon be an obstacle for what we intend to do... to your body."

K'wyil spoke well in the universal language used in the Federated Worlds governed peacefully by the Polarians, his sworn enemies. In spite of his hoarse, guttural voice, Zimko understood every word.

"You quickly held back your first reaction of fear, Zimko," the emperor continued. "I don't know if it's out of courage or arrogance but you're hiding your inner feelings well. You know very well that it would be easy for me to put you under a psychic probe and learn exactly what's in your mind because you're aware of all the plans drawn up by the general staff of your race to conquer the solar system that we're interested in."

"To *protect* the solar system that *you* want to conquer," Zimko corrected, sneering back at him.

"So be it," K'wyil conceded. "But I'll need you to be normal and not the living dead like the probe would leave you after looting your brain. That's why I'm hoping that, for your own good, you'll answer my questions willingly. And remember that even though I want to keep your mind safe and sound, the same thing doesn't apply to your body. The conquest of a solar system is not accomplished in a day. So, we're in no hurry and if you refuse to talk we can take all the time we want to force you with slow and patient torture. Even if your body ends up mutilated with grisly wounds, our surgeons and biosthetic specialists will fix it up after every interrogation session, replacing your broken limbs and healing your wounds. In such circumstances you'll be able to live through weeks, even months of suffering."

At the calm pronouncement of this frightening perspective Zimko could not hold back a shiver of horror. A brief glimmer of dread flashed in his black eyes, which K'wyil caught.

"I hope that I'm making myself very clear," he continued. "If so, here's my first question: when do you plan on establishing official contact with the primitives of the planet you call T27?"

Zimko just grinned in amusement but said not a word.

Frustrated and flustered K'wyil went on, "Another question, since you seem not to have heard the first. On what planet of this solar system we're interested in have you holed up that famous secret weapon, *Negmat*, and what kind of weapon is it?"

K'wyil glimpsed a little surprise in his prisoner's eyes. "This surprises you, doesn't it, that we know about the ultra-secret weapon you think is so extraordinary? Well, we've made real progress in interstellar espionage."

The emperor waited a minute or two and faced with the Polarian's persistent silence he roared, "Guard! Get on with the first phase of persuasive arguments!"

A Denebian approached Zimko in chains and undid the magnetic seal of his spacesuit. Right away the Spaceman's suit dropped to the ground at his feet. The prisoner's muscular body was fit into a blue bodysuit and red vest. The guard started by taking the big disintegrator pistols from his belt. Then he tore off the clothes. The Polarian Chief of the Space Commandos stood bare-chested with bulging muscles. The guard stood back and aimed a yellow metal tube at the naked belly.

K'wyil narrowed his slanted eyes to examine the series of numbers and letters tattooed on the patient's solar plexus.

"What do those three letters followed by four numbers mean?" he asked.

"It's a registration number," Zimko smiled.

Raging mad K'wyil jumped up, snatched the tube out of the guard's hands and only three feet from his prisoner he aimed it at his chest and pressed his thumb on the surface of the metal cylinder. A long, blue spark sprang from the tube and crackled on the captive's skin. He writhed, tried to back away, made superhuman efforts to dodge the searing pain that his body suffered under the electric shock, worse than an agonizing burn.

The crackling beam struck his chest for more than 30 seconds, leaving a series of bloody zigzags on his flesh, where the blood coagulated instantly. Sweat beaded on the forehead of the panting victim.

"Are you going to talk, Demon from Space!"

Zimko stayed silent, gritting his teeth and tensing his muscles, expecting a new discharge.

K'wyil fiddled with the thermal-electric ray gun, turned up its power and sneered as he aimed it at Zimko once again.

"Now, for one minute, you're going to get 300 volts with a stronger amperage than the first time. Your skin will burn at 250°C!"

The emperor waited a moment hoping that the prisoner would decide to talk but faced with silence he pressed one of his claws against the tube and fired. The spark turned from blue to orange-green and struck the bare chest with intense violence.

Zimko jerked, his face screwed up into a grimace of abominable suffering and unable to control himself he howled out in pain.

K'wyil, energized by sadistic joy, kept the thermal-electric button pressed for ten seconds before stopping.

Zimko, with his legs giving out and his head sunk into his chest, groaned, "I'll talk… but under one condition…"

"You think you're in any kind of position to demand conditions?"

Zimko shook his head slowly from right to left, caught his breath and said, "I don't know how long I can hold out but I can assure you that these thermal-electric shocks, when they get up to ten minutes, will make me pass out for a long time. Therefore… if I manage to hold out… for ten minutes… and I think I can do that… I'll be unconscious for at least six hours. This could last longer than you think… forever. And even though you pretend… to have all the time in the world, I know perfectly well that you're… waiting on pins and needles. So, I'm offering you a deal. A deal in which I'll die sooner or later but at least it'll alleviate the suffering of my companions and probably let you conquer the solar system but with fewer casualties among the primitives of T27."

"Ask away and we'll see if we accept."

Zimko took a deep breath and shook his head, throwing off drops of sweat that were streaming down his face. He said, "I'm ready to talk but only with your whole general staff present as well as your Procyonian allies. As you'll see after the revelations I give you about the fantastic secret weapon Negmat, it's not only a matter of the safety of the people you want to conquer but your own too…"

K'wyil thought for a minute before answering, "I don't really like keeping our Procyonian allies, as you call them, up-to-date on our secret plans but since I have the means to erase any dangerous memories from their brains, I'll accept this. I'll decide later whether I should let our allies remember your revelations or if I should wipe their minds clean.

"Tomorrow the allied interstellar chiefs of the general staff will meet here with me to interrogate you. I'll send for them right now. But don't forget the tortures that await you if you try to trick us."

CHAPTER IX

Every Polarian base in the solar system—permanent planetary bases as well as mobile astrobases—was bustling with activity.

600 miles from Earth on astrobase 2, Fohag, the Wolfian, in the presence of the other chiefs or officers, Wolfian, Polarian and Centaurian, from the Space Commandos, presided over a meeting of utmost importance.

The main headquarters of the Galactic Forces of the Federated Worlds had informed Fohag of the visit of a very important person belonging to the general staff but whose identity could not be revealed. Wielding almost absolute power he was going to come in person to astrobase 2—the seat of the general staff operating in this solar system—to give the ultrasecret orders he had in hand.

In the huge, circular room of the artificial satellite, the three types of extra-terrestrial beings waited impatiently for the arrival of this mysterious special envoy. Soon the door to the wide central corridor opened and in stepped Honky, chief of the Information Service, who respectfully bowed away in front of a Polarian, dressed like him in a light gray spacesuit. Inside the transparent helmet his face was totally hidden by a black, plastic mask with only two holes for his eyes.

The stranger, followed by Honky, approached Fohag and saluted him by raising his right hand. The Wolfian responded in kind and invited him to sit behind the rectangular panel covered with all kinds of controls and unusual devices.

"Excuse me for coming to this meeting wearing a mask," the enigmatic envoy began in a deep voice distorted by the suit's microphone. "This precaution is necessary because the Denebians appear to have investigative means whose exact nature we are unaware of. And at no cost can they know my identity. I've been appointed by the Supreme Chief of the

117

Space Forces of the Federated Worlds to bring you extremely important orders.

"First of all, because of the primitives' state of mind, not yet ready to accept our visit, we are forced to postpone our official contact with T27 for at least two years. Our fleeting intrusions and the psychological tests that result will start again in around two years, I mean for the Earthlings, in June of July of 1956 of their main calendar because these primitives use several types of calendars each as inexact as the others.

"This two-year break is indispensable. Moreover, we know for sure that the Denebians and Procyionians are ready to launch an expeditionary force on T27 to subjugate the inhabitants and very soon. Therefore, we have to wait two years and do all we can to prevent this invasion of Earth or any other planet in the system.

"It appears to be a no-win situation. If we continue our visits on T27 and our demonstration flights to prove to the Earthlings that extra-terrestrial beings are watching them, we'll end up looking like invaders. Then the battles that are fought in space and maybe on T27 between our enemies and us will unleash an indescribable panic among the primitives. In fact, they will see no difference between the Denebians and us and will put flying saucers in the category of evil, hostile machines come from space to conquer them... Not to mention the awful destruction that will result on Earth from the confrontation between our enemies and us.

"Therefore, the supreme command that I am spokesman for has decided first of all to reinforce the defense of the solar system by creating, on every planet, a huge defense system with not just traditional weapons but also a new weapon of extraordinary power, an ultra-secret weapon called Negmat, short for Negative Matter. The negative matter, or *reversed matter*, is built backwards in a way. Where the usual nucleus of atoms is charged *positively*, in this matter the nucleus is charged *negatively* and the electrons of the reversed matter have a positive charge. So, at the very moment when the negative matter strikes regular matter, an incredible explosion re-sults.[24]

"This negative matter is the atomic component of a some distant galaxies that we've reached very recently thanks to spaceships specially built to fly in 'negative zones' compared to the 'positive' components of most galaxies like our own. In our ships made of 'neutral' matter we can hold a certain quantity of negative matter, for example a simple block of metal from these distant galaxies, and come back into positive zones without anything happening as long as its charge is protected by the neutral casing of its transporter. But if it gets near some strategic target and we free the negative matter, it'll shoot off at lightning speed towards the target and disintegrate all positive matter in a range of 60,000 miles, depending on how much there is, without any way to defend against it. This weapon is absolutely unparalleled. And it is invulnerable.

"There are negative charges of different sizes adapted to all circumstance, able to be used against an enemy squadron as well as an entire planet…"

Everyone was silent, stupefied by the unimaginable, destructive capabilities. Seeing the general bewilderment the spokesman continued.

"Yes, this extraordinary weapon, able to pulverize a planet, a solar system, even an entire galaxy, really exists! We'll be able, if we want, to wipe out the solar system of the Procyonians and Denebians but we hope that such desperate measures won't be necessary. We're thinking that a demonstration of our power will be enough to extinguish the desire of conquest of our relentless enemies.

"When I say 'demonstration of our power' I'm not being exact because more than a demonstration it's an action that we've undertaken against the Denebians. You will know the results when we tell you the nature of this action. For the moment, it's a matter of defending against any eventuality. In two *Sfangs* a squadron transporting Negmat spheres will arrive

---

[24] True. (Author's Note)

119

here and create a depot for this weapon on every planet. All our bases will be armed, including the astrobases. Special instructions will be left on board these bases to teach the technicians how to handle the Negmat. The spheres are basically nothing but psycho-guided spacecraft or rockets that our mechano-psychic machines can push to the speed of thought or absolute speed.

"By working the controls correctly you just have to *think* the trajectory and the chosen target and the sphere of Negmat will hit it instantly and explode, disintegrating everything in range of its particular size."

In the swarm of stars of the Galaxy ten giant spaceships, almost half a mile long and 300 feet in diameter, were heading for the solar system that the Space Commandos defended. On board were hundreds of Negmat spheres of all sizes being transported to the Polarian bases set up on or near the nine planets of the system.

Leaving from Khoda—the home planet of the Polarians orbiting the sun called the Pole Star by the inhabitants of T27—after a five-hour trip at speeds far superior to that of light, the space squadron had just entered the pull of the farthest planet of the solar system that was being targeted by the Denebians: Pluto.

One of the giant spaceships veered off and headed for this small, frozen planet while the other ships separated, each following a different route to the eight other planets where they were going to set up defense bases.

One of the ships changed the strength of its gravito-magnetic field to counterbalance the force that Jupiter pulled, its destination point, the giant of the string of planets. The colossal globe of Jupiter, with its 87,000-mile diameter, seemed to swell up immensely as the ship approached. The different colored bands of its thick atmosphere blocked any clear observation of its surface. As the cloud covering thinned around the equator an oblong smear of huge dimensions appeared: the famous red spot of Jupiter, which intrigued so many astronomers on T27.

Slowing down considerably and increasing the intensity of its gravito-magnetic field, the giant spaceship emerged in the few clouds over the red spot, a thinner atmosphere than the gaseous layers surrounding the planet.

This red spot was really a gigantic continent around 30,000 miles long and 6,000 miles wide, floating on an ocean composed of layers of gas piled on top of each other. The core of Jupiter was made up of a great variety of ice fields under unimaginable pressure.

An atmosphere of hydrogen in the middle of which drifted clouds of ammonia, methane and other partially liquefied gases blanketed this enormous planet. These mixed gases produced different bands of color, from milky white to light green through vermillion and brown, that perpetually streaked the globe in slightly slanted strata.

The red continent floating on the ocean of gas looked like a gigantic platform of frozen ammonia riddled with tortured peaks, with darker stains fading to red. On the surface a thick layer of vermillion crystal gave it the red color through the atmosphere, confusing the imagination by its contrast and its persistence on a world apparently made up of liquid and viscous matter.

The spaceship landed gently on a relatively level area not far from a transparent dome protecting the Polarian base. The rays of the sun, 500 million miles away at this time, gave only a dim light to this orb frozen at a temperature close to -135°C.

A lateral hatch opened in the side of the giant ship and a long metal ramp descended to the ground. Dressed in their pressurized, air-conditioned and gravity-regulated spacesuits the Polarian technicians appeared at the top of the ramp, 200 feet above the ground. 30 of them slid down the polished metal of the gravito-magnetic conveyor belt and, once on the ground, headed for the base.

All of them were holding disintegrator machine guns in their gloves and advancing cautiously. All the cannons on the ship were also aimed at the airtight globe protecting the pyramid city.

The reason for this attitude lay in the fact that in spite of announcing its arrival the spaceship had received no answer. The officers on board, fearing a trap, had therefore decided to send a reconnaissance patrol covered by the powerful weapons of the ship.

Despite their paroptic vision the Polarians had been unable to probe the base from a distance. Such obliteration of their supra-normal vision had never happened before. So, they were right to fear the worst.

The patrol reached the decompression chamber and stopped short. The huge hatch that led to the entrance airlock and its farther door into the dome were broken, mangled and smashed. The decompression valve was now just an open passage open on both ends! Thus, the artificial atmosphere of the base had escaped, replaced immediately by torrents of ammonia and methane.

Entering the city by stepping over the wreckage the Polarians noticed that the temperature under the dome had dropped to 127°C below zero. Therefore, it must have taken some time since the artificial air had been replaced by Jupiter's gas for the 22°C to drop down to the outside temperature.

It was on the astrodrome that the patrol found the first Polarian corpses. Petrified in positions of great suffering, the unfortunate victims had suffocated with the absorption of methane and ammonia. The sudden drop in temperature had then turned them into ice statues.

Since the base was almost exclusively inhabited by Polarians the artificial atmosphere was the same as their home planet, which allowed them to dispense with spacesuits. The few Wolfians and Centaurians of the city, from the fact that they kept their spacesuits on, must have escaped death.

Little by little as the scouts ventured down the streets of the city the number of corpses grew. Of the Centaurians and Wolfians, with or without spacesuits, they found no trace.

All of a sudden one of the scouts left the group and leaned over the body of a young Polarian woman, a beautiful blond cut down by death in a hideous grimace. She died choking on the gas, her eyes dilated, her mouth open, her right hand clutching her delicate neck. The fingers of her left hand had torn the thin blouse, probably trying desperately to loosen the grip of suffocation.

The Polarian's companions, squatting beside him, sensed that the unfortunate girl was not a stranger to their friend, who sat bewildered and helpless. Tears of rage rolled down his tanned cheeks. Jaws clenched, grinding his teeth, he sobbed and said, "Ykluna was my partner…"

He tenderly caressed the young woman's face and taking her hand that grasped her throat he tried to lower her rigid arm. The little effort he made to place the frozen arm along her side was enough to break it clean off at the elbow. He was stupefied. His tearful gaze went from the arm he was holding in his glove to the corpse of the girl he would no longer share his life with. His companions helped him stand up and simply told him they must continue their search.

The streets and lobbies of the buildings were piled with corpses turned blue from the cold, petrified in all positions with the stamp of intense physical pain on their faces.

"That's why the doors didn't close automatically," one of the Polarians stated, walking in front and pointing at a huge room opened on the ground floor of a rectangular building. "The machines of the Climate Control Center were destroyed."

The vast room cluttered with all kinds of machines, its walls covered with controls and instruments, looked like the site of a fierce battle. Polarian men and women, torn to pieces, were lying among the wreckage of their gutted, shattered machines that were rendered useless and unable to perform their vital functions for the population.

In the middle of the room, sitting on the ruins, was an iridescent metal cube in which they could see the inner electronics glowing colorfully.

The chief of the patrol, before approaching this weird contraption that he had never seen on any base, used his paroptic vision to study the mechanism. Right away he felt a sharp pain in his brain and instinctively backed away, cutting off his psychic waves.

"This device is a scrambler that interferes with our paroptic vision. It was left here by the Denebians after committing their crime."

He aimed his disintegrator gun and fired. The colorful cube disappeared in the bright blue ray. On the ruins its base had left a black rectangle that seemed to fade into a smaller, greenish geometric shape.

Continuing their investigations the Polarians suddenly stopped, dumbfounded, at the corner of a street. In the lobby of a building with chrome metal walls the patrol saw a gray-blue form, luminescent, lying across the entrance. They approached silently.

A being, at least 13 feet tall, had collapsed in the lobby. Its soft head, ill-defined, had one blue-green, gelatinous eye in what could be called its forehead. Its mouth and nose formed a triple orifice at the top of a small trunk or snout. Its huge chest had three long arms on each side that ended in a kind of pincer with jaws, at first sight like a lobster.

Its two thick legs were almost cylindrical with blue bulging rings more phosphorescent than the rest of the body that wore no spacesuit. In its abdomen was a deep wound from which a trail of dark green blood had flowed, later congealing on its skin and on the metal floor of the building.

"A Procyonian!" the chief exclaimed. "It was these monsters from Procyon and not their Denebian allies who destroyed this base. Our enemies are becoming bolder of late. This is the third planetary base of this system that has suffered an attack, but it's the only one that lost its entire population."

"What's this filthy creature doing in this building?" a Polarian wondered aloud.

A quick visit to the building told all. It was on the 17th floor, in a big room that the Wolfians and Centaurians of the city were found, suffocated to death after being tortured. For what obscure reason had the Procyonians brought them to this place? One of the victims must have managed, before dying, to inflict the mortal wound in the monster who had then dragged himself down to the lobby where the patrol had found him.

The reconnaissance group hurried back to the spaceship to send a message to HQ and then, with the help of the technicians, start on the repairs needed to make the base inhabitable again.

A small team immediately unloaded the Negmat spheres for defense while the rest of the crew of the giant spaceship got on with a particularly difficult task: the restoration of the Jupiter base.

The spaceships of V'kend, the grand chief of the Procyonians and of the generals' staff summoned by K'wyil, the Denebian Emperor, had just landed in the astrodrome of Lycknah, the capital of the planet Ptopa, cradle of the scaly, green-skinned monsters.

The Procyonians, sympodic creatures able to live in extremely different physical conditions than on their home planet, left their spaceships—some spherical and others cigar-shaped—to meet their ally, K'wyil, Emperor of this world and master of many other solar systems.

Compared to them the Denebians whom they saw in the streets of Lucknah were like dwarves in spite of their height reaching six and a half feet. With a bouncing gait, their six arms hanging down with their multiple pincers, the Procyonians walked on, their bodies emitting a gray-blue bioluminescence, their blue-green eye opening and closing to a steady rhythm.

K'wyil welcomed them in his hexagonal palace with all the signs of the extreme courtesy even though deep down inside he found them disgusting and hideous. The Denebian Emperor led them into the big circular room in the middle of which Zimko, his chest scarred with horrible wounds, was still hanging from the ceiling by cables shackled at his wrists.

K'wyil invited V'kend and the 37 members of his general staff to sit with the senior officers, 43 of them, who were already in the first three rows encircling the room.

Zimko slowly raised his head, which had been sunk in his chest, and as far as his painful position allowed he looked around the assembly. All these monstrous beings made him feel nothing but disgust and hatred.

When the guests of honor were seated K'wyil stood up and approached the prisoner. "Now that my allies are present, I'll give you one minute to keep your promise and tell us everything you know about the plans of your general staff."

Zimko lowered his head as a sign of submission and started talking. "To respond to the first question you asked me yesterday, I can only give you a rough date. Contact with the inhabitants of T27 will be officially established two years from now, meaning in June or July 1956 T27 time. But this will happen only if we're sure... (Zimko paused a moment before continuing)... we can keep you out of this solar system where we don't want your attempts at invasion to cause battles that might destroy the primitive races of T27."

"Before getting on with other details, tell us what this ultra-secret weapon is—the Negmat."

"Negmat is short for Negative Matter," Zimko answered and he gave details about the formidable weapon.

When he had finished K'wyil looked at him for a long time, very impressed by his revelations. "This extraordinary weapon has to come into our hands at all costs. We will do whatever it takes to get a hold of one of these Negmat spheres in order to study its casing in neutral matter. Furthermore, to accomplish this delicate mission we will use you, whom we will psychically prepare to carry it out. So, now do you understand why we wanted to keep you alive? You're going to be the centerpiece in our new game."

"That would surprise me!" Zimko sneered, proudly raising his head. All trace of pain or dejection had mysteriously disappeared from his face.

Taken aback, K'wyil shot him a look, at first surprised by this rebellion, then terribly intrigued. "How dare you mock us when I just need to wave my hand to torture you again."

"I laugh at your tortures, you vile, turtle-faced creature!" Zimko shouted. "I advise you not to torture any more before I say what I have to say to this filthy lump of reeking waste that is V'kend, the Grand Procyonian Chief!"

The named monster jumped up. His flabby skin emitted no longer a blue but a green bioluminescence in his outrage. His six arms flailed about, trembling with rage.

"Listen up, you foul thing!" Zimko tensed his muscles and shook the cables suspending him from the ceiling. "Even though I've been a prisoner in this den of demons for three sfangs, I know that you disgusting creatures destroyed our base in Jupiter…"

K'wyil and V'kend, more and more dumbfounded, stared at the captive dubiously.

"How do you know this if you couldn't communicate with your people even psychically?" the Denebian Emperor questioned.

"Are you so sure that I can't communicate with them?" Zimko defied. "From the moment I got here I haven't stopped sending messages and receiving them thanks to a recently developed mechano-psychic device that you can't control…"

"That's impossible!" K'wyil barked. "We searched you thoroughly and found no device, however small, in your clothes."

After a burst of laughter the Man from Outer Space explained, "You didn't find the device because it wasn't in my clothes. In fact," he suddenly wondered, "what did you do with my companions, the Polarians, Wolfians and Centaurians captured along with me?"

"Some are in an armored cell, 300 feet below my palace. Others have been transferred to various laboratories in

Lucknah where they'll be used for experiments by our scientists."

"Perfect," the prisoner smiled. "In that case, you couldn't find the psychic amplifier because it's *in my body!* You thought Zimko so naïve that he'd let himself be captured by your henchmen, K'wyil?"

"And yet you did fall into the trap I set for you," the Emperor grumbled as his arrogance was starting to wear thin.

"Me?" the prisoner said. "Not at all. I didn't fall into your trap. It was part of the plan of our general staff to let me be captured. I am, therefore, in your hands, but Zimko is free, for the greater good of the Federated Worlds and the solar systems that he will have to defend against you and your revolting allies.

"No, K'wyil, you didn't capture Zimko but a... *biologically constructed robot in his image!* All the Polarians, Centaurians and Wolfians who are in your power are biological robots, machines copying the exact same actions as their originals. Thus, the words that I, Robot, are saying right now are in reality those that Zimko, *the real one*, are speaking into a mechano-psychic amplifier of his own invention.

"You've been played, K'wyil, and if you still doubt it, take a sharp blade and cut a rectangular opening in my chest, just above my number... which, as I told you during the first interrogation, really is a registration number."

Absolutely astonished by what he had just heard K'wyil grabbed a razor-sharp instrument and sliced into the synthetic skin of the biological Robot that looked like Zimko.

As the blade cut into the plastic "epidermis", identical to flesh, the Robot said, "Don't cut too deep or you'll damage my works, which would prevent me from giving you more interesting information."

The Denebian Emperor cut a surgical area six inches wide in the prisoner's chest and peeled off the one-inch thick plastic skin. Through a kind of strong plastex he could see the inside of the thorax, an unbelievable tangle of electronic tubes, wires, connections and tiny instruments and intricate mechanisms that animated this masterpiece of Polarian genius.

"Are you satisfied, K'wyil," the pseudo-Zimko smiled. "Now listen carefully to what I'm going to tell you and you, too, you maniacs from Procyon!" he raised his voice to the monsters. "You wanted to know what the ultra-secret weapon Negmat was? You were ready to do anything to get your hands on one? Well, coming right up...

"In bringing you all together here, you grand Denebian chiefs and you monsters from Procyon, I pulled off a master stroke. Without you the worlds that you govern would take years to reorganize—if, for example, you were no longer able to lead them. Your replacements would need a long time to undertake any effective actions against the solar system that you desire and that we're defending. In this room, therefore, is assembled the indispensable brains of your so-called Liberating forces.

"You wanted, I say, to get possession of a Negmat sphere? You have not one but more than 100, of smaller size it's true but still unheard-of power because I forgot to tell you that every biological robot that you captured has one of these little spheres of unimaginable destructive power installed inside them. And you're about to see them in action!"

All the monsters in the vaulted room jumped up in panic. They understood that they had blindly jumped into a diabolical trap. Howling in terror, screeching like a herd of angry elephants, the monstrous creatures leaped over their seats, pushing and shoving, scratching and trampling each other desperate to escape.

But before they could reach the exit, Zimko, the real Zimko, Chief of the Space Commandos, in control of this bold performance, pushed a red button blinking on his control panel billions of miles away.

At the same time, psycho-remote-controlled, the Negmat spheres inside the biological robots were released from their neutral casing and coming in contact with the positive matter around them they disintegrator in a dreadful explosion.

In the roar of disaster Lucknah, the Denebian capital, and all the beings it held, were wiped out in a huge explosion, glowing purple visible thousands of miles away, pulverizing the spaceships over the city, razing to the ground everything within a 300-mile range, crumbling mountains, transforming ammonia lakes into giant liquid balls that quickly evaporated, and mowing down forest as if with a giant scythe.

The whole planet was shaken by an earthquake compared to which the previous disasters were just feeble trembling. The shockwave shook the continental bedrock for seven hours. The planet's atmosphere was totally obscured by thousands of tons of dust thrown 100 miles up into the air for 93 hours (T27 time).

Instead of Lucknah, the seat of the Denebian Imperial Government, a 50-mile wide crater, 10 miles deep gaped in the ground. Out of it flowed rivers of purple lava glinting red, slowly bubbling up from the bowels of the planet whose crust had been split all the way down to the viscous matter on which the continents drifted.

On astrobase 2, in its orbit 600 miles above the Earth, for the second time in 24 hours, the masked stranger—but without a spacesuit this time—summoned the Section Chiefs of the artificial satellite in the name of the General Staff.

Polarians, Wolfians and Centaurians, gathered around Fohag, the Chief of the base, were waiting impatiently for the stranger to speak. He did so in short time.

"I'm happy to announce to you that Lucknah, the Denebian capital, where the chiefs of the green monsters were all together with their Procyonian allies, has been reduced to rubble by a commando team of biological robots whose leader was the copy of… me."

On saying this the mysterious spokesman from the General Staff of the Federated Worlds took off his mask. The energetic face of Zimko appeared smiling, satisfied with his clever strategy that had just saved many Polarian, Wolfian and Centaurian lives.

"Now that the war-mongering Denebian-Procyonian association has been decapitated, it will take at least two years T27 for them to reorganize. We will be able to use this respite to make all Earthlings believe in our existence and without unleashing general panic among the primitives. When the time comes to make official contact with the governments of Earth in June of July 1956 of their main calendar, if our projects succeed, the nine planets of this solar system will have strong defense bases from which we can repel any threat coming from space.

"Now, my friends, we have to continue our incursions and the 'demonstrations of our presence' on this planet. A great task awaits us on all the other worlds in this galactic zone as well.

"Everyone should go back to their post. Our Fim'has have to keep flying over the continents of this backward planet that we've been defending for so long against the Denebians. Its inhabitants, however, are far from suspecting that those whose existence they deny are fighting hard to keep them from falling under the control of the awful, green-skinned monsters and into the 'claws' of their hideous allies… these almost mythical monsters whom a sacred book on T27 calls the *Beast of the Apocalypse*."

The spaceship of Hogounn and Injya, the two little creatures from a planet orbiting the sun Alpha Centauri, crossed the blue sky at lightning speed, then stopped short over a town in the north of France.

Injya examined the green countryside on her viewer screen. Then she looked at her companion and placed her tiny six-fingered hand on Hogounn's saying, "I'm really starting to like this planet. I'm eager to establish a base on its surface so we can finally live here together… Its inhabitants are really different than us, just like the Polarians and Wolfians, but they are still our brothers since they are thinking beings. We, along with our Polarian and Wolfian friends will just have to educate them to add one more globe to the grand family of Federated Worlds."

"Yes, Injya, I'm also eager to take part in building an Earth base and I'm sure that there will be a lot of Earthlings who will accept us and love us like we love them... without suspicion."

The Fimn'has of the two Centaurians, altruistic and sensitive to the poetry of a foreign landscape, shot up, hovered for ten seconds, wobbled a little while zigzagging for a few miles and then stopped its pranks to soar off into the clouds toward astrobase 2.

The next day in the local papers there would be, as always, a superior attitude, in the name of Science (with a capital S), to say that a "meteor" or a "weather balloon" had drifted over such a place and such a time.

An astronomer would boost this claim with all the weight of his knowledge and make fun of the ridiculous "flying dishes," proving by A+B that it was a meteor that soared over this region. Moreover, if witnesses dared to tell him that the meteor in question flew in leaps and bounds, shot straight up or zigzagged, the founts of astronomical knowledge would quickly direct all these fine witnesses of the event to a psychiatrist who would pompously cry out, with his face twitching:

"Mild form of collective hysteria! Brain trauma! Senility and schizophrenia!"

And naturally the psychiatrist in question would be even more flabbergasted if someone with a healthy mind claimed that such a diagnosis would better be applied to him.

For, no one is deafer than he who does not want to hear and no one blinder than he who does not want to see.

Nos Ancêtres de l'Avenir

JIMMY GUIEU

ANTICIPATION

Editions
"Fleuve Noir"

OUR ANCESTORS FROM THE FUTURE

For HIM who was contacted seven times by a Creature from Outer Space and who holds the material proof of these contacts. If only he could read this book, understand and reestablish the link that has been broken.

J.G.

CHAPTER ONE

The huge Khantangskoïe steppe, north of the Arctic Circle, spread its deserted landscape of immeasurable sadness over snowy and muddy hills, punctured by clumps of green or more often gray-brown plants. Broken in the west by the wide Khatanga River carting along huge ice floes, the Siberian tundra resumed its desolation farther on in the Taymyr Peninsula.

In -41°C weather 100 men poorly dressed in rags—old military coats, hats with only a few patches of fur left, shoddy boots, legs protected slipshod against the terrible Siberian cold with burlap sacks tied around the calves—were wielding shovel or pick, digging trenches toward the river in order to drain the putrid swamps for the next thaw.

In the frozen, rock-hard mud they worked in pairs: one swinging his axe on the ground, the other clearing out the excavation by throwing shovelfuls of matter into a wheelbarrow that he would then empty into the big bucket of a tractor specially designed to work in low temperatures.

Two miles away from here, farther up Katanga Bay, stood the austere mass of the Rehabilitation Center—a concrete cube 165 feet long on every side—towering over the 20 bunkhouses that harbored the 2,000 residents to be rehabilitated.

The sun was low on the horizon this late afternoon and cast unusually long shadows of the workers over the fissured ground.

Exhausted, his back breaking from working his shovel since dawn, Colonel Zavkom straightened up, sore and shivering in the biting wind. After two years in this Rehabilitation Center all that was left of his powerful shoulders and herculean muscles was a bony frame holding up skin cracked by the relentless cold of the steppe. Leaning on his shovel he breathed noisily in a painful grimace, as worn out as he was.

His work partner, the physicist Petkov, six years older than him, stopped swinging his axe to take a breather. His once energetic face also bore the deep scars of forced labor along with a few days' growth of beard. Only his blue eyes still reflected some intensity that contradicted the look of a man suffering in body and mind. He turned around to look at his partner in misfortune but he barely had time to raise his arm to shield his face. The club hit Colonel Zavkom first before flogging him.

The guard dressed warmly in a thick uniform with a fur cap, a machine gun hanging over his shoulder, swung his cudgel a second time at the convicts, yelling, "The work's not done, pigs! You've still got ten minutes of digging. Another break and you'll go to the tub!"

Without saying a word the two men went back to work, gnashing their teeth. They shivered thinking of the inhuman treatment that the tub punishment meant, too frequently, alas, in the Siberian penal colonies.

In the distance the muffled shrill of the siren at the Rehabilitation Center sounded, announcing the end of the workday. The convicts straightened up, some of them wobbling, and with tools on their shoulders lined up in four columns, surrounded by the ten guards with machine guns who gave the signal to march toward camp.

When they reached the double electric fence and (for more security) the tangle of barbed wire, night was already falling. The spotlight from the watchtower on top of the guards' cube lit up a vast, open space in front of the concrete building. The 2,000 prisoners in close ranks stood still, numb with cold, in the huge square in the middle of which 50 armed guards formed a circle around a kind of cement vat, 15 feet wide, whose frozen surface had just been broken by a team of prisoners.

The last column came up to the vat just as Gulinski, the chief of the concentration camp euphemistically called a Rehabilitation Center, was coming out of the cube. Comfortably warm in his heavy uniform, his brutish face partly covered by his fur hood, he made a sign to an officer and stopped 15 feet away from the water-filled vat with ice floating on the surface after being struck with pickaxes.

The officer, a giant with the face of a tartar, swung his baton and made seven prisoners step up to the edge of the vat. The speakers set up around the square started crackling and the cynical voice of the chief spit out, like every evening for two years, his recorded speech:

"These men have dared to break the rules of the Rehabilitation Center. Through their rebellion and their laziness they have slowed down the work of draining the swamps. Since this Center is not a place for recreation but for work, they are going to suffer their justly earned punishment. Let this example serve as a lesson to those who still hope to escape or even just laze around. The 'tub' is only a warning. Repeat offenders will be put to death."

Colonel Zavkom at the front of the column groaned to his friend Petkov, "A warning! As if these poor devils could survive the awful punishment."

"It would have been better to die on the Moon than come back here to Russia after our failure[25]," Petkov the physicist whispered back.

A guard whom they had not seen come up from behind the left column rushed over to them, his weapon raised.

"What is this?" the chief of the camp barked.

"These two men were whispering mean things about you, Chief," the guard lied—he had simply seen their lips move—standing at attention before his superior.

"To the tub!" the brute shouted.

A glare of anger mixed with fear flashed in the eyes of the two prisoners who knew that if they protested against the lie they would still join the seven men condemned to the tub.

"Get undressed!" the tartar officer ordered, accompanying his words with blows from his baton. "You four first," he said to the first comers.

---

[25] See Volume 1.

The poor men did as told, their hands swollen from the cold, taking off their rags with tears in their eyes. One of them, a scrawny old man whose ribs poked through the white skin of his thin chest, begged them, gripping the edge of the vat. "Please, have mercy… I'm sick and…"

A kick in the back sent him toppling into the icy water that sprayed onto the three other naked prisoners shivering at the edge of the tub.

The old man sank, came back up, sank again and struggled to hang onto a big piece of ice. He coughed and breathed heavily, his eyes burning with fever, then choking he let go and with his mouth twisted in pain and suffering he died of congestion.

Then the guard pushed the other three and turned around to Zavkom and Petkov and their three companions he shouted, "Get your clothes off! Looks like the water's just fine tonight!" He turned away laughing, which caught on with all the guards in camp.

The five convicts stood there, arms folded across their naked chest, teeth chattering, looking horrified at the ice floating back over the dying men who were struggling only feebly.

"Next!"

The guard brandished his baton. The five prisoners closed their eyes and instinctively protected their heads with their skinny arms from the blow to come. But the blow did not come. An outcry of amazement came pouring out of all lungs and even though their eyes were closed Zavkom and Petkov and the other three were blinded by a bright flash that they could not identify.

They popped open their eyes and were stunned to see that the guard was not there. In his place a black stain was in the frozen mud where the ice had melted.

The spotlight from the central watchtower shined its beam over the columns of prisoners, crossed over the 20 barracks, then came back to flood the square where the tub punishment was being carried out.

All of a sudden the metal tower holding the spotlight and a battery of twin machine guns was surrounded by a bright light. Its crossed beams seemed to suddenly glow white and in a fantastic flash the thing disappeared in silence as if it had been wiped from the landscape by a magician.

A growing commotion swept through the 2,000 convicts. The chief of the concentration camp turned livid, thrown into a panic by the incomprehensible wonder. He ran in fear to the concrete building. Watching his flight the officers and guards stood still for a moment, not knowing what to do, then suddenly the officers were seized by panic and ran after their chief to the building, the invulnerable shelter where they could confront the... What, in fact? They wondered running at full speed.

The panic soon spread to the guards who left the prisoners and did as the officers who had just disappeared under the huge concrete vault of the building's façade.

Colonel Zavkom, the physicist Petkov and their three companions having escaped by a miracle—the word was not too strong—from the tub punishment got dressed as quickly as they could. Their numb, frozen fingers grabbed the clothes that the poor dead men in the freezing vat were no longer wearing and threw them over their own rags.

It was at this moment that the thing happened. Colonel Zavkom and Petkov, at the same time, stopped wrapping the burlap around their calves. Dumbfounded, they stood up and looked at each other blankly. In spite of the commotion among the 2,000 convicts left free, a clear, deep voice, a weird voice rang out *in their minds*. For, this voice, unheard by the others prisoners, came to them by telepathy.

Colonel Zavkom and you, Petkov, brave pilot of the first Russian rocket to the Moon, Zimko is speaking to you!

Nervously grabbing his friend's arm Zavkom whispered in a hoarse voice while looking around at the deplorable setting of the concentration camp, "Petkov, it's... the telepathic voice of Zimko, the Man from Outer Space and the Chief of the Space Commandos whom Kariven once told us about..."

"In that fiasco on the Moon? That fiasco that brought us into this death camp? Could it be? But where… where are you, Zimko?"

On the roof of the building where your executioners are hiding. Can't you see me? They heard clearly in their heads.

They looked up at the spot. Against the background of the starry sky they could make out a silhouette that was saluting them with a raised right hand as is the custom among Polarians, those super-evolved, humanoid creatures who were watching planet Earth on board their disc-shaped spaceships called "flying saucers" by Earthlings.

Abruptly the spotlight from a corner watchtower swept over the camp and lit up the stranger on the roof of the building. The cone of light stopped, settled and framed the form of Zimko who, brightly lit up by the beam, appeared clearly to all the prisoners. Looking up at him, stunned, the convicts wondered who this man dressed in a kind of gray-green spacesuit with a transparent round helmet could be.

"Get down!" Colonel Zavkom shouted.

The rattle of a machine gun from the corner watchtower drown out his words and a hail of bullets shrieked over the roof where Zimko was standing. Even though the bullets were whistling by his ears, he seemed content to just stand there. In the square and between the buildings, at the first volley, the prisoners threw themselves to the ground. Another round of gunfire, longer than the first, ripped through the silence.

"Zimko!" Petkov howled desperately, "Get down!"

Astounded, Petkov and Zavkom watched as the lethal bullets stopped, inexplicably, ten feet in front of the Man from Outer Space and showered down harmlessly along the face of the building.

"It's unbelievable!" Petkov said. "Zimko is probably protected by a strong magnetic field that's stopping the bullets."

The man from another planet, under the machine gun fire, unholstered the huge pistol hanging from his wide belt, aimed carefully at the watchtower and fired. A blue ray shot

141

out of the barrel and struck the top of the tower. Zimko moved his wrist and brought the ray down along the metal supports and the construction suddenly lit up bright orange... then disappeared.

He put his disintegrator weapon back in the holster and pressed two buttons on a rectangular device stuck to his belt. He slowly rose up by activating his jet pack. The strange inhabitant of a solar system around the Pole Star curved through the air and landed three feet away from Zavkom and Petkov.

Astonished, not believing their eyes, they shook his hand, unable to speak. Zavkom finally stammered out feebly, "Let's crouch down... We're still in the line of fire from the blockhouse."

"We've got nothing to fear, friends," the Polarian declared in perfect Russian. "You're now protected by my own magnetic field."

A microphone emitted these words out of the tiny speaker built into the collar of his spacesuit. Then he sent out this telepathic order that echoed through the minds of the 2,000 prisoners still lying flat on the frozen ground:

Get yourselves quickly behind the barracks but don't stand up. Crawl! Get going! he repeated telepathically when he saw that the stunned convicts did nothing. *Any minute now the machine guns are going to fire on you from the blockhouse.*

Finally recognizing that the "voice" was not an illusion, they hunched up, turned around and crawled and clambered out of the open area. The sinister crackle of three machine guns caught the prisoners retreating and sowed death in their helpless ranks. Zimko whipped out his two pistols and swept the concrete face of the building. The blue rays dug horizontal ditches in the façade, destroying everything up to 15 feet deep.

"Before the machine guns higher up are ready to fire," he said, "we should have at least ten minutes. Gulinski, the chief of the death camp, is in a panic and doesn't know what to do to get control of the situation. Come on!"

Taking the two men by the arm to keep them inside the protective magnetic field, he followed the swarm of convicts that was gradually—in complete chaos—moving away from the danger zone.

The machine guns, sooner than expected, started spitting bullets from a higher floor of the central block. Luckily, the last prisoners were just reaching the first barracks where they could find cover.

While firing on the torturers whom the concrete walls could not protect from the disintegrator ray, Zimko gave a psychic order to everyone before addressing his friends:

"Let's get farther away from the blockhouse. It'll be disintegrated soon by the cannon from my spaceship. I just gave orders, in fact, to Tlyka, my co-pilot, who dropped me off two hours ago in the steppe."

He seemed to concentrate for a few minutes, then looked up. In the freezing night of the Siberian tundra the myriad stars twinkled like sparkling gemstones on the velvety screen of a cloudless sky. One of these stars moved, grew bigger, became like a phosphorescent green chip and gradually took on its true form: a ship like a lampshade topped by a dome with windows around it and with three shiny spheres underneath.

In perfect silence, as the prisoners looked on bewildered, the bright green spaceship hovered 650 feet over the blockhouse…

Gulinski, the chief of the concentration camp, with his fur hood thrown back, wiped his forehead. He glanced frequently at the TV screen on the wall that showed him the deserted camp piled with corpses. Only two prisoners at the side of the mysterious stranger were still walking away, the others having hidden behind the barracks.

"I've got Moscow on the line!" the radioman jumped out of his seat and handed his headphones to his chief.

Grabbing the microphone and nervously adjusting the headphones over his ears, out of his dry throat he shouted, "Hello, Moscow?"

"Meltnikof," a nasally voice came back, "Commander in Chief of the Rehabilitation Centers of the Siberian Sector. Is that you, Gulinski?"

"Yes, Commander. I... I wanted to talk to Chief of the MVD[26] to..."

"For any incident you should contact my command," Meltnikof cut him off. "I'll decide what services we have to alert. What's this about? A revolt?"

"Worse, Commander. An enemy agent got through the electric fence and enter the camp..."

"The Rehabilitation Center," the Commander corrected arrogantly. "You stopped him or killed him, I hope?"

"Well... We haven't... yet been able to capture him. He's... destroyed the central watchtower and one of the corner ones too. Now he's got the pris... the workers hiding behind the barracks."

"And your machine guns, you toads, are they firing gumdrops?" the Commander barked.

"He... The enemy spy has... also destroyed eight of our machine guns on the south side. He... He's got a secret weapon... a kind of pistol firing a blue ray that destroys everything it touches."

"Don't try to shirk your responsibilities with a bunch of idiotic nonsense, Gulinski. You're incompetent, get it? I'll have you removed and brought up before a Purge Committee."

"Commander!" Gulinski groaned. "Please believe me. My officers are witnesses to the grave events that are shaking up the camp. At this very moment the screen we're all watching, me and my men, is showing some kind of disc-shaped ship hovering over our blockhouse! Do something, Commander! This... this ship might bomb us! Send out a squadron

---

[26] Ministry of Internal Affairs. (Author's Note)

of jet fighters from Nordenskiöld to help us. Quick… the disc is…"

"The disc?" Meltnikof questioned after a pause. "You believe in those stories of flying saucers that delude the lecherous snakes in the west or have you been drinking?"

Angry now and thinking of nothing but saving his life, Gulinski cut off communication without worrying about the error of his ways and called the base at Nordenskiöld himself.

"Base 7 over," he heard with relief after a few minutes of trying to "hook" on the right frequency.

"Rehabilitation Center at Khantangskoïe here. Commander Gulinski speaking. We're under attack by an enemy agent using a powerful secret weapon! His disc-shaped plane is hovering over our blockhouse and we fear the worst… Send out a squadron of armed fighters immediately and…"

"That's hard to believe, Commander," the voice broke in. "The west would not be so reckless as to come and attack a Rehabilitation Center in the middle of Soviet territory. Have you reported to the Commander in Chief of your division?"

"Yes, but if we wait for orders to come out of the hierarchy, your planes won't find anything here but ruins! Come help us right now! This disc is…"

The Nordenskiöld base never knew what Gulinski said after this. The disc-shaped spaceship called by Zimko had just fired the powerful disintegrator ray from its cannon at the concrete block. A blinding, bluish light enveloped the vast cube. Its walls glowed bright orange, pulsed briefly and faded. Five seconds later the blockhouse had disappeared, leaving a shallow black crater in its place, the only remains of its ephemeral existence.

The ship landed gently in the square, which had just served as a place of punishment for the convicts, and between the spheres of its landing gear a platform made of three telescopic tubes came down.

Zimko dragged Colonel Zavkom and the physicist Petkov forward while giving the 2,000 men hiding behind the barracks a psychic lecture:

"You're free, friends. Zimko, Chief of the Space Commandoes in your solar system, declares it for you. I don't have time to enter into details, but know that I wasn't born on this planet. You can come out of hiding and gather in the open space. The blockhouse and your torturers have been destroyed.

"You're free of their chains but being free in this country will soon find you back in the hands of those who condemned you for 'deviation'. I am asking you, therefore, to trust me and obey my orders that, as you will soon understand, are meant only to make you free men, ready to fight to protect this freedom that you and your fellow Earthlings have a right to. For, your freedom and your lives are in serious jeopardy. Everything will be explained to you in good time."

The convicts, still reeling under emotional shock, came out in groups, stupefied, looking skeptically (despite its physical reality) at the spaceship in the square where the blockhouse had disappeared.

"The ship you see is a Polarian spaceship from a distant planet in the solar system of the Pole Star. Your partners in misfortune here," Zimko put his hands of the shoulders of Zavkom and Petkov, "will also tell you that you can believe me. The people of my race want only to protect you. If you follow my advice you will be able to enjoy and keep your newfound freedom."

Colonel Zavkom and Petkov nodded their heads, too shaken up to voice their faith in their savior.

"A huge cigar-shaped spaceship will land here in 30 of your minutes in the steppe around half a mile from this camp. Leave immediately for the south. The electric fences are harmless now. At the far left of the camp you will find an opening around 80 feet wide made by the disintegrator cannon on my spaceship.

"Get going, Earthling friends, and get onto the spaceship that will be landing very soon. You'll be safe inside and can then make yourselves useful to your fellow men. The planetary base where you will be brought already has many of your compatriots, most notably the world famous Professor Serge

Yegov whom we freed this morning from another concentration camp.

"Good luck, friends. We will see each other again soon in a free world where these abominable death camps don't existed!"

Zimko and the Russians marched side by side down one of the inner corridors of the disc-shaped spaceship that had just lifted off. The electro-luminescent metal walls emitted a uniform light that cast no shadows. When they entered the cockpit located on the axis of the ship, it started heading west at 50,000 feet altitude.

Zavkom and Petkov stopped inside the oval hatch, the thick, reinforced door that Zimko had just closed.

Turning around from the half-moon shaped command post sitting in the middle of the chrome floor, a young, brown-haired woman, ravishing in a purple bodysuit that hugged her admirable form, smiled at them kindly. Helmet made of pink, phosphorescent plastic sat atop her long hair. Two flaps hanging down her cheeks and connected under her chin highlighted beautifully the dimples that gave her a little mischievous look. On her stomach the buckle of her wide belt with a strip of multi-functional electronic controls had a triple row of different colored buttons.

"Tlyka," Zimko began, throwing his arm lovingly around the young woman's waist, "let me introduce you to Colonel Zavkom and the physicist Petkov."

And to the two men, embarrassed by their wretched rags, their uncleanliness and their shaggy beards, he added, "This is Tlyka, my co-pilot and my companion… for better and for worse as you Earthlings say."

147

CHAPTER TWO

"Our clothes and appearance are pretty miserable," Colonel Zavkom said, bowing shyly before Tlyka. "But we're still very pleased to meet you. You and Zimko saved us from a disgraceful death and..."

Cutting him short at three thanks yous Zimko said, "Let's not talk about that, friends. We would have done it a lot earlier if we could have found you. After the destruction of your spaceship on the Moon, when we brought you back to Russia, while Jean Kariven and his team returned to Earth[27], we had no idea things would turn out like this. It was only very recently that we learned of your fate: sentenced by the Purge Committee for failing to annex the Moon for Soviet power. In spite of our psychic investigative means we had a hard time finding the camp where you were sent."

"One hour later and you would have found us as frozen corpses," Petkov shivered to think of it. "What became of Kariven and his American friends of Operation Aphrodite?"

Zimko smiled as he noticed that the American and Russian astronauts fighting together on the Moon had cemented a warm friendship. "They are all very worried about you. We'll see them soon because an urgent task awaits us. That's why we freed the oppressed and are reuniting the few Earth allies we made over the past few years on your planet."

"You mean the famous Earth-Polarian Alliance that Kariven kept talking about?"

Zimko was about to respond but a psychic warning from Tlyka gave him no time. He rushed to the radar screen and saw three bright dots growing bigger every second.

Tlyka, already before the controls, changed their flight trajectory and gained more altitude. The three *blips* were still getting closer.

---

[27] See Volume 1.

Zimko turned on the viewer and on the tilted rectangular screen three delta-winged fighter jets were speeding at 2,500 mph toward the spaceship.

"MIG17s!" Colonel Zavkom cried out. "These fighters can go over 3,000 mph! Watch out, they're armed with air-to-air missiles that can't miss their target…"

Zimko veered the ship sharply at a right angle to escape the three jets that had just launched their missiles. The fighter jets turned in tight formation, corrected their course and sped off in pursuit of the flying saucer. The six missiles were approaching at terrifying speed but as they entered the magnetic field that radiated up to 1,000 feet from the disc, they exploded without reaching it.

"Space velocity!" Zimko ordered. "These idiots are going to enter our field and…"

Zavkom and Petkov, staring at the screen, instinctively backed away, dazzled by the triple orange blast of terrifying brightness. The screen no longer displayed the three demolished wrecks raining down wings and fuselage.

"The poor guys were caught in the magnetic field of our ship that spontaneously increased when they suddenly sped up," Zimko was appalled. "Trying to shoot us down they got too close and signed their own death warrants. The jets were alerted at the Nordenskiöld base by the Chief of the concentration camp. We should have gone straight from planetary speed into space velocity when our radar detected them. These kinds of accidents won't happen again. There were already enough victims, to our great distress, at the start of our exploration of the planet.[28]"

On his psychic order Tlyka brought the ship up to 60 miles altitude and at a slower speed headed west.

---

[28] The case of the pilot Mantell; the case of 3 fighter jets broken apart in mid-air in California; the case of the transport plane struck down in India. Read *Flying Saucers Come from Another World* by the same author. (Author's Note)

"You must be anxious to take a bath and get out of those old rags," the Man from Outer Space addressed the Russians. "We've slowed down so we'll arrive at our next mission in three hours. So, you have time to freshen up. You'll see in this cabin," he pointed to an oval hatch, "two sterilizing showers, all necessary toiletries and enough Polarian clothes for you to make your choice and after getting dressed we'll give you a bio-regenerator treatment that you need badly."

Shaved and with their hair evened out as best they could, after the sterilizing shower of pink jets, Zavkom and Petkov appeared to Zimko in their dreadful gauntness. Dressed in bodysuits their frames were scrawny, their bones poked out of the skin stretched thinly over their chests, bearing witness to the suffering and privations endured for two years in the awful concentration camp.

The Polarian, upset by their sorry state, trembling with rage at the idea that Earthlings could torture other Earthlings like this, promised himself to crush the black sheep of this planet in order to make its still savage civilization progress into a state of wisdom and peace that has so far eluded humans.

He led them into a cabin next to the shower room in the middle of which stood two, shiny metal cubes, six feet long, three feet wide by two and a half feet tall. Five feet above them hung a kind of concave, rectangular projector out of which came a bunch of transparent arches that cascaded down to the edges of the two strange, shiny boxes.

Zimko opened a wall panel. Transparent cubes around two inches square, filled with a thick, dark red liquid, were lined up inside. In one corner of these cubes a kind of tongue stuck out, which the Polarian yanked, tipping the angle over a glass as the syrupy liquid started pouring out. He did the same with a second glass and said, "First, drink this strong restorative and lie down on the cubes there. You'll drop off to sleep but when you wake you'll be back to your athletic selves like you were before your internment in the death camp."

The Russians obeyed and with a little disgust at the ge-latinous look of the red liquid they brought the glasses to their lips. The restorative, however, tasted pretty good despite its unappetizing appearance. Then they slipped under the "tunnel" formed by the cylindrical arches coming down from the projectors and lay down on the chrome boxes that were surprisingly warm. The gentle warmth spread throughout their bodies. Their blood beat in their arteries and their heads felt light at the same time as a curious euphoria arose in their minds.

"What blood type are you?"

The distant, deformed voice of their savior filtered through a cottony wall.

"A... B...," they muttered before sinking into an abyss with tenuous walls out of which came a peaceful melody of chimes, organs and harmonious murmurs.

Zimko chose two vials containing a brownish serum and injected the unconscious Russians. Then he flipped a switch in the wall and went back to type on a keyboard next to the metal cubes. The projectors flashed, then emitted a soft yellow light over the inert bodies. The arches in turn lit up and spread their golden glow over the two patients.

Once this was done Zimko pressed a button on the control panel and a soft vibration hummed in the room. Submitted to a rotational gravito-magnetic field the two skeletal bodies rose up a foot and a half off their beds and slowly started turning so that the entire surface of their anatomy could be washed by the golden, bio-regenerative rays of the astonishing installation.

Satisfied, Zimko looked at his electronic space-watch and left the cabin. Tlyka welcomed him with a sad smile. "The poor men, in such pitiful condition, they must have suffered the worst hardships.'

"There are still a lot of these unfortunate men who were deported like them to death camps. The abuse, this treatment that's unworthy of anyone calling himself Homo Sapiens, has to stop. Now that the time has come to make official contact with the Earthlings, we'll make sure that all these injustices come to an end. We might have to force them if the leaders don't obey our orders, although we have nothing but their well-being in mind."

"A thankless task for us because even if we gain some supporters, we'll also attract the animosity and bitterness of the oppressors."

"At the start, probably so," Zimko admitted, "but the threat looming over Earth—when it will be unanimously recognized—will finally unify the Earthlings... at least I hope so."

"Dear, we're flying over Paris," Tlyka announced as she turned on the screen.

The capital appeared, a oval smudge cut in two by the shimmering U of the Seine seen from over seven miles altitude.

Doctor Jean Kariven, an anthropaleontologist well known for his momentous explorations and adventures, was eating lunch with his young wife, the ravishing Yuln, and their best friends: Michel Dormoy, Robert Angelvin and their two loves Jenny and Doniatchka. Tommy (a.k.a. Kariven junior), a five-year old boy, was carefully licking the last spoonful of delicious chocolate ice cream under the amused, watchful eyes of his parents and friends.

In their luxurious apartment in Place Adolphe Cherioux Kariven and his wife often saw Dormoy and Angelvin with whom they had shared so many good and bad times that had peppered their busy life over the years.

After bringing out the liqueurs, Yuln turned on the television that was broadcasting the third newscast of the day. The speaker, with its pleasant voice, was in the middle of a story that the guests had missed:

"... this disc-shaped machine, propelled by 46 peripheral jets, can truly be called a 'Flying Saucer'," he smiled, "and will finally give some substance to the inconsistent stories of so-called saucers usually seen after a full meal with plenty to drink! The HQ of the United States Air Force can be proud of this beautiful construction whose secret trials over the past few months are now finished. We can hope that in the near future long-range airplanes will be replaced by this machine that is simply called a 'Circle Wing.' Flying Saucers are dead. Long live the Circle Wings!"

Yuln turned the knob of the TV, shaking her head. Then she sighed and looked up, "How spiritual it is! The boring speaker—and a bunch of his listeners—is making a big show about the Air Force's declaration."

"And nobody would know except you, Yuln," Bob Angelvin remarked. "You're not an Earthling but a humanoid from a solar system of the Pole Star. A perfectly human woman come from another planet actually on board a Flying Saucer that they're mocking with so much ignorance."

Kariven shrugged his shoulders. "Bah, the day will come when these champions of human stupidity will be very sorry about their mistake and…"

That day has come, Kariven.

Kariven stopped, stupefied. His friends jumped up along with his wife. The same words had simultaneously come into their minds.

"Zimko! Dear Zimko!" Yuln babbled, her eyes filling with tears of joy.

Yes, little sister, the "voice" resumed telepathically. *Tlyka and I are drifting seven miles above Paris right now. Excuse me, friends, for reading your thoughts,* the psychic voice addressed the guests.

"Do you mean to say that it's time for official contact of our race with the Earthlings?" Yuln asked aloud while her young son Tommy, flabbergasted, went looking for where the words he heard in his head were coming from.

Yes, Yuln. Right now we're gathering the members of the Earth-Polarian Alliance that we have on the planet, as few as they might be. When everyone is together on our secret base, real official contact will take place. But first, a message for Jenny: Tell your father immediately so he can alert the mem-

bers of his organization[29] *who should be ready to carry out our orders at the appointed time. The Investigative Committee on Flying Saucers that he's directed in France for years will be of great use to us. Every one of his investigators or correspondents spread around the country will be needed to contact and help the people. With their advice and explanations they'll avoid panic among the deniers of flying saucers who are unconsciously afraid. The plan of action patiently waited for years by evolved minds whom we trust is finally entering its active phase. I'm also giving the same psychic message to our friends of the Investigative Committees in Italy, Belgium, England, Africa, the three Americas, India, Australia and New Zealand.*

Here, then, is the general order. Tonight at 10 pm local time head for the site of our first landing in France, at Guyancourt[30]. *A spaceship will come to get you and take you to our secret base, Agharti, in the heart of Tibet, where we will join you a few hours later. I hope that the time will allow you to take care of any urgent business before leaving France.*

As you know, Yuln, during the next few days the Social Services of Agharti will take care of Tommy. Therefore, you can leave behind all the things that an Earthling mother would bring with her. I'm giving you this advice because since you've been living on this planet, you must have acquired a real Earthling frame of mind.

"You can stop teasing me now," she smiled, automatically petting her son's blonde curls.

One more piece of advice, friends, Tlyka cut in telepathically. *Zimko forgot to say that the pilots of the spaceship that will pick you up tonight are not human. So, don't be too surprised by their appearance. Yuln will explain to you about their morphological differences.*

"Thank you, Tlyka," it was Kariven's turn to smile. "Yuln described to us in detail a long time ago the different

---

[29] SeeVolume 1.
[30] See Volume 1.

races of your admirable society of Federated Worlds. We won't commit any indiscretions in the presence of your allies and friends who are also ours."

In his house in Los Angeles, Professor Red Harrington, eminent physicist and mathematician, was chatting amiably over a double whiskey with Commander Mark Taylor of the Strategic Air Command. A warm Pacific breeze was gently rustling the bushes outside the bay window, which was open on this beautiful spring evening.

"Come on, Mark, don't look so worried," Professor Harrington said, pouring another glass of whiskey for his old friend.

"I'd like to see you in my place, Reed," the officer grumbled, sitting in his Air Force uniform decorated with his rank, Command Pilot: two blue wings framing the stylized American insignia topped by a five-pointed star circled with a crown of leaves. "Do you know that by abandoning my post I can be indicted by the war council? Court Martials are no joking matter!"

"I know, Mark, but you belong like me to the Earth-Polarian Alliance. By obeying Zimko's orders you'll be serving your country better than by remaining here in your daily routine. Plus, our Polarian friend's message suggested that our stay in Agharti would not be long. Afterward you'll be brought back to Muroc[31] and you can rejoin your unit that will have received government orders following the official contact of the Polarians with Washington. Given our personalities, you in the secret services and me in science, we'll be promoted to important positions in the Alliance. Only the regional investigators and correspondents studying flying saucers will be left in place and receive orders from the head of their organization. For us, you have to understand, it's very different."

---

[31] Experimental base of the US Air Force located in Southern California. It is now Edwards AFB.

"I know all that, Reed, but I'm military and a superior officer in the Special Services to boot. Discipline is something I can't break."

"Does that mean you're dropping the whole thing?" Harrington asked.

"Of course not!" the officer raised his voice, torn by conflicting feelings. "I'm going to set things straight with my boss, General Miller."

"But Zimko's orders are confidential for the moment. No one is supposed to know that Earthlings have been colluding for years with these highly evolved beings from another planet."

"Listen, Prof, General Miller, the Commander in Chief of the western experimental bases, knows that flying saucers exist and that they come from the system around the Pole Star. And you don't know that. Besides, wasn't he there when *Daisy* landed, the first US rocket to come back to Earth after exploring the Moon?[32] Didn't he examine the films showing the extraordinary Polarian base set up on our satellite in the Aristarchus crater? And finally, wasn't he convinced of the authenticity of the photographs in which our entire team is pictured in spacesuits with three Polarians in front of the squadron of flying saucers lined up on the astrodrome outside the dome?"

"Sure," the mathematician agreed, "but he won't look kindly on an inferior officer, even a Commander of the Special Service, knowing about the future and having contact with Polarians while he remains in the dark."

"Well, he won't go after me. And I think he'll..."

The sound of the telephone ringing interrupted him. Harrington picked it up and after a moment held it out to his friend, "It's for you."

"Commander Taylor here."

---

[32] See Volume 1.

"Hello Taylor, this is General Miller. I called Muroc where your second-in-command informed me you were at Harrington's."

Mark Taylor leaned over so that his friend could listen in.

"I have a funny feeling," General Miller continued in his deep voice, "that you're about to ask for special permission for an unspecified leave. Am I wrong, Taylor?"

Taken aback by the sudden declaration he coughed and stammered, "Um... um, General, I recognize that..."

"Granted," the general broke in. "I'll make the necessary arrangements with your base. Have a good time and... bon voyage!"

The General Miller's hearty laugh echoed in the phone before a click put on end to it—he had hung up.

"Now that's something else," Taylor huffed in astonishment as he hung up the phone.

"So, everything's following the well-orchestrated plan," Professor Harrington observed. "If it wasn't, Zimko would surprise me. Here you are rid of your fears and anxiety. You won't be abandoning your post since your big boss just gave you an 'unlimited' leave!"

The officer gulped down his whiskey, wrung his hands and grabbed the telephone, beaming with joy. "Finally, this damn official contact is going to take place! I'll alert Kurt Streiler, Rudy Clark and all our brave partners from Operation Aphrodite!" He looked at his watch and as he dialed the first number he added, "They'll have seven hours to get to the site chosen by Zimko where the spaceship will pick us all up."

The Guyancourt airfield, lacking hangars and control tower because it was very rarely used, was a stretch of deserted land with clumps of grass. The night was warm and the moon, high up in the sky, shined brightly on the group formed of Kariven, Yuln, their son and their friends smoking nervously next to their cars.

Tom, who was enjoying immensely this nocturnal outing in the country, was jumping around in the grass despite his mother's scolding as she tried to keep him by her side.

Robert Angelvin and his wife Jenny were talking with her father, Fred Reynal, Director of the Investigative Committee that had been studying UFOs in France for years.

Michel Dormoy and his wife Doniatchka were chatting with two of Reynal's investigators who were supposed to drive the cars back to Paris after they left.

"Ten o'clock," Doniatchka said. "The spaceship should be in sight."

"They were delayed over Russia where MIGs have been patrolling constantly since this morning," Yuln explained. "I just picked up the pilots' thoughts. They won't be long now. Being Wolfian—meaning from a planet in the solar system that you call Wolf 359—they aren't telepathic but can communicate psychically with us Polarians thanks to a mechano-psychic amplifier."

Fifteen minutes later a fluorescent green disc appeared in the sky and came down quickly with a strange, pendulum swinging motion and landed softly on the ground not far from those waiting there.

A hundred feet in diameter, the spaceship's green glow slowly faded after it had landed. Between the three landing spheres a platform came out attached to two telescopic tubes and standing on which was a small creature dressed in a gray spacesuit. Around four feet tall, the being whose body was hidden inside the suit waddled toward the group.

Yuln stepped forward, speaking into its mind, *I'm happy to meet you Ruanoor. My friends and I are ready to follow you.*

The tiny being pressed a series of buttons on its belt and a voice came out speaking French, "I'm very honored to be able to offer my Fimn'has to the sister of our venerated chief, Zimko."

"But… you speak French," Yuln was surprised.

158

"Zimko decided around a *k'bog* ago to teach us a few languages spoken on this planet in view of the future contact with its inhabitants. All the members of the Space Commandos, Wolfians, Polarians and Centaurians, are now able to understand and speak French, English, German, Russian and Spanish. Some can even speak many more languages."

Everyone listened, pleasantly surprised, to this creature from another world expressing himself in perfectly correct French. Not wanting to look too obviously curious, they tried not to stare at his big, bulging, vertical eyes in a furry black face that the transparent *Xoning* of his round helmet let them see.

Kariven, Angelvin, Dormoy and their friends said good-bye to Reynal and his two investigators, then headed for the spaceship behind Ruanoor. The platform carried them into the body of the ship that did not wait long to take off, resuming its weird green luminescence. In the cockpit, leaning over the screen, they saw the three automobiles get smaller along with those they had left with the mission to prepare the people for extraordinary events.

The air in the spaceship had been treated for the Earthlings for this voyage, so Ruanoor posted at the controls with his spacesuit on. At his side was Woodna, his Wolfian compatriot and assistant working as space radar specialist. She examined the radar screen with her right eye while her left, bulging curiously from its socket, watched the newcomers whom she had had just welcomed.

At 3,000 mph the Fimn'has sped eastward at more than nine miles high. At this altitude and speed no city was discernible. Only the outlines of mountains or big rivers appeared briefly through holes in the cloud layers that drifted over Eastern Europe.

Ruanoor fiddled with a wavelength selector and caught the Soviet network. Doniatchka Dormoy saw and heard a televised speech by Marshal Gorochenko, Chief of the USSR's armed forces.

Her friends saw her suddenly turn pale and even though they did not understand a word of the speech they knew that it was the cause of her emotion. None of them dared to question her, afraid that she would miss something that would keep her from telling them the whole meaning of the whole speech— quite violent, judging by the tense face of Marshal Gorochenko and by his explosive voice accompanied by forceful gestures on the screen.

The supreme chief of the red army ranted for ten minutes and concluded with a menacing attitude. He stood up and disappeared to be replaced on the screen by a speaker whom Doniatchka turned away from. In a flat voice she translated:

"Gorochenko, the spokesman for the Supreme Soviet, just confirmed with belligerent threats the official protest of Moscow against Washington at five o'clock, Moscow time. In the terms of this protest Gorochenko reproached the United States Air Force for shooting down three soviet fighter jets over northern Siberia. These jets were pulverized in mid-air by the Circle Wing prototype whose successful trials the TV revealed today.

"Marshal Gorochenko is calling for the execution of the guilty parties and demands immediate reparation from the American government. Moreover, he says that if another incident occurs diplomatic relations will be broken off and he confirms that the Soviet Air Force also has a Circle Wing as powerful if not more so than the American's. There's no need to highlight the poorly veiled threat of this revelation."

Everyone looked at each other, appalled by the abrupt surge in international tension. Suddenly Zimko's face appeared on the screen.

"No!" he shouted. "The Americans did not shoot down the soviet MIGs. They fired on my Fimn'has after I picked up Petkov and Zavkom in the death camp. The jets chased us. They entered our negative gravito-magnetic field and were instantly torn apart. There were witnesses on the ground who reported to the Russian authorities all the details of what they took for aerial combat. By a stroke of fate the Air Force had just announced to the public the existence of a long-range Circle Wing. The plane looks vaguely like a Fimn'has, so the Russians concluded that the Circle Wing had violated their air space and being surprised by the fighter jets had shot them down.

"This unfortunate incident, however, will have no serious consequences because in 24 hours I will have ordered the official contact with the Earthlings on both sides of the iron curtain. I will explain personally to the Supreme Soviet about the causes of the accident and will thus erase all suspicions of our unjustly accused American friends. Consequently, after our peaceful intervention, the cold war will end."

Forty-five hundred miles from Earth, in a small reconnaissance spaceship, two green creatures with scaly skin and toothless, turtle-like faces, were running their clawed fingers over the electronic keyboard of a viewing device. On the round, convex screen appeared a being identical to them: a green, lizard-skinned pseudo-man.

"Og'nka here," one of the two pilots said, "on board the patroller Zign'og of the Space Freedom Forces of Omynk. We were able to intercept a televised message from Zimko, our implacable enemy, who said he was about to get in contact with the primitives of planet 3 of this solar system. In a very short time a space squadron should be approaching this world where two continents are fighting with each other. An insignificant incident—three fighter jets accidentally destroyed by the magnetic field of Zimko's spaceship—will give us the opportunity to escalate the discord on the planet and thereby compromise Zimko's chance of success. Here's what we recommend immediately…"

In the Fimn'has that was transporting them to Agharti, Kariven and his friends, reassured by Zimko's speech, had no idea that the televised message had been intercepted by an enemy patrol.

The Denebian monsters were now speeding through outer space to their secret base on an asteroid between the orbits of Mars and Jupiter.

CHAPTER III

From all the countries on the globe where they had just boarded the representative members of the Earth-Polarian Alliance, 20 flying saucers were converging on Asia. Flying silently at 23 miles altitude the spaceships met over Everest and in triangular formation headed northeast into eastern Tibet.

On the viewer screens the landscape scrolled by rapidly, chaotic, mountainous, rent by deep valleys with snow-covered slopes or barred by glaciers.

To the north of the Kham province, the Fimn'has flew over Djogar-Tong and around 60 miles from Barka-Tala they stopped, hovering over a twin chain of mountains with jagged peaks, a few of which pierced the thick blanket of clouds.

The austere and Dantean landscape exuded savage grandeur. Absolutely isolated from all trails taken by the Sherpas or Buddhist pilgrims, this mountainous region could go for centuries without seeing a human footprint on the ground. The Tibetans avoided it with a particularly superstitious fear: dreadful legends spread from Kouen-Lun to Assam about the mysterious mountains, the home of "Gods from the Heavens".

Only a few contemplative hermits, the Gomchen, could nod their head with an enigmatic smile when a traveler questioned them on the truth of these legends. Nothing in the world could make these old ascetics reveal the exact location of Agharti, the underground city where the King of the World lived alongside the Polarians, known then as the "Dragons of Wisdom"[33].

From the unmoving squadron one spaceship broke away and slowly descended diagonally—guided by radar—through the thick clouds sitting on top of the mountains. The ship came out vertically and hovered over a huge egg-shaped rock around 250 feet in diameter. Imperceptibly the rock trembled,

---

[33] See Volume 1.

pivoted and revealed a circular opening around 150 feet wide. Its smooth walls looked metallic and emitted a blue light, dropping deep down into the heart of the mountain.

The spaceship started moving again, swinging slightly, and all of a sudden it dropped straight down into the gaping hole. Right behind it, one by one, the other Fimn'has came out of the clouds and followed the leader. When the last disc was gone the gigantic oval rock pivoted back and silently closed the access to the secret base.

After a dizzying 3,000-foot descent, the 20 spaceships streamed out through an opening in the pit that emptied into a huge, artificial cavern, over 2,000 feet high and twice as big in diameter. Its super-metal ceiling, coated with a blue glazed material, spread a light like the day over a fantastic pyramid city: Agharti, the Polarian base established on Earth unbeknownst to humans. The buildings were entirely metal, pierced with countless *xoning* windows, constructed in terraces that connected to each other via spiral airways. Soaring arches, busy with transparent, spherical vehicles, spanned the buildings in a harmonious, multi-colored maze.

Around the city was a vast astrodrome where hundreds of spaceships were lined up, flying saucers to the Earthlings and Fimn'has (their real name) to the Polarians.

From the 20 ships that had just landed a crowd of Earthlings of all nationalities came out. Among them were Kariven, his wife, their son, Tommy, the Dormoys, the Angelvins, Professor Harrington, Commander Mark Taylor, Lieutenant Rudy Clark and the physicist Kurt Streiler.

Yuln looked tenderly at Agharti, the unforgettable secret city where she had stayed with her brother and their fellow Polarians before meeting the man who would become her husband.

With a word from Ruanoor, the Wolfian pilot who had brought together the squadron over the Himalayas, the Earthlings followed him over the path leading into the city. On the airway passing between the terraced, metal buildings the Polarians, Wolfians and Centaurians—the tiny creatures, three

164

feet tall with orange human faces and wearing spacesuits—whom they met greeted them by raising their right hand. Their faces glowed with great joy at the prospect of brotherly contact between their people and the human race.

The hundred Earthlings were brought into a semi-circular amphitheater of Babylonian proportions.

At a kind of long, metal table full of buttons, dials and multi-colored, blinking lights and surmounted by ten television screens Zimko, the Chief of the Space Commandos appointed for this solar system by the Supreme Council of the Federated Worlds, was waiting for them. At his sides were seated the chiefs of the Lunar, Martian, Venusian, Jovian, Uranian and Plutonian bases, flanked by superior officers of the Wolfian and Centaurian races. These latter did not breathe the same air as their Polarian allies who had human morphology and physiology, so they were in their spacesuits.

"Welcome to Agharti, Earthling Friends," Zimko greeted them raising his right hand. "Some of you are coming here for the first time. Others have already been to this base, such as Kariven, Dormoy, Angelvin and their wives who are the French representatives of the Earth-Polarian Alliance. You won't stay long in Agharti. 24 hours more or less during which time you will study together how we plan to make official and public contact with your fellow Earthlings who still don't know of our existence."

Turning to a tall Polarian wearing a black bodysuit, his thumbs casually stuck in his belt, the Man from Outer Space added, "I want to introduce you to Nheg Honky, Commander in Chief of the Information Services of the Federated Worlds, who will tell you the decisive reasons for our anticipated arrival on your planet."

Honky spoke for more than an hour, first telling the history of the Space Commandos, then giving his audience the information they would need to present to their governments when the Polarians made contact. He showed how this combined action would allow the heads of the terrestrial powers to judge the good intentions of the "Man from Outer Space" and greatly facilitate their communication.

After he had finished Zimko stood up. "Earthling Friends, do any of you have any questions or remarks? Any suggestions?"

Colonel Zavkom and the physicist Petkov in their dark red bodysuits stood up together. The accelerated bio-regenerator treatment had done its duty. Their muscular torsos and limbs filled out the Polarian uniform wonderfully. They looked nothing like the starved, skeletal prisoners they were in the dreadful camp of Khantangskoïe.

"Friend Zimko," Zavkom began, "maybe our American, French, English or Italian brothers can, without fear, introduce themselves to their governments as members of the Earth-Polarian Alliance, but it's not the same with us Soviets. Being freed from the death camp by your charitable action, if we go back to Russia we'll be executed without getting anywhere near the Supreme Soviet. Our sacrifice will be in vain."

"I've thought of your delicate situation, Zavkom, and I don't intend for you or Petkov to announce our arrival to your government. I'll leave this process to the Earthlings living in free countries. You will still have a similar role to play, but not alone. I will be with you.

"Now, Friends, you should probably get some rest or something to eat because it was nighttime when many of you left. Tomorrow a major task awaits you. At dawn the final orders will be given and the same spaceships that brought you here will take you back to your home countries."

To Kariven and his French friends he said, "You'll get back home between 8 and 10am and before noon, GMT time, you'll have to gather all the members of the Alliance you're in touch with to make a delegation at precisely 3 pm to the President."

To everyone again he announced, "Here now, by nationality, are the times that have to be kept by the members of the Alliance. For those in the USA, first of all, on the west coast…"

In the control tower of the Orenburg airport in the Bashkirs, more than 185 miles to the southeast of Moscow, the radar men were going crazy evaluating the speed of the blip appearing and disappearing on their fluorescent radarscope.

"Look, Vassily!" one of the operators shouted, pointing at the numbers that had just lined up on the paper. "The thing is going almost 6,000 mph heading northwest! At this speed it'll be over Moscow in… eight minutes! What do you think it is?"

"*Nie znayu,*[34]" the other answered, goggling at the figures. "I'll alert Moscow…"

He feverishly adjusted the knobs on the transmitter and a few seconds later the control tower at the airport in Moscow captured their call and explained, "We were told five minutes ago about the trajectory of this object when it passed over Tashkent in Turkestan. We took immediate measures to defend against it. It's no doubt the Circle Wing whose capabilities were revealed on American radio. This violation of our air space by the dirty, capitalist rats will cost them dearly!"

Zimko's spaceship slowed down over the suburbs southeast of Moscow and ended up hovering around seven miles over the soviet capital. The sun, almost at its zenith, shined brightly on a layer of clouds concealing the Russian metropolis.

Colonel Zavkom and the physicist Petkov were nervous as they attentively watched the Polarian adjusting the controls of the special transmitter designed to send his voice over the frequencies used by the Earthlings. Tlyka, in the meantime, was turning a calibrated dial and watching the slow change in an oscillating needle on a little screen.

"All broadcasts and radio communication are cut off," she said when the needle stopped. "You can send your message, Zimko. The authorities and the Russian people can hear

---

[34] I don't know.

it and nothing else... Watch out!" she suddenly cried out on seeing six MIGs appear on the viewer, shooting straight up out of the cloud carpet toward their ship.

With unimaginable swiftness Zimko made his Fimn'has jump up 50 miles and then stop. In the cockpit—protected from the powerful effects of the acceleration by the negative gravito-magnetic field created by the spaceship—the occupants felt nothing of the upward leap. In any other plane the force of inertia of the passengers would have literally crushed them to the metal floor.

The fighter jets 12 miles below were wheeling under the ship that had escaped not only to protect itself from their missiles, which the pilots believed, but also to avoid destroying them by contact with the magnetic field surrounding the ship.

Zimko leaned over the microphone and spoke in Russian:

"This is Zimko, Chief of the Space Commandos from the solar system of the Pole Star, speaking to you from a disc-shaped spaceship hovering over Moscow. This message is particularly meant for Marshal Gorochenko, Commander in Chief of the Soviet Armed Forces. In spite of the resemblance to the Circle Wing of the US Air Force, our ship is not a terrestrial airplane. It is a spaceship that brought us to your planet. Our intentions are peaceful. We want to be in contact with the Supreme Soviet. At this very moment, in all the capitals on Earth, similar contact is being established with other governments. Out ship suddenly shot up at the approach of the six jets launched against us not to escape them but to protect them from being destroyed by entering our magnetic field. The three MIGs that blew apart over Khantangskoïe were not shot down by an American Circle Wing as you believed. They got too close to our disc and instantly suffered the effects of our negative magnetic field. It was a regrettable accident and we are extremely sorry.

"Marshal Gorochenko, are you listening? If so, answer me on whatever frequency you desire. Our electronic selector will automatically tune yours to ours."

Less than 30 seconds after this request the voice of Marshal Gorochenko came through the speaker over the blank screen:

"Marshal Gorochenko here. I didn't hear the beginning of your message but you must recognize how strange you sound. Nothing proves that you're telling me the truth. Nevertheless, I honestly have to admit that you're not acting like an enemy plotting a surprise attack. You claim to come from... from another planet? You know that this sounds like pure fantasy. But it's hard for me to believe that the Americans would push this joke—doubtful and dangerous for them—so far as to taunt us over Moscow. This being said, and holding back any talk of your origin, what do you want and expect in hovering like this over our territory where you have no business?"

"We simply want to land safely and have contact with you in the presence of the Supreme Soviet," the Man from Outer Space repeated. "To do this and in the interests of your pilots, we ask you to send away those jets that have been circling under us for 15 minutes."

There was a long moment of silence before the Marshal's voice came back. "Your request to land is also very unusual since you're asking *unconditionally* for us to send away our jets. Until we are better informed about the danger that your magnetic field presents, as you say, we do not believe you. You seem to be in a revolutionary... extraordinary plane, based on its speed evaluated by our bases, but..."

"Enough of these empty words, Marshal Gorochenko," the Polarian broke in calmly and without hostility. "Your distrust is out of place. Order your fighters to stay 1,300 feet away from our spaceship. We're going to land in Red Square. If you don't give the order, you yourself are signing the pilots' death warrant. Our magnetic field has a range of almost 800 feet on the move and 1,000 hovering at a fixed point. You are, therefore, warned. If your MIGs breach these limits our field will destroy them.

"I repeat, we are coming as peaceful ambassadors of an extra-terrestrial race. We will be unarmed, our hands empty

169

and you will see that our tight-fitting bodysuits can hide no weapons. Two of your compatriots will be with us. They are members of the Earth-Polarian Alliance, a secret, eminently peaceful organization that has recruited certain evolved Earthlings over the years. You know these two soviet citizens personally... seeing that it was on your order that they were deported to the concentration camp in Khantangskoïe. I'm talking about Colonel Zavkom and the physicist Petkov."

"You... You're the one who destroyed the camp... the Rehabilitation Center!" Marshal Gorochenko barked. "And you pretend to be peaceful after slaughtering soviet officers and guards in..."

"We *are* peaceful," Zimko interrupted calmly, "but we also have an immoderate love of Justice. Your guards and officers were just butchers, executioners, torturers whose abominable crimes sully your race! We are on Earth to protect humans from a menace coming from outer space but also to keep such abuses from happening again. Now, Marshal Gorochenko, we're going to land. You alone carry the responsibility of your pilots' death if you don't order them to back off immediately."

With this warning Zimko cut communication. His spaceship, with the usual rocking motion, started coming down fast. Long before he reached the cloud carpet the six MIGs shot off in all directions as fast as their jet engines could move them.

Zimko, Petkov and Zavkom smiled at each other seeing the planes fly off, already into the Moscow suburbs more than four miles away.

The snow-covered soviet metropolis was bathed in dim light. A recent snowfall had dropped another white layer that the cold had frozen. The spaceship landed gently in Red Square to the east of Lenin's mausoleum.

Countless Muscovites who were stunned to hear their radio broadcasts replaced by Zimko's weird speech, came from all over, running on the packed snow, stuffed into their fur coats and wool caps. An envoy of military trucks led by a half-track vehicle with a turret gun was speeding toward the landing site.

Zimko left the window amused by the deployment of force and by the astonishment on the onlookers' faces. "These Earthlings don't seem to know very well the rules of hospitality," he smiled at Tlyka. We're going out there. If anything goes wrong, fire the paralyzing rays at maximum range. You can listen in psychically to our meeting with Marshal Gorochenko and you'll know as well as I if an intervention is necessary. We'll keep our promise of going unarmed to the Supreme Soviet but in spite of everything we'll be protected by our individual magnetic field."

Turning to Zavkom and Petkov he continued, "Turn on the heating elements in your bodysuits. The thermometer in Moscow right now is down to -17°C."

The two men turned a little knob on the left side of their belt, flipped a switch activating the magnetic field generator and were ready to leave.

When they had stepped off the platform that came down between the landing spheres, the thermostat automatically regulated the temperature of their suits and a gentle warmth washed over them. The onlookers, wisely stayed 300 yards from the flying saucer, watched them curiously and were stunned to see that they were not shivering in just a meager bodysuit at this temperature.

The three men marched toward a group of officers standing motionless before a splendid Zim, as long and classy as a Cadillac. Without suspecting that one of the strangers was reading their thoughts like an open book, the officers examined them from head to toe. Suspiciously their eyes lingered on the big buckle of their belt that was full of tiny controls. Then they concentrated their attention on their faces.

Zimko stopped in front of the Commander of the MVD, strapped into a black uniform, whom he saluted by raising his right hand to his shoulder. The other, surprised, did not finish his traditional salute but hesitated before responding clumsily with the same gesture.

"Commander Prokofiev, attaché of Marshal Gorochenko," he introduced himself. "The Marshal is waiting for you in his headquarters. He asked me to come and welcome you."

"Glad to meet you, Commander Prokofiev. Colonel Zavkom, Dr. Petkov and myself are ready to follow you."

Prokofiev cast a final, ambiguous glance at their belt buckles and opened the back door of the Zim, inviting the "ambassadors" to enter.

Marshal Gorochenko was standing in the middle of the members of the Supreme Soviet that, by a happy coincidence, was in session that day.

The long walls of the huge room where the assembly met was lined up with men in the black uniform of the MVD. They had been summoned urgency and as the Nagans in their holsters proved they were more than ready to take on the role of bodyguard.

Accompanied by Zavkom and Petkov, Zimko walked quickly and confidently. Their boots echoed on the floor of precious wood with multicolored inlay. Their decisive attitude and their imposing bearing made a strong impression of these politicians used to seeing their subjects grovel at their feet.

Zimko and his companions greeted the members of the Supreme Soviet following Polarian custom.

President Koulski responded with a slight bow. "I presume that in the presence of extra-terrestrial ambassadors, the traditional 'We welcome you' is in order. Nevertheless... Sirs (Zimko read a trace of irony in these words) as Marshal Gorochenko quite rightly told you, although your landing in the middle of Moscow doesn't fail to surprise, we are not so convinced of your... true origin. Nor are we absolutely assured of your intentions."

Zimko gave him a friendly smile and said, "It is likely that in your place, President, I would act with the same reserve. However, are we supposed to prove our extra-terrestrial origin by taking you on board our spaceship and flying you off to our solar system? Would you even accept such an offer?"

The President coughed with great distinction and replied, "Such an offer—tempting in theory—bears certain, um, risks, don't you think, considering our suspicions?"

"I have the feeling," Zimko smiled again, "that this game of cat and mouse will only end in a stalemate. My human form shocks you because in the mind of an Earthling the inhabitants of other planets should necessarily look like a 'Martian' monster as your cartoonists depict. This is not always true. The Denebian races, from the Deneb solar system, and the Procyonian, from the sun Procyon, are indeed monstrous to the human eye. Furthermore, these monsters are our ene-mies... *and yours*, without you knowing it, because they're after your whole solar system and your planet in particular."

The Polarian turned his head a little, stared at Marshal Gorochenko, then brought his attention back to President Koulski. "Marshal Gorochenko is still convinced that we're unbelievably reckless American spies. And he sees our space-ship as the Circle Wing whose existence was revealed by the Air Force. A doubt remains in you, Mr. President, but more restrained because for years you've examined, growing more ill at ease, the reports sent by your bases about the observa-tions of our ships called flying saucers by your kind. Without believing completely in the extra-terrestrial origin of these discs, your mind was still shaken up. Moreover, your spies operating on American territory have always submitted un-questionable reports: no US research center of unmanned air-craft could have perfected such a revolutionary spaceship."

Very impressed by this "clairvoyance" the President of the Supreme Soviet shot a hard look at the speaker. "Are you trying to..."

"Exactly, Mr. President," Zimko cut him off. "I'm trying to prove to you that I'm telepathic, a pretty rare phenomenon among men, especially for FBI agents! I can easily give you more proof..." Turning to Marshal Gorochenko he observed, "Marshal, you're cooking up a plan right now that can't succeed. You're hoping that we'll make the slightest gesture so you can give the order to your MVD men to shoot us."

His face turned pale, the Marshal showed his absolute astonishment.

Without giving him time to speak Zimko continued, "Imagine, Marshal, that we just made a suspicious movement and you order your men to fire on us... Go on, do it," he insisted. "No harm will come either to us or to the shooters."

After a shock of surprise the President ordered, "Shoot these men!"

The MVD agents hesitated only an instant. They unholstered their Nagans and fired almost at the same time. The huge room resounded with gunfire and the sharp odor of gunpowder mixed with the smoke coming out of the muzzles.

Zimko, Colonel Zavkom and Dr. Petkov looked wryly at the hail of bullets that slammed against their magnetic field and fell ten feet from them.

President Koulski was panting heavily, not trying to hide his confusion. "I... This experiment seems conclusive. Human technology has not yet developed such a system of protection. Does it use the same principle of the force fields of your... spaceships?"

"Pretty much the same principle, Mr. President. I'm glad to read in your mind the decision to welcome us as peaceful ambassadors. At the appropriate time and with your consent I will bring you to our space base where you can judge for yourself the technical level of our civilization. For now, we have more pressing problems.

"We Polarians have decided to intervene in the internal affairs of Earth nations in order to unite all their inhabitants... and this in order to confront a dreadful danger that is looming over your planet. The first phase of this program is a global meeting of all the heads of state. This meeting must conclude with a pact of planetary defense, therefore a union, to which we will contribute by providing weapons capable of matching those of the enemy."

"May I?" the President asked. "This meeting, which I am not, in theory, hostile to, will take place in Moscow, of course?"

Zimko shook his head. "Not in Moscow, not in Washington DC but in an absolutely neutral location: our space base 1 that orbits 600 miles away from Earth. Thus, the heads of state won't refuse to come, as they usually do when they have to go to one country or another."

"Hmm, it's rather unexpected as a meeting place…"

"True but do you see any region on this planet where the heads of state would eagerly accept to go?" Faced with a skeptical, sullen look he continued, "The assembly, therefore, will take place on our space base 48 hours from now. Spaceships will land in every capital and board the heads of state who have been informed of our offer. It's only during the global meeting that we'll give the outlines of our mutual cooperation before concluding with the Earthly unity for the greatest benefit of humanity… and its safety. Before anything, Mr. President, I ask you to release immediately the hundreds of thousands of political exiles being tortured in your concentration camps."

This remark startled the President, who reacted with indignation, mixed with a certain embarrassment. "The Rehabilitation Centers are not concentration camps…"

"Maybe you'd prefer us to go ahead and free them ourselves?" Colonel Zavkom insinuated, red-faced with anger at the obvious dishonesty of the President. "My comrade Petkov and I suffered two long years in those vile penal colonies unworthy of *homo sapiens!*"

Zimko raised his hand to call for calm. "I'm sure, my friend Zavkom, that President Koulski will do his duty to free the innocent men. He's going to order their immediate release to prove his sincere repentance. Isn't that right, Mr. President?"

The latter clenched his fists and jaws and spit out, "Is that a threat?"

"Not at all. Just some advice dictated with a view to justice and humanity. This humanity for which you claim a desire for peace and love," the Man from Outer Space said calmly. "You cannot build a powerful, united and prosperous civilization except with people living together in harmony. A race that seeks to dominate others and that oppresses those who don't share its authoritarian views or its dictatorial doctrines is a fallen race. Such a race doesn't deserve the freedom and independence that it refuses to some of its children.

"We Polarians refuse to tolerate injustice and the abuse of power that results from it. If all the peoples of Earth unite to reject our offer of peace and selfless aide aiming to improve the destiny of Earthlings, we will bow out and leave your planet to its pitiful fate... and to the mercy of the Denebians and Procyonians. But such is not the case. Millions of inhabitants of this planet have been hoping for our arrival. These good people, from the humble worker to the brilliant scientific researcher, aspire to an era of peace, abundance and joy when suffering, hunger and injustice will be a thing of the past. This era has come. It will start, unfortunately, with an interplanetary war—interstellar even—but will end in peace for the planets that men, finally united, will be able to visit like so many Promised Lands.

"Does this plan satisfy you at all, Mr. President?"

Struggling inside, the Chief of the Supreme Soviet felt the eyes of all those around focused on him. Would he lose face by obeying the "advice" of this being from another planet? Wouldn't it be turned around by members of the more or less open opposition?

"In all honesty," Zimko asked after seeing through his thoughts, "does your office as President have any value beyond the safety of hundreds of thousands of innocent people? That such a thought would cross your mind leaves me puzzled."

Taken aback by this moral slap, the President stiffened up and called out to Colonel Rostof, head of the MVD and director of all the so-called Rehabilitation Centers in Russia,

"Colonel Rostof! Give an order immediately to free all the political prisoners and make sure that they get home safely. All guards and officers who do not follow this order and do not treat the prisoners humanely will be shot! I'm holding you personally responsible for any failure to follow this order."

Turning to Zimko, he muttered, "I'm ready to contribute as far as is in my power to your... magnificent project of global union. I hope you're sincere and have in mind only the love our race, which is the sister of yours."

CHAPTER IV

Kariven, who had just got back to Paris with his wife and friends, was holding a meeting in his apartment. Their return from Agharti, the Polarian base hidden in the heart of a high mountain in Tibet, came off without a hitch. At this meeting was Fred Reynal, Director of the Research Institute on the Study of Unidentified Flying Objects.

"It wasn't easy," he began, "getting an appointment with the Interior Minister. I had to move heaven and earth to get my contacts moving and a little cunning to set up the meeting without confessing why. Although I couldn't get to the President of the Republic, we at least have the means to see the Interior Minister. I hope that our entire delegation will be let in."

"Did you give the instructions to your investigators and correspondents?" Michel Dormoy asked.

"All done, Michel. We were able to get together 40 cars and vans, each equipped with a loudspeaker and at the appointed time they'll run through the streets of Paris shouting out our information to reassure the people and keep them calm. Every investigator knows his route by heart. Plus, a plane from the Aero-Club will be dropping tens of thousands of flyers over the city at the same time to back up the info from the radio-cars. Half an hour before the action all the journalists from the newspaper and radio along with television cameramen will by summoned to the landing site designated by Zimko."

"I think this is going to make a big splash!" Jenny laughed, trembling with impatience.

"The cars and flyers will be seriously breaking the law that forbids this kind of 'publicity' in Paris. But since the situation demands it, we have to break the rules."

"Especially since the reason for this infraction will be seen by the authorities who will be ready to forgive us,"

Kariven remarked. Then he raised his glass and said, "Now my friends, let's drink to the most astonishing peaceful revolution in human history!"

Kariven's green and cream Versailles and Reynal's sky-blue Ford stopped on Rue des Saussaies and the passengers entered the courtyard of the Ministry of the Interior.

After a slightly surprised glance at the three young women accompanying the four gentlemen the guard asked them to follow him into a sitting room where he left them, taking the letter of introduction that Reynal had given him. Around ten minutes later the guard came back to usher them into the huge office of the very important person.

The Interior Minister, a friendly man around 50 years old, received them courteously by offering them to sit in the armchairs in front of his desk. A fleeting expression of surprise had not escaped his visitors when he noticed that the delegation was not exclusively represented by the stronger sex!

"Ladies and gentlemen," he bowed his head, "I admit that I was not expecting to be honored with such charming delegates. The short letter of my excellent friend Moneret in Foreign Affairs did not specify who would be coming." He raised his right eyebrow in a kindly manner and added, "Moneret didn't even mention the nature of the important revelation you have to make."

"Monsieur le Ministre," Kariven began, "the brevity was deliberate. We also have to admit to be honored to be received by you without needing to expose beforehand the reason for our demand. We had to... use a little cunning... and, um, lie to our influential friends."

The Minister, at first a little shocked, finally smiled, "Hell! Now this looks a lot like influence peddling... or a breach of trust. But I like your frankness and I don't doubt the honesty of your intentions."

"We're grateful to you," Kariven bowed his head politely. "You have certainly heard a good number of crazy stories on the subject of what are called flying saucers. Would it be indiscreet to ask you what you think personally about it?"

"But... not really. It's not indiscreet. I believe very sincerely that we've got a lot of false information and little truth about things. In my opinion it's all about a physical phenomenon that's still unexplained... or maybe the sightings are due to a foreign power. But what do flying saucers have to do with this meeting? I have to say that I don't get the connection between it and your coming here?"

Kariven glanced at his watch: 3:17 pm. He responded nervously, "I apologize for having to set you straight, Monsieur le Ministre, but flying saucers have nothing in common with physical phenomenon or with experiments on special planes being carried out by foreigners. I don't have time to explain in detail the reasons I can say this but please let me tell you first the reason for our visit."

"I'm listening."

"First of all, formal proof will be given you within 45 minutes that flying saucers exist. They are disc-shaped spaceships from the planet Kodha orbiting around the sun that we call the Pole Star in the Ursa Minor constellation."

The Minister opened his mouth and had to force himself to get his words out, "You... Please consider this meeting over! I have no time to waste with fantasies like this."

"Please, Minister!" Yuln stood up and in a touching voice pleaded, "I know the revelations of my husband might sound like babble but I myself am from Kodha! In spite of looking human, I was not born on this planet."

The Minister, flabbergasted, convinced that he was dealing with religious fanatics, slowly spread his legs and with his right knee pressed a button under his desk. His maneuver could not have been seen since he was sitting behind his solid desk, but the young Polarian's paroptic vision and her telepathic sense immediately discovered his ploy.

"We're not fanatics, Monsieur le Ministre, " she raised her voice in indignation. "And your secret call won't bring anyone to your office. Not that the button you pressed with your knee doesn't work but simply because I just tele-projected to your two guards. Yes, we Polarians can even read your mind and see through solid objects."

Kariven glanced at his watch again: 3:31 pm. He looked at the Minister whose forehead was beading with sweat and said, "I'm sorry, Monsieur le Ministre, for this incident. I beg you not to see any violence whatsoever in my wife's interven-tion. And she really is from another planet. We just want to reestablish peace on Earth. May I continue?"

"I… Please," he muttered hoarsely, wiping his forehead.

"It's 3:32 pm right now. At four o'clock sharp a squad-ron of six flying saucers will land in Place de la Concorde. Please…" he insisted, waving his hand politely as the Minister was about to interrupt.

"These human-like Polarians have many friends on Earth gathered into a peaceful organization called the Earth-Polarian Alliance. We are among them. We have at our disposal a net-work of investigators and correspondents covering the entire territory and who are presently ready to welcome the Men from Outer Space. Our radio cars will drive through the city at 4 pm to calm the people so that the landing spaceships won't cause a panic. An airplane will drop flyers with information explaining the situation.

"We are asking you, Monsieur le Ministre, to alert the police immediately and set up a line of guards around the Place de la Concorde. Give strict orders not to shoot the pilots of the ships that are going to land. Avenue Gabriel and Rue de l'Elysée should be cleared because we intend to take the Polarian ambassadors in our cars to meet the President of the Republic.

"When the six ships have landed, order the police to set up a second line around 30 feet from the squadron. The jour-nalists will then be able to work near enough without being bothered by the crowd of thousands of onlookers who will surely be rushing to Concorde.

"It's 3:36 pm, Monsieur le Ministre. I beg you, give the-se orders immediately if you don't want to see the worst panic

Paris has ever suffered. With the police in place everything will go smoothly. Without them, the worst accidents are bound to happen."

Seeing that he was still hesitating and that time was relentlessly running out, Yuln concentrated and using her fantastic supra-mental faculties she influenced the Minister. Right away he picked up the telephone and in a firm voice gave a series of precise and imperative orders.

At 4 pm sharp the 40 cars equipped with loudspeakers and parked at their respective positions drove off. On their doors had been painted in bold letters: EARTH-POLARIAN ALLIANCE—CAR NO. X OF THE RESEARCH INSTITUTE FOR THE STUDY OF FLYING SAUCERS.

As they passed by the people were intrigued by the words and listened to the message that was constantly blaring from the loudspeakers:

"Attention! Attention! At this very moment there are six flying saucers hovering over Place de la Concorde. Do not panic! Do not panic! These ships are piloted by beings from another planet. You have nothing to fear. They are peaceful beings that look like humans. Civilization will benefit greatly from their arrival. Listen at 7 pm tonight to the special broadcasts on French radio and television following the contact between the Men from Space and the Earthlings."

The plane from the Aero-Club, piloted by a member of the Alliance, flew over Paris at 1,500 feet altitude and dropped tens of thousands of flyers supporting the announcements from the radio cars.

The cars, cruising slowly through the streets, continued their warning:

"Attention! Attention! The six flying saucers that you might have seen over Place de la Concorde are about to land. Do not panic! They are our friends…"

Intrigued at first the people reacted in different ways after a few minutes. Some just shrugged their shoulders and went on their way, grumbling about the cheap ploy used for an original advertising campaign.

Others, less rational, tried not to admit their apprehension faced with such an extraordinary event—that they refused to believe but that they feared subconsciously.

Still others, far from being calmed by the reassuring announcements, hurried to get back home or ran into the first café they saw hoping to find adequate shelter.

Some people, however, a little braver, quickened their step to reach the site to see if the cars were speaking the truth.

On Avenue des Champs-Elysées the Earth-Polarian Alliance car in the area was causing a real commotion. All the pedestrians and customers on the café terraces (who were standing up at their tables) were staring down the street. After hearing the message a second time, which was repeating over and over again from the loudspeaker in the car—now stuck in a traffic jam at the metro station George V—they looked up and were stunned, hardly believing their eyes. About a mile up in the air six shiny, metal, disc-shaped ships were on the move, coming straight down, wobbling a little.

Policemen, jumping out of lines of cars by the hundreds, spread out to form a circle around the huge Place de la Concorde. Looking up, as uninformed as the growing number of onlookers who were hassling them with questions, they held hands in a giant circle and started flexing their muscles to hold back the wave of curious people.

The journalists meanwhile were arriving and with them vans from TV and radio. Following orders the police let them enter their circle but keep them back from the second circle that was still not formed. Gossip spread quickly and more than one Parisian that night would complain about their feet being crushed by clumsy gawkers.

The six spaceships—whose metallic surface was almost blinding as it reflected the sunlight—descended slowly. Without a sound, without a bump they landed on their three spheres in a circle around the obelisk. Each ship measured 50 feet in diameter.

The onlookers, as if obeying a mysterious order, stopped talking at the same time. In dead silence their eyes were riveted on the wondrous ships from another planet, on these ships that for years had been ridiculed as drunken visions or collective hallucinations. They were fascinated by the semi-circular domes protecting the cockpits and surrounded by windows.

"Looks like a washing machine," a young rascal snapped, but his joke had no effect on the crowd.

All of a sudden everyone looked down at the lower part of the six discs where a round platform was slowly starting to come down, suspended by shiny, telescopic tubes.

At this moment five policemen broke the line to let Kariven's Versailles through. Inside was the Interior Minister sitting with Yuln, Angelvin, and his wife Jenny. Behind it came Reynal's Ford with Dormoy and Doniatchka.

A hundred policemen lurched forward to close up the second cordon around the spaceships. When they were in place around the two cars and six spaceships the journalists were let loose. From a side street they scrambled over each other trying to get the best view.

On the platform coming down slowly by design from one of the spaceships they could see the legs of three beings, then their big belts and finally their chests and heads.

Zimko and Honky were standing on either side of Tlyka, smiling, fit into the sky blue bodysuits of the Space Commandos. On their chests were embroidered the golden, cigar-shaped spaceship with a stylized lightning bolt. A plastic pilot's helmet—green for the two men and pink for Tlyka—covered their heads but left their energetic faces clear.

Yuln was the first to jump out and run into the arms of her brother with tears in her eyes. Zimko lifted her up like a feather and laughed with joy as he kissed her cheeks loudly.

This unexpected scene broke the nervous tension of the onlookers who spontaneously exploded. Shouts of joy burst from everywhere but when they saw the Interior Minister get out of the car and Kariven introduce him to the three "Martians," the general euphoria turned delirious. The eight to ten year old kids evaded the police surveillance, ran under their arms and whooped like Indians on the warpath as they bolted toward the flying saucers.

The young ladies were overwhelmed by the male bearing of the "Martians"—because there was no doubt in anyone's mind today that these ships came from Mars!—pushed and shoved to get through the police line.

The reporters had a field day, their eyes glued to their cameras. The newscasters from the radio and TV were elbowing each other to get an interview with the ambassadors from another planet without wondering whether they might not only speak "Martian." About this point they would soon find out.

After cordially greeting the Interior Minister, Zimko gave a big smile to his friends of the Earth-Polarian Alliance (Kariven, Dormoy, Angelvin and their wives) and spoke in a deep, warm voice:

"Monsieur le Ministre, my brave friends of the Earth-Polarian Alliance and all you Earthling friends who are listening to me, I bring you fraternal greetings from all the races of the Federated Worlds. We have crossed outer space from Kodha, our home planet orbiting the Pole Star, 250,000 billion miles from Earth, on board our giant spaceships called 'flying cigars' by you. These here," he pointed back at the squadron, "known here as flying saucers, are just reconnaissance ships transported on board the bigger ships. We only use them alone very rarely to cross the 400 light-year distance.

"But for now let's put aside these minor explanations. Everything you're eager to know about us you will learn tonight on the television and radio, which has just received an official message from our space HQ, an artificial satellite orbiting 600 miles off Earth."

Zimko's words, sent through his tiny belly transmitter, echoed loudly in the loudspeakers that had emerged from the cockpits of the six spaceships at the start of his speech.

"Earth friends," the Man from Outer Space continued, "at this very moment in Washington DC, New York, Peking, Sydney, Tokyo, Moscow, Rome, London, Berlin and all the big cities on the planet, similar contact is being made between the representatives of our race and yours. For years we have had many friends on your planet, members of a secret, peaceful organization—the Earth-Polarian Alliance—whose cars were just now announcing our arrival. The three Earthlings at my side, Jean Kariven, Michel Dormoy and Robert Angelvin, along with their wives, are the veterans of this Alliance. One day soon peace will finally be established between the peoples of Earth, your race and ours will form a union... against an enemy from outer space. For, a threat is looming over your civilization. But that, too, will be revealed in the message tonight. This is not, therefore, the time to panic but rather to take appropriate measures."

With these enigmatic words the enthusiasm running through the crowd died down. There were worried eyes now staring at the beings speaking of peace... by preparing for war. But what kind of war? Certainly not a conflict between east and west since the Man from Outer Space said that Earthlings would soon be united. What should they understand by "enemies from outer space"? Could it be that an *interplanetary* war was about to take place?

"I repeat, Earth friends, don't give in to panic. We Polarians, with all the means of offense and defense at our disposal, are ready to protect you... if any attack is made on your planet. Stay calm and trust in our desire to help you and henceforth you will benefit from our knowledge."

Zimko sent out a psychic call to the occupants of the five other Fimn'has and from each of them came out the axial platform holding two Centaurians and two Wolfians, creatures from three to four feet tall, wearing either metallic or rubber spacesuits. The transparent part of their round helmet showed their faces, similar to humans but orange for the Centaurians and brown fur with huge vertical eyes for the Wolfians.

At the sight of these 20 little beings that were so different from the Men from Outer Space—but closer to the idea formed of "Martians"—a reflex to fall back struck the thousands of curious bystanders around the Place de la Concorde. Some in the front looked like they were about to run away.

Zimko raised his hand and his voice, "You have nothing to fear! These beings are our allies and therefore your friends. The smaller ones in the jointed metal spacesuits come from the solar system Alpha Centauri. The others, a little taller, come from the system Wolf 359. They also speak French and other Earth languages. We have known your languages for a long time.

"Take a close look at these Wolfians and Centaurians and don't think of them as monsters or freaks. They are intelligent beings, kind and wise, whose civilizations are as evolved as ours.

"Take a close look and etch deep in your minds their faces and bodies and spacesuits. For, these two races and our own are the only ones that will come as friends to your planet. We also have allies of different types but they won't come here. Our three races are the only peaceful races that operate in your solar system. Remember this. And if by chance you witness the landing of a squadron of flying saucers whose occupants are different from Wolfians, Centaurians and us, run away and immediately alert the police or the nearest authority. Because they would be extra-terrestrials who are not part of our Space Commandos and therefore *enemies!*"

All over the world they snatched up the newspapers to devour the reports on the arrival of the cosmic visitors to our planet. Radio and television had been reporting all night long, giving commentaries and showing the different phases of contact made in all the big cities on Earth. People wanted to see new pictures of these pseudo-men and their weird, dwarf companions. One special edition after another sold out. Crowds even camped in front of the big dailies' printers hoping to get the latest scoop. Police and security services were stationed around the editorial offices, radio stations and TV studios to keep back the impatient crowds.

In the morning, fanatics even showed up at the various ministries—without knowing which could really satisfy their desires—to demand that they be among the first to depart for Mars. For, in spite of all the explanations in the media, some people stubbornly continued in their belief that the flying saucers were Martian.

The astronomical observatories were overwhelmed. They were assaulted with constant telephone calls. Some people wanted to know where the planet Kodha was, the home of the Polarians, how long its orbit around the Pole Star was, and why the Pole Star was a sun, etc. To the evasive answer given by the astronomers to the first two questions the questioners got angry. They could not understand that they telescopes could not spot a planet whose existence we did not know about before its inhabitants came to visit.

Moreover, the good people kept making fun of the famous astronomer Sosthene Cornu who, on the night before the memorable day, had given a speech on the radio in which he railed against "the human stupidity of the feeble-minded who believed that so-called flying saucers came from outer space"! Facts had just given him a well-deserved slap in the face by shattering his ridiculous anthropocentrism of a narrow-minded scientist.

Fluorescent discs with an emerald green halo, 15 spaceships carrying on board the Heads of State of the powerful nations on Earth sped into starry space to converge on their space base orbiting 600 miles around the planet.

A huge sphere of metal, over a mile and a half in diameter, the base looked frozen in space, an extraordinary globe hanging in the cosmic void on a background of bright stars that did not twinkle. On its equatorial part a rectangular hatch opened, 165 feet high by 650 feet wide, revealing a vast, brightly lit hold in which the discs entered five at a time. The hatch closed up behind them and when the artificial air had been reestablished the axial platforms came out of the ships with their occupants standing on the chrome metal striped with thin grooves.

Zimko, along with Kariven, Dormoy and Angelvin, led the representatives of the Earth nations—still dazed by this voyage that was unthinkable only 48 hours ago—through the corridors and walkways of the "equatorial section". A group of tubular elevators took them to drop them off in another corridor with electro-luminescent walls. At the end of this they went through an armored door and entered an enormous amphitheater with a concave ceiling giving off a soft, bluish light.

Seats in soft metal that felt both spongy and rigid were set up in a semi-circle. Before each of these was a movable, rectangular tray with a notebook of blank plastex pages, different colored pens and a small device with a screen. Above the screen was a sign with the name of the Earth nation whose representative would occupy that seat.

"This half-circle is a little reminiscent of the United Nations," the President of the French Republic whispered to his neighbor.

Of course, he was astonished to hear in his mind, *but here the discussions will not be fruitless.*

The President nodded and smiled at Zimko. These thoughts projected into his head must certainly have come from him.

For the first time in history all the Heads of State had willingly agreed to hold a truly "general" assembly, which pleased them greatly. This unanimous decision had met no resistance and no veto had delayed it.

The kind face of the American President betrayed a brief, amused surprise on seeing the seat next to him occupied by President Koulski, Chief of the Supreme Soviet.

Zimko sat behind a kind of long desk cluttered with strange instruments. Suspended above a big, convex screen a fluorescent spiral emitted red pulses on the chrome control panel coated in *isolex* before him.

At his side sat the veterans of the Earth-Polarian Alliance: Kariven, Dormoy and Angelvin. To his right, however, the seat remained empty.

In front of the desk-control panel the superior officers, Wolfian and Centaurian, sat down—in chairs designed for their size—in their spacesuits. They were the general staff of the Space Commandos.

Honky came in and sat to the right of Zimko who then raised his hand and addressed the assembly in English. His words were automatically translated electronically on each of the devices for the different Heads of State. These devices—psychic buzzers—sent the translation directly into the minds of the participants so that they did not need to wear headphones that become tiresome during a long speech.

"Gentlemen," the Chief of the Space Commandos began, "for the first time in your race the powerful politicians have finally come together not to backbite and criticize but to build the foundation for lasting peace. Before giving the floor to my old friend Nheg Honky, Chief of the Information Service of the Federated Worlds, I would like to give you a brief history of our civilization. This might allow you to understand why we are, in some way, your... *Ancestors from the Future*...

CHAPTER V

This unexpected paradox—*Ancestors from the Future*—came as a great surprise to the high dignitaries assembled under the huge dome of the Polarian astro-base. So it was with lively interest that they listened to Zimko's talk.

"In a very distant past, around 500 million years ago, our race had already reached an extraordinary level of evolution. The age of interplanetary travel, now surpassed, gave way to interstellar travel thanks to the discovery of one of the most distinguished scientists of our planet. The crowning achievement of decades of research, this scientist perfected a space-time disruptor that permitted our spaceships to enter subspace, a strange field where Time has no duration and Space no extension. Consequently, our spaceships could move from one solar system to another at absolute speed. In essence, after taking off and flying for a certain distance following traditional methods, the spaceship dropped its standard mode of propulsion to replace it with the space-time disruptor, which we still use. The ship could then leave normal space and jump at absolute speed into subspace, which, in a fraction of a second, brought it to the frontiers of the target solar system. There it cut the space-time disruptor and went back to traditional technology based on electromagnetic fields.

"Our ancestors started inventorying the many solar systems of their galactic zone and meticulously exploring them, one by one, planet by planet. This took time, millennia in fact, but it allowed us to locate the planets that were physically similar to Kodha, our home. Then we established Polarian colonies on these planets. One of them was a star in your system: Mars, which, being older than Earth, had already reached its vital stage hundreds of millions of years before. Mars supported pretty evolved flora and fauna in an atmosphere not unlike Earth's, but the latter was still in a stage of geological upheaval.

191

"A Polarian colony, therefore, was set up on Mars and over the ages developed an important Martian civilization. Later, at four different epochs, we sent Polarian colonist to your planet. It was these colonists who successively founded the first terrestrial civilizations long ago disappeared: Gondwana, Mu, Lemuria and Atlantis.[35] Swallowed up one by one by disasters these civilizations only left a handful of Polarians—or 'humans'—who soon degenerated into a prehistoric stage.

"After each cosmic cataclysm the disrupted solar system was flooded with electromagnetic energy—a by-product of cosmic rays—blocking our spaceships from coming back to the affected planets. From this fact, powerless to help our poor brothers, we watched on our screens as the civilizations they built decayed and died. Nature is made in such a way that it destroys everything it creates. When the cosmic rays eased up—sometimes taking millennia—new space squadrons headed back to the worlds with a mission to rebuild the civilization destroyed by disaster.

"We were able, thereafter, to spot the preliminary signs of certain cataclysms but not all. The most usual—the arrival in a solar system of a foreign body—was easy. And this was how we warned our ancestors on Mars 300,000 years ago. A giant comet with a solid core blazing across the solar system caused them to abandon Mars and emigrate to Earth where, tens of thousands of years earlier, a civilization had been completely destroyed. Before the problem star, the comet Yahoun, reached Mars, they went to Earth and founded... Atlantis.[36] In its turn, almost 15,000 years ago, Atlantis was swallowed up, leaving only a small number of survivors who no resources. They dispersed over the various continents of the globe where they led miserable lives. Some of them fell back into almost barbaric states; others, obviously luckier, notably in Egypt, built new a civilization that your archeologists consider highly

---

[35] See Volume 1.

[36] Another reference to *Nous, les Martiens*.

evolved whereas, in fact, it was only the bones of decadent culture.

"Only one branch from Atlantis kept a semblance of its former splendor because they were hidden in a temperate valley of Antarctic ice.[37]

"You Earthlings, therefore, white and red, are descended from Martians and ultimately of Polarian origin since our brothers had founded the colony on Mars. Black and yellow Earthlings are a mix between Polarians and the natives of Venus where our ancestors also established a colony.

"Basically, Earthlings are not originally from Earth but from the planet Kodha in the solar system of the Pole Star, the cradle of our ancient civilization, the oldest and most evolved in the Galaxy. We Polarians are, therefore, your ancestors.

"But since your civilization, after Atlantis, has not yet reached a high level of evolution, we consider it in its infancy. Our civilization, compared to yours, is practically… in the Future. That's why I used that strange paradox by calling us your Ancestors from the Future.

"To wrap up this history, as sketchy as it was, you should keep one fundamental truth in mind: we Polarians bring to the Earthlings a love whose profound sincerity they have no inkling of. Our most cherished desire is to help you, to guide you to Knowledge, Wisdom and Goodness because not only are humans are brothers but we all come from the same race, the Polarian race that is now going to take them under its protective wing like an older brother wrapping his strong arms around a younger, still clumsy brother being harassed by an enemy.

"Excuse me for this long but not pointless digression. Now I give the floor to my good friend and brother in arms, Nheg Honky, Chief of the I.S. of the Federated Worlds, who will tell you the goals and motives of our coming to your planet."

---

[37] This refers to *Le Monde oublié*.

At the thunderous applause Zimko smiled, glad to see telepathically the unanimous surge of enthusiasm and sympathy among his listeners and even some affection toward his own people.

For the Wolfians and Centaurians, wearing their space-suits, it was a little harder to feel the emotional current pulsing like an aura, invisible to human eyes, around most of the Heads of State. In their great wisdom they were not offended in seeing some of the VIPs, although attracted by the Polarians, feeling a vague, instinctive repulsion toward them. Earthlings, in fact, considered these little creatures a little like "monsters", maybe freaks, very different from *homo sapiens*, and though they were not hostile they also did not show the same interest that they did to their (physically) kin of the Polarian race.

Equality and mutual understanding between different thinking races of the Galaxy had never been something accepted in a day. It would be the same with these Earthlings among the Wolfians and Centaurians. But the latter knew that with time their races would end up being considered "natural" in the same way as Polarians.

Honky, with his big build, as big as Zimko, put his hands flat on the control panel and addressed the assembly:

"Gentlemen, you who represent the Earth nations, as Zimko just said our race is spread all over the Galaxy, continually landing on new planets where it peacefully establishes bases out of kindness, wisdom and altruism. These base are there to help the under-developed natives. One day during our space voyages we Polarians explored the solar system of stars that you call Deneb in the constellation Cygnus and Procyon in the constellation Canis Minor. These two solar systems, to the surprise of the Polarian explorers, were inhabited by two evolved races that had also reached the stage of interstellar travel. Denebians and Procyonians categorically refused our offers of alliance and cultural exchange and forbid us to come back to their planets. Wanting above all not to bother the evolved races capable of progressing on their own, we decided not to return. However, we expressed our good intentions by assuring them that we would answer any call from them if they decided one day to establish cordial and neutral relations between our races.

"A few decades passed and we landed on a planet in the solar system of Canopus that we had already visited several times and whose natives, a rather primitive creature that looked like an upright frog, kept shy but friendly relations with us. Imagine our surprise in finding that their capital, consisting of round mud or brick cabins, was reduced to heaps of burned rubble.

"The terrorized survivors, whom we had great trouble finding as they were hiding in their swamps, explained to us the cause of the disaster: a few days earlier the Denebians landed on their planet with ten spaceships that looked like ours because they were disc-shaped. The Canopians approached, curious and trustful, believing they'd see Polarians who often enough came to help them and gradually teach them basic knowledge accessible to their minds.

"On seeing these different creatures—we'll show you what they look like very soon—they ran away, very disturbed. The Denebians abruptly paralyzed them, then made them take them to their lakeside city. Their goal was to colonize the planet and enslave the rightful inhabitants. Although unable to measure up to their powerful, invulnerable invaders, the natives refused to give in. They fought heroically, but in vain, with their primitive weapons—a kind of spring loaded weapon that shot big, poisoned thorns.

"The thermal cannon from a single Denebian spaceship only had to fire its blazing ray twice to reduce the Canopian capital to cinders, along with its 25,000 inhabitants. The few survivors who told us their misfortune said they would prefer to commit collective suicide rather than submit to these monsters. They begged us to protect them and fight back the cruel creatures who didn't hesitate to wipe out a population of 25,000 Canopians using their thermal weapons against... poisoned arrows!

"Naturally," Honky continued, "we made a formal agreement to protect the Canopians. Our HQ sent a message right away to the Denebians—their real name is Ptopans, being from the planet Ptopa in the solar system Omink called Deneb by the Earthlings.

"In this message we denounced the Denebian methods of enslavement and announced that from then on the Canopians were under our protection. Our spaceships made regular patrols in this solar system in order to repel any attempt at invasion.

"Far from being intimidated by these warnings the Denebians, without a declaration of war, launched a guided missile loaded with concentrated atomic cyanogen against our new protectorate. When it struck the ground it was supposed to explode and poison the air. Our paroptic vision, an ability unknown to the Denebians, saved us and the Canopians from a horrible death. We ended up exploding the missile in space where the noxious gas dissipated without doing any harm.

"And that's how the Polarian-Denebian-Procyonian War started centuries ago. Because the monsters from Procyon have the same thirst for conquest as their Denebian allies.

"We inflicted considerable losses on them but the demonic creatures kept running around the Galaxy hoping to conquer new planets and, if necessary, enslave the inhabitants. So far they have only attacked—like cowards—very primitive, non-humanoid races. But the last dozen Earth years they have set their sights on your planet and are trying by any means possible to conquer it. Twice they almost got a strong foothold in your solar system and even on Earth itself without you knowing[38]. We chased them away both times and inflicted heavy losses. But lately some agents from our Information Service—biological robots that look like Denebians and Procyonians—warned us that these creatures are getting ready to try a massive invasion of Earth, Mars and Venus.

---

[38] See Volume 1.

"We decided, therefore, to intervene and make official contact with Earthlings in order to put them on guard against the monsters. The moment has come to prepare the defense of your planet where we already have some valuable allies and friends in the Earth-Polarian Alliance," he bowed politely to Kariven, Dormoy and Angelvin who would lead the organization in Europe.

"During out recent contact," he continued, "Zimko in France and his superior officers of the Space Commandos in the other countries, they urged the Earthlings to engrave in their memories the image of Wolfians and Centaurians. This should allow you to recognize the three friendly races who are very different from the Denebians and Procyonians—specimens of which you are about to see. These specimens will also be shown to all Earthlings to forewarn them against any eventual contact with individuals… maybe already present on Earth.

"Two enemy crews were recently captured during a brief skirmish between our patrols and their vessels in the asteroid zone."

While saying this Honky had sent a telepathic order to the Polarians guarding the prisoners. A few minutes later an armored panel, 30 feet wide by 20 high, slid open silently in a metal wall of the big meeting room. A kind of brightly lit platform appeared, above and behind the half-moon desk where the Polarians sat with the members of the Alliance, facing the assembly of Heads of State.

The terrestrial leaders jumped back when they saw a group of six, hideously ugly creatures step forward. Under the psychic control of their guards the prisoners stopped at the edge of the raised platform and stood still, deprived of their consciousness.

There were three Denebians, vaguely human creatures, six and a half feet tall with green skin—covered in big, horny, triangular scales like a lizard. Their red or scarlet eyes were striped with yellow bands and their lipless mouths made them look like disgusting turtles. A fleshy, brown growth swelled out of the top of their oval heads and their bony fingers ended in retractable claws.

They looked nice and pretty, however, compared to the Procyonians! These giant monsters, 13 feet-tall with blue, phosphorescent, hairy skin, had four arms ending in pincers a little like lobsters. Their huge, flabby head with weird, bulging face, had only one eye, one remarkable eye, cloudy and yellowish, from which a milky liquid leaked. The puss dripped down the oily face and mixed with the purple drool that seeped out of the repulsive, thick-lipped mouth.

The Heads of State twisted their faces in disgust, standing up from their seats and troubled by this nightmarish vision.

"Don't be afraid," Zimko quickly advised. "These creatures are harmless now. Under the mechano-psychic control of our bio-electric brains, they obey only us."

With a friendly wave of his hand he invited Honky to continue.

"Right now cameras are filming these creatures as well as this assembly and our words are being recorded. Copies of the sound and images will be sent to Earth where all the radio and TV studios will broadcast them in a few hours to the population. Tomorrow, Dear Representatives of the Earth Nations, you'll just have to personally confirm the truth of this information to your citizens.

"Zimko and I are sure that these ugly creatures and the threat looming over your civilization will motivate the union of all peoples without delay. It would be preferable to have peace on Earth and the unity of its inhabitants come from their wisdom. Alas! I have to admit that Earthlings are not wise enough yet to unite in a Global United States as was encourage in 1955 by a great Frenchman, Bernard Dewavrin[39].

---

[39] Dewavrin's "bold, constructive plan" called for the adoption by the free nations of a common army, a common foreign policy and a common economy. As his first recommendation, Dewavrin urged that France become the 49th state of the United States of the World. He was frank enough to say that "the

Therefore, it would take a threat from outer space to unite human beings! And this threat is here, under your very noses. Will you hesitate, Gentlemen, to drop your quarrels and your ideological, economical and sectarian differences in the face of this planetary invasion?"

And they witnessed a scene never before seen in the UN assemblies: they saw the Heads of State, in a sincere and spontaneous spirit, shake hands warmly, hug one another and even—breaking all protocol—the US President give a friendly slap on the back to President Koulski while he hugged the British Prime Minister.

The day after this historic moment, in cheerful moods, Earthlings were glad to learn by the newspaper, radio and television that following an international agreement from the World Assembly in the Polarian astrobase, the constitution of the Global United States had been drawn up and approved unanimously. The Earth and Polarian economists, sociologists and scientists were going to study the methods of cultural and economic exchange between the two related races. Borders would be abolished and the currency unified.

The planet Kodha was already sending to Earth a squadron of giant spaceships transporting gifts offered by the Polarian authorities to their Earthling brothers. Machines, medicine, real "miracles" and everything our civilization

U.S.A. would not derive any initial advantage from the fact that the American Constitution would be used as the cement, the 48 American states as the foundation and France as a cornerstone," but was careful to point out that "the 49th state would receive the same rights as the 48 American states." Dewavrin added that "unless the Americans are concealing imperialistic aims (and this plan for a United States of the World could help as a test) they should approve of it, even though the representatives of the 48 states would soon cease to enjoy a majority in the United States of the World's parliament."

needed would arrive to benefit humanity that had finally united.

An Earth-Polarian general staff got together to study a plan of defense on a global scale.

A team of technicians was chosen from the greatest specialists of all the countries to leave Earth and travel to the Polarian bases on the Moon, Mars, Venus and other planets of the solar system.

The entire globe was quivering with unprecedented energy. Despite the threat—that many humans still considered to be distant—an atmosphere of joy spread under the skies. Hundreds of thousands of Soviet refugees living in Western Europe went back home, guaranteed not to suffer retribution. The quarrels and disagreements were quashed and in a spirit of fraternity people found a new lease on life.

Civilization was at the dawn of a grand and sublime renewal.

Of course, everyone felt their hair stand on end in fright on seeing the videos of the abominable Denebians and Procyonians, but with the powerful Polarians as allies these monsters would have to watch out. The tacticians in the bars animatedly described the casualties in their ranks at the hands of our "Ancestors from the Future" as they were already calling the Polarians.

"Leagues of Cosmic Love" formed mostly by old spinsters or idealistic mystics preached the mating of races with the secret hope of one day seeing themselves swept away by some handsome knight from outer space aboard a shining spaceship. Maidens (and others) once dreamed of a prince charming. Now they were dreaming of Conquerors from Outer Space!

The religions, after a moment of confusion before these human-like strangers to Earth, agreed to admit that "nothing could limit the all powerful Divinity." If God, in His infinite wisdom, had endowed Earth with thinking creatures, He could very well had extended His creation to other worlds. And nothing in the Holy Scriptures flatly denied this very wise reasoning. Quite the contrary.

Many exegetes and Church Fathers re-examining the Holy Texts called up Jesus' ambiguous words full of deep esoteric meaning: *I have other sheep that are not of this sheep pen* [John 10:16]. They also mulled over this enigmatic saying: *My Father's house has many rooms* [John 14:2] and they understood why Christ once said: *My kingdom is not of this world* [John 18:36].

A revival of faith, purified by Knowledge, spread through the human race that swelled with love and set to work with courage and hope on contributing to the development of a new society.

The sublime faith of cathedral builders, earning salvation through their work, took hold of Earthlings, brought them together and united them by the truly sacred bonds that unite brother to brother.

How good it was to work with the wise help of our older brothers, the Men from Outer Space with altruistic and charitable sentiments.

Yes, for sure, Procyonians and Denebians had better watch out!

A small, dark disc, around 30 feet in diameter, whose security system absorbed radar waves and thus kept it from being spotted, was slowly drifting through the dark night of space. It had just captured the radio and television emissions from Earth and was filming the start of their alliance with the Polarians, Wolfians and Centaurians.

The two pilots of the reconnaissance ship, with their green, scaly shell glistening under the bank of lights of the axial cabin, had an ironic look in their red eyes as they watched the images on the screen above their control panels.

A vertical tube over the screen suddenly flashed a series of red pulses. The creatures' claws slammed down on a button and the spaceship launched into space at extraordinary speed. With the security system absorbing the radar waves—instead of bouncing them back to their point of origin—they would have been spotted by two flying saucers from the Space Commandos.

After exchanging messages with their mobile base set up on an asteroid between Mars and Jupiter, they headed back to Earth and were soon flying over Russia. It was nighttime on this side of the globe and their ship, with its jet-black hull, passed totally undetected.

Working methodically the Denebian spies had been spying for 48 hours on the movements of the enemy spacecraft. In the evening they had seen the giant "cigars" unload some material for the USSR and take off for the USA where they did the same thing before heading back to their planet. Since the coast was clear they landed silently in the suburbs about two miles west of Moscow.

After sweeping the surrounding area with the beams from their psychic probes to make sure that no Polarian was around, they turned off all the lights inside their ship and opened the exterior hatchway.

From the ventral hold they pulled out the bodies of three Polarians in Space Commando uniforms and dragged them to the edge of the hatch. From there they went down to the snowy ground and then back to the hold. Inside were two Earthlings, skinny and dressed in rags, bearing marks of whipping on their chest and neck, lying on the metal floor. The Denebians activated the small device (a cube covered with phosphorescent pins) that they wore on their chest and the two men got up, slowly, like robots. On the order of the guards one of them grabbed a rectangular case, about one by two feet, and along with his companion jumped to the ground.

Obeying the mental orders of the green monsters the three Polarians stood up but did not move. Facing the Earthlings, they, too, looked unconscious.

Pressing the control buttons of their weird cubes—thought projectors—the Denebians watched carefully as one of the Earthlings approached the Polarians. The man, spurred on by a sudden fervor, threw them to the ground and started tearing at their bodysuits until they were ripped to shreds. Then, with all his strength, he punched them in the face, pummeled their bodies and taking a knife out of his pocket he finished them off.

Calmly, having followed the orders of his guards, he went back to them. The green monsters retracted their claws, then punched him hard in the face, over and over, splitting his lower lip and over his eye and ripping his shirt to pieces. The unconscious man, horribly knocked around, stood up and took the box that his companion was holding. Then he waited. The Denebians went up to the second prisoner and gave him the same treatment.

Covered in blood, ragged and shaggy, the two men looked like they had just come out a fierce battle. One final psychic order came to them and the poor men seemed to regain consciousness. Straightaway they started running through the snow toward the lights of Moscow.

Shivering in his torn shirt one of them was holding on tight to the mysterious case.

Satisfied with their clever ploy the Denebians took off silently and at high speed set their course for their secret base.

Marshall Gorochenko, standing at attention in front of President Koulski, watched on worriedly as he paced nervously up and down the wool carpet covering the floor of his office.

"It's unthinkable!" the President shouted. "I refuse to put faith in the ravings of these men!"

"But, Mr. President," the Marshall said, "I tell you that I *personally* checked their accounts. I saw the indisputable traces of a fight in the snow around the three Polarian corpses. And I swear to you that these poor survivors have wounds and bruises proving without a doubt the violence they suffered at the hands of their… executioners."

"Bring these men in! I'm telling you that if I find they're lying I'll have them executed without mercy!"

The two Earthlings, acting under the psychic orders of the Denebians, were brought into the President's office. Bandaged and dressed more warmly than when they were found by the MVD patrol, they bowed before President Koulski.

"Are you Russian?" the President growled. "How did you manage to... do what you did?"

"Yes, Mr. President, we are Russians and we belong to the Earth-Polarian Alliance. We were invited one day to take a study trip with other members of the organization, French, American, English and Australians, on board a flying saucer. When we got to Kodha, the Polarians' home, they took us around the splendid cities to show us their architecture. We were never alone and this made us curious.

"Petruski and I decided one night to slip away from our guides who were very kind but far too inclined to control out visit. We managed to escape their discreet surveillance and at dawn, to our great surprise, we found something that they had carefully hidden from us: a penal colony! A kind of camp where Polarian guards were constantly whipping *Earthlings and a few Denebians slaving away.*

"We'd been fooled! The Polarians with their pretty speeches had managed to coerce us out of love for our race whereas their real goal was to enslave us. After their contact with us they figured on making us the witnesses of their good intentions, their altruism and their desire to help us and protect us from the Denebians. And we were buying it just like the Heads of State bought it a few days ago during that famous contact. In truth, the Polarians are diabolical men whose dirty but very clever Machiavellianism has only one goal: to break down the Earthlings' suspicions of them by raising the specter of an interstellar war started by the Denebians and Procyonians.

"Really, this is all a great big fraud. The Denebians and Procyonians *are not our enemies!* On the contrary they are the ones fighting against the power-hungry Polarians, these pseudo-men who have fooled us in this vile way. Oh, they're clever! They've brought hundreds of tons of material, gifts from their race to their younger brothers here on Earth... as they say. In fact, these gifts have no other purpose but to build up our trust in them. When they're implanted in every country of the world, they'll change tactics and reveal themselves in their real light: as conquerors of Earth!

"And you, Mr. President, and all the other Heads of State on the planet, *will have helped them without knowing it!*

CHAPTER VI

Unconscious victims, repeating with unbelievable ease the psychic orders implanted in their minds by the Denebians, the two men, impassioned and persuasive, had shaken up President Koulski. The victim of an emotion that he did not try to hide, he ran his hand nervously through his gray hair and in a flat voice said, "Continue with your account…"

"So, we were found by the Polarians at the edge of the camp and immediately locked in there where we found other Earthlings who, like us, had uncovered the hidden goals of our so-called allies. Procyonians and Denebians, captured in space battles, were our partners in misery. Except for looking like monsters to the Earthlings, these creatures, quite peaceful, would have no problem being presented to us as monsters thirsting after Earth. And all the Heads of State, unfortunately, took these false accusations as proven truths!

"Taking advantage of the commotion in the city from the contact, we escaped and hid in one of the many spaceships about to depart for Earth. Hiding in the hold of a flying saucer, we landed last night not far from Moscow.

"In desperation and feeling better that we were back home, we decided to risk leaving. Armed just with a knife we took advantage of a break by the crew of three Polarians, to escape. Unfortunately, on opening the exterior hatch the pilots woke up and jumped on us. After a violent fight we came out the winners without them being able to use their awful disintegrator rays."

Petruski cut in, "And we can prove the existence of this damned camp on Kodha where Earthlings, Denebians and Procyonians are working and dying. In fact, when we escaped the penal colony we were able to steal a camera, with film, that the chief was using to film his prisoners. This might seem weird to us but as my comrade told you the surveillance in the camp loosened up a lot right before the departure of the space squadron for Earth."

On President Koulski's order the said box was brought and the two escaped prisoners from the planet Kodha quickly took out a strange device, looking like both a camera and a machine gun. Along the inner walls of the case were eight plastic holders with magnetic film.

Petruski opened a side section of the device and fit one of the eight rolls of film into the cavity, asking the President to turn off the lights. Then he shouldered the camera and aimed it at the wall. After focusing the picture, the images were projected on the improvised screen in relief but strangely striped with transparent yellow and black.

First there was a view of the whole camp with the Polarian capital blurry in the background. Then came a foreshortened view, quite unexpected since it looked shot from above, which seemed illogical because the camp should—normally—have been filmed from the ground.

President Koulski and Marshal Gorochenko, without being able to explain these two different angles *on the same film*, put it down to some unknown property of Polarian optics or geometry.

A column of Earthlings, Denebians and Procyonians guarded by Men from Outer Space stopped in the middle of the camp. The guards raised their disintegrator rifles to their hips and shot. The horrible pain that twisted the prisoners' faces turned into agony. Then they were surrounded by a blinding flash and disappeared, disintegrated.

"These poor guys," Petruski said, "tried to escape the night before. Now you're going to see some 'preventive treatment' given by the torturers to their poor victims."

Another roll of film showed a second column of captives being cruelly whipped by their Polarian "executioners" in order to remove every last desire to escape.

"It's despicable," President Koulski panted. "We have to alert our allies in the other countries immediately. It's now or never to prove that the nations of Earth are united, not against

207

the Denebians and Procyonians but against the Polarians, these pseudo-men working secretly to destroy us! Marshal Gorochenko, inform our ambassadors abroad, in code, so that all the heads of state can meet in absolute secrecy tonight in Washington. I'm leaving myself in ten minutes for the United States and bringing these two men and the damning proof that they managed to acquire. Ready my special plane!"

And under his breath he whispered, "If the Polarians suspect anything at all, the human race is finished."

The French government had just appointed Kariven to the post of Director of the French Section of the Earth-Polarian Alliance. In his office in the Foreign Ministry—Extra-Terrestrial Division—he was talking with his Cabinet Chiefs, Dormoy and Angelvin. Cabinet Chiefs was the right title because the anthropologist, although he was called a Director, was in fact considered the Minister of Extra-Terrestrial Relations. His final position was nothing but a question of administration and therefore of time...

"Our friend Zimko will arrive in Paris any time now," he told them. "His spaceship is crossing the orbits of Mars and Jupiter where he's setting up space patrols that are on a mission to search for the secret Denebian base that they figure is on one of the countless drifting 'rocks' in the asteroid belt. It's a long-term undertaking that might last months."

The interphone on the right on his desk rang. Kariven pressed a button and the voice of a page announced, "Two gentlemen from DAT[40] to see the Director. The gentlemen say they have a message of the highest importance. Plus, they've got a special pass from the War Minister himself."

"Kindly show the gentlemen in," Kariven said.

Impeccably dressed in plain clothes, the two tall agents from DAT entered the office. After a courteous salute they

---

[40] Défense Aérienne du Territoire, Territorial Air Defense. (Author's Note)

showed Kariven their pass and the letter signed by the War Minister as well as the Soviet ambassador in Paris.

"We have it from reliable sources, Director," one of them began, "that the Polarians are fooling us horribly. They're planning to invade Earth and enslave mankind."

Kariven, Angelvin and Dormoy were speechless at this ridiculous accusation. They just stood there in shock. Kariven automatically lit a cigarette, forgetting to offer one to his guests. Then, pale and hardly containing his indignation, he attacked, "What stupid series of circumstances brought on this nonsense?"

Unflustered by his violent reaction the two agents told him briefly about the secret message from Moscow transmitted by the Soviet ambassador to the War Minister without even going through the Foreign Ministry.

Floored by the abominable mistake that they knew perfectly well lacked any foundation the three friends did their best to convince the agents—to no avail—that the accusations were false.

"We have to ask you to accompany us right away to Orly where a special plane will take you to Washington DC," one of the men said. "The President of the Republic, the War Minister and President Koulski are already on their way. We have strict orders: if we see even a single doubt in you about the authenticity of the message, we'll have to… force you to go with us."

"Is that a threat?" Kariven slipped his hand discreetly under his desk.

With unexpected speed two automatic pistols were in the hands of the two agents. "Don't move, Director. We're following orders and we can't turn back. Despite the respect we have for you, we are forced to bring you and your Cabinet Chiefs, Messieurs Dormoy and Angelvin. Understand, however, that this is in no way an arrest. The War Minister insisted on this. As soon as the secret meeting in Washington is over— and when the Polarians lies have been clearly proven—you will be free because aware of your patriotic duty as Earth-lings."

Kariven stood up, livid, clenching his jaws. "We'll follow you but you're going to realize the horrible mistake you're making by being the accessories to this tragic delusion."

Two and a half hours later Kariven, Dormoy and Angelvin entered the underground department of the Pentagon where all the heads of state of the terrestrial nations and the chiefs of the Earth-Polarian Alliance were gathered. Once again could be seen the perfect union of minds of these men who only a week ago were still squabbling over all kinds of contentious matters.

The three Frenchmen were eager to see their American friends, Professor Harrington, Commander Taylor, Lieutenant Rudy Clark and the physicist Kurt Streiler, as well as the Russian friends, Zavkom and Petkov, in the assembly. But it was with a look of alarm that they shook hands and sat down in the big, vaulted underground room where the high dignitaries of the planet were already sitting.

In the place of honor next to the President of the USA, President Koulski started speaking in a shaky voice but in very correct English.

"Gentlemen, Friends. It is with great sorrow that I learned from the mouth of these two men here (he pointed out the two Russians who escaped from the Polarian prison camp) about the unbelievable lies of our so-called allies from outer space. Of course, I know that this cruel revelation is not accepted by the veterans of the Earth-Polarian Alliance. I'm referring to Mrrs. Kariven, Dormoy and Angelvin for France, Professor Harrington, Dr. Kurt Streiler, Commander Taylor and Lieutenant Rudy Clark for the USA, Colonel Zavkom and the physicist Petkov for Russia and all those who like them have seen their trust betrayed by the tyrants from outer space. These clever, devious pseudo-men knew ever so well how to put their suspicions to sleep and make them involuntary accomplices."

The men thus named fidgeted in their chairs and exchanged meaningful glances that hid nothing of their indignation at this monstrous misunderstanding.

"I don't want to go on about their errors," Koulski continued, "but on the contrary come even closer together to help them out. The ideal, obviously, would be to contact the Denebians and Procyonians to tell them how strongly we desire to purge the solar system of the Polarian invaders. But alas, the latter are watching us, from space, with their squadrons guarding against our selfless liberators. How easy it was to deceive us by showing the frightful figures of these creatures—ugly in human eyes—but whose hearts are pure. It is a well-established fact that we feel an instinctive disgust of everything that breaks drastically with the aesthetic sense in our selfish eyes. So, it's almost normal for us to consider these hideous creatures from Deneb and Procyon as bloodthirsty demons. What a mistake, my friends, what a regrettable mistake!

"We'll have to defy the Polarians, these beings so like humans who, we have to admit, are tarnished with the same vices and the same thirst for domination that reign over us. For, here, tonight, we have to admit our mea culpa! And I myself as President of the Supreme Soviet admit... not without some shame, that for years the behavior of the USSR was not free of blame.

"But those times are over. Discovering the real threat from outer space, Earthlings have to unite more than ever to face the invaders who are already occupying the major cities of our planet without any opposition.

"Fortunately, there are not too many of these Polarians. We have to take advantage of this to... exterminate them without delay and wait for the help that will surely be coming from our friends the Denebians and Pro..."

"That's murder!" Kariven shouted, boiling with rage, jumping out of his seat and imitated right away by the veterans of the Alliance.

The President of the USA furrowed his brow, shocked by the untimely and quite improper interruption. He banged his mallet on the desk to demand silence.

President Koulski raised his hand and his voice at the same time. "I understand Mr. Kariven's reaction and his faithful friends. But I ask them for a few more minutes of their attention in order to see the incontrovertible proof that opened my own eyes."

He made a sign to the two Russians and the lights went out. The film was projected on the panoramic screen at the back of the room, followed by comments that produced murmurs of rage and indignation at the hateful treatment inflicted on the Earthlings, Denebians and Procyonians by the Polarian "frauds".

When the lights came back on President Koulski turned to Kariven and his companions and asked, "Well, gentlemen, are you convinced now?"

"Less than ever!" the anthropologist stood up again to take the floor. "I claim, on behalf of my comrades present here, the pioneers of the Earth-Polarian Alliance, that this film is fake and they were never taken prisoner by the Polarians. At most it's a pretty clumsy fiction we owe to the Denebians. The proof? The first shot shows the camp normally. It's taken from the ground and looks like any other landscape filmed in a straight line along the horizon. In this case the Polarian capital in the background should logically be along a horizontal line from the camp. But this is not the case. Although the camp was filmed horizontally, the city was filmed *at an angle!*

"And you should've understand why. It's easy to see that the Denebians could not film the capital calmly from the ground. They had to do it with a powerful zoom lens from high up in the air on board their spaceships or maybe even from outer space thanks to a space viewer. That's why the camp, *which is actually their own*, is seen horizontally and the city at an angle."

"And how do you explain the treatment inflicted on the prisoners by the Polarian guards?" the President of the USA asked.

"That's also staged, Mr. President," Kariven shot back. "The Denebians made their Earthling and Polarian captives unconscious and submitted them to their mechano-psychic machine to make them follow their orders. A few Denebians and Procyonian allies played the role of prisoners, along with the real ones, suffering the punishments of the so-called Polarian guards. "

"That sounds like some crazy fantasy," the President shrugged.

"Just like flying saucers until the day of contact," Commander Taylor said quite rightly. "Can we deny today that eminent scientists thought the sightings of these machines was pure folly and didn't hesitate to accuse the people who saw them on the ground or in the sky as lunatics?"

"*Errare humanum est*[41]," President Koulski philosophized.

"Exactly!" Kariven cut in. "All of you, gentlemen, are making the same mistake right now by trusting the film and story of these men… *under the psychic control of the Denebians*, the green monsters whom my friends and I have fought and who are no doubt watching us right now thanks to their space viewers. Hiding in the cosmic void they are following our debate and happy to see that their ploy hasn't been found out by you, the Rulers of this world.

"I guarantee that you can believe in the existence of these Denebian psychic machines. They paralyze the will of whoever is influenced and the Denebians have psychic control over them. They can make them say and do anything to deceive the brothers of their unconscious victims. My compan-

---

[41] To err is human. (Author's Note)

ions and I can guarantee this because our Polarian friends have the same machines."

All the members of the Alliance confirmed the statement of their French chief.

"But," Koulski spoke with a strange glint in his eye, "if you admit that the Polarians have a similar invention, then we're right to wonder if you members of the Alliance aren't right now *under the psychic control of the Polarians!*"

"Craft bringeth nothing home," the President of the USA cited, shouting an order immediately afterward, "Arrest these men!" Turning to Kariven and the other members of the Alliance he said, "I'm sorry it came to this, gentlemen, but finding it impossible to prove either your involuntary guilt or your sincerity, we have to protect ourselves against any possible rebellion. You will be put in prison but not as criminals. You will be well treated and as soon as the situation clears up and the first contact with the Denebians and Procyonians is made, you'll be released and given a psychic examination by the Denebian neurologists. They will know how to get out of your subconscious the psychic orders imprinted by your filthy masters, the Polarians whom we were too quick to trust."

"This is the most pathetic mistake in human history!" Kariven shouted, struggling in the hands of the FBI agents taking him away.

The last words that he and his arrested friends heard before leaving the room struck them with horror:

"Now, gentlemen, we have to have a plan of action to take any means whatsoever to destroy the foothold that the Polarians have established on our planet."

It had been two days since the crews of the Polarian spaceships in every capital of the world, after finishing their duties, were enjoying some well-earned free time. They were supposed to return to their ships the next morning at six and were using their time well.

Some, in response to invitations from Earthlings of all kinds and from all social classes, were spending the evening with a native family. Others, more eclectic, were visiting museums and research centers that were left open during the night for them. Others again, attracted by the beauty of Earth women, left behind the relics in the museum to devote their time to pretty girls. In couples, happy and carefree, they went to the movies, the theater, nightclubs and thus mingled intimately with the terrestrial way of life, experiencing some of their amusements with a courteous smile behind which lurked funny thoughts about the immature performances on screen and stage.

The Polarian co-pilots and radar technicians, ravishing in their shiny or phosphorescent bodysuits, appreciated the company of Earthlings who were, in their turn, won over by their charms and simplicity. Romances were born in all countries with these beings who were both sympathetic to the backwards terrestrial civilization and also ready to help their "descendants". And this sometimes caused envy in the men or women who, given the small number of Polarians, could not get over their weaknesses. But everyone, for the most part, got along well and no obvious hostility was shown.

Things suddenly happened with unexpected quickness, without any sign to give the slightest hint of a suspected attack.

In every capital in the world where the Polarians had landed, the Assault Divisions with hand-to-hand combat specialists carried out swift attacks. The combined operations took place simultaneously, at the same time in every place.

Breaking into movie theaters, nightclubs, houses, anywhere Polarian men and women were found with their new Earthling friends, the Assault Divisions set upon the enemy. Tear gas was used in the theaters to overcome the Polarians who had suddenly understood the cause of the attack thanks to their paroptic vision.

Everyone who tried to flee, not daring to use their disintegrator weapons and thus sparing the lives of the Earthlings, was struck down shamefully. Nor did the Polarian women escape the revolting carnage. Earthling men belonging to the

Alliance tried to interfere for their trustworthy friends from outer space but they suffered the same fate and were either arrested or killed.

Of the 7,000 Polarians staying on Earth, more than 4,000 were slaughtered and the others, when they surrendered or managed to be taken, were shot with knock-out gas from a safe distance. The masked men of the Assault Division brought them immediately to the closest prisons where medication kept them unconscious. All telepathic communication with their fellow Polarians flying in the atmosphere or in space was cut off.

Zimko, who had to delay his return to Earth for more than 15 hours because of a battle between his squadron and some enemy ships on the outskirts of Vesta, was now heading toward our planet.

All of a sudden he stiffened up at the commands of his Fimn'has. His face tensed, his eyes staring forward, he was getting a bunch of psychic messages, some clear, others weirdly blurry like fadings in radio signals. At his side Tlyka felt the same thing and had the same problem "reading" the confused messages from their brothers on Earth.

The Earthlings are attacking us! they heard, stunned.

Other snippets, more and more unclear, wormed their way in, like some inaudible chant, causing interference in their hearing.

We're surrounded... impossible to use our disintegrators without causing terrible damage to the people around us... The Denebians convinced the Earthlings... Now we're enemies of Earth... The Earthlings think we're smearing Denebians by calling them enemies... They were able... that we're the real conquerors of Earth.

Soon complete messages, clear and precise, came to them from the few crew members who got back to their ships and into space. In a minute Zimko and Tlyka knew all about the disaster.

"The idiots!" the Man from Outer Space was furious.

216

"Those poor people, you should say," Tlyka corrected him gently. "They don't know what they're getting themselves into by acting like this. All alone the Earthlings will be easy prey for the Denebians, who have fooled them by making us the lying conquerors pretending to be their allies."

"That's the sad truth," Zimko agreed. "It's too late now to explain it to them. If we land again the maniacs will slaughter us… even though we could easily get the better of them without the slightest risk to us. If only they'd waited before killing everyone. It would have been so simple to accuse us openly. We could have tried to justify… despite the diabolical ploy the Denebians had played so masterfully. Even if we'd invited the governments to send investigators to Kodha to see that there are absolutely no prison camps holding Earthlings, they wouldn't have believed it and would have categorically refused to 'throw themselves to the lions'."

"What can we do in this no-win situation?"

"First of all free the members of the Alliance who remained loyal to us and of course free our imprisoned brothers."

One hour later a squadron of 1,000 disc-shaped spaceships surrounded the Earth under Zimko's command. A cold determination was etched on his face and his distress racked his throat. He had received no psychic message from his sister Yuln and his paroptic vision had quickly shown him the reason for this unusual silence.

Yuln, Jenny and Doniatchka had been the first to be arrested right before they started the "witch hunt," which had left thousands of Polarian men and women lying dead. Now drugged with the other Polarians and the Earthlings of the Alliance who had fallen into the hands of the Assault Division, they were sleeping, unconscious in a prison, locked up together in the same cell. Tommy, the son of Yuln and Kariven, had been given into the care of a governmental institution where he would be well treated but living far from his parents, with the other children from members of the Alliance killed or in prison.

All this Zimko had just found out. A flood of rage reddened his face.

At 600 miles altitude the spaceships split up, their crews instructed with specific orders. And all the ships at zero hour were hovering at a fixed point over the cities holding the prisoners. Then they fired a torrent of paralyzing rays over the cities.

Fifteen minutes later the spaceships landed, some in airports, some in empty lots if they were big enough. Most of them, however, landed in big public squares.

The Polarians walked among the people frozen in all positions in the streets, sometimes at their windows or leaving a building, store or bar. They marched toward the prisons where they knew they would find who they were looking for in order to save them from the injustice of their brothers blinded by the enemy trick.

The vehicles, cars, motorcycles, buses and trains stopped by the gravito-magnetic rays, cluttered the streets with their passengers frozen in bizarre positions.

All the capitals on Earth looked like weird and wonderful wax museums.

The Polarians easily opened the prison doors and took away their own kind along with the Earthlings of the Alliance on stretchers, frozen as they were. The families of the Earthling allies, locked up in different institutions, were also recovered.

An astonishing spectacle of men from outer space carrying away their loyal friends, paralyzed but conscious. Through the city streets sunk in graveyard silence their procession walked without even looking at the people changed into more or less ridiculous statues.

This bus stopped just as it was taking off, with all the passengers leaning backward from the acceleration, and this girl with one foot on the bottom step, the other in the air, clinging to the bars on the rear platform; these two men ten feet away running after it—all this looked like a hallucination or the effect of a magic wand wielded by some evil, terrifying fairy.

After two hours all the surviving Polarians and Alliance members were on board the Fimn'has that were taking off over the big cities. At 200 miles altitude the Polarians watching their screens waited for life to return to the paralyzed. At the expected time the vehicles started up, rolled a few feet, then stopped right away as their drivers regained consciousness. Nervous and dazed they jumped out and called out to each other asking what had just happened to them. Those who had seen the Polarian patrols bringing out the stretchers despite their paralysis came up with all kinds of far-fetched ideas.

Once the paralyzing effects were gone Zimko gave orders to his squadron to head for the Martian base. "And now," he grumbled, "the Earthlings are going to reap their bitter fruits! They couldn't trust us and act in good faith. Lured in by the so-called help of the Denebians, they're going to be slaves. *The Earth is now at the mercy of the monstrous green monsters from Deneb!*"

CHAPTER VII

In accord with a treaty signed by all the heads of state meeting in Washington 48 hours after the unspeakable aggression against the Polarians and Alliance members, the United States of the World had just been created.

In an underground department of the Pentagon where the eminent personalities were assembled, the President of the USA—unanimously elected for seven years to the post of the President of the United States of the World—stood up. The TV and film cameras were trained on his energetic face that was etched with fatigue from the exhausting work of the past few days. His graying hair cut short, a wrinkle of worry on his forehead, he addressed the assembly of the first session of the USW in the following words:

"Gentlemen, thanks to the swift action and timely alert of the Russian Head of State, our nations, finally united, was able to thwart the evil plans of the Polarians. However, as events are quickly proving to us, we underestimated their power and remarkable organization.

"In fact, these pseudo-men, a few hours after the masterfully planned operations sped out of earth's orbit and headed into outer space. The Denebians, therefore, attacked their relentless enemies... and chased them out of our zone, which is pretty good in itself. But now we have to fear that these pseudo-men will try to come back on the offensive to take over Earth.

"Still, and this is our only hope, I think the Denebians won't give them time to do it."

"Our Russian friend and ally," the Canadian President said, "might be right to hope for this. Our base in Shirley

Bay[42] has spent two days following the frequent flights of discs that are quite different from the Polarian Fimn'has. A film taken by two of our spectro-telescopic cameras[43] have indeed shown the presence of discs at a very high altitude whose undersides are completely smooth. Now, you will remember that the Polarian ships had three big landing spheres.

"Gentlemen," the President of the USW spoke again, "let's not get out hopes up. But let's get ready, no matter what happens, to welcome our generous, future defenders with open arms. The Denebians and Procyonians, although they are different from humans and almost became our enemies, have been more open than the pseudo-men from the Pole Star. They did not create secret organizations on Earth to infiltrate the people and later come out as allies. No, quite the contrary, they have always remained in the shadows, probably afraid that looking like 'monsters' to us would make us hostile.

"If we are lucky enough to welcome them to our planet, we must make sure to show our good intentions by treating them like humans and not like circus freaks. Christian charity makes it our duty…"

Forty million miles away, in the domed Polarian base on Mars in the heart of the Hellas desert, another assembly was gathered. Nearly 300 Earthling men and women, loyal members of the Earth-Polarian Alliance, were together in a huge room shaped like a horseshoe and with a lighted ceiling. On the back wall, 65 feet high and twice as wide, was a giant screen of transparent material. With remarkable clarity it was

---

[42] Giant observatory and laboratory for the study of flying saucers created in Canada in August 1954. It took two years to build and set up. (Author's Note)

[43] A camera that reacts automatically to the magnetic field of flying saucers to take pictures when they pass by. With the optical system is coupled a spectrograph that analyzes the ship's light. It is a camera specifically designed to observe flying saucers. (Author's Note)

now showing the USW meeting held in Washington DC. The Heads of State surely had no idea that their so-called enemies, the Men from Outer Space, were watching their every move and listening to every word.

When the President of the USW gave his final remarks, Zimko turned it off and the space viewer screen clouded over while the ceiling brightened its blue light.

All the Earthlings had taken off their terrestrial clothes and put on the one- or two-piece bodysuits in Polarian fashion, which was much more practical and rational than many of our ridiculously outdated clothes.

Since their arrival on the Martian base the men and women were getting regenerative and rejuvenating treatments whose positive effects they were starting to feel. One Earth month from now, the Polarian biochemists had assured them, those of them who were over 30 would be back to their younger strength, energy and physiques! Soon, thanks to the marvelous science of the Men from Space, the Earth colony would only have young couples. And they would see this strange thing: parents as young as their children! Because there were some couples who were 50 or 60 years-old, physicists, engineers and scientists with their families, of all nationalities and ages, veterans of the Alliance who joined the organization soon after Kariven and his friends.

The latter were sitting on both sides of Zimko under the big screen, watching their compatriots who were listening carefully to their chief, their beloved chief to whom they owed their freedom and their wonderful new lease on life and longevity.

"Earth friends, my loyal companions of the Alliance," Zimko began, raising his right hand in fraternal greeting, "the screen just showed us the instability of your fellow man, always ready to tear down tomorrow what they build today and to hate what they do not understand.

"Maybe we were wrong despite our wisdom and goodwill, to present ourselves to them as caring, selfless older siblings. Violence breeds violence, as they say on Earth. It's a beastly aphorism but, alas, it still applies. Maybe we should have landed in force and taken over the governments to guide the civilization and condemn humanity to happiness. Later it would see us as brothers and not as conquering enemies. But we didn't do this and our first contact has been shattered.

"With their savage aggression, with the slaughter of thousands of your and our fellow beings, loyal friends of the Alliance, the Earthlings have once again become fratricidal. We could, with no problem, overcome them and punish them for their iniquitous crimes, but this would only strengthen their blind hatred of us, a hatred being cleverly manipulated by the Denebians. Besides, a heroic return to Earth would only support the idea that the Earthlings have of us now: super-evolved pseudo-men set on conquering their planet.

"Therefore, we are forced to abandon men to their fate. The future alone will dictate our behavior. You, my Brothers of the Alliance, who have all grieved the loss of a dear one at the murderous hands of your compatriots or who have suffered under their stupidity, you all should understand me."

Weeping, gasping and shouting in terror, two ten-year old boys and a seven-year old girl were hurtling down the side of the hill. One of them tripped on a rock and dragged the others down with his fall. They jumped up right away and without looking back the boys grabbed the girl's hands and continued their mad dash, choking on pure panic and fear that nothing could assuage.

Red in the face, sweating bullets, their hearts beating a mile a minute, they reached Dompierre-sur-Yon, a small town in Vendée, where they ran screaming into the little church, the first refuge they saw on entering town.

On this warm, summer afternoon the church was deserted and echoed eerily with their sobbing. All three, literally drained by their frantic run, staggered behind the altar and collapsed.

Alerted by the unusual noise a priest came out of the sacristy and following the sobs found the three children huddled together, trembling convulsively and unable to control themselves.

"But... what... but," the priest stammered, "well, what's going on? You're Jean-Marie Bonnet, right?" he asked one of the boys, the short, blond, freckle-faced kid hugging his sister in a gesture of heartbreaking protection.

He nodded repeatedly, sniffling.

"And you, Dominique, can you tell me what's so scary that you burst into our quiet church? I hope it's not a fight with some bullies," he squatted down and tussled the hair of young Dominique. By Saint Peter!" he let slip out, "Jacqueline's fainted!"

He took the limp little body and with the two boys right behind he almost ran into the rectory, calling out, "Noemie! Noemie! Quickly, call Dr. Chabert!"

The old servant rushed to the door at the end of the small garden next to the church, drying her hands on her blue apron, and after straightening her glasses cried out on seeing the priest running toward her and carrying her own daughter in his arms, "Good God! What happened?"

"Don't know," he priest panted. "Call Chabert, quick!"

While the old servant went off trembling the priest put the girl on an old couch. He filled a glass with some quinquina[44] and used a spoon to force a little of the liquid between her lips. After two or three tries he managed to get her to gulp some down.

When Dr. Chabert, a 30-year old man in shirt sleeves, showed up carrying a leather case, the girl was coming around.

"Well, well," he smiled at the priest, "if the doctor of souls is competing with the doctor of bodies, I'm going to retire. The child is perfectly healthy," he said after examining her. "She fainted out of fear apparently. Her brother and their friend held out but I think they had a terrible fright."

---

[44] An aromatized wine, a variety of apéritif wine.

"But of what? They've been crying for 15 minutes and can't seem to calm down."

One of the boys managed to speak in a shaky voice, "We saw the Devil, Father!'

The priest furrowed his brow, cleared his throat, and said, "Come now, come now, children, don't speak nonsense. The Devil doesn't have the habit of meeting up with people personally. They're corrupted enough not to need him to reap what they sow in their life... May God forgive me this impious statement."

"How about it, Jean-Marie," Chabert suggested, "why don't you tell us everything, starting from the beginning? Why did Jacqueline faint? What did you see that was so scary?"

"The Devil, Dr. Chabert, the Devil! We saw him like we're seeing you, right in front of us, in the woods by Charette."

"Yeah," little Jacqueline squeaked, still getting over her fright. "Even he was all green..."

"With no horns," the younger boy said. "With big red eyes."

"Not red, black," Jacqueline corrected.

"Red and black with yellow stripes," Jean-Marie described.

"And no tail..."

"Skin like a big lizard," Jacqueline shivered.

"And claws and a crest like a rooster with..."

"Just a moment," the priest broke in, trying to piece together this "Devil" from the anatomical fragments that the three children were throwing out at the same time.

"You said that..." The sound of a crowd quickly approaching the church interrupted the doctor's question.

Shouts, cries and stamping feet came closer now. The priest and doctor looked at each other and without a word they hurried to the garden door. When they got there they saw a group of country folk with a few children running fast with a village police officer at the head. Red-faced and scared to death he saluted them as he ran by.

"My word, it looks like they really did see the Devil in person!"

An old woman, well behind in the stunning, staggering race, her hand clutched to her heart, stopped and swayed before falling down in front of the two men who rushed to help her.

Exhausted, in a quivering voice, she whined, "Caint be in this day and age! Big as this," she sat on the roadside and waved her bony hands to picture something very tall without realizing that her hands were only a foot off the ground. "Like a toad! With warts or mebbe scales! And those eyes! Red and yellow!"

"Come on, Mrs. Martin," the priest advised. "Catch your breath and get a hold of yourself. What did you see and where was it?"

"Was only one at first, then two others came out of the woods around Charette. We were in the fields when *they* come out. We were scared, imagine! And then we ran when they got closer."

She had trouble getting up, even with the help of the priest and doctor, and new wave of terror made her shiver. With wild eyes and shaking hands she started panting and struggling to get free of the men helping her. "Lemme go! They following us! They gonna come here!"

She crossed herself and broke free. She scurried away leaving the priest and doctor dumbfounded.

"First the kids and now the farmers. Simple folk but not crazy. It must be a collective hallucination," the priest reasoned. And grabbing the doctor's arm. "Are you scared of the Devil, Chabert?"

The doctor, surprised by the odd question, shrugged his shoulders. "I'm a doctor and absolutely logical, as you've complained to me often enough."

"Right," the priest smiled. "You won't hesitate to come with me, then. Let's get a drink first."

The other nodded and in the rectory kitchen they drank a big glass of Noah wine, which they love in Vendée.

226

"It's still strange, this general fear," the doctor thought out loud. "There's certainly some natural cause but strong enough to have completely addled these good people... who aren't cowards."

Putting down his glass the village priest glanced over at a rifle hanging on the wall. The doctor saw him hesitating and with a forced smile, staring at the rifle, said, "Maybe it'd be wiser, right?"

With a nod from the priest he grabbed the rifle, put a box of cartridges in his bag and joked, "This exorcism defense will back up your *vade retro, Satanas!*[45]"

Right behind him the priest spoke to his servant giving buttered toast to the three children who were still shaken up. "Noemie, go to the police and tell the sergeant that we're off on a 'Devil hunt' in the woods around Charette. If the they want to join in, they'll know where to find us."

"Cowards! That's what you are!" Sergeant Mathieu shouted at the ten farmers recounting their adventure. "You're not children, by God, who run away from bad jokes! Because you can't make me believe in the stories of the Devil and such nonsense! We'll go over there and I guarantee you that the three kids who threw the fear of God in you are going to be in big trouble!'

After speaking all this common sense Sergeant Mathieu jumped on his bicycle and with his three deputies went bravely on the offensive, rifle slung over his shoulder.

Dr. Chabert and the priest stood petrified with horror, paralyzed by a nameless fear, completely still, unable to move a finger. 100 yards away up the road, three nightmarish creatures around six and a half feet tall, looking vaguely human but with their bodies covered in horny scales, were slowly walking in their direction. Their oval heads were softer, topped by a fleshy growth that bobbled a little as they walked.

---

[45] Get thee behind me, Satan!

Their dark red eyes stripped with thin bands of yellow were staring straight at them.

The priest clutched his crucifix and mumbled, "*Vade... retro... Satanas!*"

The doctor's throat went dry and his stomach suddenly contracted. He lifted his rifle with his finger on the trigger, ready to fire. He whispered, "These... monsters are like the things the government is expecting to come. But are they really them?"

An unsettling event quickly gave them the answer. One of the three Denebians (since it really was these monsters whose cunning matched their thirst for power) raised his arm and in a hoarse, cavernous voice, and *in French*, said, "We are your friends, Earthlings! See... we have no weapons and are trusting in your wisdom not to attack us."

He was still walking forward although his two companions stopped. He stopped only when he was less than two feet from the barrel of the gun aimed at his sparkling green chest by Dr. Chabert whose forehead was streaming with sweat.

Holding out his arms, the crucifix at the level of the monster's face, the priest could not say a word. Horrified, he stared at the repulsive creature—half-man, half-lizard—who just turned his attention to the cross.

Looking long and hard at the crucifix the Denebian finally growled, "Isn't this a symbol of one of your divinities?"

Both surprised by his knowledge of the religion and shocked by the polytheistic idea, the priest forced himself to speak. "We have only one God and this symbol is that of His Son Jesus..."

"Have I offended you by my mistake?" the creature asked shyly, expertly playing his role of humiliated guest.

Caught off guard by this rather troubling question the priest lowered his arms. "No... No, not at all. The Son of our God, among many other sacred truths, teaches us to forgive those who offend us. But this isn't the case since you just don't know."

The Denebian was honestly pleased. This first contact with these "ugly white creatures" was unfolding under the best conditions.

At the moment that Dr. Chabert was about to lower his rifle, a gunshot was heard and startled him. The Denebian jerked, brought his clawed hand up to his shoulder and wobbled, twisting the two drooping folds that were his lips.

The two men turned around and saw the three policemen jumping off their bikes, the sergeant in the lead, still holding up his smoking gun.

"Stop!" the priest shouted, jumping between the police and the two unharmed Denebians who had just dropped to the ground. "You fool, what have you done!"

Dr. Chabert's vocabulary was much less bookish, "Jackasses!" he yelled, looking worriedly at the fallen monster with a bullet in its shoulder.

"But they..." the sergeant stammered, dazed and turned pale with fright and disgust before these monstrous creatures. "I... We thought they were attacking you."

"They're Denebians. Certainly frightening creatures to look at but their feelings toward us are pure," the priest explained, chatting away as he knelt next to the wounded.

Cautiously and keeping their weapons in hand, the policemen came forward. The two other Denebians also came up to their companion and examined him thoroughly.

The wounded creature slowly turned his head to the priest and in a weird, gravelly voice that could make anyone shiver, he said, "This... this little accident mustn't affect the relations that we are counting on establishing between our races." Lowering his big, red, yellow-striped eyes to the crucifix that the priest had put back in his belt, he added, "We don't worship the same God but ours also teaches us to pardon," he lied again. "The Earthling who wounded me certainly had good intentions. He must have thought you were in danger..."

Moved by the great wisdom of this "poor creature," looking from the police to the doctor, the priest said, "What a grand soul! What good and wonderful beings! If only Earth-lings could have a soul as charitable as theirs one day!"

Stupid white monsters, the Denebian thought, whose scaly carapace was only scraped by the bullet. *With ideas like that, we'll be able to conquer them before they even know it! And when they become aware of our true intentions, they won't be able to do anything about it!*

CHAPTER VIII

Less than five hours after this incident, special editions announced the good news to the world. In huge capitals all the newspaper headlines spread the sensational information:

A DENEBIAN FLYING SAUCER LANDS IN A VILLAGE IN VENDEE! THREE PILOTS—GREEN SCALY CREA-TURES TWO METERS TALL—SPREAD PANIC AMONG THE PEOPLE.

A PRIEST AND A DOCTOR ESTABLISH FIRST CON-TACT WITH THE PEACEFUL BEINGS COME TO HELP EARTHLINGS!

More discreet than the deceitful, Men from Outer Space, and so much more human despite their troubling appearance, the Denebians have sent three ambassadors to Earth (see pho-to below sent by special wirephoto).

After a moving description of the contact and the acci-dent that ensued, the reporter launched into a poetic-realist flight to sing the praises of these *"wise ambassadors of an extra-terrestrial people whose altruism toward our race is constantly verified."*

The journalist concluded, *"There's no doubt that this first contact will be the prelude to a closer collaboration be-tween our two races; a prelude that foresees huge benefits for our civilization that, safe from a sneaky Polarian attack, will be able to take huge steps forward with the selfless aide of the good Denebian scientists."*

In an emergency meeting in Paris at the old UN Palace, now the French Department of the USW, the awestruck heads of state were watching the three green creatures from Deneb sitting in the place of honor in front of the President's seat.

231

In spite of all efforts made to consider these ambassadors as "brothers" and allies, the VIPs could not help feeling an uncontrollable disgust in their presence. Before these glistening, green, scaly creatures with red eyes, a shiver ran down their spines. From the depths of their being an insurmountable fear rose up, one of those latent fears in every individual, a subconscious relic of ancestral terrors.

If the heads of state reacted like this, what reactions would the people have to these creatures when they started crowding the streets of cities and towns? For, the day was coming since these beings were offering their help and protection. And there was no question—without hurting them deeply—of asking them not to show themselves in public.

The President of the USW, no less uncomfortable than his illustrious colleagues, was making visible efforts to smile kindly at the Denebians. But did they even understand the meaning of a smile?

"Excellencies," he began his address to the "two-legged lizard" ambassadors. "I am extremely happy to welcome you to our planet in the name of the United States of the World. It is with the utmost sorrow that I learned about the unfortunate accident that befell one of your Excellencies. I can assure you that the guilty party of this regrettable attack will suffer the severest penalties…"

M'nag, the Denebian commander specialized in hand-to-hand combat, the bitter enemy of Zimko, playing the bighearted ambassador here, stood up and bowed melodramatically. "I would thank the President of the USW not to be too hard on the Earthling who wounded me. It was an accident. Your brother only did it because he thought the two other Earthlings were in danger. Our desire is to establish friendly and lasting relations with your race. We would be sorry to start off with a disciplinary punishment because of us. Would you do us the favor of pardoning this Earthling for his nervousness and his mistake?"

The President bowed in turn, "We are deeply moved by these honorable sentiments. I will make sure to grant your wish and see to it that the man who dared to shoot at Your Excellency will not be punished.

Then turning to the assembly he continued:

"Gentlemen, our civilization will obviously be proud to ally with people whose ambassadors show such wisdom. The Denebians, as their Excellencies explained to me, have learned several of our languages thanks to the mechano-psychic devices similar to those the Polarians used to spy on us. But where the latter got the collaboration of some Earthlings to assuage our fears and manipulate our imaginations to their favor, the people of Deneb don't use such tricks. They didn't use flashy publicity and in poor taste to announce the arrival of their representatives. No, only three ambassadors were sent to our planet, landing timidly near a village in France, Dompierre-sur-Yon, which will become famous for this historic encounter. This discretion immediately won us over. His Excellency M'nag and his Plenipotentiary Ministers R'zog and T'gonk, who presented their credentials translated from Denebian into French, English, Russian and Spanish, are now going to state the offer of their government."

The President of the USW bowed and invited "His Excellency" M'nag to take the floor.

The Denebian stood up, towering over the frightened Earthlings watching him. Where the bullet had grazed his shoulder was a kind of greenish swelling covered with a clear, anti-septic film. He and his partners were dressed only in a kind of underpants resembling leather with a wide, very thick belt. Around his scaly neck hung a triangular metal plate. Incomprehensible signs were engraved on it in red characters that shined brightly even in broad daylight or under the artificial light.

His hoarse voice boomed forth, making his attentive listeners automatically shiver. "His Majesty K'Wyil II, Emperor of the Omink Solar System called Deneb by Earthlings, Beloved Master of the Seven Solar Protectorates, is very happy to present to the President of the USW, to his brothers and the people, the assurance of his deep feelings of Cosmic Love."

You could not say that this pompous, grandiloquent greeting was welcomed cheerfully by the heads of state. But they forced themselves not to reveal their thoughts about these ambassadors full of goodwill but with a very eccentric vocabulary. No doubt these grandiose words were allowed if not encouraged in Denebian diplomacy.

"Through our unworthy mouths His Majesty K'Wyil II informs the Earthlings of his intention to offer help and protection against any attempted invasion by the Demons from Outer Space called Polarians on your planet.

"If the Earthlings do us the great honor of accepting our selfless offer, we will report their agreement to our Venerated Master who will immediately order our freedom squadrons to surround Earth. Then our ships will land on the day, time and place of your choosing to set up a strong defensive network on your planet without delay.

"Posts of magnetic detection will be spread over the globe to create a veritable net of protection that no enemy spaceship will be able to slip through without automatically setting off a flood of disintegrating missiles that will destroy it down to the last atom.

"If the Earthlings don't want our help and refuse our offers of protection, we will do nothing to force them to accept our presence on their soil, staying faithful to our policy of non intervention if it's considered undesirable. Then we will just set up, with their permission, a simple observation base orbiting 600 miles above Earth. This will allow us to detect any approaching enemy squadron and fend off any attempt to enslave them.

"Thus, President and you Heads of State, without forcing our presence on you—for, we know how much our appearance shocks you—we will still protect you. We will only ask of you in exchange to tolerate a Denebian embassy of ten people in one of your capitals."

Turning now to the President of the USW in particular he said, "Do you think you can give us an immediate answer to one of these offers or would you rather meet in private to deliberate before telling us you decision?"

Charmed by the deferential tone of this being who was so different from humans… and by the purity of his offers, the President told the assembly, "Gentlemen, it is up to us to decide. All who want a discussion here and now raise your hands."

Almost everyone raised their hands without a second of hesitation. Only three heads of state did not move: the representative from France, England and Israel. Finally, France and Israel agreed as well.

"Gentlemen, an almost unanimous decision has been made," the President of the USW observed. "I declare the discussion open to give an immediate answer to Their Excellencies M'nag, R'zog, and T'gonk of the Denebian Empire. Two possibilities lie before us. First, to welcome an expeditionary corps to our planet to build our defense. Second, to simply give the right to this corps to set up a space base orbiting our planet with the creation of an embassy on the ground with only ten people in it. All those in favor of the first option raise your…"

A loud explosion shook the floor and shattered most of the windows of the United Nations of the World Palace.

The President's question remained unfinished and a wave of anxiety washed over the assembly. In the commotion that followed the inexplicable explosion, His Excellency M'nag raised his thundering voice above the shouting:

"I ask the President to let me leave immediately for a few moments. I believe that the auto-defense system on our spaceship has just been set off by an enemy ship!"

"I… Please," the President acquiesced in his distress.

M'nag stood up and ran out, leaving his Plenipotentiary Ministers with the Earthlings. His green body glimmered eerily when he crossed the sun-washed courtyard. When he got to the central path looking over the flowerbeds of the Trocadero, M'nag stopped. An expression of complete satisfaction twisted his face—a grimace that an Earthling could not interpret.

The Denebian spaceship sitting in the middle of the esplanade was shooting purple beams into the sky from the top of its dome. A crowd of curious onlookers was running up and gathering at the foot of the Eiffel Tower into which a 50-foot wide flying saucer had crashed.

Everything is going just fine, the green monster snickered to himself. *It couldn't get better than this. I will make sure to make a rave report to our Emperor and suggest X'hug get a promotion. He guided this captured Polarian ship into this ridiculous metal structure at the perfect time,* he thought as he sneered at the Eiffel Tower.

He went back to the heads of state who were huddled together on the front steps of the Palace and returned to the assembly room with them.

"Just as I thought, our defense system reacted to the presence of an enemy spaceship. As it came in it caused our automatic detector not to fire our disintegrator missiles so as to protect this magnificent capital from devastation. And we acted rightly. But our explosive missiles still struck it down. Being full of Sh'lang explosives, however, it caused some damage when it crashed. I'm sorry but this is nothing compared to the destruction it could have caused if it had time to drop its atomic payload on your city."

In an emotionally charged voice the President declared, "We are infinitely indebted to you, Excellencies, for having the foresight to turn on the automatic detectors on your ship. Without this wise precaution we can be sure that this meeting would have ended in a massacre. Without a doubt these Demons from Space wanted to bomb our assembly where they could kill your Excellencies along with all the heads of state on Earth.

"This vile aggression proves to us, if there were further need, the Polarian wickedness and the urgency of an agreement between your people and ours. Personally I recommend an immediate agreement and ask you, my Earth brothers to accept the first offer of our generous defenders. Namely: authorization for the Denebians to set up a strong defense system covering the surface of the globe as soon as possible."

Before the President even put the question to a vote, in an assembly that was now completely unanimous, the heads of state raised their hands in acceptance.

"Gentlemen, I thank you for your enthusiasm in accepting this necessity. Before long we will get the security that will allow our civilization to progress on the paths of knowledge and peace. Will we ever be able to return the enormous benefits that we owe to our brave defenders?"

M'nag bowed ceremoniously, "We were sure that you'd come to an agreement with the intelligent and sympathetic race that we are. I leave it to you, Mr. President, to fix the date and location that you want for our first defense installations as well as for the establishment of our permanent base."

"I propose we welcome the first squadrons in two Earth days at eight o'clock, local time, in the following capital cities to start with: Paris, Washington DC, Moscow and Sydney. After that, depending on how fast the Denebians can set up their defense system, the spaceships can land in the other capitals to cover the whole Earth as soon as possible with an effective detection network."

"With your permission, Mr. President, we will take your wise decision back to His Majesty K'Wyil II."

"But," one head of state objected, "during your trip our planet will be vulnerable to a sudden Polarian attack."

"Rest assured, Earth Allies," M'nag responded, "we won't be gone for more than three of your hours because we don't need to go back to Omynk, our solar system. A simple trip to our secret base on an asteroid between the orbits of your Mars and Jupiter is all we need. We will give the order to our first squadrons to get ready to come to Earth at the appointed time."

"Won't you be spotted going back to your base? The Polarians must be patrolling our system non-stop."

"Have no fear, Mr. President. A very long time ago we perfected an invisibility shield that is even better than the one

237

used by our enemies. Whenever we judge it necessary, our ships become invisible and undetectable even to the space radar of the Demons from Space!"

In his HQ on the Martian base, Zimko was talking with his friends Kariven, Dormoy, Angelvin, Commander Taylor, Professor Harrington, the physicist Kurt Streiler and Lieutenant Rudy Clark. They were watching in dread as the viewer showed them the meeting taking place on Earth between the heads of state and three Denebians.

"The blasted lizards are wasting no time!" the Man from Outer Space said worriedly. "And things are happening much faster than I thought."

"It's obvious," Kariven pointed out, "that the set-up of the so-called attacking spaceship, struck down just in time over Paris, made a strong impression on the heads of state. With this new ploy the Denebians forced them to make a reckless decision for them to come to Earth immediately. The lunatics don't understand that the so-called detector network, far from protecting the Earthlings, will help enslave them!"

"We still have one strong point," Zimko said. "The monsters are convinced that their invisibility shield is invulnerable. And we've done our best to let them believe that our detectors and space radar can't spot them. Therefore, they're right to imagine that, being invisible, their spaceships pass unnoticed. We still have time to prove the opposite to them."

The Man from Outer Space looked at his space-watch and saw the small, green screen showing the different time zones on Earth.

"So, M'nag's ship will leave Earth for three hours. That might sound short by it's still enough for us to try something to 'limit the damages', as you say, when things go sour on your planet. I need ten volunteers for a pretty dangerous mission, I have to admit. Are you…"

"When do you leave?" the six men asked at the same time.

"I was sure that you'd accept even before knowing the nature of the mission. And if it fails, it will mean our death. I'll ask for four other volunteers…"

A smile suddenly crossed his lips.

"Yuln, naturally, read me telepathically. She and her friends Jenny and Doniatchka are threatening to join the Denebians if we don't take them with us."

The joke cracked them up.

"I think that in their place I would do the same thing," Kariven smiled. "Plus, Jenny, Doniatchka and Yuln have proven themselves for a long time. For my part, I accept them on our mission."

Everyone agreed. Zimko was about to agree as well but a wave of confused thoughts battered his mind. He projected his paroptic vision across the base and did his best to find the psychic source. Again he smiled and stared at Clark, the young Air Force officer who had participated in several dangerous missions years ago along with his friends and Kariven.

"Lieutenant Clark," Zimko said, amused by his embarrassment and his obvious desire to ask something. "Do you, too, agree to bring with us a certain Polarian girl with the charming name of Bentya?"

The lieutenant could not help blushing and he had to clear his throat before answering. "That's… I… If you think it's possible."

"But of course it's possible. Bentya's just sent me a telepathic ultimatum."

Becoming serious again Zimko continued, "Earth friends, we have two hours and 45 minutes to prepare ourselves and get to Earth. Tlyka, Yuln, Jenny, Doniatchka and Bentya are already at the Biosthetic Center. Let's get there right away… to powder our noses."

Surprised by this idea, absurd to say the least, they got up and followed their friend and chief.

It was hard for Kariven to open his eyes. It seemed to him that the skin on his face was stretched tight. His nose, especially, bothered him. It was not really painful, just uncomfortable. When he propped himself up on an elbow, he suddenly realized that he was lying on a metal table. From the ceiling was hanging a kind of transparent mold, swaying five feet above his head. This mold had the shape of a human face. Clear tubes of different colors as well as a bunch of electrodes stuck inside the face of this mask were connected to an articulated, telescopic arm.

"Hello, *Jeff*."

Kariven jumped and swung his head to the sound of the voice. 13 feet to his left a gorgeous young brunette in an emerald green two-piece was smiling at him, sitting up on a similar table under a similar machine.

"He... Hello," he stammered, astounded to find himself with this beautiful stranger in a strange place.

Then his memory suddenly came back. He got up and ran into the arms of the young woman who kissed him passionately.

"Yuln, my love! I mean *Myriam*, my love! You... You're as lovely in your new artificial face as you usually look."

"You're not so bad yourself, *Jeff*," she smiled and pointed at the mirror on the wall. "Our biosthetic machines have made us new people."

"And the psycho-tracers have given us new personalities without wiping out our memories. It's incredible!'

"No acquaintance on Earth will ever be able to recognize you. And that goes double for the Denebians."

In the cabin of the spaceship piloted by Zimko, Kariven, his friends and their companions were joking about their new faces, which they were enjoying enormously. It is a weird feeling to know one is a different person than before.

Yuln, Jenny, Doniatchka, Tlyka and Bentya (the young "conquest" of the handsome Lieutenant Clark) were truly divine. Their exquisitely pure features, their eyes and smile literally fascinated their companions. And extraordinary, absolutely irresistible magnetism emanated from them, which scared them a little bit. Wouldn't they break the hearts of the Earthmen they met on the streets of Paris? Because it was in Paris that the Space Commando team was going to operate.

The Denebians—as Zimko's new psychic inspection of M'nag's mind had informed him—were in fact going to set up their planetary HQ in this city.

"New Style" Jenny looked again at her husband and smiled tenderly. When he touched her hand he felt an unpleasant tingling and immediately drew back. Surprised and hurt by this incomprehensible revulsion she stared at him, her big blue eyes suddenly full of sadness.

Dressed like his friends in a perfectly tailored, "terrestrial" suit Zimko at the commands of his Fimn'has was watching on, worriedly, at the different reactions and confused thoughts of the passengers.

"My friends," he declared, "I can easily imagine the trouble you're having because I didn't tell you everything about the treatment you got. Besides changing your features, it also changed your psycho-physical faculties. From now on all your actions will have to be carefully controlled by your mind in order not to disturb those around you. Let me explain.

"To protect you and to give you the same psycho-physical weapons that we Polarians have, we changed your neuro-circuitry, especially the intracortical neurons that preside over the psychic functions and the metabolism. You now possess the extra senses and faculties that you admire in us. They're only starting to wake up. Jenny, a little more receptive, felt something weird. But an hour from now you'll all be able to read the thoughts of others, see through matter, follow several different currents of thought at the same time—and all this while talking. Finally, just by concentrating you can cast a stream of lethal electrocuting waves on at least two human or Denebian subjects. This will be useful to you. But you will obviously have to control your thought actions. Bob, in fact, just by touching his wife's hand, felt an unpleasant tingling. Jenny is an excellent experimental subject. She reacted quickly to the treatment. However, in a short time, you will all be able to control yourselves and by shaking someone's hand you won't have to worry about electrocuting them."

"I understand all this, Zimko," Yuln spoke up. "But I don't fully understand this... strong sensual effect that we provoke without trying at all. This is new, even for me, a Polarian, who already has the paranormal sense unknown to Earthlings."

Zimko smiled, deliberately not thinking about the reason for his unusual seductive ability to keep it from his sister and his friends whose telepathic sense was awakening.

"The purpose for this psycho-seductive magnetism will be revealed in good time. But rest assured, Yuln, and you too my friends, you will soon be able to control this new ability. What you don't seem to see is that your husbands also have this power. They won't become aware of it until later, in around five or six hours. Personally, I still don't feel the effects. Have you set your watches to French time?" he asked, looking at his "Swiss" timepiece... specially made in Kodha. "It's 8:32 pm."

Then Zimko checked the screens on his control panel to make sure the Fimn'has was absorbing the radar waves and staying undetected.

Tlyka, no longer brunette but blonde and her face had lost its tan, checked the functioning of the invisibility field around the ship.

"In 15 minutes," Zimko announced, "it will be dark and we can set down on the Saint Cloud racetrack... where we are expected."

Totally invisible, the spaceship landed on the racetrack, avoiding the grass where the landing gear would leave obvious traces. The night was calm. A breeze wafted in the polyphonic concert of frogs and crickets.

With its lights turned off the unseen platform came slowly out of the disc. Its passengers looked like they appeared above the ground, legs first, by magic. They jumped silently onto the hard dirt holding their breath. A useless precaution since the racetrack was deserted. But not completely because 20 yards away, just as spectacularly, another pilot appeared out of a second invisible spaceship. He was dressed in a dark suit and carried a leather briefcase.

Raising his right hand he saluted the newcomers and handed Zimko the briefcase. "Here's your passports and ID cards. The amount you asked for is divided into 10,000 Francs and $1,100. You'll find the two cars, a blue and white Versailles and a dark red Ford, parked down the road about half a mile from here."

"Thanks, Shongo," the Man from Outer Space smiled. "You can take our Fimn'has. We'll make do with the cars. Has the squadron arrived?"

"The last formation just landed in Agharti." He smiled and added, "You can't even park a car on the astrodrome. The last 1,000 ships couldn't land and have to keep their gravito-magnetic field on to hover over the underground base. They got there around ten minutes ago. The Denebians will be landing on Earth soon. But everything's ready. The situation is in your hands now. Good luck!"

He walked off, climbed onto the invisible platform, spotting it thanks to his paroptic vision, and disappeared into the spaceship. Silently and undetected, it rose up and sped off to Agharti, the secret Polarian base inside a tall mountain in Tibet.

"Let's go get our new cars," Zimko proposed. "We'll be staying in three different hotels, close to each other so we can stay in permanent psychic contact. I'll give you your passports, IDs and divvy up the money that you'll need to live in France or maybe travel abroad. Because there's no way I can put it in your bank accounts since you're not yourselves.

"From now on we can only rely on ourselves. The Denebians are going to swarm the Earth. We won't even be able to trust the Earthlings.

"Tonight we'll rest. We need it and starting tomorrow we'll start in on our secret battle…"

CHAPTER IX

The population of the world had heard about the decision of the USW council with a mixture of hope and anxiety. Hope because the threat of invasion that the Polarians (those evil Men from Outer Space) presented was now being stopped. Anxiety because people felt revolted and disgusted by these green monsters from the stars, in spite of the kindness they were showing to humans.

A week ago the Denebians had started setting up their detector network in every country. From one place to another across the continents the metal frameworks of giant towers stood tall. At the top was a slowly turning satellite dish pointed at the sky, sending out a fan of orange rays every three seconds.

Every city where the Denebian squadrons had set up was full of feverish activity. Some Earthlings forced themselves to fight against their disgust, the real horror that these frightening "two-legged" lizards caused every time they met them on the streets.

"If," they told themselves, "these creatures are hideous to us, the inverse must also be true. We Earthlings must look just as nauseating in the eyes of the Denebians. But they don't show their feelings about us at all. Does this come from their high degree of evolution? Do they look on us as simply a different but normal form of life or do they hide their repulsion better than us—out of kindness?"

In fact, only a minority of Earthlings reasoned like this. Most of them could not overcome their instinctive horror.

When the Polarians arrived their Earthling counterparts felt spontaneously attracted by them; everyone wanted to make friends with a Man or Woman from Outer Space. It was not the same with the Denebians. Far from it.

When someone strolling down the street saw one of the green creatures coming toward him, he did not hesitate to change sidewalks to avoid rubbing shoulders with the repugnant "friend."

Several times already in concert halls and even dance clubs where these beings naïvely entered, there were scenes bordering on panic. And every time, without saying a word, without even looking hurt—but obviously suffering inside—the Denebians left.

The Earthlings clearly felt in them—at least they interpreted their behavior thus—a profound desire to get along, to mingle with human society, to participate in its good times, its fun times and to be closer.

The Freedom Squadrons had brought with them many female Denebian "assistants." A little smaller than their male counterparts but with their bodies similar to Earth women these creatures were dressed in a very short, skirt made up material that looked like gold leather. Without any shame whatsoever they showed their scaly skin for all to see—a lighter sea-green than the opposite sex.

Their slanting red eyes with a yellow stripe sometimes stared hard at an Earthling male. Faced with this awful caricature of a woman with her scaly breasts shamelessly exposed, the man would shiver with disgust. Turning his back on the Female—as the Earthlings started calling the Denebian women—he hurried away, remembering the unpleasant feeling of those huge red eyes staring at him stubbornly.

It did not take long for the Earth women to see that they, too, became a physical object of scrutiny that often went beyond what was proper. A rumor gradually formed in Paris that girls and young women had been followed by Denebians. This kind of thing was, of course, not uncommon among humans, but it was easy for a woman to put a man in his place with a few choice words or even a slap, which proved more difficult with these green creatures.

Strange, disturbing stories, if the narrator was to be believed, started making the rounds.

Men had even been followed by Females. They would have to run away when they found themselves in a deserted

245

street at night and a Female's boots pounded the pavement faster as they caught up to the man they were following.

So far, however, nothing really bad had happened to either sex. Denebian men and women were content to follow humans and let their attitude suggest an intention that went beyond the norms of propriety.

News came one morning, exactly 18 days after the last chain in the "protective network" was installed over the face of the globe. In all the countries on Earth, after an Earth-Denebian meeting, the heads of state addressed their people. Radio, TV and newspapers published their surprising declarations. Some papers did not hesitate to call the speeches "a miserable disgrace to the human race," or "intolerable and immoral conspiracies".

"After three weeks of contact with our Denebian friends and allies," the official statements said, "we are sorry to say that no real connection has taken place between the Earthlings and Denebians on an individual basis. In whatever public place our guests show up, they face the same cold and reserved attitude, when they are not simply left alone in a place (bar, theater, club, etc.) quickly deserted by the Earthlings.

"Such anti-social behavior has to stop. We owe much gratitude to these beings from another planet, different from us for sure but like us they have a heart able to love even those who avoid them.

"We owe it to them to show more understanding, more kindness, even affection. It is clear that we will not understand or love the Denebian race until we have given up this ridiculous idea of considering them monsters or freaks. We have the proof that on one of their protectorates planets, humanoids (therefore identical to us Earthlings) have not only accepted their benefactors but even mated with them for generations. From their mutual affection a hybrid race was formed, strong and powerful, producing beings that are obviously different from the two parent races but whose appearance is not shocking.

"We ourselves recently visited a city on the planet X'naog where Denebians, humanoids and their hybrid races live in harmony.

"Thanks to the remarkable work of Denebian biologists and geneticists on histology and chromosomes, such racial mixes are now possible. Nothing now is preventing our races from creating a new race together, a mixed race, Terrodenebian that will consolidate our two peoples and seal our union in a powerful and lasting way.

"Moreover, such a project is under consideration. We would like to see it undertaken. And so it is with great joy that we welcome volunteers, of both sexes, to participate in this marvelous experiment.

"We hope that our call will be answered. The mayors in Paris and in all big cities, the medical schools, hospitals and Biology departments of the CNRS[46] will accept and advise the volunteers who, if they want, will be guaranteed anonymity."

"It's sickening, despicable," Kariven barked, throwing the paper down in a rage. "Our heads of state must have gone mad to publish such obscenities."

"No, Kariven," Zimko sighed, shaking his head. "They aren't crazy... *They've just fallen under the psychic domination of the Denebians!*"

This revelation troubled Kariven, his wife and their friends meeting at the Ritz in Zimko's luxurious apartment.

"And you think that even one Earthling will go along with this disgraceful 'crossbreeding'?" Doniatchka snapped, suddenly surprised that neither she nor her friends could hear Zimko's thoughts.

He had, in fact, just raised a psychic barrier to block all telepathic inspection of his mind. "Not only do I think so," he responded, "but I know so."

"If I ever met a man or woman who debased themselves in this filthy project, I'd demolish them!" Lieutenant Clark

---

[46] French National Center for Scientific Research.

threatened as he put his arm around the waist of beautiful Bentya.

"Oh, no, Clark, you won't do that," Zimko smiled enigmatically.

"And why not?"

"Because then you'll have to 'demolish,' as you say, everyone in this room, starting with yourself."

"What?" the officer gasped, looking around at his stunned friends.

"The time has come to explain to you why we're all endowed with almost supernatural psycho-seductive magnetism."

The others looked at each other, trying to understand what he meant.

"The superhuman charm making us specimens of incomparable beauty and irresistibly seductive *is why we're going to be volunteers for this experiment.*"

Raising his hand for silence—because everyone started protesting at this repugnant idea—Zimko continued, "But rest assured, we'll have no need to finish out the exper..."

"Zimko!" his younger sister shouted. "You just let an idea slip out that contradicts your assurance."

"I got it too!" Jenny confessed. "You said we'll have no need to finish out the experiment, but in your mind you added, *at least I hope not.*"

"Please," Zimko was embarrassed. "All of us here have faced danger many times. This danger is no worse than what we've seen before. It is there and I think it's normal to recognize it. I wasn't trying to hide anything from you. So, we're going to go as volunteers to this experiment they euphemistically call 'hybridization'. But since we're the only 'Earthlings' to be blessed with superhuman beauty, backed up by an irresistible psycho-seductive faculty, we can be sure we won't be selected for a few lowly pilots or officers but rather... for the members of the Supreme General Staff."

"Or for Emperor K'Wyil II himself and his entourage?" Yuln insinuated.

"Why not, little sister? If we're clever and make the right moves, we can hope for anything."

"Now I finally understand what our electrocuting power is for," Jenny mumbled, thoughtful and determined to enter this mockery of an experiment.

"Could we at least have a little time before," Yuln squeezed her husband's hand.

"We should and we will," Zimko insisted. "We're not starting on this today. We have to wait a little while so that the Earthlings finally recognize the monumental mistake they made in murdering our kin and welcoming these green monsters."

Eight more days passed and not a single woman or man had made the "commitment" to volunteer for the unnatural experiment. On the contrary, Earth men and women stopped going out at night. The streets of the cities where the Denebians were staying became deserted at sundown.

Sometimes the tenants of a building were startled awake by cries of terror that were quickly muffled under a gag. Whoever dared to take a peek out their window or even on the landing, said they saw a Denebian rushing down the stairs carrying the slumped body of a young woman. Another time there were two hideous Females who were dragging a man in their strong, clawed hands as he struggled in vain and more and more feebly, obviously drugged after a surprise attack.

Some witnesses, bold enough to intervene, were lashed by the sharp claws of the filthy creatures. On several occasions men fired guns at the abductors, leaving their victims at death's door and the corpses of the "Liberators of Earth" on the sidewalk.

Few newspapers mentioned these infamous abductions. It was as if a gag order was given to radio, TV and the press because such news was never reported.

The people were finally starting to doubt the good intentions of the Denebians. Public opinion started shifting, first in different neighborhoods. Anger was rumbling, ready to explode. But the Earthlings, not knowing that these abductions were happening everywhere on the planet, did not know how to react. They thought that maybe they really were isolated cases only in their own city, with only a few delinquent Denebians to be held responsible like in all races.

Earthlings would have panicked if they had known that tens of thousands of men and women had mysteriously disappeared since the arrival of the "two-legged lizards."

But an official statement from the Council of the USW, broadcast in every country, soon threw the whole world into confusion.

"No volunteer for the Hybridization experiment has yet come forward, so it has been decided in the last USW assembly that subjects of both sexes will be chosen officially. We remind everyone of the fact that this experiment, whose importance everyone should recognize, bears absolutely no danger.

"While regretting the need to apply the Law of Improving Social and Cultural Exchange, which was voted in this morning, we condemn the anti-social behavior of the xenophobes who shock our Denebian friends and allies by refusing to associate freely with the representatives of their race.

"We remind you again that the volunteers, if they come forward—and despite the law—will be treated well and free to decide. They will not be forced in any way and can choose as they want. The Denebian authorities will be honored to consecrate voluntary marriages, for Earth men or women, with the Denebian subjects of their choice. The first 100 volunteers will even get a voyage offered by His Very Powerful Majesty K'Wyil II, who will do us the great honor of coming in five days to visit our planet, the new protectorate of the Denebian Empire."

Around noon, after this stupefying news had thrown the people into turmoil, Denebian patrols were posted outside the factories around Paris. Armed with thermal ray guns, ten monsters were lined up on either side of the exit door. At first intrigued, then more and more worried, the workers hurried out with their heads lowered, trying to avoid the prying eyes of the two-legged lizards.

Choosing young men and women on sight the Denebians would grab someone and lead them directly to a police car parked nearby. At the wheel of the car was an officer who kept his eyes forward, apparently oblivious to what was happening.

A young female worker, kidnapped in front of her fiancé, whose arm she was holding, started screaming and struggling. A scuffle ensued. The men, letting their bicycles or mopeds drop to the ground, jumped bravely into the fray. The poor men were soon writhing in agony, their bodies burned by the thermal rays shot mercilessly by the green monsters.

News of these horrible kidnappings, in spite of the silence in the papers, spread like wildfire through all the capitals where they took place.

It was said that the Denebians, not being immediately accepted by the Earthlings, were forcing them to create a hybrid race of half-man, half-lizard monsters. To do this (they whispered) they were kidnapping young people. After two or three generations of intensive crossbreeding, the pure human race will practically disappear and be replaced by the "hybrids," totally devoted to their masters from Deneb who will raise and indoctrinate them!

But in Paris, just like in London, Washington and Moscow, the Polarians and Earthlings of both sexes, loyal to the Alliance—with their bodies transformed by a special treatment in the Polarian planetary bases—were starting to show up at the Terro-Denebian authorities as "volunteers."

They were welcomed with open arms by the representatives of the Ministry of Racial Exchange, recently formed in the main terrestrial capitals.

This rush of "volunteers" coincided with the arrival of Emperor K'Wyil II and his entourage on Earth. The Denebians concluded a little too hastily that the Earthlings were attracted by the promise of a magnificent voyage in their solar system offered by the Emperor himself to the first 100 candidates.

The Emperor, his ministers and the marshals of the Free-dom Forces set up in the Palace of the USW in Paris to honor the country where the first contact had been made.

A big party followed by a ball—since this kind of festivi-ty seemed to please the Earthlings—was scheduled for that night. The heads of state were invited to show the people that the governmental machines of the two races were still getting along excellently.

When night fell, in the brightly lit Palace decorated for the occasion and after Earthling and Denebian appetizers had been served, the ball commenced.

An impressive line of green monsters armed with ther-mal rifles surrounded the Palace.

Emperor K'Wyil II, a hideous creature over seven feet tall, glistening green, with hard, scarlet eyes, had insisted on inviting the first 100 volunteers who were ready to submit to the hybridization experiment.

Thirty Females from Denebian "high society" were also there at the diplomatic ball. Arrogant, with her busty, scaly chests stuck out, one of them—a favorite of the Emperor it was said—stared unashamedly at an Earthling "volunteer" as handsome as Apollo.

The man held her gaze and even tried to smile. The or-chestra was playing a slow song and staring straight at the awful creature the man walked up to her. He bowed respect-fully and asked, "Although I am just a wretched Earthling, may I have the honor to invite Your Splendor to dance?"

In a cavernous voice the Denebian growled something and literally threw herself into his arms.

You could not say that Zimko was jumping with joy—because it was he who had invited the Female to dance—but the foul, oily contact with this creature was part of his plan.

While dancing and whispering flattering nonsense to his monstrous maiden, he cast his paroptic vision around to keep an eye on the talents and tactics of the other "volunteers". His sister Yuln, radiating beauty, was dancing now with the Emperor himself. Kariven, Dormoy and Angelvin were dancing with "aristocratic" Females.

As for Commander Taylor and Lieutenant Clark, they looked like they were enjoying the company of two other Denebian Females.

Zimko smiled inside. Although treacherous and shrewd these monsters from Deneb were not very skilled in human psychology. To believe that these volunteers, men and women, were consumed by love for them was the most ridiculous thing in the world!

He changed the range of his paroptic vision, tuned it to his telepathic waves and saw the feverish activity in Agharti, the secret Polarian base thousands of miles away in Tibet. His psychic introspection was disturbed by a guttural shout from the Emperor. He was standing in the middle of the room holding Yuln by the shoulders, his claws resting on her blue spangled bodice, crying out a second time, very short, which was a sign of great joy among the Denebians.

"Earth Friends!" he announced in his voice from beyond the grave. "I would like to introduce to you Myriam, a volunteer who has the honor of becoming my Servant!"

Becoming the "Servant" of a Denebian was a conventional term meaning "to become his concubine"! Although the Earthlings were ignorant of this linguistic subtlety, Yuln and Zimko knew about it.

K'Wyil shoved the Polarian onto the dance floor and stepped back, growling, "Dance! Dance, Myriam! Tonight will be our wedding night!"

Humiliated, red and confused, Yuln caught her balance and stood there embarrassed by everyone looking at her.

Dance, little sister, she heard in her mind. *We need to gain more time at all costs.*

That night, pathetic scenes played out in the big cities of Europe and Russia. At the same time in the USA, obeying the Emperor's orders, the Denebians committed the worst abuses.

New space squadrons kept arriving and hundreds of thousands of men and women were abducted, others burned for trying to interfere or revolt.

A general order, come from who knows where, granted free rein to all Denebians, including the officers in the detection posts. Besides saying that the Denebian HQ temporarily established in Paris had the situation under control, the order gave the members of the Liberating Space Forces, as a reward for their hard work and courage, the authority to choose a Servant. As a result the detection stations sometimes went more than five hours without personnel.

The Denebian Females enjoyed the same freedom and ran through the streets in groups or alone wherever they were stationed.

The terrorized Earthlings were living in agony. Some people committed suicide, preferring death to surrendering to the lewd, demoniacal creatures.

In this reign of terror and horror, every man and woman thought desperately about the horrible mistake humans had made in slaughtering the Polarians!

Emperor K'Wyil II had his scarlet eyes fixed on the Earthling girl whom he had brutally forced to dance for him. The yellow stripes in his slanted eyes started quivering with lust. Then he made a sign and some Denebians rushed at her.

All the other green monsters, as well as the Females, jumped on their volunteers. The heads of state, ministers and other Earthlings under the psychic control of the extra-terrestrial brutes, did nothing before this orgiastic storm.

Suddenly, the pseudo-volunteers received the telepathic order, *Do it! Time's up!*

The shouts and commotion stopped as if by magic. The Denebians men and women stumbled away from their dance partners who were tensing all their muscles in a violent effort of will that straightway unleashed a powerful electrocuting energy on the filthy creatures.

Wheezing and panting like wild animals in a cage, Emperor K'Wyil II and his high dignitaries and aristocratic Females collapsed, their bodies jerking in pain. After a moment they lay motionless, struck down.

In three giant bounds Zimko jumped into the next room. He tore open a kind of closet and flipped a bunch of switches, which plunged the Palace in darkness.

Let's meet on the upper terrace, he ordered telepathically, running to the monumental staircase.

Easily moving through the darkness thanks to their paroptic vision, everyone was in the meeting place a few minutes later.

Out of breath, Yuln dropped into her husband's arms. "What an awful experience, Jean!"

"It's over, my love. The rumble of revolt is spreading all over the world and the Denebians are going to find out how stupid it was to abandon their posts for the sake of debauchery."

Zimko was scrutinizing the starry sky, not with his eyes but with his super-normal vision. "Our squadrons are all over Earth," he announced to his friends.

Endowed with the same ability now the others saw in their mind, like on a panoramic screen, thousands of disc-shaped spaceships. In formations of 50 Fimn'has, the Polarian ships split up, heading for the capitals and big cities around the world.

"In ten minutes," Zimko noted, "a squadron will be flying over Paris."

A rush of air blew over the huge, flat roof of the Palace of the USW. Everyone looked up and to their great surprise, even though there seemed to be no cause, the stars were no longer visible!

Tune your paroptic vision, Zimko ordered psychically.

Astonished, they saw the dark shape of a reconnaissance spaceship. Invisible, hovering between them and the stars, it darkened the sky.

As the platform came slowly down from the Fimn'has, six Denebians rushed onto the terrace at the same time as the lights flooded the area again. Surprised to see this group of Earthlings on the roof, the monsters brought their thermal guns up to their hips, ready to fire.

Zimko and his friends dropped to the ground and threw out a violent electric discharge at the intruders. Two of them fired—too high—but one second later they all collapsed, growling in pain. Curled up on the ground, they died, electrocuted.

Zimko and his friends ran at full speed to the spaceship, jumped on the platform and hugged one another. In a few seconds they were safe inside the ship, which took off, staying invisible until the squadron of 50 Fimn'has arrived in Paris.

With a victory smile on his lips Zimko gave a general telepathic order to all the squadrons around the Earth:

Immediately fire paralyzing rays on the cities where you've picked up the "volunteers". Intensity 19! Go!

After one minute, in all the urban centers where the monsters from Deneb had got hold, life stopped. Earthlings and Denebians were frozen in place together.

"Land!" Zimko ordered. "Operation Clean-Up!"

In tight formation the Polarian flying saucers landed and unloaded the fighters of the Space Commandos. Meanwhile, Zimko's ship headed for the stars.

The Commandos in groups of ten Polarians, broke into the detection posts around the globe and systematically disintegrated the machines. In every location the paralyzed Denebian invaders were brought to the spaceships that took them straight to the Gobi Desert. A huge metal sphere, more than half a mile in diameter, had been dropped there, partly buried in the vast stretch of wind-swept sand.

Flying saucers were landing non-stop around this extraordinary, shiny sphere. Once their cargo of monsters was unloaded, they left again, leaving the paralyzed brutes to other Polarians who piled them onto a kind of moving walkway that spiraled around the sphere and poured them into an opening at the top.

In less than four hours all the Denebians who had brought terror to the Earth were prisoners in this sphere. Then the Polarian crews left the sphere to itself. The gigantic machine slowly started glowing green, illuminating the desert with a ghostly light. It vibrated for a few seconds then shot straight up into outer space.

The faint light of dawn chased away the night from the Paris skies. The effects of the paralyzing rays were finished. Able to move, the Parisians hugged one another in fear, anxiously asking what had just happened.

Was it a new torture by the Denebians? What had they invented to hurt and humiliate the Earthlings?

Some people dared to go outside. Reassured by the calm in the city they joined other neighbors and friends and wandered through the streets that were slowly waking up. Soon a group of men and women, disheveled and in pajamas and bathrobes, came running down Avenue Gabriel, shouting at the top of their lungs.

"They've come back! They're here in the Place de la Concorde! Come on everyone! We're saved!"

Intrigued by the commotion people started looking out their windows, stumbling down into the street, wavering between fear and hope—a mad hope, they thought—and walking toward the place. In less than an hour the Place de la Concorde was chock full of Parisians from all corners of the capital.

A squadron of ten flying saucers, shining like aluminum in the sunlight, was surrounding the obelisk. The cockpit of one of the spaceships slid open, revealing Zimko, Kariven, Yuln, Dormoy, Angelvin and their wives. One after another all the Fimn'has cockpits were open with the Earthlings who had remained loyal to the end to the Earth-Polarian Alliance.

In the Place de la Concorde and in the streets around it, tens of thousands of onlookers shouted for joy. They had recognized the particular form of the Polarian spaceships and were waiting impatiently for their crews to appear.

Zimko and his friends, dressed in uniforms now—blue and dark red bodysuits—looked around at the huge crowd come to greet them. With a big smile Zimko saluted the crowd by raising his right hand.

He brought a microphone to his mouth and in a deep, warm voice, declared, "Earth Friends, the Polarians and their loyal companions of the Alliance salute you! We forgive you for the massacre of our brothers and sisters because you were fooled by the Denebian trickery. You were wrong, however, to blindly accept the so-called revelations of these power-hungry, bloodthirsty monsters. Their goal in blackening us with crimes was only to remove your suspicions... which you hadn't even shown.

"These hideous green creatures were about to destroy your race by debasing it with their own. This would have created a new race of unbelievable ferocity that would have wiped out the last humans and replaced them with their masters all over the planet.

"The frightening adventure is over. The Denebians, the monsters you put up with for so long, have been defeated. In their thirst for conquest and domination they sowed bloody death in seven solar systems. We can no longer let them continue their abominable crimes.

"Therefore, two hours ago a giant sphere in which the criminals are imprisoned left Earth. The guided spaceship is almost entirely built of negative matter[47]. Emitting a strong, repellent magnetic field, no weapon will be able to destroy it. Right now it is entering the Omynk solar system, the Denebian Empire. In a little while, near the planet Ptopa, the seat of the abhorrent green race, its outer walls of neutral matter will fall away and leave open the inner sphere of negative matter. When it gets close enough to the 'positive' planet Ptopa, the negative matter will undergo an atomic transformation and in

---

[47] See *Space Commandos*.

an apocalyptic explosion of cosmic energy it will wipe out Ptopa and the race of green monsters!"

The crowd broke out in a loud ovation. Zimko raise his hand asking for silence and continued:

"Freeing the seven solar systems enslaved by the Denebian mercenary colonists will only take a few days. The freed races will finally be able to enjoy the fruits of liberty and benefit from our aide.

"Earth, likewise freed and finally united, will see an era of joy and love. The specter of war, planetary or interstellar, is banished forever. We Polarians have educated, helped and protected countless races in solar systems all over the Galaxy. Now we're going to devote our efforts to help humans who are our close relatives since they're descended from the first Polarians who came into this solar system a long time ago. You will enjoy the immense benefits of our civilization. Your ills and your suffering, moral and physical, will be eased thanks to our biological and neurological sciences. The constant imbalance that still exists on your planet between technical, moral and spiritual evolution will disappear, bringing men into a righteous stage where he will understand the machine in ways that have so far been wanting.

"This will not happen overnight but clear progress will be seen even before the end of this year. Around ten years from now we hope to see humans out of their rut. Then they will race down the path to Wisdom and Love, the two inseparable qualities that should unite all thinking peoples in the Galaxy.

"A huge task lies before us, Earth Friends. I'm sure that our sister races are finally going to experience the serenity and happiness that God created them for.

"The Time of trials and tribulations is over.

"A new dawn is rising for your civilization…

"Peace on Earth and good will to men!"

Prisonniers du Passé

JIMMY GUIEU

★

★ANTICIPATION★

Editions
"Fleuve Noir"

PRISONERS OF THE PAST

CHAPTER ONE

The B47 quadjet ionocruiser that was carrying the Inter-national Research Commission appointed by the GCSR [48] had taken off from Tokyo at 10:30 am local time for Nagasaki.

Because August 9, 1961, was exactly 16 years after the destruction of Nagasaki by the second American bomb, the UN and the GCSR were sending out a multi-national team of researchers. For 15 days they would carry out a systematic study of the city and its surroundings, its natural resources and its population, which would result in, like every year, a census of the survivors affected by the radiation and a meticulous examination of their bodies in order to detect any possible cellular degeneration.

These specialized researchers were going to devote themselves to the study of humans (on the physiological, psy-chological and cultural level), animals, plants, raw materials and the soil formerly submitted to radiation.

On board the ionocruiser and under the leadership of Professor Saigo Kato, a world famous Japanese teratologist, were sitting Dr. Jean Kariven, anthropologist; Michel Dormoy, geophysicist; Robert Angelvin, an ethnographer rep-resenting French Science; Professor Red Harrington, mathe-matician and chair of applied physics at the California Institute of Technology; and Kurt Streiler, physicist and electronics expert representing the USA.

---

[48] Global Center of Scientific Research.

The Russian delegation was made up of Professors Serge Yegov, atomic physicist and head of the facilities in Atomgrad, and Colonel Zavkom, biologist and ex-colonel of the Soviet Air Force.

England had sent John Shelley, a specialist in cosmic rays; Italy, Dr. Renato Tagliero, nutritional biologist; Brazil, Ricardo Alves, Nobel Prize winner in chemistry.

In a world finally united, thanks to the generous intervention of the Polarians, the Men from Outer Space who came from the solar system of the Pole Star, these international specialists were going to cooperate in a peaceful goal to improve the lot of the Japanese survivors.

Sitting comfortably in their plastex seats, the scientific delegates were chatting amiably. Zavkom, in plain clothes, his blond hair cut short, offered a long cigarette with a gold filter to his friend Kariven, sitting on his right. While pulling the cigarette out he followed the eyes of his neighbor that were staring out the window at the sky, which was rapidly turning gray.

"I have the feeling that the summer monsoon is preparing a nasty day for us," Zavkom mumbled in English.

"That's weird," the anthropologist responded. "The sky is turning gray, but there's no clouds in sight."

This observation caught the attention of Dormoy and Shelley, sitting behind them.

"Maybe a mass of volcanic dust is blocking the sun at a high altitude?" the geophysicist wondered.

"This is nothing compared with the darkness of our London fog," the Englishman smiled. "In the streets you can't see anything. Anyway, we're landing in... Look at that, my watch stopped! What time do you have, Dormoy?"

He slid up the double cuff of his shirt to look at his watch and smiled back, "Bad luck, Shelley, my watch has stopped too. You have the time, Kariven?" he leaned forward.

"Sure," the Frenchman turned around. "It's... Damn, my watch stopped at 10:30, the time we took off."

"Get this! My watch is also stopped at 10:30!" Zavkom was puzzled.

In the double row to their left the delegates looked at their watches and then at each other in surprise.

"Santa Madonna!" Tagliero exclaimed comically, speaking in English but rolling his Rs, "It's a trick! Out watches all stopped working at 10:30!"

Indeed, he spoke the truth. The delegates' watches were all showing 10:30.

Kariven stood up, went to knock at the cockpit door and asked the stewardess, "Can you tell me the time, Miss Robson?"

"Of course, Dr. Kariven," she raised his wrist. "Oh, I'm sorry. I'll have to ask the pilot because…"

"I think there's no need. His watch and the instrument panel probably stopped on takeoff. Could you check?"

A minute later the charming stewardess came back a little pale. "I don't understand it at all. The clocks and watches all stopped at 10:30."

"Where are we right now."

"We're flying over Usuki Kyushu. Landing in ten minutes in Nagasaki."

Kariven went back to his seat pensively. He turned around and asked, "Mike, what do you think of all our watches suddenly stopping at the same time on board the plane?"

"Our watches reacted as if they'd been put near a powerful source of magnetic energy. And yet that's not the case. Even if we were flying over a mountain of magnetite, at our altitude this shouldn't have happened. I can't see any… rational cause for the sudden freeze."

Kariven went back to the cockpit to listen to the radioman communicate with the Nagasaki airport.

"ZHIB3, special ionocruiser from the GCSR, Tokyo Division, calling Nagasaki…"

A lilting voice in Japanese came out of the speaker but the radioman, who did not understand the language, just repeated his call in English. In the cabin the passengers were starting to get nervous. Dr. Saigo Kato stood up, adjusted his glasses and slipped into the cockpit. "Allow me," he bowed to the operator who gave him the microphone.

He repeated the call in Japanese and added, "On board this airplane are American, French, English, Russian, Italian and Brazilian experts. Why didn't you answer in English? We want to land. Can you tell us what runway…"

The speaker echoed with a flood of words in Japanese, then angry, shrill shouting.

Saigo Kato opened his eyes wide and stared at the speaker. Then, losing his usual aloofness he bent over the pilot and spit out, "Captain Howard, change course and gain altitude immediately!"

"But I can't…"

"I beg you, Captain. Our safety is at stake!"

Seeing his frightened attitude the pilot understood that the unusual order must have serious reasons behind it. He veered off course, headed east and pushed his four jets to bring them almost vertical in a deafening whine.

Above the plane small white clouds suddenly appeared, breaking up abruptly to dissipate in the air.

"But… they're firing at us!" Kariven was alarmed. "Look at those anti-aircraft shells exploding under our plane!"

All of a sudden a bright light, infinitely brighter than the sun, lit up the misty sky five miles below them. A blinding, terrifying ball of light with ringed turbulence at the base, filled the southwest horizon off Kyushu. The orb of fire swelled up and spread out over a giant, pink-orange-purple corolla, rising up at dizzying speed to form a dome at the top, flashing with lightning.

All the passengers of the ionocruiser had instinctively closed their eyes or turned their heads.

Professor Yegov, with his hand over his eyes, in a strangled voice stammered, "It's unbelievable… an atomic bomb… just exploded in Nagasaki!"

Trying to control his trembling hand Dr. Kato brought the microphone up and repeated his calls, but in vain: the speakers remained stubbornly mute. The Japanese put the mic down gently and staggered back to the cabin where everyone was waiting anxiously for news.

"Nagasaki isn't answering…"

"That's weird," Kariven thought aloud. Then, "You look troubled, Dr. Kato, when you were talking with the control tower. Could I ask why?"

"Of course, Dr. Kariven. The control tower didn't understand English, which surprised me. When I explained to him that our plane, with international scientists on board, wanted to land, the operator started cursing me… and set off the anti-aircraft alarm that immediately tried to shoot down our plane."

"Are you sure that the order was given?" Zavkom frowned, finding it hard to believe.

"Should I remind my esteemed Russian colleague that I know my ancestral language perfectly well?"

Dormoy was fumbling open a leather case. He pulled out a scintillation counter and quickly turned it on. On the head of the machine, shaped like a huge pistol, a red light started blinking fast.

The geophysicist shouted, "Captain Howard, climb immediately to maximum altitude! We're in the middle of a radioactive zone!"

Without waiting for further explanations the pilot opened up the jets and shouted back, "Hold on!"

Standing in the middle of the cabin Dormoy did not have time to get back to his seat and lost his balance, falling against Dr. Alvez. The Brazilian chemist held him fast while the quadjets reached full speed, climbing vertically at 1,700 mph.

In record time it reached 40 miles altitude and in the ionosphere reduced its speed as it leveled off. Dormoy straightened up, grimaced and after making sure that his *scintillator* had survived his fall, he went back to his seat.

"Ah, we barely made it. Despite the anti-radiation protection in the cabin, the rays from the explosion got through the walls a little. Thank God the intensity of the radiation was dampened and too weak for us to have to worry about it. But that was a close one!"

"For God's sake," Tagliero thundered, "what happened? Is it really an atomic bomb? My eyes hurt and I swear I can still see that blinding mushroom cloud!"

"A strange coincidence," Kariven rubbed his eyes gently. "August 9, 1945, at 11:01 hours an atomic bomb exploded in Nagasaki. Today, August 9, 1961, sixteen years later, and around the same time, another atomic bomb explodes in the same city. The world, however, is not at war as far as I know."

"Enough to drive you nuts," Angelvin grumbled. "All the atomic and thermo-nuclear bombs on Earth have been confiscated by our friends the Polarians. So, no country could have launched one on Nagasaki. And even if one could, what would be the point, by God?"

"Note also that no laboratory working on nuclear weapons exists in Nagasaki," Kato reminded them. "A hypothetical accident is out of the question."

"And yet someone had to launch the damned bomb that blew up Nagasaki," Yegov the atomic physicist growled.

"Plus, why did the control tower in Nagasaki order the anti-aircraft missiles to shoot us down when all the nations of Earth are united now?"

Kato, obviously disturbed by this attack made over his country, sighed, "My poor mind can't explain this act of wicked violence against your honorable selves. I'm sorry, truly sorry, and I'll report it to the Ministry as soon as we arrive. I'll demand the responsible parties be punished."

"Don't worry, Kato," Professor Harrington consoled. "I can't explain this strange incident any more than you but you have no reason to doubt the friendship that unites the peoples of Earth today. I refuse to believe that it was a clear-cut attack. I propose we turn back to Tokyo where we can get some useful information."

"I don't see any other solution, given that our research program was just canceled by the destruction of Nagasaki."

Obeying Kaito's orders, the pilot set course for Tokyo. The plane started descending toward the East and came out of the ionosphere. The jets, after being quiet in the relative void at 100 miles altitude, started whistling. Then they howled and ended up wailing loudly, deafeningly in the lower atmosphere. All of a sudden the radioman furrowed his brow while scrutinizing the fluorescent radar. Six bright dots—radar blips or echoes—appeared, getting bigger and bigger at every swing of the line around the screen.

"According to the size of the blips," the operator told the chief pilot, "they're fighters. The idiots are heading straight at us at 300 mph! So they must not have radar to tell them that we're flying head on to meet them!"

"Nah! New recruits probably," Captain Howard said untroubled. "They're still 100 miles away and it won't be long before they spot us. Then they'll change course. But I'll still gain a little altitude… just to keep them from getting balled out by their instructors."

The maneuver was handled expertly and the ionocruiser went up from three to four miles altitude. The blips representing the six fighters disappeared from the radar but seven minutes later they reappeared on the edge of the screen, even bigger this time. Keeping his eye glued to the telescope, the co-pilot soon spotted the planes that he kept in the crosshairs of the scope.

"Captain! They're heading straight at us, literally!" the radioman announced.

The co-pilot was almost crushing his eye against the scope and swearing, "Damn! On the side of the planes I see the emblem of… the Mikado! The Emperor of Japan!"

"You're crazy! The Mikado in 1961! You're seeing things…"

A hail of machine gun bullets suddenly cracked against the plane's armor and one of them flew through the cockpit's Plexiglas but it did not hit any of the occupants.

"Get your masks on!" Howard ordered, making the plane climb at maximum speed into the ionosphere.

He put his oxygen mask over his nose, imitated by his men, while he activated the airtight closure separating the cockpit from the passenger compartment. The others were now isolated from the cabin that was losing pressure.

The quadjet was now at 85 miles altitude after easily losing the Japanese fighters. The radioman hurried to seal the bullet hole by applying a patch of Plexiglas with a machine that looked a little like an electric sander.

Then, turning the interior speakers on Captain Howard spoke to the passengers. "Gentlemen, although the incident did not last long, you must have realized that a bullet penetrated our cockpit... without hurting anyone. A quick repair has been made, bringing the pressure pretty much back to normal. However, just as a precaution we'll leave the safety hatch closed. Miss Robson, is everything okay?"

"We're a little shaken up but everyone's fine, Captain. Professor Harrington wants to talk to you."

The mathematician stepped up to the wall speaker. "Captain Howard. I just had a brief talk with Dr. Kato. Though we can't explain these... alarming incidents, we've decided not to head back to Tokyo but to get to the closest American base. Where is it?"

"I don't get it, Professor. What do you mean by the closest American base? In Japan?"

"No, in the Pacific is better. At Okinawa for example..."

"In the Pac... But Professor, we don't have enough fuel even to reach Formosa![49] We've already used up three quarters of our reserves with these maneuvers, climbing up at full speed. All we can do is to drop down and glide to Tokyo. And still, I'm not sure we have enough fuel to reach the city. Coming from Rangoon we made the stopover in Tokyo only to pick up Dr. Kato without thinking that we needed to refuel. We had enough reserves to reach Nagasaki but with all this trouble in the air..."

---

[49] Taiwan.

"Captain!" the radioman cried out as he turned up the volume on the radio. "Listen to this!"

...spreading out for almost two square miles. We are recording almost 40,000 dead and 25,000 wounded. The destruction caused by the atomic bomb Fat Boy, although quite considerable, is not as extensive as that caused by the atomic bomb Little Boy that destroyed Hiroshima three days ago. The wounded amounted to...

The broadcast in English was suddenly interrupted and only crackling was heard over the speakers.

Captain Howard's voice spoke out worriedly, "Make up your mind, Professor. Our fuel is running out and I have to cut down to two jets to stay this high for a few more minutes.

"How long can you hold this altitude, Captain?"

"Five minutes, maybe ten, but I don't believe in Santa Claus anymore, you know... I have to choose a heading so we can land on relatively flat land without too much damage."

"Captain! A typhoon just came out of the north, heading straight for us!" the radar man alerted.

The chief pilot manipulated his controls and the plane veered away, gaining more altitude.

"I have to go back to the south or southwest, Professor. To avoid the typhoon I'll have to get higher. Now, with the state of our reserves, we can't climb very high or very fast or fight against the storm. Our only hope is to land before the typhoon can hit us. So, heading southwest."

"But we're going to be in the middle of the radioactive zone!"

"Would you rather crash into Mount Eshira on our left or go for a dip in Iyo Nada to our right? I'll try to stay as far as possible from the hot zone but I can't guarantee anything... Miss Robson, would you please hand out the anti-radiation suits immediately... Quickly! And say a prayer, if you have time."

Hastily the stewardess with the help of some of the passengers distributed the big plastic bags containing the protective suits. In record time everyone was wearing their light-weight suits, checking the seals and fastening their seatbelts.

"Our compass is going crazy," Captain Howard announced over the speaker. "Now we don't know our exact heading. Visibility is really bad. Everything's gray... but, the sun was shining in a cloudless sky. This is some unexplained phenomenon. Hold on!"

A violent shock and the passengers clenched the armrests of their seats. The plane had just landed hard and was still bumping along the rocky ground. Then it came to a halt.

Streiler smiled at Miss Robson through his soft, transparent helmet and asked, "Anything broken?"

"No. And you?"

"Not this time."

One by one they left the plane and stood dazed. A mile to the west were the ruins of Nagasaki: the ground devastated, cluttered with twisted beams, with black, shapeless bulks of melted metal along the ravaged streets, the wreckage of all kinds of cars.

"It's horrifying," Kato murmured in a strangled voice.

Dormoy turned on his scintillation counter and it clicked furiously, crazily. "This zone is terribly hot," he noted. "Without our anti-radiation suits we'd be exposed enough to have to write our wills pronto."

"It's horrifying, horrifying," the Japanese teratologist kept repeating, his eyes filling with tears. "August 9, 1945, Nagasaki was destroyed by an atomic bomb and here we are today, 16 years later, for a second time Nagasaki's been razed by a similar bomb! May my ancestors forgive me for the evil thoughts in my head that want to kill whoever's guilty of this cowardly, unjustifiable act of destruction!"

The group of scientists, the crew and the stewardess started walking in their opaque, glistening suits looking like clumsy monsters out of a horror film. They reached the road full of fugitives who were running around, crying, shouting and moaning. Kato stopped a trembling man who looked at the scientist and his companions with wild eyes.

"What happened?" he asked, so upset that he did not see how ridiculous his question was.

"It's… I was in the basement when it happened. I didn't see anything… I was thrown against the wall and a terrifying light blinded me. The neighbors say the sun fell onto the Earth… It took me seven hours to get out and…"

"Seven hours? You… mean the explosion happened seven hours ago?"

"Six maybe, or eight, I don't know…"

Leaving the poor man to flee with the terrorized crowd, Kato translated the conversation to his friends.

"How could the guy say that the bomb exploded six to eight hours ago when in fact it struck here barely an hour ago?" Kariven objected, more and more curious.

"I don't know, my friend," the Japanese shook his head slowly. "Let me take you to the ruins that used to be Nagasaki."

The last refugees, hidden away for hours in their basements, were deciding to leave the site of the disaster. Making their way through the fugitives, the scientists and crew entered the devastated city. Fires raged everywhere but the atomic mushroom was diluted in the atmosphere. Kato, leading his colleagues, kept stepping over corpses that cluttered the ground the closer they got to the center of the city. They finally reached the Urakami valley in the middle of which was a huge crater full of slag and vitrified rocks mixed with piles of melted metal.

"Just like the bomb that exploded 16 years ago, in the same place in Urakami," the Japanese observed.

"It's an extraordinary coincidence," Kariven thought out loud.

They went around the rocky spur of Nakashima—over 1,000 feet high—and entered a part of the city that was a little less devastated. The rocky mass had shielded it from total destruction. In this place although the buildings were in a pitiful state, they had stood up to the extraordinary blast. The shockwave had smashed against the rocky barrier.

Groans coming from a half-buried building attracted Kaito's attention. Helped by Kariven, he tore off the hinges of the broken door and entered the hallway full of debris. An eight- or ten-year old child was whimpering, stuck under a beam. To his right lay a young woman in a blood-red kimono, her chest crushed by the heavy beam. A stream of blood out of the corner of her mouth was hardening. Streiler, Zavkom and Tagliero used their combined strength to lift the beam while Kariven and Kato carefully pulled the boy away.

Walking backward, the Japanese scientist tripped over a smashed typewriter and caught himself at the last moment by the frame of the door on the right. He regained his balance and got ready to continue dragging out the wounded boy but stopped short, staring at the ground. In the wreckage, covered with plaster, a rectangular object stuck out. It was chrome metal with four openings through which he could see Japanese characters. He picked up the small object with a hesitant hand, stared at it for a long time and then gave a puzzled look to his friends.

"What is it, Kato? What've you found?"

"A... desk calendar."

"Is that so surprising?"

"In itself no, Kariven. It's the date that's extraordinary: August 9, 1945."

"You... 1945! That's impossible, come on. The explosion must have damaged it and substituted 45 for 61. The month and day are not surprising since it's August 9... 1961."

When they left the ruined house a team of rescue workers were in the street. The men were wearing gas masks, a completely whimsical protection against radiation. Kato called them over and gave them the boy with a broken arm.

"What time did the explosion happen?" he asked in Japanese to the head nurse.

"You weren't here?" he sounded surprised.

"Yes, but... I was dizzy... the fire," Kato lied.

"I understand. The horrifying bomb exploded this morning around 11 o'clock, eight hours ago now. The number of casualties is incredibly high, tens of thousands for sure."

"Why didn't they send for help from Tokyo immediately?"

"The general staff must be overwhelmed since it's only been four days since the other bomb almost totally destroyed Hiroshima."

"Hiroshima?" Kato raised an eyebrow. "Are you mad? We were all in Hiroshima last week at the world conference of atomic scientists…"

The nurse furrowed his brow, "So you survived the terrible disaster?" Then he looked more carefully at the strangers in protective suits and jumped, "Who are these Whites dressed like you in these weird clothes?"

"They're French, Italian, Brazilian, English and American scientists who…"

"English! American!" the nurse exclaimed, astonished. "Prisoners then, right?"

"Prisoners?" Saigo Kato was astonished himself. "Why prisoners? They're my friends…"

"Your… friends?" he stepped backward, indignant, and pulled an automatic pistol from his pocket.

A shot was fired and his weapon flew out of his hand. The nurse grimaced in pain and grabbed his bleeding right wrist. The Englishman, John Shelley, quickly stepped up, a Smith & Wesson aimed at the rescue worker. He thanked heaven for thinking of putting a gun in the outside pocket of his anti-radiation suit. Without understanding Japanese, the change in the man's attitude told him that something unusual was about to happen.

The rescue workers put their hands in the air and keep fearful eyes on the White man whose index finger was glued to the trigger of his revolver.

"You're a traitor making pacts with the American devils!" the head nurse barked and he spit at Kaito's feet.

"Will you tell me the reason for your offensive attitude?" he asked calmly but feeling an indefinable emotion rise up inside.

"You dare to pretend to ignore the fact that we're at war?"

Kato's calm left him and his voice turned hoarse when he asked, "Today... uh... What day is it?"

The head nurse looked stunned, forgot his wound and answered, "But... August 9, 1945 of course..."

CHAPTER TWO

Yuln, Kariven's young blonde wife, rushed into the apartment of Jenny Angelvin, the wife of the ethnographer, who was talking with Doniatchka Dormoy. Pale and ruffled she held out the latest edition of *France Soir* to her friends.

"It's horrible," she whimpered, pointing at the headlines.

"An atomic bomb destroyed Nagasaki!" Jenny read out loud. "My God, are Bob, Jean and Michel there?"

Yuln shook her head in despair. Tears were forming in her big blue eyes. "We have no news from their expedition. It's weird but I can't probe Jean's mind anymore, or anyone with him. For the first time in my life my telepathic abilities have failed me. Such a psychic breakdown is unheard of among my fellow Polarians. Intuitively I know that they're not dead... and yet I can't hook up with their thoughts."

Jenny was upset but kept her voice clear of emotion as she read, "This morning at 11am local time a terrifying explosion devastated the port of Nagasaki, exactly 16 years to the day after the first destruction of the great Japanese city. A US Navy fighter jet on a training flight over Kyu-Shu alerted the Tokyo base immediately after seeing the blinding flash preceding the radioactive mushroom cloud that accompanies every atomic explosion. Because in all likelihood it was a nuclear weapon that pulverized Nagasaki. According to the first reports, it appears that the city suffered considerable damage. The victims number in the tens of thousands.

"We are, however, without news from the ionocruiser transporting a group of international scientists to Nagasaki. They were supposed to be completing a study of the long-term effects on people and things from the first nuclear explosion dating back 16 years now. An ionocruiser took off a few hours ago from Rangoon heading for Japan to fly over the devastated region before reaching Tokyo. The RTF will broadcast tonight, at 8:22 pm, a special news bulletin about the disaster.

Many planes are already en route for Kyu-Shu to bring aid to the victims of radiation. They will land around 10 pm local time."

Jenny, Doniatchka and Yuln looked at one another, depressed and distressed by the sorrowful news.

"I can't find any reason for this atomic explosion," Doniatchka lamented. "Every country on Earth is united now and lives in harmony. Besides, the arsenal of A and H bombs have been confiscated by our friends, the Polarians."

"No one could have launched the bomb… and yet Nagasaki was destroyed once again by a nuclear weapon."

The insane response of the Japanese nurse, translated by Kato, left Kariven and his friends bewildered. They gave one another a look of unbelief mixed with worry, bordering on dread. Kato gave a curt order in Japanese to the rescue workers:

"Turn around and get away from here double quick. We won't hesitate to shoot again if you follow us."

The Japanese complied willingly and ran as fast as they could, probably to go get help.

"Let's get out of here, my friends," Kato suggested. "This place is unhealthy for us in more than one way. Let's get back to the plane. We'll be safer there than in the radioactive streets.

Hurriedly, stumbling and jumping over the debris and corpses, the scientists and crewmembers in their gray anti-radiation suits looked like Michelin Men moving through an apocalyptic landscape.

Was it the sun, low on the horizon, that caused this opaque grayness sticking to the ravaged land or was it a late fall of pulverized matter drizzling back down after the explosion?

When they reached the remains of the suburbs of the city, they had a hard time spotting the oblong shape of the plane, ten feet away, drowned in the mysterious grayness.

Stopping to catch their breath a little, the specialists huddled together, almost blindly, in order to discuss the situation.

"This darkening of the day is not due to the ashes and radioactive dust," Yegov noted. "Look, the wind is coming from the west and we don't see any whirlwinds. It's like… this gray is a form… how can I say it? A thing in itself from the air or space around us." He brought his wrist up to his face behind the transparent, flexible helmet and muttered, "My watch is still stopped at 10:30."

A few groans told him that it was the same for the others.

"Damnit," Dormoy swore as he noticed that his scintillation counter was gone from his belt. "When I was running through the ruins I lost my scintillator!"

"Too bad," Kariven said, "but this is not the time to go back to look for it."

All of a sudden the ground shook, jerked, like there was a small earthquake. At the same time the grayness suddenly dissipated and sunlight flooded the area.

Completely astonished after being thrown off balance they all expected an aftershock because they thought it was an earthquake, pretty common in Japan.

"The… the sun!" the anthropologist shouted, feeling his mind start to reel.

They looked up and were stupefied seeing that the sun was now at its zenith when just a minute ago it was ready to set.

"There! Look!" Kato shrieked, pointing to the southwest. "The… the city is… intact!"

Indeed, splendid new buildings had replaced the smoking ruins of the city ravaged by the atomic bomb.

Miss Robson had Streiler's arm and she was squeezing it nervously through her gloves.

"Well now," Tagliero grumbled, "we certainly didn't dream the whole thing."

"Certainly not," Kariven agreed. "Unless we accept the idea of collective suggestion… which could have forced us to put on our anti-radiation suits."

The sound of an engine made them turn around: a Jeep was coming, driven by a Japanese with three passengers in regular clothes—two Japanese and a European. The vehicle screeched to a halt and the three men jumped out.

Surprisingly, Kato recognized his two compatriots. "By the spirits of my ancestors, it's Dr. Matsu Haido and Dr. Yu Sakawa!" He bowed respectfully to them and said, "Let me introduce you to my honorable colleagues, Dr. Matsu Haido, atomic physicist, and Dr. Yu Sakawa. And this is Professor Hoeskield, a Norwegian neurologist with the Nagasaki Institute.

The latter, a tall, thin man with big glasses sitting on his nose, greeted the newcomers, "You had some problems with your plane, no doubt, to have to land here? We've been waiting for you at the airport since 11, your scheduled landing time, and it's already 11:45."

Automatically, Kato and the others looked at their watches, which now showed 11:45!

"I understand less and less," Yegov grumbled. "And the explosions?"

The Russian scientist looked embarrassed at his friends and once more contemplated the city that was miraculously reconstructed in a few minutes. He could not say a word.

Kariven, armed with courage and daring to look like a madman, said, "Dr. Sakawa, my question is going to seem... bizarre maybe but, um... was there an atomic explosion in Nagasaki?"

The two Japanese and the Norwegian raised their eyebrows in surprise. "I'm afraid I don't get what you mean, honorable colleague. Except for a weird, brief darkening of the day nothing out of the ordinary happened... certainly not a nuclear explosion!"

"Today is August 9, 1961, right?" Kato asked shyly.

"Well of course," Mitsu Haido was still surprised. "Would it be rude to ask the reason for your... strange attitude, esteemed friends?"

Almost reluctantly the Japanese teratologist tried to explain the extraordinary adventure they had just lived through. When he had finished, Sakawa was bewildered but bowed politely. "I won't insult you by doubting your story, but I have to flatly deny it. My response is... a logical paradox. Nothing of what you say happened. In truth, I'm afraid that the trip or overwork has played a nasty trick on all of you."

The strident hiss of a twinjet made them all look up. An American plane was circling over Nagasaki. After three complete rounds it came down slowly and landed in the airport to the southeast of the city.

"That plane wasn't expected," Dr. Haido said. "I wonder why it was circling over Nagasaki before landing."

The arrival of four automobiles interrupted his reflections and he invited his colleagues to climb in.

"Do you mind if we all go to the airport where that plane just landed?"

Without showing his surprise Dr. Haido accepted Kato's suggestion and ten minutes later the vehicles stopped before the customs office located on the edge of the airfield.

Three men were coming out of the twinjet: the pilot and two civilians, all three dressed in the same anti-radiation suits that the delegates of the GCSR wore. The two groups of men headed for each other, equally astonished.

"William Stockfield," one of the passengers introduced himself, holding a Geiger counter in his left hand. "This is Professor Ernst Robinson, atomic physicist, and Ted Haller, our pilot."

When the introductions were over Stockfield raised his voice, "Are we crazy or is this some kind of bad joke? Because judging from your getups that are the same as ours, I see that you got wind of the disaster too."

"We even lived through it up in the air," Kato explained. "How did you learn about it?"

"A fighter on a training run over Kyu-Shu alerted Tokyo, saying that an A bomb had just exploded in Nagasaki. Help was organized immediately: a squadron of rescue planes with radiation specialists will be arriving here soon. We came as scouts to check out the ruins and get an estimate of the damage done by the bomb… and we found Nagasaki unharmed? You got to admit that it's a little hard to swallow!"

"The more so since the detector planes from Luzon in the Philippines and from Tokyo recorded the powerful explosion… which apparently didn't take place," Robinson added.

"It's just baffling," Kariven admitted. "We're absolutely certain that we saw the bomb explode, saw the usual mushroom cloud of pink gas rise up over the ruins and we all visited the city reduced to ashes… And now this city is brand new again."

"Right before the explosion," Harrington spoke up, "a Japanese fighter jet even sprayed some bullets at us. A jet with the emblem of the Mikado on its wings and hull… just like before the last war!"

"In short," Kato summed up, "we had the very unpleasant feeling of traveling back in time 16 years as if by magic."

This comment made the whole group feel anxious.

"Our watches stopped when our plane got caught in this weird grayness," the anthropologist continued. "And everything started then. For example, it was when we came out of it that everything went back to normal. We could believe that basically for a few hours the past took the place of the present."

Harrington shook his head skeptically, "That comes down to imagining our plane was caught in a kind of fold in Space-Time for a certain period."

"Yes, in a fold simultaneous with the Present since the entire Earth seems to know about the atomic explosion… which dated back 16 years. The fold in Space-Time that you allude to, Harrington, is here somewhere, in Nagasaki, but encroaches on the Present all over the planet. But the return of the past event itself only happened in this exact spot where it happened 16 years ago."

"In other words, for X hours Nagasaki and its population were suddenly thrown back 16 years into the past while the rest of the planet remained in the Present?"

"I don't see any other explanation, Bob. And you Kato?"

He shrugged in ignorance. "The paths of understanding sometimes have limits that Wisdom advises not to cross. However, the hypothesis of my honorable colleague Kariven seems tempting... although unconventional and irrational. But what fool would dare pretend to know the mysteries of Time?"

"None of this explains how we could slip involuntarily into this Space-Time Fold," Zavkom, the Russian biologist, objected. "Because when Nagasaki was thrown back in time for a while, we were too. We were pulled out of the Present and plunged into the Past. The scared faces of the Japanese rescue workers, when they caught us in the ruins, proves that they were complete 'foreigners' to our Present... just like we were to theirs. So, there was an interpenetration of our two... Presents!"

Haido and Sakawa had followed the conversation with growing stupor. Sakawa struggling to control his emotions, addressed his foreign colleagues, "Would you be kind enough to follow me to the GCSR labs? I'll show you something that won't fail to surprise you."

In front of the international scientific delegates, Sakawa opened a small, metal box that he had just put on the laboratory table.

"But that's my scintillation counter," Dormoy turned pale.

Indeed, in the box lay the detecting instrument in the form of a big pistol with a red light near the back.

"Well, when I lost it back there I didn't think I'd ever see it again." Utter confusion suddenly froze his face. "Where... and *when* did you find it, Dr. Sakawa?"

"This instrument was a mystery to the Japanese engineers who found it in the ruins of Nagasaki... *16 years ago today!*"

"But... but come on, Sakawa, I lost this scintillator around two hours ago... right after the explosion..."

"I get it, Dormoy. You lost your counter just now after the explosion of the atomic bomb. I have to agree with the views of Dr. Kariven now... that are partly confirmed by the following facts: entering the Space-Time fold, which you say was around two hours ago, was actually 16 years ago! And at that time such scintillators didn't exist yet. However, this one was found on August 9, 1945, by a team of Japanese specialists who were searching through the ruins of our city that has since been rebuilt."

"It's staggering," Kariven pondered, looking at the counter that was slightly tarnished by time. "Imagine what the fate of our plane would have been if it was right over Nagasaki at the moment of the explosion."

"You would have been pulverized!"

"And the wreckage of our plane would have been another enigma for the Japanese investigators along with the Americans," Professor Harrington noted. "Because in 1945, ionocruisers didn't exist yet."

Tagliero spoke up in English, "My specialty in nutritional biology is far away from atomic physics but I think I'm right to wonder if experimental nuclear explosions, after Hiroshima and Nagasaki, might not have contributed to this phenomenon. The 100 explosions strung out between 1945 and 1956 could have caused some kind of... Space-Time Warp. An invisible disturbance creating this Fold that Kariven proposes."

Harrington thought for a long time before responding personally to the suggestion of his Italian colleague. "You might have put your finger on the exact cause of this phenomenon, Tagliero. I obviously can't explain the thing rationally, but it does seem possible that the forces of nature unleashed during our experimental explosions could have influenced our Space-Time... or the Fourth Dimension. This would explain, practically speaking, the fantastic adventure we just lived through."

"Luckily, this 'interpenetration' of two time periods happened at the same place but at different times," Kato pointed out. "I mean this: Nagasaki of 1961 remained *temporally* unaffected by the bomb that destroyed Nagasaki in 1945. We can therefore conclude, theoretically, that the Space-Time Fold miraculously spared our present time. Otherwise the bomb of 1945 would have also destroyed the rebuilt city of 1961."

"That is fortunate," Harrington gasped.

The next day, the newspapers all around the world reported the stunning statements of GCSR scientists who had lived through the fantastic adventure. Reassured about the fate of Nagasaki, the people of the world breathed a sigh of relief. No atomic bomb had been launched—of this they were certain. But as for a solution to the mystery of the Space-Time Fold, nobody was able to resolve the problem with equations and present a simplified explanation to the general public.

Everyone talked about a "space warp," of disturbance in the "curve of our local universe," of "cracks in the Fourth Dimension," but nobody really knew the real meaning of these expressions. The public, for the most part, was happy just knowing that "something had gone wrong with Time," and faced with the incredible complexity of the phenomenon, it preferred not to lean too far over the unfathomable abyss of the mystery.

For 15 days, the international delegates of the GCSR performed numerous biological, chemical and psychological tests and experiments on the people of Nagasaki. The atomic physicists and geophysicists studied the soil, the subsoil, the objects and material while Kariven Robert Angelvin undertook a comparative study of the lifestyle of the Japanese who had survived the explosion of August 9, 1945.

Afterward the delegates went back to their respective countries and resumed their usual work.

Two more weeks rolled by until the end of August. In their luxurious apartment at Place Adolphe Cherioux, Yuln and Kariven—their young son Tommy being on vacation in the countryside—were finishing up an excellent lunch. Sunlight flooded the living room through the big window. Kariven lit two cigarettes, offered one to his wife and went to sit in the cushy armchair. Yuln cuddled up in his arms and smoked in silence, happy.

The telephone rang and the anthropologist picked it up. "... speaking... Oh, hello, Jenny. Yes, she's here."

"Hello Jenny. Well, of course I'd love to go with you. I also have some shopping to do at the Trois Quartiers.[50]. We'll go together. Come pick me up in 30 or 40 minutes..."

Yuln kissed her husband and went to get dressed. On the TV screen where the show Tele-Paris had just ended appeared a pretty announcer with a sweet voice listing the evening's program. As she passed by, Yuln was about to turn it off when the screen suddenly went blank, leaving her bent over in mid-gesture, astonished.

"A technical problem that has nothing to do with my will," she smiled.

A few minutes later the doorbell rang. The anthropologist went to open it and stood facing his upstairs neighbor, a young painter who had set up his studio on the rooftop terrace. Tanned and disheveled, his plaid shirt unbuttoned, he looked worried. His hands were trembling a little.

"Hello, Picasso," Kariven joked, getting along well with the young bohemian whose real name was Pierre Arnald. "Is everything all right?"

"Uh, hello Dr. Kariven. I... don't feel so good and..."

"Well, come in. Have a cup of coffee and tell me what's wrong."

"I think I need a drink... or eyeglasses."

Kariven opened the door of the bar under the TV and with a theatrical wave of his hand, presented the row of bottles. "A drink, you say? Liqueurs? Cognac? Rotgut?"

"An aperitif, please. I haven't eaten yet."

---

[50] Department store on Boulevard de la Madeleine, Paris.

Kariven served him a Cinzano, which he gulped down. "So, Pierre, are you feeling better now? Tell me what…"

"I'd rather show you the thing," the painter jumped in. "Come up to my place and… then judge for yourself and tell me whether I need an eye doctor… or a psychiatrist."

"What the… Did you hear that dear?" he asked Yuln who had just come back into the living room wearing a gorgeous, clinging dress of emerald green plastex.

"I heard," she smiled. "Well, let's go and see… see what, in fact, Monsieur Arnald?"

"You'll see, Madame Kariven… at least I hope you will," he frowned.

When they reached the terrace, Arnald did not take them into his studio but pointed to the magnificent view of the capital that stretched as far as the eye could see. Yuln and her husband contemplated the sight and turned back to the painter, puzzled.

"Well, I still don't see what's troubling you, Arnald."

"Ser… seriously?" he was starting to panic. "You… you don't see anything over there… northwest?"

Kariven looked in that direction then shrugged his shoulders. "Honestly, no. I don't…" All of a sudden he jumped, realizing the importance of the thing. Then he spun around. "The Eiffel Tower!"

Yuln looked and stifled a cry of surprise as she brought her hand up to her mouth.

The young painter relaxed, obviously relieved. "Oh, I really thought I was going crazy. But I see that I'm not bound for the asylum yet. So, you can also see that it's not there?"

"The Eiffel Tower has disappeared," Kariven mumbled.

"And the interruption of the TV program was not some technical problem," Yuln remarked. "If the Eiffel Tower disappeared, then the broadcasting antenna on top of it has disappeared too."

"But… how could such a thing happen?"

287

The young bohemian who was back to his calm, nonchalant self, in spite of the frightening event, said coolly, "Better ask you scientists friends, Dr. Kariven. Who knows, they might even be able to give an answer."

The anthropologist was no longer listening. He could not stop looking at the unusual grayness in the distance, gradually creeping over the Champ de Mars where the Eiffel Tower used to stand, that giant metal construction weighing 20 million pounds... suddenly vanished.

"What happened, dear?" Yuln asked. "Do you think that..."

"Yes," he finished his wife's thought. "A Space-Time Fold is swallowing up the Champ de Mars."

"Oh my! And Jenny lives on Avenue de la Bourdonnais, right near the Eiffel Tower!"

At the wheel of her light green Citroën DS19, Jenny squinted and hit the brakes turning onto Avenue Edouard Branly. She watched through the Plexiglas roof as the gray fog invaded the area—in the middle of the summer day.

The bushes and grass along the avenue were barely visible. A Versailles passed by Jenny's car but quickly slowed down in the unusual "pea soup."

Afraid of hitting an obstacle or even a pedestrian, Jenny pulled over to the curb, leaned on the steering wheel and looked around in vain trying to see through the gray that was getting thicker by the second.

Kariven made an unexpected decision. "Come quickly, dear!" he told his wife, running to the elevator.

A few moments later inside their Simca Regence they were driving toward Champ de Mars.

"Call Michel and Bob right away and tell them to floor it to Champ de Mars."

Without asking for details—which she could read, anyway, in her husband's mind—Yuln picked up the car phone and entered Dormoy's number.

"It's Yuln," she said when he answered. "Leave immediately for Champ de Mars! Don't ask questions, Michel. Jean and I are on our way to the Eiffel Tower... that disappeared in a space-time fold. Get to the corner of Avenue Edouard Branly and Avenue Anatole France."

Now holding the wheel with his left hand, Kariven snatched the phone away from his wife and shouted, "Good God, Michel, every second counts! Drop everything and meet us! Bring a gun and ammunition!"

He hung up and screeched around a corner at breakneck speed. At Avenue de la Motte-Piquet a barrier of gauzy fog stretched across the pavement and hid the rest of the road.

"Hold on, Yuln! We're going through... or into the void!"

Yuln huddled up to him, gritted her teeth and stared into the gray fog floating out to meet them.

The Regence dove into the opaque and cottony but intangible gloom and cruised down the street, then slowed down. The fog before them seemed to lighten up a little. But behind then it looked like a solid mass.

In the blind, the Regence stopped on Avenue de Suffren at the entrance to a street impossible to identify but leading to Champ de Mars.

The anthropologist wiped his forehead and leaned back. "What a mess! But we managed to enter the Space-Time fold... *on purpose!*"

"Do you really think we're in a different era?"

"I'm sure of it, Yuln. This grayness around us is just like what we experienced in the plane before we found ourselves in Nagasaki in 1945. I hope Dormoy will get in before it dissipates... or solidifies, separating our time from this one... Ah hell, I completely forgot to call Bob!"

"I took the liberty of suggesting to Michel *telepathically* to pick him up before meeting us. It shouldn't be long since Bob lives right near here. Because," Yuln smiled, "I forgot about good old Bob, too, after calling Michel. As for Jenny, she's somewhere in the area. I feel her presence but my paroptic vision is blurred by this weird grayness…"

Yuln suddenly stopped talking and thought for a minute before continuing with a touch of anxiety in her voice, "Dear, aren't we taking the risk of becoming… prisoners of this time forever?"

"Let's not worry about that yet. We don't even know *when* we are." His face clouded over and he added, "Maybe I shouldn't have dragged you into this adventure."

"Oh, Jean, look," she whispered, stupefied.

CHAPTER III

The grayness surrounding them for the last half hour was disappearing, gradually fading and giving way to the clear light of day.

The Champ de Mars appeared with its carpet of grass, its trees and evenly pruned bushes, but this Champ de Mars had something unusual about it. The Eiffel Tower had vanished. The layout of the flowerbeds and lawn was different from what Kariven and his wife were used to.

To the southwest and northeast the blocks of houses and buildings they saw were not at all the same as before either.

Yuln hugged her husband. From Rue Joseph Bouvard, crossing the park of Champ de Mars, ten or so people had come out. With their elbows tucked in they turned to the left at Avenue Suffren and ran, worried and scared, in the direction of the young couple sitting in the car.

"Well, that's too much," Yuln murmured on seeing the group on the run.

The fleeing people kept looking behind them. The men were mostly dressed in frock coats, mauve, brown, even green, wearing tight-fitting pants and ridiculous top hats. They gallantly helped along an older woman or young girl trying to keep up. The clothes of the women were no less extravagant: puffy sleeves, wide, brightly colored skirts, crazy hats streaming ribbons and lace and held on by long hat pins.

Flouncy and out of steam, two frail maidens—very "florid postcards"—clutched tightly between their thin, gloved fingers, a hot pink parasol fringed with sky blue lace. Supported by two admirers with waxed sideburns and bushy moustaches they scurried along in their high-heeled white ankle boots. Fifty yards from the anthropologist's Regence they stopped short and were bumped into by the momentum of the people behind them.

A surge of panic seemed to pass through them and it turned into a stampede. Some bolted off to the right, others to the left, vanishing into the streets crossing Avenue de Suffren. Others again opted for the park where they scampered between the bushes, brazenly trampling the lawns.

Yuln and Kariven gave each other a look of surprise.

"We must have plunged into the last century, around 1830 or 1840, to tell by the clothes of these panicked people."

"Panicked by what?"

A horn honked loudly in the distance and a green DS 19 took a tight turn before heading down Avenue de Suffren.

"It's Jenny! I recognize her car."

The aerodynamic car stopped in front of the Regence and brown-haired Jenny Angelvin stepped out, a little pale. "Yuln, Jean, thank God! But what's happening? On my way to pick up Yuln, I got caught in a weird fog that forced me to stop on Avenue Edouard Branly. After 30 minutes the fog cleared up but everything had changed. Bizarre people in crazy clothes ran away when they saw my car. I was just driving around anywhere."

"What's happened in this district of Paris is a... Space-Time warp and our Present has been replaced by a slice of the Past. We've landed in a space-time fold around 1840."

"What makes you say that?" she looked astonished.

"The outfits... of the Parisians you scared away. Just think that at this time, instead of automobiles, there are only steam engines. The ancestor of the car didn't appear until 1891 with the old V2 Panhard & Levassor! It's easy to see why these people are so scared of these 'monsters' that our cars must look like to them."

Short, repeated honks from a horn interrupted him.

"Are you sure that there weren't any cars at this time?" Jenny asked. "Then where's that honking coming from?"

Without answering Kariven jumped back into the Regence and started honking his horn. Quick beeps, three at a time, answered him a little closer. Kariven honked again and the other horn answered even closer.

The back and forth went on for a one or two minutes before the blue Versailles of Dormoy showed up, speeding around the corner of Avenue Edouard Branly.

"Michel!"

The car pulled up behind the DS 19. Dormoy and his wife Doniatchka climbed out as the back door opened for Angelvin.

All of them talking at the same time, disturbed as much as excited by this extraordinary adventure, they shook hands, happy to have found each other and be able to stand together against the Unknown.

"How is it, Michel, that you happened to have Bob with you?" Kariven asked, pretending not to know about Yuln's telepathic suggestion to Dormoy's mind.

"When I was passing Avenue de la Bourdonnais, just after your phone call, I suddenly thought of picking Bob up on the way. As for Doniatchka," he smiled, "she threatened to make a scene if I didn't take her. After getting Bob in the car I had to speed up because the fog bank of Space-Time was fading away. The odd thing was that my car slowed down and shook as if it was getting stuck in some gooey matter that was holding it up. So, I floored it to break through the… jelly and we ended up in the space-time fold after you."

"Hey! Hey! Over there!"

They turned around and saw a group of men, women and children running as fast as they could in their direction. Dressed in the normal clothes of 1961 they surrounded them, showing signs of great relief.

"Well," Yuln sighed, "I have the feeling that we weren't the only ones caught in the Space-Time fold."

A man around 40 years old, who had taken the lead of the small group of 15 to 20 people of both sexes stepped forward and held out his hand to the anthropologist. "I'm Maurice Leconte, engineer. You're Dr. Kariven, aren't you? I recognize you from seeing all the photos in the papers, as well as Messieurs Dormoy and Angelvin."

The men, women and children who had followed Leconte were babbling and rambling.

"I don't think I'm wrong to assume that we've been caught in a space-time fold? I came to this conclusion when I remembered your statements to the press about Nagasaki."

"That's right, Monsieur Leconte," Kariven agreed. "We're... prisoners of the Past. Probably in the last century."

At these words the crowd fell silent, but not for long because a chorus of protests and crying broke out.

Raising his voice, the anthropologist spoke wisely, "Whining or wailing isn't doing us any good, my friends. We need to come up with a plan of action to get together all the Parisians... from 1961, who were dragged back into this era like us. In groups or alone our contemporaries are going to start panicking and might commit desperate acts that we have to prevent at all costs. In the first place, does anyone know exactly what year we're in?"

The engineer took a newspaper out of his pocket and gave it to Kariven. "I found this paper in Champ de Mars—*La Tribune* of Raspail, dated August 29, 1843. It's in perfect condition, so it must be either from yesterday or today."

"Good. So, it's the end of August 1843 and we were carried 118 years into the past. Let's see, in the reign of Louis-Philippe. I propose we split up in groups of three or four and go searching around Champ de Mars for our... partners in misfortune. When the groups find anyone from 1961 they can give them the same advice: bring our contemporaries together into a 'clan' so that we can make a decision about our... security in this past century.

"We'll all meet between 7 and 8 pm in Place Joffre... which in 1843 obviously had another name but you all know where it is—at the SSW end of Champ de Mars. Does everyone agree?"

The plan was accepted unanimously.

Kariven concluded, "You'll obviously be meeting other people, soldiers and... the police in your search. In no case should you be hostile to them. You'll probably be causing quite a stir, with your strange clothes in this time, wherever you go. If any of you are arrested, tell the authorities the time and place of your meeting point and stay respectful, courteous… and diplomatic. Do your best to explain our situation by pointing out how many people like you there are, which should naturally seem suspicious. As for my friends and I, we're going to contact the police or some other authority to try to… sort things out."

Turning directly to the engineer, he added, "Monsieur Leconte, would you take charge of directing the 'roundup' operation while we go check out the Bigwigs of this epoch?"

"Gladly. It'll keep me from thinking too much about this damned pickle we've got ourselves into. Good luck!"

The anthropologist took off in his Regence followed by Dormoy's Versailles and the Angelvins' DS 19. The three cars got onto Avenue de la Motte-Picquet, confusing the Parisians of 1843 who froze in astonishment on seeing them approach. Women and children ran away screaming, sometimes imitated by men.

Carriages, stagecoaches and men on horseback hastily pulled over to the sidewalk although the horses neighed and stamped the ground furiously.

"You can't say we're passing unnoticed," Yuln remarked worriedly. "Where are we going, dear?"

"To the Academy of Sciences before getting in contact with the authorities. If anyone can understand and accept our strange adventure, we'll find them there and not among the police and politicians."

"On the condition that the scientists or authorities of this time have a more open mind than their colleagues in the future. Remember their ridiculous position, their determination to fight against the extraterrestrial origins of flying saucers… before our Polarian brothers came on board their spaceships to Earth? Neither a demonstration of my telepathic abilities nor the proof of my paroptic vision was enough to convince them before."

Leaving their cars in front of the austere building of the Academy of Sciences, the three young couples climbed the front steps—before the bewildered gaze of passers-by—and entered the lobby. A page in an old-fashioned uniform, with graying sideburns, mumbled something, staring at them like sideshow freaks.

"Would the Permanent Secretary see us?" the anthropologist asked politely, ignoring the man's troubled stare.

The page loosened his collar and swallowed hard before stepping back and stammering, "The Permanent Secretary... is very busy. I... I'll see if... Who should I say is calling?"

Puzzled, the anthropologist thought for a moment and decided to give him his card. A few minutes later, still alarmed, the page asked the extravagant visitors to follow him.

When they entered the big room with walls covered in books and in the middle of which stood a huge ministry desk, a man stood up. Dressed in a dark gray frock coat, his neck wound with a kind of white silk scarf-tie, his graying hair a mess, he looked around 50 years old. His piercing eyes were riveted on the newcomers and his energetic face showed both surprise and annoyance.

François Arago,[51] Permanent Secretary of the Academy of Sciences, Deputy of the East Pyrenees, a great scientist of the last century, specialist in optics with a passion for electro-magnetism, furrowed his brow. "What's this bad joke all about? This isn't a masked ball! I'm surprised that you have the audacity to come here dressed up like this!"

He glanced at the business card handed to him by the page, turned it over and played with it thoughtfully.

Then he asked, "Which one of you is Dr. Jean Kariven?"

The one in question bowed slightly and stepped forward. "I'm Jean Kariven, Monsieur Ar... Permanent Secretary. And

---

[51] (26 February 1786-2 October 1853), was a French mathematician, physicist, astronomer, freemason, supporter of the carbonari and politician—25th Prime Minister of France.

before explaining the reason for our visit, allow me to introduce my companions."

Having thus respected the rules of decorum, he was about to continue when Arago, after once again examining the card, asked, "What is this... number 306-81-77 under your address?"

"That's my pho..."

Kariven did not finish, not wanting for the moment to explain to the great scientist what a telephone was, an invention that would not see the light of day until 1876, long after the death of Arago, who was growing impatient and irritated.

"If you won't explain the meaning of this number, are you going to tell me object of your visit?"

"I'm getting there, Monsieur Arago. First of all, and in order to clear your mind of any idea of fraud or pranks that you would be right to suspect, would you be willing to examine our... vehicles?"

"Your... vehicles?" he looked sour. "Oh, well, that! Do you think I'm a carpenter?"

"Certainly not!" Kariven was amused by his indignant response. "They're nothing like the horse-drawn vehicles but rather... mechanically driven machines."

Argo looked exceedingly offended. "Enough of this, messieurs! Would you please leave me alone!"

At this moment the office door opened and the page entered, followed by six municipal guards with their feathered caps and their hands on the hilts of their swords.

"What is it?"

Very embarrassed, the page bowed deeply and stammered, "Please excuse me, Permanent Secretary, but I thought I heard you call the guards. The strange... machines of these visitors inspires no confidence in me and I feared..."

"What machines?"

Without waiting for an answer, Arago opened the glass door, stepped out onto the balcony and leaned over to inspect the street. He gripped hard onto the cast iron railing, leaned over more, and turned around, astonished, to face his visitors. "What are those... metal machines?"

Disturbed by the turn of events, Kariven responded with a proposition, "It would be preferable if we explain everything to you... confidentially."

After a brief hesitation Arago waved away the page and the guards who left but remained stationed in the corridor around the office door, ready to intervene at the first call of the deputy. Preoccupied and fascinated by what he had just seen from his balcony, he invited his guests to sit down. With his elbows on his desk, his fingertips touching each other before his lips, he waited.

Kariven, after countless digressions, juggling his words so as not to alarm his illustrious host, begged him not to fight against the apparent enormity of his explanation as he struggled to tell him the course of their adventure. His friends jumped in from time to time to emphasize a detail or to present a different angle to a point of view that seemed obscure to their host.

When he had finished speaking, the anthropologist wiped his forehead and to calm his nervous tension lit a Lucky cigarette after automatically offering one to the Deputy, who refused.

Shaken up, François Arago stood up, paced a little in his office, stopped, ran his hand nervously through his hair and said, "It's unthinkable! You seem sincere but... I'm afraid I can't accept your statements as truth. It's all so fantastic, so astonishing!"

He thought for a long moment, bit his lower lip and declared, "Let's go see your... automoving machines. That might convince me."

A big crowd was gathering on the opposite sidewalk. A line of guards was encircling the vehicles at a respectful distance, keeping a worried, watchful eye on the crazy machines whose chrome glistened in the sun. The guards separated to give way to Arago and his visitors from the future.

Kariven lifted the hood of the Regence and invited the scientist to examine the engine as he explained how the gas worked in an internal combustion engine. François Arago was both troubled and deeply interested. For one hour he questioned his demonstrator, making him explain the nature and function of various parts of this mechanical marvel. He even accepted Kariven's invitation to sit next to him and watch his automatic gestures to start it up.

The crowd shrank in fear to the wall when the Regence took off, gained speed and honked its horn at the intersection. It made a tour of the neighborhood at 55 miles an hour before pulling up at the Academy of Sciences again.

Full of contradictory emotions, Arago stepped out of the vehicle and leaned against the hood for a minute. His heart was racing. "This is the most extraordinary thing a human being could ever experience," he confessed. "A vehicle moving silently by itself and at such incredible speed… it's unbelievable!"

"For us this is very natural," Angelvin assured him, amused by his fascination. "In 1961 and for decades before, millions of people on Earth drive in cars that don't surprise anyone anymore. Airplanes—flying machines—soar off from one continent to another at more than 600 mph. Rockets are shot hundreds of thousands of miles into space. Beings from another planet even landed on ours, coming in spaceships from a solar system around the Pole Star and since then, thanks to the progress they gave our civilization, all nations are united."

"But," Dormoy explained, "before that the most dreadful wars pitted people against each other and destroyed continents. Bombs converting matter into energy, in part, razed cities and killed tens of thousands people in a split second. Big cities were utterly destroyed by these atomic bombs but also by traditional TNT bombs. Some…"

"Be quiet!" the scientist groaned, closing his eyes. "Follow me."

Back in the Deputy's office Kariven and his friends sat down without saying a word, intrigued by the sudden turnaround in their host's attitude.

Arago's teeth were clenched as he stared hard at them with cold, almost hateful eyes. "And this is the civilization of the future? A civilization built on collective murder and founded on millions of corpses? What demented brain dared to invent a bomb that you tell me partly converts matter into energy? What authoritative monsters pushed their people to massacre other people like that? Are you proud of this horrible slaughter? Is this the painful price to pay for future generations to build a... civilized society? Flying? Mechanized? Is this really the civilization of *your* Time?"

Uncomfortable now they could not help admitting to themselves the justice of this violent indictment.

Arago took a deep breath and seeing their frowns added, "A strange accident that I don't understand very well at all threw you and your vehicles... and your knowledge into our era. I cannot reasonably hold you responsible."

He paused, breathed heavily, flaring his nostrils, then slammed his fist down on his desk. "But at no price do I want your knowledge or your revelations to make the science of our times progress even one iota. No doubt some of your specialties could be used to our benefit, but in accepting to use them we would be starting on a dangerous slope. It might end up very treacherous to change evolution, whether by stopping or speeding it up.

"What would happen, for example, if thanks to your information we built a bunch of these... automobile vehicles? First the ruin of carriages, stagecoaches, blacksmiths and a whole series of occupations that relies on, if I may call it thus... animal locomotion.

"Then an economic upheaval would follow, probably preceded by a much more deadly war than in the past. There would always be enemy agents trying to steal the secrets of manufacturing these vehicles. In a few years we would have to confront the threat of invasion. Imagine a strong foreign power with an army of these vehicles moving at lightning speed? And equipping them with powerful cannons?

"And not to mention the crazy sword of Damocles that this diabolical bomb of energy from matter represents for the people. By revealing to us your secrets, you would be committing the murder of…"

"Rest assured, Monsieur Arago," Kariven broke in, "even if we knew the principles of the atomic bomb, we wouldn't be able to give you the secret of its fabrication."

Arago waved away the objection and continued, "It doesn't matter! We have to leave Time to follow its normal course and civilization will follow without hindering it or hurrying it up. Your place is not here in this era… Mesdames and Messieurs. Your presence alone constitutes a danger to our country and even the world. Although your arrival astonished the Parisians, they don't know where you came from or the exact nature of your knowledge. I'm the only one who knows your secret… and I will remain the only one to know it. Guards!" he boomed out.

The six guards burst into the room, swords in hand.

Kariven and his friends jumped up. Dormoy took a step forward pointing his Colt 11.25.

"Don't shoot, Michel!" the anthropologist shouted.

The guards circled them, waiting for orders from the Deputy.

"I advise you to throw down your weapon, Monsieur Dormoy," Arago said. "Your friend has perfectly understood that all resistance is useless."

"Don't fool yourself," Kariven replied. "It's not to surrender that I said that to Dormoy. We could very well fight back and probably without firing a shot get out of this predicament. But by fighting these men we would be disturbing the course of History and make changes with unforeseeable consequences in the present society. We don't know, for example, if one of these men might not become the father of a scientist, a great thinker or a genius. By killing him to escape, we would

301

be removing this future person from History and this we don't want. That's why I prefer to give in… and wait."

"But just coming into our era has already influenced History, since we can't manage to completely suppress the event. You've made contact with me, with these guards, with people who saw you together, who saw your machines in the street. How do you think that these events can be erased from *our* present time?"

Arago's pertinent objection troubled the mind of Kariven and his friends.

The Deputy stared at them with pity. "I'm truly sorry for you because I'm forced to put you under house arrest… all the while knowing that you've committed no offense voluntarily."

"Under… house arrest?"

"At least for the time being. I'll think about this extraordinary adventure and decide your fate later. But rest assured, no harm will come to you. You'll probably be exiled so no human being will be able to contact you. Goodbye… and I'm sorry for these extreme measures."

"But… That's impossible! Wait!" Kariven was outraged. "We have to get back to Champ de Mars! That area is stuck in the Space-Time fold and will sooner or later be freed and go back to our era. If we don't get back there, we'll be stuck here forever and…"

"Sorry but I can't run the risk of letting you loose."

He bowed as a farewell and left them to the guards.

A double row of guards were blocking the street to the right and left of the main entrance to the Academy of Sciences. Other men, under Arago's orders, were covering the "automobile vehicles" with tarps to hide them. Then some horses were "hitched" to the vehicles and started huffing and puffing, trying to drag them away. With the brakes on, however, the tires screeched across the pavement.

After a few hours of hard work the three cars were dragged into the courtyard of the Academy, safe from the prying eyes of the crowd that the guards dispersed with waving arms and threats.

"Lieutenant, set up a permanent patrol around these machines," the Deputy ordered. "And make sure your men don't let anything slip out. There're already enough people who saw the demonstration of how they work. I myself will make sure to deny any rumors that will certainly start running around about these... machines and their owners.

"Send an officer to headquarters with an order to organize patrols around Champ de Mars in order to catch—as quietly as possible, I insist—any, uh... people whose clothes look different... from us.

"These people will be led immediately to the Chateau de Vincennes where you'll put them under guard with strict orders forbidding them to leave. They won't be prisoners, properly speaking, but under house arrest. Then we'll see."

In the paddy wagon bumping down the street, the "exiles" brooded. Four guards with their hands on the pistols were sitting with them. A small troop of horsemen rode in front of the wagon at a good pace. Another followed.

The sun was slowly setting at the end of the day.

The anthropologist watched the landscape through the narrow window. "Where are they taking us?" he asked the guard sitting next to him between Dormoy and his wife.

"Vincennes," he answered curtly, not saying another word.

Kariven sighed and took Yuln's hand, squeezing it tenderly in his. "What's going to happen to Leconte?" Angelvin worried. "I'm afraid we acted without thinking enough. Maybe we shouldn't have told Arago the truth. I'm sure there are guards out there right now looking for the good people of our time who were thrown back into this one."

Angelvin could not have said it better. Indeed, hundreds of municipal guards were riding toward Champ de Mars. Their mission was to split into three groups at Place de Fontenoy and surround the area on three sides at the same time. A fourth troop, coming from the Chamber of Deputies, headed for the Quai de la Seine to close the circle around Champ de Mars.

The first troops reached the Place de Fontenoy just when a kind of fog—coming out of nowhere and from all sides at the same time—rose up in the calm evening air.

Nightfall came on quickly and soon the horsemen were stuck in semi-darkness. The horses whinnied, stamped, shook the reins and breathed heavily out of their flared nostrils.

Contradictory orders were given telling them to slow down, line up on the left, on the right, go back, go forward, creating total disorder and throwing the worried riders into wild confusion.

Groups of men, women and children were running up, scared, gathering in Place Joffre where a crowd was already surrounding Leconte.

Parisians from 1843, astonished gawkers, were watching, without believing their eyes, the bizarre group of people in bizarre clothes. They were watching from a distance, not daring to cross Avenue de La Motte-Piquet to see them up close.

The stomping of boots on the surrounding streets was getting closer.

Leconte looked nervously at his watch. He was surprised, looked at the others, and seeing them shake their heads, muttered, "All our watches stopped at the moment when we were thrown into this time. Damn, it must be almost 8 o'clock now and Kariven is still not here."

"What are we going to do?" a young woman holding a boy by the hand asked.

"Wait. We've all been lucky enough not to be arrested by the police or the municipal guards when we were wandering around the area. I don't think we should fear being imprisoned now…"

"I'm not so sure," a man objected, smoking his last cigarette with a shaky hand. "If our presence here so far has intrigued or frightened the guards and everyone else, that moment of surprise has probably passed…"

"Look!" a young woman shouted as the crowd also saw the big group of cavalry arriving in Place Joffre.

"Guards on horseback! They're probably coming from the Military School to the southeast of here…"

A few latecomers were still arriving, out of breath, rushing up to the engineer.

"A huge number of horsemen are on Avenue de Suffren!"

"They're also coming down Avenue de La Bourdonnais!"

"So, we're surrounded!" Leconte was alarmed.

All of a sudden, from every direction, a gray fog slowly washed over the guards on horses who vanished from sight in a minute.

Cries of fear broke out. Children started crying. Then, little by little, a crushing silence fell over the crowd. Feeling hemmed in, they dared not move an inch.

A thought crossed the mind of the engineer, a thought that he did not voice aloud. *Kariven and his team aren't here! What's going to happen to them?*

All of a sudden a bunch of electric lights were shining in the evening air while a hellish clamor of honking horns, curses and angry shouts boomed around them. A police whistle blew twice to calm down the mob.

Lines of cars, buses and motorcycles—all the headlights turned on—screeched to a halt. Bumpers were dented by some who were too close to this group of people who just appeared out of nowhere as if by magic.

Huge traffic jams were formed around Place Joffre on Avenue de La Motte-Piquet at rush hour.

Crying with joy the women hugged one another, the men shook hands vigorously, children jumped around, paying no attention to the angry shouting of the drivers cursing them and telling them to "get lost somewhere else."

The area around Champ de Mars had come out of the Space-Time fold and traveled back to the present. Leconte looked around at the usual jumble of big Parisian streets. But a

305

shadow dampened his joy of being back in 1961. Walking away he talked to himself, "We're saved, but Kariven and his friends stayed in 1843. After leaving the area sunk in the Space-Time fold and not coming back when it returned to our present... they'll be prisoners of the Past forever!"

CHAPTER IV

In one of the huge rooms—furnished like a salon—of the Chateau de Vincennes where they had been put under house arrest, Kariven and his friends had been moping around for 24 hours.

The anthropologist paced the room, stopping frequently before the tall window looking out on the inner courtyard and mumbling, irritated by being forced to do nothing. His pack of Luckys held only seven more cigarettes—he offered them to his wife and friends and grumbled bitterly, "I'm an idiot! It's my fault that we're here, prisoners of the Past! I wanted to take an active part... and fully knowing the cause this time... in one of these Space-Time folds. But I didn't have the right to drag all of you into this... insane experiment with me."

"Bah!" Dormoy replied, "Living through one of these experiences was also the goal of me and Bob. And we were getting ready to tell you about it the very day you called me. So, don't beat yourself up. Drop this obsession you have with your guilt."

"Miichel's right, Jean," Angelvin agreed. "Over the years of our eventful life we've lived through a lot more, less tragic moments. We pulled through safe and sound, on Earth as well as on the Moon.[52]"

"Yes, I know, but we've never been prisoners of Time! Even if we manage to get out of this chateau, wherever we go we'll be in 1843!"

"Not if we escape and hide around Champ de Mars," Angelvin said, "Let's not give in to this depressing apathy. We absolutely have to get back to Paris as soon as possible to be able to pull out of this Space-Time fold when it turns back to our Present time."

---

[52] See Volume 1.

"Yes, but when will it happen? If it hasn't happened already... If we wander around the park or through the streets we'll be picked up again."

"Just like Leconte and the other Parisians dragged along in the time warp probably were..."

Three short knocks at the door and Arago entered. His face bore the marks of a sleepless night—crow's feet etched around his eyes. He said hello to his "guests," sat across from them, lowered his bushy eyebrows and in a worried voice began:

"Your misadventure puts me in a very precarious situation, Mesdames and Messieurs. According to you, a crowd of people from your era, thrown into ours, was supposed to meet last night around 8 pm in Champ de Mars?"

Everyone nodded anxiously.

"These people mysteriously disappeared in front of the municipal guards surrounding the area."

The three couples stood up, turning pale.

"Did you say... disappeared?"

"Evaporated, if you prefer, Monsieur Kariven."

They felt like a slab had just sealed up their prison, blocking forever the only exit through which they hoped to escape.

"So, the area around Champs de Mars got out of the Space-Time fold and reentered our time," Yuln murmured dryly, sadly pressing her husband's hand.

Arago looked like he honestly shared their dismay. "I'm truly sorry that I didn't listen to you. I should have let you go back to the area to wait for the unsettling, reverse phenomenon to take you back to your Time."

Kariven asked curtly, "Were any disappearances of people from your era reported?"

"Uh... no, not that I know of. I've just had a conversation about this with the Police Chief. Searches made turned up negative. It seems, therefore, that only the people from your era were displaced in Time."

"These retrogrades in the Space-Time fold can be seen as a kind of opening in the Past that stayed fixed while the Present moves into or is placed inside this corner of the Past for some indeterminate time. Only people from *our* Present of 1961 were moved while those of the Past remained fixed in their era."

"Apparently, yes," the scientist agreed thoughtfully. "Otherwise we'd be seeing people disappearing... transported into the Future, meaning into your year 1961."

"It even seems that only people caught *outside* at the moment of the phenomenon were brought back in Time," Angelvin pointed out. "It's an inexplicable mystery..."

"What's to become of us?" Doniatchka asked with tears in her eyes.

"No decision has yet been made, Madame. But as I said yesterday, you'll be treated not as prisoners but... obligated guests. We will, however, be forced to keep you outside of everyday life and far from society. For this you will really seem exiled—not banished but exiled—on an island... Martinique probably."

Yuln buried herself in her husband's arms and wept, her head against his shoulder, in despair.

The global press repeated the astonishing displacement of this district of Paris, vanished in a Space-Time fold.

For almost ten hours a fog that kept growing thicker fell in a circle around Champ de Mars, quickly forming a barrier, then a kind of dome around the area that nobody could enter. For, this fog, at first intangible, turned into a real wall, brightening as well. When the fog dissipated, the wall remained, impassable despite being apparently immaterial and completely invisible.

From the roofs of the buildings in the unaffected neighborhoods, frightened Parisians had watched the Eiffel Tower disappear and the rapid transformation of the streets and houses that had vanished for an instant, then were a little distorted and replaced by other streets and houses, some elegant and new, others old-fashioned, all of them different.

The reverse effect occurred in the evening. The invisible dome, immaterial but solid at the same time, appeared in the fog that gradually thickened. The vaporous dome stretched upward, rolled into a whirlwind in which the buildings and streets of another Time melted away. The misty dome finally thinned out and disappeared, leaving the area to "fade in" like a movie effect, with the Eiffel Tower showing up in double exposure.

A crowd of wearied, startled people had suddenly shown up in Place Joffre, gathered around the engineer Maurice Leconte thanks to whom they had found each other and waited anxiously for the troublesome return to the Present time of the affected zone.

Coming unharmed out of the time warp, they had described in detail their fantastic adventure to the newspapers, radio and TV. That was how they were surprised to learn that the famous anthropologist Jean Kariven, his friends the geophysicist and ethnographer Robert Angelvin along with their wives, stayed behind in the Space-Time fold, prisoners of the Past.

The news had been welcomed with a fierce outcry in the world. The public had appreciated and loved the three men justly celebrated for their numerous scientific expeditions, in which their charming wives had frequently participated, and especially for the important role they played in preparing our planet for the coming of the Men from Outer Space.

The day after his return to the Present, Leconte went to the Bibliothèque Nationale where he methodically combed through the newspapers of 1843 and particularly those of the second half of the year. With growing anxiety he searched for a trace, any clue hinting at the intrusion of "foreigners to this era," but in vain. No reporter made any allusion to the "automobile machines" or to the "strangers in bizarre clothes" who were surrounded by guards sent to Champ de Mars on August 29, 1843.

The papers were hopelessly silent about the meeting that Kariven must certainly have had with the "authorities of the time".

La Tribune of Raspail, *Le Bon Sens* of Cauchois-Lemaire and Louis Blanc, *L'Avenir* of Lamennais, *L'Univers* of Abbé Migne, *La Presse* of Emile de Girardin and all the others seemed (unbelievably) to know nothing about the extraordinary event that had shaken up the past century.

With special authorization and the fact that he himself had dove into this bygone era, Leconte was authorized to consult the police archives and reports. He also got access to the (known) letters and royal archives of Louis Philippe but to no avail. The king, however, would certainly have taken a lively interest in people coming from the Future!

"And yet," Leconte told himself, "Kariven and his friends did stay in that era. I should have found at least a hint, a rumor, some mention in one of the yellow old papers I examined. It was as if the poor couples had been hidden away… maybe even murdered! But how could they have prevented leaks? The people who saw them, who saw the three cars driving around the streets of Paris in 1843 must have talked to one another. Gossip and rumors must have spread to writers and journalists of the time who should have mentioned them in their writings. This total silence about such a sensational event is unacceptable, unbelievable. Wasn't it as if nothing had happened? And yet didn't I myself participate in the fantastic adventure? I refuse to believe in such… draconian censorship in 1843. The hothead Lamennais would not for a second hesitate to report, dissect and analyze such an incident. But nowhere in his works is there a mention of it."

These troubling, agonizing thoughts were communicated by Leconte to the journalists who published them in almost all the dailies. Following these statements and his own articles, the paleographer archivists, historians, exegetes and bibliophiles wrote to him to confirm that despite meticulous research no trace of this event could be found in the past.

The newspapers published numerous editorials on Kariven and his friends who disappeared in the Space-Time fold. Some articles even took the form of eulogies.

Three days later, while the distant spotlight of the Eiffel Tower was sweeping around the night sky, a long line of military trucks was entering the unused Guyancourt airport, 12 miles from the capital. 500 men got out, armed with paralyzing rifles—a gift from the Polarians—and surrounded the dark airfield.

Their mission was to keep everyone out but they did not know why. Only their chief, Captain Martin, had received the exact orders although he did not know the real reason for this deployment of force.

Around 11 pm the American ambassador in Paris drove up in a Sabre. The splendid turbine automobile whined on the road before rocking its purely aerodynamic body to a stop.

Captain Martin went up to the two men who were getting out of the Sabre. He saluted them and shook the hand of the ambassador, "Everything's ready, Sir," he gestured to his detachment that formed a circle half a mile in diameter.

"Great, Captain," the ambassador smiled. He was around 50 years old, very distinguished, dressed in a dark, double-breasted suit, with graying hair glistening brown in the headlights. "Allow me to introduce Monsieur Maurice Leconte, whom you've no doubt heard of lately in the media."

Visibly stunned to find himself in the middle of the night on an old airfield guarded by the military, Leconte asked, "Captain, maybe you can tell me why…"

The officer shook his head and smiled in apology, "I know no more than you, Sir."

Holding back a fit of anger, Leconte turned to the ambassador, "So, what's the meaning of this kidnapping—polite of course but a kidnapping nonetheless—that I'm victim of?"

"Kidnapping is a serious word, Monsieur Leconte," the ambassador smiled. "And you'll allow me to remind you that you were *invited* to come with me and not *forced* to follow me. I told you that you were free, absolutely free, to refuse to help us."

"I admit it, Sir. But how can I be of use?" he looked around and continued, "Here on this abandoned airfield guarded like a fortress?"

"You'll find out soon, very soon," the enigmatic ambassador answered, looking at his watch before looking up.

Intrigued, Leconte followed his gaze and tried to make out what could be of interest in the star-studded night sky. He did not wait long before seeing something come speeding from the west: a huge, dark rocket ship on the front of which was a cockpit or passenger compartment lit up with fluorescent lights.

Without a sound the strange machine slowed down and hovered. A bright spotlight from beneath lit up and swept all over the ground that formed the landing strip. Then it came down slowly and still without a sound landed in the middle of the old airport.

The ship was 230 feet long and around 80 feet in its widest diameter. It was impressive with its radar antenna that pointed out its "nose" that contained a transparent, metalloplastex compartment. Dark windows ran along the cabin reinforced with super-metal that looked like nickel-chrome. On its sides was written RT1 in phosphorescent letters.

It sat now on giant pads that had come out of its belly when it descended vertically. In the hull, over the triangle of pads, a rectangle of light appeared. Then telescopic stairs came slowly down to the ground.

Two forms were outlined in the hatch against the background of light and climbed down the stairs, holding onto the rail.

Seeing the ambassador's obvious astonishment, Leconte realized that he was not the only one seeing this ship for the first time.

The two pilots, none other than Professor Red Harrington and the physicist Kurt Streiler, bowed before the ambassador who introduced them to the "kidnapped" engineer, saying, "I don't think I should explain anything, Monsieur Leconte. Professor Harrington and Dr. Kurt Streiler, to whom I hand you over, can tell you everything that I couldn't tell you before, regretfully. But let me thank you in the name of the USA and the confederated nations for the assistance that you will be giving these two remarkable scientists."

Leconte became more and more bewildered. He ended up shrugging in surrender. "So be it. Since I'm assumed to be helping, I might as well do it willingly." Smiling, he added, "Let's go, gentlemen, whatever I can do… if you really think I can be of some use."

"You will be, I guarantee it. Would you accompany us?"

They said goodbye to the ambassador and Captain Martin and climbed the stairs of the big metal rocket.

The three of them hurried through an inner passageway, quite like a luxury cruise liner, and climbed nine more narrow steps that led them to the upper deck. At the end of a long corridor with luminous walls they entered the cockpit.

Leconte carefully examined all the controls, screens, the blinking lights on the semi-circular control panel and, accepting a cigarette from Streiler, observed, "Very recently I also had the chance to visit a Polarian Fimn'has, or Flying Saucer as we used to call these spaceships, but I've never seen anything like this."

"This is not a spaceship," Harrington corrected him. "And before telling you more, I have to ask you to give us the same personal assurance that the ambassador to your country gave, namely that you will swear to reveal nothing of the true nature of this… ship."

"You have my word. And I will never break it."

"The efforts you made to find any traces of our friends Kariven, Dormoy, Angelvin and their wives in the writings of the past inspired us to contact you through the ambassador. In order to send you on a… top-secret mission whose importance you will understand. This machine that so intrigues you is not a spaceship but a *Retrotimeship*, meaning a machine capable of moving through Time. Or rather into the Past only because we haven't been able to discover the means of traveling into the Future even though we've been slaving away at it for five years."

This information left the engineer dumbfounded. He stammered, "You... Into the Past? So, you've already experimented on this truly fantastic machine?"

"Several times but in absolute secrecy[53]," Streiler confirmed. "Even though peace reigns on Earth now and all nations are fraternally united, it would be dangerous to reveal the existence of a Retrotimeship. Just imagine what would happen to world peace if let's say a secret political group, that doesn't exist thank God, managed to get hold of it. The present stability would collapse from the actions of this imaginary group in some period of the Past.

"That's why there is and will always be, most likely, only two prototypes of the Retrotimeship in the world, whose use is exclusively reserved for missions of... the utmost importance. Our mission falls into this category."

"I think I've understood the purpose of our mission, Professor," the engineer was just realizing the staggering truth. "We're going back into the Past—to 1843—to free Kariven and the others."

"Yes and no," Harrington smiled ambiguously. "Haven't you noticed the total absence of traces of our friends in the writings of that time?"

"Yes, but I don't see the link... Unless we admit that they were never there, which is impossible since they are prisoners of the Past."

"Yes and no," the celebrated physicist from the California Institute of Technology repeated. "Sit down there and you'll understand this paradoxical mystery."

Leconte obeyed, confused by these obscure statements.

Harrington and Streiler sat at the controls of the Retrotimeship, but only Streiler worked his. A low rumbling

---

[53] See Volume 1.

echoed through the machine room. A green light lit up and the ship slowly ascended.

On the ground the 500 military guards watched curiously as it went up.

At 3,000 feet altitude the ship turned upward and at a steady speed shot into space. Safe from the dangerous effects of acceleration thanks to an anti-g device, they passengers felt nothing when the ship stopped in outer space, apparently without slowing down, 30,000 miles from Earth.

Through the transparent cockpit Leconte was admiring the curve of the Earth, an enormous globe with a pale halo of atmosphere. A dark crescent divided the Earth, leaving the old continent in shadow while the sun shining in the black sky lit the West Atlantic and the three Americas. The Moon, partially lit, was also shining brightly among the familiar constellations.

"You're up, Harrington," Streiler said, leaving the space propulsion commands to his friend for the delicate job of retrogradation in Time.

Harrington typed something on a keyboard that looked like an electronic calculator and entered in the column marked Present: Departure 23:57. In the next columns with the respective titles: Temporal Transfers/Arrival/Date/Target Hour-Minutes-Seconds—he entered 1843/August 29/15:30 and pressed a button.

The green indicator light went out, replaced by a red one that started blinking. The ship started vibrating gently. The vibrations grew stronger and suddenly the darkness of cosmic space disappeared, replaced by an endless gray, the weird environment where the Retrotimeship traveled in its voyage to the Past.

A few minutes passed in this dimensionless environment, then the gray thinned out, seemed to move away, gradually absorbed by the blackness of interplanetary space becoming visible again with its numberless stars. The vibrations stopped. The red indicator light went out; the green came back on blinking.

"Your turn, Kurt."

Streiler, in normal space propulsion, started a steep descent at 25,000 mph. Ten minutes later he slowed down and glided into Earth's atmosphere, still reducing the speed to a very modest 125 mph.

The trajectory through the atmosphere brought it almost without transition from darkness into sunlight. The ship flew over the suburbs and hovered directly over Paris—a smaller Paris than today and lacking the Eiffel Tower.

"Here he are in 1843, August 29," Harrington glanced at the control panel and clarified, "3:33 pm and 20 seconds. We're three and a half miles above and won't be noticed. At this altitude our ship looks like a thin, shiny spindle, practicable undetectable."

"Why not land? At 3:33 pm, the area around Champ de Mars was already in the Space-Time fold. Kariven, his friends, me and many other Parisians from 1961 were already stuck in 1843 for about 15 minutes."

"It isn't necessary to land and it would complicate things. Intervening effectively to free our friends would change the course of Time. Such an event could have unforeseen consequences. Kariven's intrusion has already shaken up the Parisians of this Time enough, believe me. We have to erase this unexpected and *excessive* episode from History but not *act* in this era."

"In that case, and supposing that such an... *erasure* is possible, what did we come back here to do?"

"To film it, which will be useful for us later on," Harrington answered as he pulled a chrome lever.

The tilted screen on the control panel lit up and the image of the Champ de Mars, seen from about 300 feet up, appeared in the screen.

Leconte leaned over excitedly and pointing at himself stammered, "But... that's... me!"

Indeed, just like a movie the screen showed Maurice Leconte talking with Kariven. In a circle around them were Yuln, Angelvin, Dormoy, their wives and a few other people thrown back into the bygone era. To their right were the three cars parked at the curb while people dressed in the day's fashion were scurrying through the paths, fleeing these "diabolical machines" and the funny looking but troubling human beings.

Harrington turned a knob, zoomed in and framed the group formed by Leconte, Kariven and his friends. A speaker boomed out the voice of the anthropologist being automatically recorded: "... right, Monsieur Leconte. We're... prisoners of the Past."

The background was filled with the shouts and cries of the group around them.

Then Kariven's voice came out again, "Whining or wailing isn't doing us any good, my friends..."

Harrington turned off the sound although the cameras and audio detectors continued recording.

"The recording will be very useful when we show it our friends... to convince them of their adventure."

"To convince them?" Leconte parroted. "Will we really need to convince them of the reality of the... mess we're getting them out of?"

"You're not used to the unsettling possibilities and complexities of Time travel," Streiler smiled. "How do you think we'll convince our friends about a misadventure... *that hasn't happened yet...* and that will never happen?"

"Listen, Streiler," Leconte frowned in bewilderment, "You and Harrington have had enough fun with me! Explain this mumbo jumbo or I think I'll lose my mind."

Streiler broke out laughing, imitated by Harrington who was starting up the temporal retrograde device.

"You'll understand everything, even better than with words."

After a new leap into space, the Retrotimeship returned to Earth and hovered over Guyancourt. The spotlight swept the night, found the detachment of soldiers guarding the airfield, then slowly came down to land.

The three men were quickly climbing down the telescopic stairs and heading toward Captain Martin.

Astonished, Leconte heard Harrington declare, "I'm Professor Harrington, Captain, and this is Streiler and Leconte."

"Very pleased to meet you, gentlemen. I've been expecting you," the officer responded.

"Am I dreaming? What is this ridiculous drama, Professor? We left…"

"Tsk, tsk," Harrington hissed. "Please, Leconte, no questions right now. You'll understand later."

"Later! Later!" he shook his head.

Captain Martin held back his surprise and said, "I got instructions to keep your ship safe until you return, Professor. The embassy *Sabres* are waiting for you," he added, pointing at the two long cars, low and streamlined with Plexiglas roofs.

"Thank you, Captain." Then he seemed to remember something and said, "Oh, Captain, one question that might sound crazy but is vital to our mission: what day is it?"

The officer did not blink, aware of being on a "top secret" mission whose details were hidden from him. He answered, "It's August 28, 1961, Professor."

"Thanks. See you later."

Harrington dragged away Leconte who could not believe what he had just heard. The two got in the second car while Streiler took the first.

"August 28, 1961," Leconte thought out loud, staring at the road without seeing it. "I don't get it! No, I don't get anything at all!"

"Listen up," Harrington advised, amused by the engineer's confusion. "I told you it'd be better not to intervene in an era of the Past when we could disturb History. Okay. But if we intervene… 24 hours before your 'slip' into the Space-Time fold, meaning last week, no trouble can come of it. For example, as you saw the landing of the Retrotimeship didn't cause a stir among the soldiers guarding the airport whereas it would have thrown them into a panic in… 1843. And this we didn't want. Therefore, we took the following measures.

"Before coming to France, on September 4, 1961, and going to Guyancourt where our ambassador took us, we took a trip into the Past. Oh, a very short hop in Time only going back to August 28, 1961. On that day in Washington we told the military authorities about our intention to intervene in the near future to accomplish a... Rescue in Time. The President of the States was informed and knowing our service record he granted our requests. Following our plan Washington contacted Paris right away in code and got the abandoned Guyancourt airport under military guard for the night and two embassy Sabres for our use.

"Our orders, you see, have been carried out since we're here in the cars after landing on the guarded airfield... *tonight.* In other words, eight days before the time we come from."

Leconte furrowed his brow, thought hard and repeated out loud in order to get a grip on the befuddling ride into Time:

"So, with the Retrotimeship you brought us back from September 4 to August 28, 1961, eight or nine days ago. You had a meeting with the President of the USA and told him that in eight days an area of Paris would be swept away in a Space-Time fold just like Nagasaki on the 9th. We know that this happened since we came from after this time in the Retrotimeship. During this time warp our friends Kariven, Dormoy and Angelvin, world famous scientists, were left behind in the Past, prisoners of Time. Our duty is to free them... by intervening at the right moment."

"That's exactly how things happened," Harrington confirmed.

"Hold on, don't interrupt me," Leconte wrinkled his brow even more, almost comically. "I'm still figuring things out, trying to put a little order in this temporal maze. I imagine that you told the President something like this: on the night of August 28, the night before the Space-Time slip we want to land the Retrotimeship in Guyancourt. It should be heavily guarded to keep anyone from approaching of ship while we're gone. And we'll need two cars. Okay, but did you figure out what to do next?"

Harrington smiled, then laughed on seeing the suspicion in the engineer's eyes. "That, my dear Leconte, will be explained soon, in the presence of Kariven and our friends."

"You're annoying, Harrington, with your explanations in installments."

CHAPTER V

The two Sabres reserved for Harrington and Streiler by the embassy stopped at Place Adolphe Cherioux and the passengers went immediately up to see Kariven and his wife. The latter greeted them with joy although rather surprised by the visit at this late hour.

In the presence of Kariven, Leconte committed a blunder. "I really thought I'd never see you again, Kariven!"

He raised his eyebrows, not understanding, "Never see me... again? We've met before?"

"One second," Harrington broke in, sitting down in an armchair. "My dear Kariven, and you, Yuln, are probably going to think I've gone nuts when you I start telling you what it's about."

Yuln and Kariven, intrigued by this prelude, exchanged an amused smile.

"Tomorrow, August 29, 1961, around 2 pm," the mathematician began, "what happened on the 9th in Nagasaki, when you were there, will happen in Paris, minus the atomic destruction. The district of Champ de Mars will be cast into a Space-Time fold and into the year 1843."

A smiling, skeptical frown crossed the anthropologist's lips while Yuln brought up a small, rolling bar.

"I had no idea, Harrington, that one of your hobbies was reading tea leaves! But maybe you're just... psychic?"

This friendly joke put a smile on the American's face. "Go on, Kariven, joke all you want, but I'll have the last laugh seeing your face when I give you proof of my... psychic powers."

On saying this he opened the leather briefcase he had brought from the Retrotimeship and took out several newspapers. "Read these."

The anthropologist unfolded the first paper and his eyes fell on the date. "September 1, 1961! But this paper doesn't…"

"Come out for three days," Streiler finished calmly. "It's true. Why don't you read out the headline, Kariven."

He did so, speaking slowly and with an emotional voice: "Kariven, Dormoy and Angelvin—Prisoners of the Past!" He looked up at his friends, incredulous, and resumed, "The engineer Maurice Leconte, escaped from the Space-Time fold in which Champ de Mars was stuck, has described the final moments he spent with the three famous scientists. Kariven, Dormoy and Angelvin, along with their wives, are considered lost forever in the Past!"

"It's unbelievable," Yuln murmured, dumbfounded. "But how did this paper get into your hands, Red, if it doesn't come out for three days?"

Harrington turned serious, leaned forward and weighed his words. "Because we are coming… from next week, Yuln."

"The Retrotimeship!" Kariven exclaimed. "I should have thought of that sooner."

"That's it, Kariven. The Retrotimeship brought us back to this August 28, 1961, the night before Champ de Mars slips into the Space-Time fold."

Terribly intrigued, the anthropologist wondered, "So the six of us were… or rather will be carried away tomorrow into this Space-Time fold?"

"Exactly. Along with a bunch of Parisians like Maurice Leconte who followed your advice and got the people together in Place Joffre. In the meantime you six went in your cars to contact the authorities. But you weren't back in the affected area when it returned to our Time. You missed the… *replacement* and remained prisoners of the Past."

"I see," Kariven figured, "that by staying out of the area tomorrow we'll avoid the time warp. But the slip into 1843 will still take place."

"Sure, but we've also thought about that and taken measures. This afternoon Washington sent a note to French authorities asking them to evacuate Champ de Mars between noon and midnight tomorrow. The real reason, you can imagine, won't be made known to the public since it doesn't know about the Retrotimeship. Besides, around the evacuation zone there will be guards armed with paralyzing rifles to forbid anyone from entering for 12 hours.

"Champ de Mars will be thrown into the Past but without any person knowing about it. In short, you will never have lived through the extraordinary journey. The 'human side' of this story will simply be erased from History... since it will never have taken place."

"Well, there's the Gordian knot," the engineer Leconte spoke up. "I finally understand why, despite my research in the archives, I never found a trace of this episode that could not have passed by in silence."

Stunned, Yuln called Dormoy and Angelvin immediately to ask them to come over with their wives Jenny and Doniatchka. The two young couples were intrigued by this nocturnal rendezvous and showed up around 11 pm.

Over the next few minutes, after listening to the incredible story told by Harrington, they went from disbelief to total astonishment. Nevertheless, they had to accept the facts. They could not deny the authenticity of the newspapers that would not be printed for three days.

Doniatchka felt dizzy and dropped into an armchair. "In fact, Yuln, I'd gladly accept a strong drink." She grabbed a bottle on the bar and poured a big glass of Cinzano that she almost downed in one gulp.

Harrington stood up and said, "Let's not dawdle, my friends. We'll finish this very informative conversation later... meaning *next week*, when we'll come back."

Captain Martin and his men watched the rising, mysterious "spaceship" in which Harrington, Streiler and the three young couples brought from Paris had entered. At a distance of 6,000 miles from Earth, Streiler stopped the Retrotimeship and Professor Harrington turned on the viewer.

For 20 minutes, Kariven and his friends watched in a daze as the images of their stay—*not yet lived*—in 1843. Over the speakers the words that they would never speak awoke a strong emotion in them. Yuln's pretty face was stunned, which in other circumstances would be funny.

Getting a hold of himself Kariven broke the tension along with his wife when they both said, "It's unbelievable!" The spontaneous outburst made everyone laugh.

Harrington turned off the screen and declared, "You have all seen and heard the events that you were... or rather would have been involved in. Engrave them in your memory because they will disappear forever from the recording."

"Disappear?"

"Naturally, Jenny," Streiler said. "The fact that the Retrotimeship is pulling you out of... circulation during the fall into the Past, you will therefore never have lived through it and this event will be utterly erased from History."

"Just look," Harrington threw down the newspapers that reported their disappearance and lamented their being lost in Time.

He flipped a switch and worked the controls of time travel. The green light on Streiler's post went out and the red light on Harrington's started blinking. The Retrotimeship vibrated and the blackness of space around the ship turned into the gray of Space-Time. All of a sudden the newspapers on the metal floor of the oval cabin disappeared without leaving a single trace, faded into nothingness.

"A magnificent confirmation of my predictions," the mathematician smiled. "The event never took place. You were never thrown back into 1843 with any other Parisian from 1961. Therefore, the articles were never published! The demonstration is, I believe, convincing enough, isn't it? And off to the Present, meaning to next week in your case. We picked you up at 11:30 pm on August 28 and will bring you back to Guyancourt on September 4."

With a smile the American started the retrograde system and slowly turned the knob on his half-moon panel. The knob, however, got a little stuck, which was unusual. He said, "We'll have to check this when we get back to the States, Kurt. I don't think the shaft got jammed but we should examine it very carefully."

"Okay, Red, we'll see about that tomorrow. Ready?"

"Ready, Kurt. It's all yours."

Streiler started the field generator and the electromagnetic energy propelled the Retrotimeship—now a simple spaceship—toward Earth. Through the transparent walls of the cockpit they saw the globe rise up toward them at dizzying speed and for a brief moment the sphere left their field of vision: the Retrotimeship had just veered off slightly to enter the atmosphere on a tangent. After slipping into the rarefied layers of the ionosphere, the ship dove into the biosphere before leveling off on a horizontal flight.

Streiler squinted in surprise at the viewer screen that was showing only a hazy landscape full of thick fog.

"Damn weather!" he complained, hovering the ship at 1,500 feet altitude. "We're right over Guyancourt and can't see a thing. We can't even make out the lights of Paris or the spotlight on the Eiffel Tower."

"But it was a beautiful night," Leconte noted, "when we took off eight hours ago. Captain Martin and his men must be swearing up a storm. How's he going to keep watch in this pea soup?"

"Nah, we'll land with the radar," Streiler proposed.

Piercing the fog, the radar screen showed the middle of the abandoned Guyancourt airfield. The Retrotimeship, with its spotlight turned on, landed gently. When the pads had touched down the side spotlights went on, their blinding glare diffused by the fog into a mass of pale halos.

"What a beautiful evening!" Kariven joked. "We can't even see the honor guard."

In the outer hatchway the passengers shivered: the temperature had dropped. The handrail of the metal stairs was sticky, almost gooey in the fog. In her pearl gray suit Yuln had goose bumps. Her friends Jenny and Doniatchka were also shivering in their summer outfits.

On the ground everyone had the unpleasant surprise of sinking up to their ankles in gooey mud.

"What a rain they must have had to soak the field like this," Leconte railed, turning up his collar against the cold.

"Captain Martin!" Professor Harrington boomed.

His call was muffled by the fog that passed through their clothes all the way to their skin.

"Captain Martin!" Three more times, cupping his hands around his mouth, he called in vain.

A heavy silence weighed over them.

"That they've all gone deaf, all right, but that Captain Martin and his men can't see the ten krypton spotlights through the fog, I can't believe it."

"Maybe they left?" Jenny Angelvin suggested, wrapping her scarf around her neck.

"Left? Impossible. They had orders to guard the airport until we got back and we couldn't have been gone from the *present* for more than a few hours. An order is an order. In the army more than anywhere else," he insisted.

The strong spotlights fused together only 15 yards from the Retrotimeship, forming a kind of dull globe. The fog seemed to be compacted, compressed in order to stop the light like a screen.

The shadows of the nine time travelers were also absorbed by the fog and their outlines looked ghostly in the milky field of light.

"Our English friends would be jealous of this fog!" Leconte joked, but he got no response. Everyone felt a gnawing worry, a strangling surge of dread.

From the gray, moving form of Harrington his voice echoed, "Damn it all this weather! For some unknown reason Captain Martin and his men disobeyed orders and abandoned their post. We've got two choices: head for the Retrotimeship's secret base in the USA or wait here for the fog to lift. I don't advise going back to the States because we'll just have to come back to France in an ionocruiser and thus lose 24 hours. In less than six hours it'll be dawn. So, let's go wait in the ship. You can rest or sleep in the cabin if you want."

"Gladly," Yuln accepted, shivering. "We could get bronchitis our here in this fog."

Back in the warmth of their ship they sat in the spacious rectangular cabin, 30 by 15 feet and 10 feet high. The magnetized feet on their soft chairs stuck fast to the metal floor. The walls and ceiling, also metal, gave off a bluish, almost neon light. To the right were lined up cabinets containing the microfilm of a large library. Four mobile viewers were also stored in the micro-library.

Streiler brought in a tray with plastic cups holding warm water. Using slender thongs he dropped a brown tablet in each. The steaming water quickly turned dark brown and the smell of excellent coffee filled the room.

"Here's some coffee—with sugar—that I think we all could use."

Of course the hot drink was very appreciated and helped warm up not only the body but the morale as well.

"It's still strange, this fog you could cut with a knife," Doniatchka mused.

"Especially at this latitude and at the beginning of September," Kariven completed. "Even in winter I've only rarely seen such thick fog in Paris."

Streiler, playing the role of maître d' to perfection, to distract his guests, turned on the huge radio-television machine standing to the left of the micro-library.

"Short of weather bulletins predicting a starry night, a little music will help us pass the time."

"Chic," Jenny approved. "Coffee, music, old friends, we've got all we need for an impromptu party!"

The accidental guests smiled thinking about their comical situation: stuck in a time-traveling ship because of the fog, they were about to change it into a nightclub for a few hours.

"And the music, Kurt, what's taking you so long?" Doniatchka teased.

Surprised by the silence the physicist turned a knob, searching for a signal but the speaker produced nothing but a constant hiss. No radio station could be found.

The video, after several tries, also stayed off. No wavering line crossed the screen even for a second. Everyone looked puzzled at each other while Harrington slowly stood up with a worried look.

"First of all the fog and then the absence of the military and now this!"

Streiler and he exchanged a look and without a word they both rushed to the cockpit. The others followed to find them leaning over the transmitter of the control panel, trying to get in contact with the Retrotimeship base in the USA.

"RT1 calling Nevada Center... RT1 calling Nevada Center," Streiler repeated into the round microphone on the chrome panel.

The speaker did not make a sound. For ten minutes the physicist kept it up but with no success.

"Try to get Washington, Kurt," Harrington advised.

Streiler changed frequencies and repeated his call to no avail.

"Le Bourget or Orly Airports?" Kariven suggested anxiously.

Neither Le Bourget nor Orly Airports responded.

The latent and so far unexpressed fear quickly materialized in them, causing an unpleasant tightening in their guts.

Sweat beaded on Streiler's forehead. He laid his hands flat on the controls and stared blankly at the silent speaker. "I... I don't know where we are," his throat went dry, "but *we're not in the Present...* since we can't get anyone to answer our calls."

"Come on, that's impossible!" Harrington got busy with the temporal retrograde device. All of a sudden he stopped and ran his fingers over the controls, remembering a apparently banal detail. "This knob that got stuck a little might have caused a... detour in Time!"

Feverishly he unscrewed the top the control panel mounted on hinges. The insides of the delicate mechanism controlling the time travel appeared in their incredible complexity. One part was connected to the control panel but another more important part was in a separate base.

Various colored connections, hundreds of them, linked countless electronic circuits together in an intricate tangle. Transistors were arranged, also by the hundreds, in criss-crossed layers. To the right bundles of multicolored wires came out of the electronic keyboard to get lost in the shiny cone that was fixed to the metal floor behind the panel.

With infinite care and using a pen-tool that looked like what radiotechnicians used, Harrington slid the copper point of the instrument along the wires and connections.

Some greasy waste on the pin of the guilty knob seemed to have caused the damage. A series of parallel ridges along the grease attracted the mathematician's attention. He gave a more careful examination to the fragile, insulated filaments around the pin (when the panel was closed) and pondered:

"I think I've found the... well, one of the causes of the problem. The technicians who check the Retrotimeship before we leave from the Nevada Center greased the controls, notably the axle pin of this knob. Nothing unusual on all this, but an abnormal variation in temperature at some time for even a short period must have made the grease more fluid. As it ran down the pin it spread over the filaments... which should never come in contact with this pin.

"One or more of the filaments must have had a crack in their insulation, probably microscopic, and the grease got in. This could have caused a variation in the feed, some of the low voltage energy escaping. As a consequence the lower power altered the working of the keyboard controlling the time travel. This is, of course, only a hypothesis, a theoretical starting point for the tests we'll have to perform."

"And how long will that take?" Dormoy asked.

Harrington shrugged. "Maybe ten hours… or ten days if I'm right."

"Ten days?" Kariven was alarmed. "When we don't even know in what Time we are!"

"Knowing it wouldn't change anything," Streiler philosophized, putting on sky blue overalls to protect his suit during the repairs.

Harrington also took out a pair of overalls from a compartment in the back of the cockpit and put them on, absorbed in thought.

"Being no use to our friends," Kariven observed, "we should leave them alone to work. Just standing around here might bother them."

All agreed and they decided to take a short rest in the cabins on the upper deck. Before lying on the foldout bunks of the narrow cabin, Yuln and Kariven looked out the single window stuck in the reinforced wall. The lateral spotlights were turned off. They could see nothing but a pale halo to the right coming from the cockpit. The fog, still as thick, kept them from seeing anything beyond the window.

"Freed from the Past, now we're stuck between Scylla and Charybdis," Yuln sighed.

As the fog dissipated the sunlight, already high on the horizon, flooded into the cabins of the Retrotimeship. The time travelers got ready and met in the inner passageway.

When Streiler and Harrington could not be fund in any cabin they headed for the forecastle. The two of them were there, covered in grease, hair a tangle, hunched over the guts of the Retrotimeship. They looked exhausted. They were struggling to keep their eyelids from closing over their weary eyes. They straightened up, rubbing their backs.

"I don't want to sound like a pessimist," Harrington sighed, "but we're not going to be leaving this morning."

"We haven't been able to analyze the exact nature of the problem yet," Streiler added. "Moreover, the problem created some nasty results in the Time Counter so that we don't know what era we're stranded in."

"The wise thing to do would be to get a few hours of rest," Kariven advised. "The work you've done has worn you out and you won't get anything useful done if you force yourselves to continue."

"Kariven's right, Red," Dormoy agreed. "Since we can't do the work ourselves, we'll watch over the ship in the meantime."

"Maybe you're right," Streiler accepted, covering a yawn with his hand.

"At this point, losing two or three hours won't matter. Let's go get some sleep. Wake us up in three hours, Kariven."

When they were in their cabins the others went down to the lower deck to leave the ship. The warm air outside caressed their faces as the sun made them blink their eyes.

The land around them was very different from what they had the night before. Shrubs and brambles and all kinds of plants were growing on the land. In every direction they could see it was wild country, luscious vegetation, dense forest and to the south an unknown landscape without roads or buildings.

They walked around the ship, trying to spot the smoke from the capital to the west, but in vain.

"Either the radar misguided us and we're not in Guyancourt," Leconte reckoned, "or if we're there it's at a time before Guyancourt... or Paris even existed."

Dormoy, the geophysicist, was leaning toward the second possibility. "I think that we're in a period before Paris was built. Judging by the geological markers I'd say we're in the quaternary period, well after the ice age as you can see by the vegetation which belongs to a humid, moderately warm climate. So, we are in *our* geological period and not in some distant epoch like the tertiary or even secondary period."

"Well, I like that better," Yuln joked. "I'm feeling closer and closer to home."

This joke made them all laugh.

Then Kariven said, "I'd like to get a more precise chronological details. Shall we explore a little? A very short exploration, of course, that for safety reasons shouldn't go much more than a mile beyond the Retrotimeship."

"Excellent idea," Doniatchka, Yuln and Jenny were ready to go.

"Sorry," Kariven informed them, "but it's *us* who are going and not *you*, lovely creatures."

"Be reasonable and think a little," Angelvin tried to persuade them while Kariven and Dormoy went to get some weapons from the Retrotimeship. "If we all go, who will watch over Kurt and Red during our absence? You three will be much more useful on board, keeping watch, than with us."

This argument seemed convincing enough and satisfied with their role the three young women climbed the metal stairs after kissing their men.

The four men, each armed with a paralyzing rifle, discussed for a moment to decide which direction to take. They quickly agreed to climb a small, green hill around half a mile to the north.

They started walking through the high grass that rose up to their thighs, talking along the way. Behind them, beyond the metal rocket shining in the sunlight, the grass waved at several points and multiple groves cut through it, converging on the ship.

CHAPTER VI

The scouts, with Kariven at the head, climbed the slope of the tree-covered hill, disturbing the hares and rabbits. They even saw a herd of frightened deer bounding off to the east over some rocks. A great number of partridges flew out of the grasslands surrounding the hill.

"This would be paradise for any 20th century Nimrod," Dormoy smiled.

"No kidding. This area is full of game and would be great for hunting."

Kariven stopped suddenly and brought the paralyzing rifle to this shoulder. His partners imitated him, on the alert. The anthropologist pressed the trigger and a faint crackling along with the smell of ozone suffused the heady air. 200 feet to the left a bush shook and a deer, paralyzed by the rifle, tumbled down the hill and hit an oak tree.

"This delicacy will spice up our usual fare," Leconte was pleased.

"We'll pick it up on the way back. It will stay paralyzed for two hours."

On the top of the hill they could see the vast extent of land. A narrow river wound through it, 500 yards to the north, which must have emptied into the Seine. To the southwest was a forest and beyond it the plain where their ship was sitting.

For a moment they contemplated the long metal rocket whose pads were sunk in the high grass, then they went down the hill. It took them 15 minutes to reach the water. At their approach the deer bounded away gracefully and disappeared into a grove of trees 300 yards away.

"I think there's no need to cross the river. For now let's explore to the north before getting back to the field. That way we'll be able to…"

The anthropologist broke off, staring at the water that was carrying along a leafy green branch.

"Well, well," he said as he dropped down on his belly to grab the object that the current was pushing to the other bank. Holding out the base of the branch he asked excitedly, "What do you think of this?"

At first his companions did not understand, then all of a sudden they got it.

"The branch... has been cut!"

"Cut and not broken! Look here, this bevel was made by a blade. This is incontestable proof that humans exist in this era... and that they work metal. Considering the small size of the river and the clean break, it couldn't have been cut very long ago... or very far from here. We should go tell our wives not to leave the ship."

Yuln, Jenny and Donitchka were searching through the kitchen, noting that the "edible" stock contained only 50 cans of food. On the other hand, there was a large choice of dishes concentrated into tablets. This discovery was a great disappointment.

"I hope we're not going to rot in this metal carcass for long," Jenny said, "otherwise we'll be forced to eat these unappetizing tablets."

Doniatchka was busy searching through a metal cabinet to the left of the window when she cried out in surprise on seeing a herd of deer leaping through the field less than 20 yards away. The three women pressed against the window. Yuln looked at each of her friends as she read their thoughts telepathically.

"I don't think our husbands would be happy with your... hunting project."

"Oh, Yuln, what's the harm? If we can get a deer, we'll surprise them with a gourmet meal."

"I hunted wild reindeer in Russia," Doniatchka smiled, "and I can brag about my cooking. So, it's decided—we're going."

"The deer will be long gone before we even get the rifles," Yuln objected. "Besides, we should be watching over Kurt and Red while…"

"Okay," Jenny sighed. "The housewife!"

Doniatchka proposed a compromise: "Listen, you two. There's nothing stopping us from keeping watch… right outside the ship. Maybe some other animals will pass by in range. What do you think?"

"Okay," Yuln gave in, "but let's stay close to the ship."

A few minutes later they were sitting cross-legged with their rifles across their knees and the grass up to their shoulders.

"We'd make a weird picture, sitting like hunters, dressed in fashionable clothes, in some bygone era and in front of this crazy metal beast," Yuln whispered in good humor.

"Our adventure is full of anachronisms. Remember what Leconte said? Didn't we drive through the streets of Paris… in 1843?"

"And here we are now hunting prehistoric deer with paralyzing ri…"

She finished her sentence screaming in fear.

Jumping up behind them after crawling between the Retrotimeship's landing pads, a group of long-haired men were throwing themselves on the imprudent hunters.

There were ten of them, blonde and redheaded. Two straps of buckskin crossed their muscular chests holding up a kind of crude loincloth. Daggers and short swords hung from their belt or were hooked onto the straps.

The young women were grabbed from behind, their lips crushed under the fingers of their captors, and dragged away. They fought, kicking their feet, clawing and biting, but to no avail.

Yuln, who had not dropped her rifle, tried to smash it into her assailant's stomach. Without breaking stride the man snatched the weapon and threw it into the grass, holding her even more tightly. Yuln groaned, suffocated, and finally gave up fighting against the brute. He loosened his grip a little and kneed her in the back, throwing her off balance, making it easier for him to carry her with his left hand over her mouth.

In fact, Yuln had no need for a voice to call for help. The second after the initial terror had passed she emitted her thoughts that instantly reached her husband's mind.

The anthropologist was just coming down the south side of the hill when he pulled up, stupefied. "Yuln!"

The others stood silently while Kariven listened in his mind.

Kariven! Jenny, Doniatchka and I have just been abducted by primitive men with long, blonde hair... Ten of them armed with knives and swords, iron I think, and heading into the forest south of the ship.

Thrown into a panic Kariven blurted out the psychic message and followed by his friends started running and muttering, "They couldn't been abducted on board the ship, damnit! What crazy idea made them leave! Leconte, go alert Streiler and Harrington while we go to the forest. One of us will stay by the big oak tree we saw to the SSE to wait for you. Then you join us."

Leconte veered off to the left and leaped up the metal stairs while the three others continued their way toward the forest. Soon they bent down and walked hunched forward in the tall grass to hide in case a lookout had been posted.

When they got to the big oak tree whose trunk was more than 30 feet in diameter, they agreed to leave Angelvin to wait for Leconte. Kariven and Dormoy dove into the forest and followed a line directly south. After covering half a mile they spotted a path in the mud where big wheels had left deep grooves. Hoof prints—probably bovid—were also visible.

Seeing a plane tree whose first branch was only eight feet off the ground, Dormoy hoisted up his friend who pulled himself into the tree and scrambled to the top, around 50 feet up. From there he had a good view and over the tops of other trees toward the east he could see a thread of smoke rising into the sky.

"This path must lead to their camp," he figured when he was back on the ground. "Let's get off it and cut through the forest."

At this moment Angelvin and Leconte arrived, walking fast, paralyzing rifles at their sides.

Be careful! they all heard at the same time in their minds. *A lookout is posted at the top of a tower in the middle of the village. You have a chance of not being spotted if you follow the river that narrows under a canopy of plants...*

Sent by Yuln, this telepathic message made them change their direction. Getting their bearings they ended up finding the river after 15 minutes of silent walking. Indeed, brambles and shrubs and branches of the trees on the bank formed a kind of tunnel that was perfect for their goal.

Without thinking about the brambles that would snag their clothes they jumped into the water, up to their thighs, and waded upstream. They struggled for almost 500 yards, the water sometimes rising up to their waist forcing them to raise their rifles over their heads.

They started to hear confused sounds, mixed with a few shouting voices, coming from a point upstream to their right. The four men, tired from the hard march through the water whose current was moving faster as the land sloped down, became twice as wary.

The shouting was closer now, sounding to them like an argument in a foreign language. Through the bushes the "castaways of Time" finally saw the village. And it really was a village, made up of 30 or so huts and shacks made of log and branches. The roofs, mostly cone-shaped, were covered with straw or grass and dried mud.

A square tower, also built of logs, stood in the middle on beaten earth. Yuln, Jenny and Doniatchka had their arms tied to the tower. Before them ten young men with long hair and tanned skin, dressed in loincloths or buckskin pants, were facing off against a group of older men. The two clans were waving their arms wildly. Those with their back turned to the prisoners were yelling at the others and clenching the handles of their long iron swords, rather crudely fashioned.

Scrawny dogs were barking furiously around them and sometimes went to growl at the feet of the captives. Chickens and roosters were pecking the ground between the huts and shacks. Three big ox-carts with their arms sticking up were left by a crude enclosure where four oxen, two cows and a calf were calmly chewing their cuds.

Nearby but at a respectable distance stood the women, children and old people who watched the men of the tribe with worried eyes. Some of them glanced angrily at the prisoners.

Yuln, standing between Jenny and Donitchka, whispered, "In their primitive thoughts I can read the cause of the argument. Our abductors are at odds with the older men of the village. And they're at odds with each other about the fate of... their catch."

Jenny and Doniatchka were startled. "Their catch? You mean... us?"

"Yes. These primitives who are just entering the Iron Age sometimes raid neighboring tribes to carry off the women. The practice—vulgar to say the least—is obviously pretty common at this... pre-Gallic time. I think I understand now the exact reason for their disagreement. Our abductors already have a wife and the elders are angry because only the chiefs are authorized to practice polygamy."

The two women looked at each other and turned to her, stunned. Jenny was upset, "You're talking about all this with surprising... apathy, Yuln! I'm not amused and have no desire to be the prize in this fight."

Yuln smiled without saying anything. Then she projected a thought into her husband's mind:

I know that you're there, dear, with our friends. Don't try anything yet. It would be too risky right now. Wait for my signal. And above all don't kill these men. Without them the women of the village would be at the mercy of neighboring tribes who lust after them... just like they lust after us and are fighting over us right now.

339

Surprised by this message Kariven told his friends, still in the water and spying through the bushes with their elbows on the ground and the paralyzing rifles ready to fire.

Yuln, even though she did not understand the language of these people at the dawn of civilization, could still interpret their thoughts. Thus she had been able to probe the rudimentary psyches of the antagonists. Using her supra-normal abilities she cast into their minds inflaming impulses that fanned the anger of one side and the jealousy of the other. In a few minutes all the men of the village were victims of Yuln's inner suggestions and they started yelling. The lookout, also seized by a sudden, inexplicable anger, abandoned his post and joined the clan of elders. Then they all threw down their weapons and shields and with bare hands jumped on one another in a free-for-all brawl.

The women and children ran to safety into the shacks while the dogs barked feverishly at the shouts of rage.

Now's the time to act! Yuln said telepathically.

Kariven and his friends climbed up the bank, adjusted the paralyzing rays to 30 minutes and fired, sweeping the land horizontally. In the ozone saturated air the fighters immediately stopped their battle and fell on top of each other, frozen in position, fists raised, faces scowling.

Three dogs that got caught in the line of fire were also paralyzed and fell over on their side, legs stiff and jaws open in a ridiculous, silent bark.

In the huts and shacks, after witnessing the wonder, the women yelled out, panicked and dropped face first to the ground.

In no time at all the captives were untied and hugged their husbands, a little pale but radiating joy.

"Let's not dawdle in this unfriendly place," Dormoy advised. "We've got around 20 minutes to get away from here before the natives wake up."

"I think we can... tame them easily enough," Yuln thought out loud.

The anthropologist gave her an anxious look.

"They're not fundamentally bad," she continued, "as I found out probing their minds. They kidnapped us because their tribe lacks women, just like the others. Partly from the fact that infant mortality is high because of a total lack of hygiene and there are the physical complications that often affect women after childbirth. These complications are often fatal. Moreover, the villages battle one another over hunting grounds... when it's not to abduct the women. There are no real unions to bind these people... from whom our Gallic ancestors will be born."

Kariven looked doubtful. "I see here the altruistic feeling of your brother Polarians, my dear, but do you think it's possible to teach these people the principles of hygiene and brotherly love in a few hours or a few days?"

"If we all work on it willingly, we'll manage... Especially since we won't be leaving any time soon..."

"What do you mean?" Dormoy asked.

"I read in the minds of Kurt and Red that they have to do a complete overhaul of the Retrotimeship's electronic network. It could take weeks... or months."

"Months!" the anthropologist echoed, appalled.

"As long as it takes. During our forced stay in this era we could be useful in saving human lives and educating these tribes."

"These tribes?" Angelvin frowned. "So, you want us to run around this country preaching the good word and giving lessons to our... ancestors?"

"In fact," Kariven reflected, "why not? We're in the middle of protohistory. History with a capital H, strictly speaking, hasn't started yet at this epoch in France or rather in the Celtic region that will become Gaul. I think our helpful intervention in this Time won't have any harmful repercussions in the future. With the helicopter on board we can travel a great distance and, yes, that's right, preach the good word to these people simmering in the crucible of Evolution. Our intervention will carry a much lower risk of causing a serious panic at this time than in 1843 when stagnant ideas had already taken root in people's minds."

"She's got a point," Dormoy agreed.

The ethnographer Angelvin thought for a moment before giving in, "Yuln's right. I opt for this new-fangled crusade. Even though we can't give a bunch of medicine to these Celts or proto-Celts, we can still teach them how to protect themselves from certain illnesses. They'll probably grasp basic hygiene pretty easily as well as... practical medicine."

"Are you sure that they're Celts?" his wife asked.

"Judging by their iron work—swords, daggers and decorations—and by their clothes, their blonde-red hair dyed with plants, they are Celts. The first Celts most definitely who lived around 800 or 700 BC."

"Therefore in the period of Hallstatt I," the anthropologist commented.

"Very likely," Angelvin said. "There were many invasions and racial mixing with maybe Illyrians, which makes the mosaic of proto-Celtic peoples very complicated. But I don't think I'm wrong to call these Iron Age people Celts."

"It might be a good time to get ready to break the ice," Kariven said. "And to start with, before they wake up, let's put the weapons they dropped out of reach."

Quickly, stepping over the paralyzed bodies, they grabbed the knives and heavy swords and put them behind the tower.

The dazed Celts slowly recovered the use of their limbs and stood up, finally becoming aware of the unusual presence of these strangers in their village. By probing their minds Yuln followed their reasoning process and their anxiety.

After hesitating awhile they started speaking to one another in simple words, looking at the ground, surprised to find no weapons. Some of them tried to jump on the intruders with their bare hands. A discharge of weak paralyzing rays struck them down and they collapsed. Faced with this supernatural response the others backed away, their eyes wide open, then scampered off in all directions.

Yuln chose this moment to send into their minds some calming, soothing impulses. Gently and slowly her supranormal abilities generated simple ideas to analyze, suggestions presenting the strangers not as invaders but as friends.

The men acted as expected. They came back, timidly, struck by superstitious terror, stopping in front of the (dead for them) bodies of their tribesmen.

Yuln communicated her thoughts. For obvious psychological reasons she expressed herself—telepathically—so that they thought the "words" were spoken by one of the four men who had come to free the captives.

"We come as friends to your territory. We did you no harm and yet you stole our women. See: to punish you for this crime we executed these warriors with our invincible weapons. But we won't kill them. No, we're going to bring them back to life to prove to you our friendly intentions."

With these simple ideas sent into their minds Yuln advised her companions, "Do what I do, quickly!"

She stretched her arms out over the frozen Celts and whispered her psychic message, "They have to believe we're all-powerful if we want them to obey our orders. This little act is to show them we can bring these impulsive young men back to life after they wanted to attack us."

One minute later, under the outstretched arms, the six young warriors woke up. Terrified by what had just happened, they scurried back, their eyes full of fright, and bumped into the feet of the other members of the tribe. The latter, on seeing this demonstration of magic, bowed down to the ground, begging for pardon from these "divinities" whom they knew not how to worship and earn their good graces.

Yuln continued "talking" in the name of the stronger sex. She spoke her telepathic messages with elementary, even simplistic ideas, using metaphors and images to explain to the Celts that they owed them obedience, not because they were gods but because being different and gifted with higher knowledge they wanted to help them and cure their ills.

When she finished, Yuln told her husband, "Watching the villagers during our brief captivity, I noticed a young man whose left shoulder was dislocated. He was in pain and couldn't use his arm. He's in that hut, the second on our right. I'm going to get him and you can cure him. It'll be great advertising."

A few minutes later Yuln came back leading the 15-year old by his right arm. He was nervous, looking all around him with panicked eyes. His left arm hung at his side; his shoulder bore the trace of a hard fall: dark bruises, scratches and scrapes.

An anthropologist but also a medical doctor—Doniatchka was also one, too—Kariven walked up to him and asked Angelvin to help. He examined the bruise, felt the shoulder—making the patient wince and the ethnographer hold him more tightly—and concluded a recent dislocation, fortunately not separated. The head of the humerus was only slightly out of the glenoid cavity and most of the ligaments were probably still intact.

All the men of the village, as fearful as the patient, watched the scene with nervous curiosity.

"Dear, would you... *calm* this boy for a few minutes?" Kariven asked.

Yuln nodded and projected into his mind soothing waves that did not block the pain but calmed the fears of the young, wounded Celt.

"Now you, Bob. Hold him tight while I readjust. The only problem is if he wiggles around because this is going to hurt."

Kariven felt around and located the abnormal bulge of the humerus and very carefully pulled the arm while adjusting it.

The patient screamed out in pain when the anthropologist popped the head of the humerus into the glenoid. He struggled to get free of his "torturers" but Angelvin hugged him tightly to his chest while his friend massaged the wounded shoulder with care.

"He shouldn't move it for four or five days. There are no splints here, so we'll have to make due with what we can find."

In 15 minutes, the engineer Leconte, with the help of a Celtic sword, had split a piece of wood in two and as best he could "flattened" them out.

Jenny, Yuln and Doniatchka went to search the shacks and came back carrying two rolls of linen and woven hemp that Kariven used to bind the makeshift splint to the arm, which was subsequently bound to the patient's torso. The latter was totally astonished to feel his pain subsiding and hurried back to his shack.

To all the Celts gathered round Yuln emitted these thoughts:

"In a few days this young man will be able to use his arm again. He will be healed. Now let's take care of the two sick women who are suffering without you being able to help them at all. Later we will teach you how you can take care of your own."

Within one hour Kariven and Donitchka—formerly, a doctor from the Moscow faculty[54]—diagnosed two intestinal infections, dermatosis, phlegmon of the throat and for the two young women an infection in the genitals following childbirth—a process in such deplorable conditions of hygiene that alas it was a problem known to all under-evolved peoples.

The two doctors had to go back to the ship to get a medical bag and some sulfamides from the infirmary on board while the others stayed with the tribe.

When Streiler and Harrington saw only Doniatchka and Kariven coming back they feared the worst, but their calm, smiling faces eased the worry about the fate of the others.

"We came to get some medical equipment and drugs from the medical lab," Kariven informed them. Seeing their astonishment Kariven explained their adventure.

---

[54] See Volume 1.

"Out of every bad comes some good," Harrington mused. "During the overhaul of the time travel mechanism that I'm afraid could take weeks, you can borrow the gravito-magnetic helicopter for the altruistic mission you so nobly want to undertake."

The anthropologist frowned, "Do you really think we won't be able to leave here for weeks?"

"Afraid so. The circuits and internal devices of an electronic super-brain are child's play compared to the Retrotimeship's mechanisms."

Doniatchka noticed Streiler clenching his jaw and for a second raising his eyebrows. "Kurt!" she was upset at the idea that the two engineers could hide the truth from them. "Do you really think the ship is… *beyond repair?*"

Streiler claimed that he had never had such a thought but his denial lacked conviction.

Harrington sighed, "That is Kurt's opinion. But I'm not beaten yet."

"Hell," Streiler fumed, "I'm not beaten either but admit it, Red, we're in a damn mess."

"I won't deny it, but we've only been working at it for ten hours and it'll take weeks to finish. At least wait until we've checked all the circuits before giving up."

His nervous temperament and a fruitless night of work made Streiler irritable. He grumbled and turned his back, leaning over the jumble of wires, lights, tubes, transistors and other parts that were a mystery to the profane. Several pieces of flooring had been removed around him, showing the incredibly complex mechanics buried under the cockpit.

Just as Kariven and Doniatchka were stepping through the hatch Harrington said, "I think I should warn you not to alarm the others… prematurely, right?"

The anthropologist looked at the young woman deep in the eyes and saw her silent but sad approval.

"Understood, Red. Doniatchka and I won't say anything. But don't forget that Yuln is telepathic."

CHAPTER VII

The sun had just sunk below the horizon and the indigo twilight was darkened the forest. On the beaten earth in the middle of the village the Celts had lit a big fire around which they were eating the last of their hunt in the company of the castaways of Time.

In their anachronistic clothes of the 20th century, worn and torn and dusty, the "castaways" ate in silence, preoccupied and gloomy.

Kariven was furtively watching his neighbor, Hyok, the chief of the clan, who was holding and using correctly his big iron fork. The modest eating tool—made by the villagers—was one of the first contributions of the time travelers to the Iron Age men. They learned pretty quickly how to make iron cutlery: forks, spoons and table knives. Moreover, they used them eagerly, imitating their teachers.

Hyok was in the prime of life, a wide chest, hairy, long red-blonde hair and a square jaw with an upper lip supporting a big droopy moustache. He was gentle but knew how to show his authority wisely. Hyok incarnated both wisdom and strength in the heart of the tribe.

The tree trunk on which he was sitting was also used by Yuln and her husband. The anthropologist seemed to be staring—without seeing it—straight through his wooden bowl. After finishing his huge leg of deer, he was meditating.

After watching him for several minutes Hyok put his hand on his arm and said, "Master ate but was not hungry… Sad? Your friend Hyok sad too."

Pulled out of his reverie Kariven forced a smile. "I'm not sad, Hyok, but worried," he answered in Celtic, a language he and his friends learned easily enough thanks to the precious knowledge of the ethnographer Angelvin[55]. "We've been here for almost five months and our 'iron bird' is still wounded. We'd like to go home to our… country but we have to wait… maybe a long time."

Hyok used the rudiments of French that Jenny and Yuln had taught him and said, "The other iron bird not good to go back?"

"The helicopter?" the anthropologist smiled. "No, that little iron bird can't take us all the way home."

"But you say Earth is round. If little bird fly and rest? In steps, rest the night, bird can go to other side of Earth, no?"

How could he explain to this Celt of the Iron Age—who had already memorized the basics of geography—that their country was not on the other side of Earth but *of Time?*

Not wanting to make him understand this abstract idea, Kariven kept it short and simple, "We will try to go back later. Tomorrow we will take you in the belly of our iron bird again. We will go west where the sun sets and visit new villages. You will help us like you've done so often to reassure the villagers and explain to them our desire to help, to heal and to teach them many useful things.

"Later, when many moons have passed, you and your men will continue our work among others of your race living in this country. You will teach them to make the tools and instruments that we taught you to make. You will show them how certain plants and 'rocks' form powders or liquids that heal sickness or can be used to make other things. And even later their children and your children will find methods that we didn't teach you."

Hyok's gray-blue eyes sparkled with pride. Puffing out his chest he said, "Later Hyok big chief in big village when men come here often."

---

[55] We can still find traces of the Celtic language in old Irish, Manx (Isle of Man), Gaelic (Scotland) and various Indo-European dialects. (Author's Note)

Yuln, sitting to the left of her husband, leaned over to look Hyok in the eyes. "Maybe you'll be the chief of all villages one day, Hyok, it's very likely. But never forget that only the good can help people become wise and knowledgeable. Conquests can get new land but they make the conquered people angry. Now, you don't build anything solid on bitterness and hatred. We come from a country where bloody wars pitted peoples against peoples, where rivers of blood were spilled during a long reign of hatred. These peoples were strong, then very weak and unhappy after killing one another.

"We know that even if you're on the right path, alas, your successors can wander off it. But maybe with the example that you and your brothers are setting they'll follow in your footsteps and imitate you... If they don't, if they act like warriors, they'll probably destroy everything you leave to them."

Hyok nodded gravely, thought for a minute, then objected, "We make good path. But warriors can come attack village. But how can good beat evil without swords, arrows and axes?"

The ethnographer Angelvin pushed away the wooden bowl on the big table placed next to the fire and sighed, "That's the eternal question. A wise people, loving arts and science—like you're starting to be if you follow our teachings—is liable someday to be attacked by aggressive people. In this case, if it doesn't make weapons, it'll very likely be conquered."

"*Si vis pacem, para bellum*[56]" Kariven quoted. "This adage, unfortunately, is relevant in every century. For the technical evolution and advanced morality of the Celts to have a chance of success, we have to think of teaching them different... and effective means of defending themselves against an eventual attack."

"In other words," Leconte concluded, "teaching them for example how to extract sulfur and saltpeter, and how to pre-

---

[56] If you want peace, prepare for war.

pare charcoal to give them—with these three basic products—the formula for gunpowder? Living in the Iron Age, the Celts will easily be able to improve the working of metals... in order to create simple cannons."

"Oh that, Maurice," Yuln jumped in. "You're going a little far and getting off track of our goals."

"Maurice and you are both right, dear," Kariven said. "Teaching new methods of destruction—or defense—to these men is absolutely contrary to our principles. However, only these methods could really protect them against foreign invasion. I'm referring to the conquest of Gaul by the Romans between 125 and 51 BCE, around six or eight centuries from now. Basically, both ideas are valid... and contradict each other because the latter will cause a huge change in History, a thing we can't allow."

Hyok, who had understood nothing of this conversation that was intentionally spoken in English, asked Kariven (splitting his name in two), "Kariv'en no answer. How to beat evil without swords?"

"We were just talking about that problem, Hyok. The solution is very delicate. To defend yourself is normal if you are attacked, but you can't take the initiative to spill other people's blood."

"Hyok agree. No attack..." He glanced over at the paralyzing rifle hanging from a branch over the table and added, "We fight but not kill enemy if we have sleeping arrow."

Kariven and his friends smiled at this *proviso* and already saw a more humane stature in his thought.

"With what we have at hand here, Hyok, we could never build these paralyzing weapons that you call sleeping arrows."

Disappointed by the response Hyok thought for a minute, then said, "We make hard swords if you teach Hyok to make hard."

The anthropologist smiled to his vocabulary. "Don't think too much on the hard iron I talked about, Hyok, which we call steel. Making it is pretty complex and for the craft will need equipment that we'll study together later if you think it's possible to build."

Entering the long dining-living cabin of the Retrotimeship they greeted Streiler and Harrington with the usual, "Well?" Short and sweet, repeated almost every evening for five months when they came back from the Celtic village.

Harrington rubbed his eyes, let out a sigh and in a cheerful voice that clashed with the weariness showing on his face, he said, "We've finally finished checking all the circuits and relays of the time travel mechanism."

"Really?" the three young women exclaimed together.

"The Kinetempograph, or time measurer, is back in working order," Streiler said.

"And even if we can't get back to our time, we now know where we got shipwrecked."

"And *when*?" Kariven asked.

"In 757AD, May 19 using our calendar. Unfortunately the Kinetempograph isn't enough for time travel. The breakdown we pretty much localized will need a few more weeks or maybe months to fix. It seems that some essential factor is escaping us and delaying our progress."

"Therefore," Harrington pretended to be indifferent, "you have all time you want to continue your altruistic and peaceful education of the Celts."

The Chrysler Turbine of Commander Mark Taylor—attaché of the Strategic Air Command—purred to a halt on South Executive Avenue, having been stopped twice already by the FBI guarding the White House and the safety of the President of the United States.

Commander Taylor and Lieutenant Clark, strapped into their elegant Air Force uniforms, climbed the winding steps of the White House. On the stoop once again two men asked to see their papers... all the while keeping their right hand in the pocket of their beige raincoat where a big caliber gun bulged.

Commander Taylor showed them his invitation, signed by the President himself, addressed in his name and that of his subordinate. Once this final checkpoint was passed they could finally enter the holy of holies of the American federal capital: the White House. Two other G-men led them through the spacious rooms with floors shining like mirrors and soon they were brought to the President. He welcomed them with a friendly, even playful smile, which added to his amiable demeanor.

"Commander Taylor and Lieutenant Clark," he began after sitting them in front of his huge desk, "I'm going to give you a mission of utmost... danger. The future of the world might depend on its outcome."

He put his elbows on his desk, crossed his fingers and stared at the two men before continuing.

"August 25, 1961, fifteen days ago, Professor Red Harrington and Kurt Streiler, whom you know from the first time travel you made together,[57] asked to see me about an extremely important matter. Now, Streiler and Harrington... were coming from the future. Taking the Retrotimeship RT1 at the Nevada Center, where their laboratories are, they were coming from September 4, 1961, to ask me to make the French government evacuate the neighborhood around Champ de Mars in Paris on August 29. On that day the area would be carried away in a Space-Time fold, just like happened in Nagasaki on August 9. Your friends Jean Kariven, Michel Dormoy and Robert Angelvin were supposed to be carried away too... and not come back. As you'll see in the report here, Kariven, his friends and their wives would have been thrown back and lost in 1843.

"The orders for evacuating the threatened area were carried out by the French authorities and no Parisian disappeared, thanks to the wise precautions of Streiler and Harrington. But, as they were coming from a time when the event had already taken place, including the disappearance of your French

---

[57] See Volume 1.

friends, they returned to the Past, the day before the slip into the Space-Time fold, on August 28.

"This day, on board the Retrotimeship, they brought Kariven, Dormoy, Angelvin and their wives with them after telling them what would happen the next day. Thus the three kidnapped couples avoided the problems they were going to face without knowing it.

"With its rescue mission complete the Retrotimeship should have come back on September 4, 1961, where it was expected in the evening at Guyancourt, near Paris, an abandoned airfield under military guard. Well, on September 4, the Retrotimeship didn't land and no one knows what happened to it. Now it's been 11 days since the ship with the castaways in Time has disappeared. In all likelihood, for some unknown reason, the ship is lost somewhere in Time.

"I'm asking you, therefore, to leave today in the Retrotimeship RT2 to search for RT1 in the Past. A special plane will take you to the Nevada Center this afternoon. It leaves at 1 pm from Bolling Air Force Base.[58] I have no need to impress on you how important this mission is. Finding the castaways of Time is our primary concern. Not only because the passengers and the machine are priceless, but also because of the repercussions that might fall upon civilization from their intrusion in the recent Past."

The two officers exchanged a look that betrayed their pessimism, then Commander Taylor said, "Mr. President, you know very well the incredible difficulties that await us in searching for the RT1. These weird time slips in certain areas of the globe proves that the dimension of Time is seriously disturbed. A disturbance that we still don't know the cause of. Some people think it's the effect of atomic explosions on the curvature of Space. Others say that the solar system, in its

---

[58] Military base on the east bank of the Potomac in Washington, DC. (Author's Note)

course in the Apex,[59] has run into a zone of unknown proper-
ties working on the Time Dimension. In fact, Science is lost at
sea and we can't blame it. If the RT1 had a breakdown, I hope
that it didn't turn off its automatic alert system and that we can
find where or when it stopped in the course of Time. If not..."

Taylor opened his arms without finishing his thought.

"The only clue we have, Mr. President, is the date you
gave us. Our first stop, then, will be September 3, the day before Streiler and Harrington first left. Logically we should find
them and explain what's going to happen... until they disappear. So, it'll be easy for them to take what they'll need with
them and save themselves and our French friends. Going back
a little farther in the Past, for example, to save them from the
setbacks awaiting them..."

Programmed to go back to September 3, 1961, the RT2
left Space-Time. Commander Taylor left the time travel commands and Rudy Clark turned on the gravito-magnetic boost-
ers.

The ship was flying silently over Death Valley and heading southeast to land near Los Angeles. The report from the
President said that on September 3, 1961 Harrington and
Streiler were still in the city at 2 pm. Kurt was at Harrington's
house preparing for their departure the next day.

At a very high altitude the RT2 was flying over Kramer
at the intersection of highways 395 and 466 to the north of the
Mojave Desert when the light on the radar-viewer started
blinking. The screen lit up showing a weird triangular ship that
was speeding toward the Retrotimeship. The electronic brain
instantly plotted a new course and safety measures were taken
by the automatic pilot. In a split second the RT2 leaped into
outer space while the strange spaceship, at breakneck speed,

---

[59] Point in space represented by Vega (in the constellation
Lyra) toward which our solar system is heading. (Author's
Note)

shot a purple beam into the space that the Retrotimeship had occupied a second earlier.

These maneuvers happened almost instantly. The electronic brain on board compensated for the inevitable slowness of human reflexes that cannot match the speed and accuracy of the trajectory calculator.

Clark looked worriedly at his superior. "Did you see that, Commander? If it wasn't for the automatic safety system we'd be toast."

"Damn," Taylor swore. "What got into that animal? It was like it was trying to ram our ship."

"Ram? For a second I thought its nose was shooting a pink or purple ray at us."

"So, I wasn't seeing things. I, too, believed I saw a beam just missing us. Clark, turn on the invisibility shields. I'm not feeling good about that triangular ship."

Clark obeyed and pressed a big red button in the middle of the control panel. Six small lights stared blinking green, confirming that the four lateral shields and one on each end were working, making the ship invisible by reducing its refraction index to zero. At the same time the system was absorbing radar waves instead of bouncing them back, making the ship undetectable.

"I'll be damned," Clark grumbled, "we're reacting like we're in enemy territory. But we're in our home country."

"Sure," Commander Taylor remarked, "but I still don't know why the flying triangle did that. It wasn't an American spaceship. And it's not Polarian either since our friends the Men from Outer Space only use discs, spheres and rockets."

"Our planets were federated with the Polarians and a lot of other solar systems and we know what ships they use. I don't know where that one could have come from."

"In fact, it could have just been an American prototype that was intimidating us to get us out of its way... Let's head for Los Angeles but leave the invisibility on for now."

At reduced speed and high altitude they flew over Palmdale, 25 miles NNW of Los Angeles. The scintillation counters on the outside of the RT2 detected a source of radio-activity. On the control panel a tiny, frosted, green screen lit up and numbers marking the strength of the radiation clicked by under the astonished eyes of the two men.

"500 Roentgens!" Commander Taylor turned pale.

The number disappeared and was replaced by 550, then 600 and wavered around 700.

"780 Roentgens! It's... it's not possible!" Lieutenant Clark muttered as he set the ship to fly off at 30,000 mph into space.

The pilots were protected from this formidable speed by an anti-G force field. They felt nothing, but beads of sweat started covering their foreheads.

"780 Roentgens," Taylor repeated in a daze. "How could such radiation show up only 25 miles from Los Angeles? No human organism could withstand it!"

"The source seems to be coming from south or southwest of Los Angeles," Clark turned on the viewer showing the landscape almost 2,000 miles beneath them.

Both of them groaned almost simultaneously. Stunned, unbelieving, they were watching the image on the screen. They saw Los Angeles—or what used to be Los Angeles. Of the marvelous buildings, parks, beautiful streets, geometric buildings of the Hollywood studios, nothing remained but a frightening chaos of ruins, masses of melted metal and dust everywhere from which clouds of smoke were rising. Lieutenant Clark cleared his dry throat but he could only emit a muffled sound. Taylor was shaken up as well and automatically checked the Kentempograph to make sure it was really September 3, 1961.

"I... I don't understand," he muttered. "Such a catastrophe never took place in Los Angeles on September 3, 1961, and yet... Los Angeles is razed to the ground, completely destroyed by a thermo-nuclear bomb probably... Unless there was another slip in Space-Time of the whole North American continent just when we were traveling into the Past? But even still? A catastrophe like this couldn't happen in the Past, near or far! It has to be a new kind of disturbance in the Dimension of Time. We have to be sure, Clark. Look for an area free of radioactivity and we'll land."

Without saying a word Clark brought the Retrotimeship down to Earth. Half an hour later the invisible ship landed silently in the Anza Desert, 13 miles west of the shore of the Salton Sea. The Lieutenant opened the rear ventral hold and the gigantic, rectangular hatch unfolded slowly toward the ground where its top sank into the ochre sand. The two men entered the hold and climbed into the helicopter that was parked there.

The machine was a helicopter only in name. It had no blades because it was propelled by a gravito-magnetic field. It looked like an oval ball, the lower part was shiny metal and the top, the cockpit, was transparent. 22 feet high by 13 in diameter at its base it could hold eight passengers.

The reconnaissance craft slid down the carriage of the inclined ramp formed by the hatch and came off to float around eight inches off the ground. The ventral hatch was closed by remote control and the helicopter rose up quickly, heading toward Mecca, a small town on the NNW bank of the Salton Sea, 183 miles from Los Angeles.

After flying over the huge stretch of water and coming in sight of land the pilots were in for another surprise: no trace of a town appeared in the place where Mecca should have been according to the map. The helicopter followed the shore, heading east, until they saw, 20 miles from the point where Mecca should have stood, a group of buildings.

"The place seems peaceful enough," Commander Taylor noted. "Since Mecca is conspicuously absent, we should land there on the empty land to the north of that town."

A few minutes later the two men left the aircraft, each armed with a paralyzing rifle after taking the precaution of slipping a disintegrator pistol (the formidable Polarian weapon) under their arms. At the entrance to the sunlit town a sign read "Mishka" in big blue letters on a white background.

"Mishka? Mecca? It's close… but different."

357

The streets were deserted between the clean, bright buildings that were only four or five stories high except for one massive, rectangular, bright green building that stood over 150 feet higher than the rest in the center of town.

The first person the officers met was an old woman in a white tunic held tightly around her scrawny neck. She was limping along, using a weird, glass cane, and stood in the middle of the street to look suspiciously at the two strangers walking toward her.

"Excuse me, madam," Commander Taylor said, "but we've had a... breakdown and would like to contact the... mayor or sheriff or any authority in Mec... Mishka."

The old woman looked at them one at a time, blinking her eyes, and croaked, "Authority? If it's Dr. Avshton you want, you'll find him over there," she pointed to the huge green building dominating the sleepy town.

Walking toward the place they passed two men and farther along a woman, all three old and dressed the same: red sandals and a white tunic gathered at the neck.

The officers rang the bell of the only door of the big building and a young woman opened. She did not try to hide the surprise on her pretty face. Her brown hair fell to her shoulders and swept the shiny, bright yellow tissue of her tight blouse.

"Is it possible to see Dr. Avshton, miss?" Commander Taylor asked after bowing slightly before the young woman looking at them with wide eyes.

She finally pulled her attention away from their uniforms and in a gentle voice said, "Would you follow me? Dr. Avshton will certainly see you."

Dropped on the fifth floor by a silent elevator they were led into a huge room that was, apparently, both an office and examining room to judge by the tables and numerous metal cabinets that decorated the place, separated from the office by a heavy, white curtain that was shiny but opaque.

Dr. Avshton, dark-haired and very young, also wore a yellow shirt that was shiny. Just like the young lady who had brought the visitors, he did not try to hide his surprise as he stared long and hard at their uniforms.

"Commander Taylor, Strategic Air Command, and this is Lieutenant Clark."

"Very honored, gentlemen," the doctor nodded and offered them to sit. "And to what do I owe this honor?"

"We were making a reconnaissance flight in the area and a mechanical problem forced us to land near Mec... Mishka. After making our repairs, we took the opportunity to visit your town."

This explanation seemed to surprise their host even more. Before responding he addressed the young woman standing next to the door. "Stay here, Shora. Sit down." Then he turned to his visitors. "I'm afraid I don't understand... Commander Taylor, what you mean. Your breakdown I get but the fact that you were compelled to visit our town, as you call it, surprises me. Don't you know that Mishka is a forbidden zone to everyone... of your age? Unless you were... sent by the authorities?"

The surprise of the two officers was clearly more than the doctor's.

Taylor tried a trick to justify their presence in this zone. "Please excuse me, Doctor, but we're on an official mission and we're not at liberty to reveal the details. So, I ask you to keep this strictly between ourselves. Even the authorities... of the area and of California don't know about it."

"So be it. You can trust me."

"Out of curiosity, Dr. Avshton," Clark said, "could you tell us exactly when this zone was created?"

"June 13, 1357, to be exact. But it wasn't so long ago that you could forget..."

The two officers had trouble hiding their astonishment but managed not to even look at each other.

"1357," Mark Taylor thought aloud. "So that would be now..."

"21 years ago," Avshton finished for him, keeping a careful eye on the strange visitors.

359

"That's right," Clark nodded. "And you're satisfied with your... post?"

"Well now, I couldn't find a better place for my work on biological aging, could I?"

"Indeed," Clark agreed, praying to all the saints in paradise not to abandon him and his chief.

"All the old people in *Calofnia* were sent here to end their days. We help them the best we can in their final months of life. The law voted in 1357 is cruel to order these old men and women to leave their home, their children, their friends and come here when they reach 60 years old... Mishka," he murmured thoughtfully, "the dead zone, as they call Calofnia. Sad reputation. We try hard, however, to let them die in their old age without too much physical pain. Our mechano-hypnotic treatments also protect them from emotional suffering... at least most of them."

He paused, hesitating, then decided to admit, "At the risk of appearing like anarchists to you, Commander Taylor, I'm sorry I didn't live in the last century, free of all these... modern constraints."

"Aren't we all," Clark ventured to agree.

The doctor stared at him for a long time, raised an eyebrow and calmly remarked, "I don't want to... offend you, Lieutenant Clark, or you, Commander Taylor, but your... attitude and your comments suggest you don't belong to the... dictatorial army."

The doctor's reluctance and carefully chosen words made the officers suspicious. This man seemed honest and sincere but he was hiding something.

"Listen, Dr. Avshton," Commander Taylor took a risk, "since we've been talking—courteously—I'm sure that we both feel like we're being duped. Am I wrong?"

Avshton glanced at his assistant, who had not opened her mouth, before saying, "I admit that I've been thinking the same thing."

"And your conclusion? Especially since our uniforms don't impress you. I told you that we're on an official mission but that's not true. *Here* we're acting on our own; I admit it."

"You have no need to admit that, Commander. I believe you wholeheartedly especially since your uniforms… belong to no army I know of."

This time the two officers could not hide their surprise.

"Who are you and where do you come from?"

Taylor answered with another question, "Do you have a calendar, doctor?"

Once again the doctor raised his eyebrows and with an expression of amused bewilderment he gave to his mysterious visitors a shiny block from his desk. Silently but unconsciously moving their lips the two Americans read the numbers that appeared on the chrome metal calendar: 3-9-1378.

"September 3, 1378," Clark repeated aloud, scratching his forehead.

His chief took a deep breath and said, "We're Americans and we come from September 3… 1961."

CHAPTER VIII

It was Avshton's and Shora's turn to shiver. "You say you come from the Future?" the doctor batted his eyes.

"Yes and no. Because if we came from the Future we would find here in this area... a village in 1378... an Indian village and not a modern city. Because America was not discovered until 1492 and colonized afterward by the whites. At this time only the old continent was civilized. And yet, could we call civilized a people who knew nothing of cars, planes, movies, television and everything that today belongs to modern man?"

"But you claim to have traveled through Time?"

"Yes, but not in *our* Time, in *our* Past, which is terribly different than *your* Time and Past. And that's what I don't understand either."

Avshton stared at the young woman, then at his visitors before raising his voice, "By Kahen and Heaven! If *you* don't understand, how am I supposed to?"

"You speak our language and despite your strange clothes and some weird turns of phrase, you are certainly Earthlings like us," Clark observed.

"Naturally I'm an Earthling. Did you think you'd find a Polarian here?"

"Polarian?" the two officers were startled. "That's the first time I've heard a link between our two eras. How do you know about the Polarians in 1378 when they don't come to Earth until 1958?"

"Not at all. The Polarians tried to make contact with Earthlings in 1213."

"Tried? So they failed?"

The Franshais spaceships chased them away from our planet to preserve their global domination," the doctor explained.

"*French* spaceships? In 1213? During the reign of the Capetian King, Philip II?"

"Capetian? Philip II? But no! Under the government of Norbi Hyoky, the dictator at the time. By Kahen and Heaven, we'll never understand each other."

"Kahen," Rudy Clark thought aloud. "That sounds like Cain."

"Cain?"

"A bible character. One of the sons of Adam and Eve…"

"Adam and Eve?" Avshton echoed without understanding. "Kahen and Heaven is a kind of… polite swear word. Kahen was the name of a kind of divinity and Heaven is where He came from with her brothers and sisters."

"I think, doctor, that you might want to teach us a little of your history, otherwise we'll end up in a ridiculous and endless maze of misunderstandings."

"From the beginning of history, preferably," Taylor added.

"So be it. But don't expect anything more than a very basic sketch—I'm no historian. So, Tradition says, partly backed up by archeological finds, that around 2,200 years ago an iron bird—we'd call it a spaceship—came down from Heaven and landed on Earth. This happened in Fransh, not far from Parish, 15 or 20 miles from the present city."

"Paris no doubt," Rudy Clark corrected.

"No, *Parish*. Out of this iron bird came demi-gods and demi-goddesses who established contact with the primitives, our ancestors, then in the Iron Age. These demi-gods, still worshipped by the believers to whom I don't belong by the way, were called, in the chain of command: Kahen, Dhomoyk, Harkton, Hanlvin and…"

Clark and Taylor felt fear and dread shoot through them as a strange shiver ran down their spines. They wanted to stand up but could not. They just sat there, full of mixed emotions, unable to say a word.

"What's wrong with you?" Avshton was alarmed.

"It's nothing," Taylor managed to say. "Please continue, doctor, and excuse us, your story hit us pretty hard. We'll explain why later."

"As you wish. So, I was saying that the demi-gods Kahen, Hool his wife, their brothers and their sisters Gh'en and Douk'ha, were in contact with an Iron Age people. Apparently their iron bird was damaged and could never be repaired, which forced them to live the rest of their lives in this tribe at the dawn of civilization.

"Where did these... demi-gods come from? From a distant country according to Tradition, but most certainly from another solar system because we now know that at that time no planet of our system had a race evolved enough to build aircraft, let alone spaceships. Kahen and his friends knew how to make our ancestors love them and they were accepted right away, especially since they got all kinds of benefits from them. In fact, while Harkton and Shrylere stayed in the iron bird—maybe they were sick or were trying the fix the mechanical problem—the others patiently educated the primitive people.

"On board a smaller iron bird, legend says, the demi-gods flew from one village to another, teaching Good to all the people along with new methods in metallurgy, medicine, woodworking, construction, mineral extraction, etc. Slowly, from place to place, from province to province, during the decades of the practical teaching of Kahen and his brothers and sisters, our ancestors organized themselves into a strong and united nation, independent and able to make a huge leap on the path of Evolution. The knowledge brought by Kahen to our ancestors allowed them to progress centuries in only one generation."

"Indeed," Rudy Clark reflected. "Without Kariven... I mean Kahen, the legacy of your ancestors left to themselves would have no comparison—quantitatively and qualitatively—to what you have inherited. In 1378, you would know nothing about cars, planes, TV, rockets and all the technical wonders that are the pride of the Modern Age."

"There's no doubt," Avshton admitted. "A few years after the demi-gods came to Earth, a chief came out of the first Shelte people visited where they stayed until they died. This chief was called Ioc or Hyoky, we don't know the exact pronunciation, but it doesn't matter. The fact is the chiefs... and the tyrants who reigned later took the name Hyoky in memory of the first King or Chief of the Shelto-Fransh."

"You mean French?"

"No, Lieutenant, Fransh. Of this we are sure because the inhabitants of Fransh are still called this. So, Hyoky I reigned for ten years, supported and wisely counseled by the demi-gods. Without a direct descendant, a young man of the tribe succeeded him. It was a man Kahen had once healed and who owed him eternal gratitude for it. He was a good and just king. With the support of the demi-gods Hyoky II advanced his people, with constant improvements and technical achievements in this young society that would be the mother of our civilization.

"Although gods are eternal, as they say, demi-gods unfortunately are mortal. One by one they died after spending 50 years among the Iron Age men. But at their death they left a huge legacy to Fransh: their knowledge. Or at least they left that part of their knowledge that our ancestors could learn. Knowledge based solely on Good."

An inexpressible emotion squeezed the throats of the two officers on hearing the great deeds of their best friends, called demi-gods by this man from a time completely foreign to their own.

"Peace," Avshton continued, "was maintained in Fransh for a long time, maybe one or two centuries. Many records left by Kahen's descendants were unfortunately destroyed in wars. And one day Hyoky IV, who faithfully followed the path laid out by his predecessors, was assassinated by the chief of a jealous province. A cleverly planned plot allowed the assassin, the usurper, Hyoky V, to get rid of his victim's relatives. That was how the reign of violence started.

"And it was at this time that we see the first truly deadly weapons appear: rifles, pistols, cannons, pretty crude but in spite of their imperfections they were still formidable weapons. Weapons that were no match for neighboring peoples who had still not reached the level of the Fransh.

"Hyoky V first ordered that Teachers no longer operate outside the country. The demi-gods, however, had wisely encouraged the education of all humans no matter where they came from. Their dream was to bring all people into an early stage of a real World Federation.

"For several years, under the indoctrination of Hyoky V the Fransh prepared for war. New teachers taught them harmful, selfish principles, patiently infusing the hearts of men with hatred, telling them that other people were enemies, jealous of the knowledge and technical riches of the Fransh. The effects of these vile policies were soon felt among the Fransh. On a superficial pretext—a group of foreigners raiding a nearby town—war broke out. The powerful army of Hyoky V invaded several countries at the same time… and conquered them in only a few months. The people could do nothing against the attack—swords and arrows against rifles and cannons and already the first explosive shells. In less than a year the Fransh occupied all of Arop and were still arming themselves. Over the centuries they sent expeditionary commando teams that took possession of the old continent—Arop, Afrish and Ashi—turning the natives into slaves or, depending on the mood of the conqueror, considering them as simple servants.

"The Anglo-Sashons were conquered like all the people on the continent but fled in great numbers over the ocean and reached this continent here where they settled and quickly multiplied. At first they had to fight the natives of the red race who had been living here since forever but soon they made peace and the two races—white and red—united. For centuries they lived in peace since the Fransh were busy consolidating its position on the old continent. Once this task was finished the Fransh armies rested, regrouped their forces and left some battalions of Surveillance Commandos in the occupied countries. Then over the next few centuries the Tyrants turned their attention to the ocean and decided to invade the New World where my Anglo-Sashon ancestors had once found refuge. Because if they hadn't come here nobody would've known there were other lands over the ocean as Kahen had said.

"And the conquest of the New World began. My ancestors didn't have the technical benefits of the conquerors but resisted heroically, even though the fight was hopeless and unequal for them. They had to surrender to save themselves being slaughtered to the last woman and child. With the New World the Fransh were masters of the Earth… and they have remained so!"

"Still?" Commander Taylor could not believe it. "Haven't you tried to throw off their yolk over the centuries? To get your independence back?"

"Yes, of course. There were always resistance movements that were mercilessly exterminated. We live in relative peace, as long as we submit to the needs of our masters and the current tyrant: Marli Hyoky II-III-I. The II indicated the second millennium after Kahen, the III marks the third century of the second millennium and the I the first dictator of this century.

"We resist and we react but alas we always lose because we don't have the means to fight with equal weapons against our masters. With the exception of hunting rifles and revolvers we have no weapons. What hope is there under such conditions of inferiority? Only last week, as a cruel example that will give some idea, the tyrant came to inspect the west coast Surveillance Commando. While standing in his car, reviewing his commando team, a group of rebels were foolish enough to fire at him with hunting rifles. The tyrant was wounded in the arm… only. The guilty parties were executed on the spot and since this attack was the 20th in less than ten years committed against the high dignitaries of the tyrant or against himself, he decided on a terrible retaliation to serve as an example to future rebels. In Langles, the town where the attack was made, the Surveillance Commando evacuated. The people were curious at first and happy, but not for long unfortunately because the next morning a triangular spaceship dropped a hydrogen bomb that pulverized the city and destroyed the entire population. This bomb, a secret weapon that only a few Fransh scientists know how to make, wiped Langles off the face of the Earth. Radio, TV and the newspapers, being controlled by the Fransh of course, quickly broadcast to the world this news that was supposed to discourage the slightest will to resist among the enslaved people."

"That's horrifying!" Taylor scowled. "Lieutenant Clark and I flew over Los Angeles, meaning your Langles, just a few hours ago. The radioactivity is still awfully high."

"We don't know much about atomic physics," Avshton explained. "Our masters keep a close eye on our education but the Fransh use bombs with short term radiation. In a week all traces will have disappeared. Teams of forced labor, recruited as always from the malcontents—and they are legion!—will clear the ruins with big machines given them by the new Surveillance Commando. In a few months a new city will be built in Langles on the ashes of its murdered inhabitants."

"Kariven would be appalled to learn of these awful crimes… that he and his friends caused indirectly," Clark thought aloud.

"Our poor friends had no idea of the changes that would result from their intervention in the Past," Taylor said. "By educating the Iron Age men they jumped almost 1,000 years—based on the chronology of our own history—in the normal span of technical evolution."

"Poor Kariven. So this is what he and Yuln, Angelvin, Dormoy and the others passed on to posterity. Covered in glory they are the pivotal points of this civilization that has made demi-gods of them!"

Avshton and Shora his assistant looked at each, puzzled. The real meaning of these comments escaped them.

"Kariven? Do you have a demi-god by this name in your Time?"

"Your demi-god Kahen and his brothers and sisters are just our friends, Avshton. Friends who left *our* Present to end up—accidentally because of a disturbance in the Time Dimension—in *your* Past… where they couldn't get out of."

This declaration left them speechless. Clark and Taylor patiently told them everything they knew about the disappearance of the Retrotimeship.

"So, you're coming from a Future that's chronologically late with respect to our Present?" the doctor asked.

"Chronologically is the right word, Avshton. We have, however, reached and even surpassed your stage but following a slower evolution because in 1378 you are already in the middle of the Atomic Age whereas we, at that time, were still in darkness. It's easy to understand: in the Iron Age we weren't blessed with the teaching of men from the Future."

"All the better," Clark pointed out, "if you look at the social state the men of today are living in, under this tyrannical reign of the Fransh."

"You're lucky you know nothing about this horrible dictatorship," the young assistant spoke sadly.

"The Fransh have always been our friends and allies," Commander Taylor informed them. "For centuries their thought shined all over the known world. Their culture was rich in learning for other people but today, with the Earth finally united, the level of evolution in the great nations is pretty much the same everywhere. What will help us progress faster toward the Golden Age is the fact that the specter of war is locked away in the storehouse of past faults."

"Point of fact, Avshton," Clark reflected. "If you date Kariven's coming to your ancestors 2200 years ago, how is it that your calendar says 1378? Logically it would be around the year 2200."

"A lot of ink has been spilled over that question and it divided the Fransh themselves for a long time. Here's the reason: a kind of Messenger from who knows where and who left for who knows where—on a fire arrow some say—showed up on Earth 1378 years ago, around 800 years after the Kahen

Era. This Messenger was a great sage by the name of Vrish-Ju and he tried to teach men kindness, preaching to the Fransh dictators about non-violence and love of other people.

"Vrish-Ju started a big, passionate movement wherever he visited and the dictator Hyoky Ralsh IX at the time had to deal with his influence that was threatening to weaken his... questionable popularity. So he decided not to kill the Messenger of Good but to accept his ideas and pretend to follow the New Doctrine. His prestige rose high, then, among all the people who considered him rightly to be a tyrant. On seeing this and to make the movement even more in his favor, he offered the people of Earth to celebrate year 1 of the New Age offered by Vrish-Ju. It was decided, then, to replace the old Kahenian calendar with the Vrishian. And so it was 1378 years ago that the Messenger of Good, Vrish-Ju, thought for a while that the people and the tyrant were going to follow that path of wisdom.

"His joy was short-lived. Seeing that Hyoky Ralsh IX was quietly pulling the reins of power and that the people felt conquered, Vrish-Ju made a now famous statement... though it's better not to quote this to a Fransh: *The giant stands proud, unjust and brutal, defying the repeated attacks of all his oppressed people. But he will fall in time. The weak who are shaking, kneeling at his feet, will suffer more of his arrogance and his abuses but Time will deliver them one day.*"

Avshton smiled faintly before continuing.

"The Wise Messenger disappeared mysteriously and sunk millions of faithful into grief and sorrow. He never made clear the meaning of the enigmatic words *Time will deliver them one day.*"

The triangular spaceship had been flying all over Langels (Los Angeles) for almost two hours, circling wider and wider and gradually moving away from the zone recently devastated as a retaliation. At the commands of the patrol ship were two men, 30 years old, with sharp chins. They nervously scrutinized the landscape using a cone-shaped instrument. The powerful, electronic telescope allowed them to see the ground as if they were only 30 feet high.

On the control panel the triangular screen showed the bust of a hard-looking man. His red and white uniform was the same as the pilots.

"Well?" his voice snapped over the speaker.

"Still nothing, Commander. But…"

"There are no buts," the officer barked. "You were dreaming, that's all. And you wasted time searching for this ghost ship—as stupid as when you alerted all the posts in Calofnia."

"But," the chief pilot said, "we're sure that…"

"Enough, Rolansh! Get back to your base and get examined by a psychiatrist! Over and out."

The screen went blank and Rolansh looked at Bertra, his co-pilot. "By Kahen and the rest, we did see it, that huge rocket ship not far from Langles."

"Of course, but I'm not sure that our ray hit it. Whatever the case, we're going to get it now for setting off a false alarm all over Calofnia. Don't you think we should search a little longer before going back to base?"

Rolansh glanced at the time and grumbled, "Let's patrol for another 30 minutes but I don't think it'll get us very far. Besides, where could that ship have come from when the entire Earth is under our control?"

"Are you going to say I was dreaming?" Bertra said reluctantly. "What if it was a Polarian spaceship?"

The pilot broke out laughing. "Are you joking? A Polarian spaceship here? Come on, it would have been seen long before by our space stations. A Polarian! That's a laugh. We chased them away centuries ago…"

"By Kahen!" Bertra shouted, looking through the electronic scope. "Look over there on the outskirts of Mishka!"

The pilot grabbed his own automatically focused cone and swore aloud on seeing the oval helicopter left by Taylor and Clark.

"Well now, it's really shrunk down, this ghost ship."

"It's not the same but it's still totally different from our Surveillance Commandos."

The triangular spaceship landed silently 100 yards from the aircraft and the pilots, each armed with an ultra-sonic machine gun, headed towards it cautiously. Noticing that it was empty they carefully approached the small city. The first house they visited had 30 old people in the big, ground floor lounge, all of them wrapped in their long white tunics. Some were reading, others chatting quietly, lying on their reclining lounge chairs.

"We're searching for two strangers who are hiding in Mishka," Rolansh announced loudly. "Did they come in here?"

A young woman in a shiny, golden yellow smock walked up to them. She was cold and distant. "Nobody came in here except our usual residents."

"Maybe they didn't come in but they certainly passed by *in front* of the house. Considering there's almost no one on the streets, your residents must have seen something through this big front window."

"I'm telling you that we haven't seen any strangers in Mishka," she replied calmly. "Now, you're free to submit us to a psychic examination if you think it's necessary. The residents and I are at your disposal. You can also search the house."

The two pilots scowled at the nurse and spit at her feet before leaving to go to the central block.

"Hello Blira," Avshton smiled at the woman's face that had just popped up on the triangular screen to the right of his desk. "Why do you look so anxious?"

"Dr. Avshton, two men from the Surveillance Commando just questioned me about the possibility of strangers in Mishka."

The doctor glanced briefly at his guests before asking, "Strangers in Mishka? And what did you tell them, Blira?"

"That we didn't see any," she hesitates a second. "Don't keep them at the Center any longer, doctor. The patrol will be there any minute."

The doctor thanked her, frustrated to see that his false surprise did not fool the young nurse. He turned off the screen and stood up. "I can't hide you here, friends. You have to leave through the dining hall and hide in house number one…"

Loud knocks at the door startled him.

"Shora, take them away, quickly," he whispered, betraying his close feelings for his assistant.

She and the two officers left through the operating room while the doctor went to open the office door calmly. The barrel of an ultra-sonic machine gun smashed into his chest.

Rolansh, alone, pushed him back with the weapon and ordered, "Stay in this room! Where are the men you were conspiring with?"

"The men? I'm afraid I don't understand…"

The ultra-sonic discharge struck his belly. The doctor bent double and howled in pain.

"You still don't understand?" the torturer teased cynically.

"Don't shoot!" the doctor pleaded, shaking in pain. "They… They're up in the…" He slowly raised his arm to point upstairs before passing out… without betraying them.

CHAPTER IX

Bertra and Rolansh had split up. While one entered the Central Block to question the personnel and the head doctor, the other went into the yard, around the back of the building and hid behind a bush.

Convinced that the doctor had caved in, Rolansh blocked the elevator and silently climbed the grand staircase. Meanwhile, guided by Shora, Clark and Taylor were in the dining hall whose huge windows looked out onto the yard. Shora went out first after scanning the grounds (a little too hastily) to make sure that no one was waiting for them. Followed by the two men she hurried into the yard. They had barely gone 20 yards when a voice behind them shouted, "Stop! Hands in the air!"

This harsh command froze them in place. But with a simultaneous reflex Clark and Taylor jumped to the side, diving into the bushes, Clark shoving Shora to the ground. Before even having reached the grass Commander Taylor had flipped off the safety switch of his paralyzing rifle. He fired and swept the park with his ray at maximum power. It was only then that he saw through the leaves the body of a man in a short, tight-fitting, red and white tunic fall forward. The barrel of the machine gun he was holding with two hands stuck in the ground. Paralyzed, he could not let go of his weapon.

"Quickly," Shora scrambled to her feet, helped by Clark. "You have to hide in house number one on the edge of Mishka.

As they started to run Taylor said, "Shora, it's better if we get to our helicopter. If we stay too long here we'll reduce our chances of escaping the Surveillance Commando."

"We'll make a detour to reach the north exit of Mishka without going through the city."

374

They were panting when they came out of the huge park and were soon on a plain full of scrub and brush where the dried grass fought for the sandy soil with thick plants, signs announcing the nearness of the desert. Beyond the leafy park, around a mile to the south, the terrace-roof of the medical block rose up.

Having avoided the streets of Mishka by this detour, it was not long before they saw their helicopter, glistening in the sun like a huge metal ball with a transparent top. Behind it was parked the triangular ship, its nose pointing toward the sky.

When they reached the oval helicopter they stopped, relieved, and said goodbye to the brave young woman who helped save them.

"Goodbye, Shora. You and Dr. Avshton have been of great service."

"Goodbye, friends from the Future," she whispered. "We're glad we could help. I hope Dr. Avshton got rid of the other guard. We'll put their bodies in their ship and dump it in the lake."

"The guard is only paralyzed," Clark warned her. "He'll wake up in around half an hour. Better go tell Avshton right away."

"There's no need."

Surprised by this voice they swung around, weapons raised. But before being able to fire they felt a sharp pain in their chest and dropped their weapons, doubling over. Rolansh was lying flat on the sand under the helicopter. He jumped up, picked up the two rifles and backed away, keeping his victims in his sights. He clenched his jaws in anger as they struggled to straighten up, racked with pain.

"So Bertra is only paralyzed," he smirked. 'We'll wait calmly for him to wake up."

Threatened as they were, they had to obey and waited, moping, not daring to pull out the disintegrators they both had been wise enough to hide under their arms. At the slightest suspicious move Rolansh would not hesitate to shoot and yet every minute lost was making it more dangerous for them to escape when the second woke up. 45 minutes passed like this, the guard watching every move they made. Bertra finally arrived, running up, mad as hell.

"They almost got me, the damned..." Not finding the right word he huffed and puffed and finally grumbled, "Should we take them back to the base or would you rather head for Sadigosh?"

"Neither, Bertra. With the doctor, the nurse and this girl here being accomplices of these... two weird guys, some retaliation will have to be taken on Mishka."

"That's for sure!" the other sneered. "Especially since the old people also lied by keeping silent."

"Therefore, we're going to offer our Grand Marli Hyoky a great show! Go alert HQ at Sadigosh and explain the situation. I'll bet they'll ask Grand Marli Hyoky right away to do us the honor of attending the festivities in person."

"And her?" Bertra nodded his arrogant head at Shora.

Rolansh shrugged and looked at Clark and Taylor. "Here's what'll happen to you two for running away."

He calmly adjusted his weapon and aimed at the young woman. In horror she backed away a few steps and instinctively raised her trembling hands in imaginary protection. Rolansh pulled the trigger and the ultra-sonic beam spit out. The poor girl started screaming, howling, and fell backward. She balled up in the sand, her body convulsing terribly. The intensity of the beam grew so strong that her golden yellow smock was burned away, without a flame, scorching her skin. In the last throes of death she moaned and remained balled up on the ground. Her shriveled corpse was covered in gruesome blisters. It was nothing but a pile of flesh whose cells exploded under the ultra-sonic vibrations.

"Bastards!" Clark clenched his jaws in hate and moved to jump on the monster.

Bertra shot a weak discharge at him that stopped him in his tracks and made him groan in pain. "Take good care of them," he said to the other as he headed to the triangular spaceship.

Fifteen minutes later he came back looking happy, his eyes glinting with ecstatic joy. "I spoke to the Grand Marli Hyoky himself!"

"You're joking!" the chief pilot replied without taking his eyes off the prisoners.

"No, really. Grand Marli Hyoky was there inspecting the Communication Center in Sadigosh just when I called. So, he listened to my message personally and did me the honor of answering in person... and congratulating both of us warmly! A ship from HQ is bringing him here with the commander to raze Mishka to the ground and destroy the nasty vermin."

"Well now, Bertra, I smell a promotion in the air."

"The way Grand Marli Hyoky spoke, it wouldn't surprise me at all," he gloated.

Clark and Taylor looked at each other, stunned. They were truly in a tight spot, the worst in their lives that had, however, been full of danger.

Clark whispered something to his partner but Rolansh thundered, "If you need some information, ask out loud! And don't even think about escaping! You're far too precious to even think of bribing us to let you go..."

"And taking away your promotion," Taylor sneered back.

"Exactly. You'll have the honor of being interrogated by Marli Hyoky in person very soon. And if your explanations sound sincere to him, you can hope for his mercy."

"Yeah," Bertra smiled cynically. "You'll die a good death choosing whatever way seems nicest to you... In fact, where do you come from?" he suddenly asked. "Are you Polarians?"

"Earthlings," Taylor answered, forcing himself to stay calm.

"Earthlings? And you want us to believe that rebels could have built a ship like this in secret?" he pointed his thumb at the helicopter.

"There they are!" Bertra shouted, ignoring their captives' response.

In the sky, coming from the west, a huge triangular spaceship around 250 feet per side was heading toward Mishka. The sunlight sparkled off its aluminum-colored armor, giving it a blinding brilliance. On the bottom were numerous concave windows. Three rectangular plates slid open to reveal the double wheels with huge green tires. When the landing gear was out the giant ship veered off and came back with a low rumble to land and roll to a stop only 50 yards away.

Next to this colossus the triangular patrol ship and the oval helicopter looked like toys sitting in its pointed shadow. A ramp with handrails came slowly down and a man appeared in the ventral hatch—a fat man with brown hair, pale skin, draped majestically in a kind of pure white fur decorated with gold embroidery and precious gems, red, green, blue, purple and black. He walked slowly down the ramp followed at a distance by ten men in richly embroidered yellow tunics. The commander's red uniform clashed harshly with the formal attire of the dignitaries.

Marli Hyoky, dictator of Earth, stopped 15 feet away from the captives flanked by the two guards. Rolansh, trembling with emotion before the Supreme Chief, bowed low. He accompanied this servile gesture with a great sweep of his right arm, bringing it to his heart to show his loyalty. He stayed bent over with his head lowered. Bertra was alarmed to see that the prisoners—the height of insolence—stood up straight, mocking His Greatness! With a hard punch to their backs he forced them down, "Bow down, you dogs!"

Taylor and Clark obeyed reluctantly and imitating their guards they bowed and brought their right hand humbly to their chest... in order to slip their hands onto the butt of their disintegrator pistols.

Marli Hyoky approached the two guards and ordered, "Stand up, Guards. You have accomplished an incredible feat that you will be rewarded for. Now get this vermin up," he pointed a foot at the captives bent over.

Without even looking at each other the two prisoners jumped forward and stuck their disintegrators in the dictator's belly. Completely stunned, he opened his mouth as if he suddenly could not breathe. Clark spun around and shot just as the guards got over their surprise and were about to fire. There were two blinding flashes and their bodies disappeared, vanished in the rays.

The dignitaries of the escort, 30 feet away, started running at them but Clark was already turning his disintegrator back on them. More blinding flashes and high-pitched whistles and one by one the tyrant's henchmen were changed into bright beams of light.

"And there's more for you," Commander Taylor growled, digging his weapon into the dictator's back. "Walk, hands in the air."

"Don't shoot! Don't shoot!" his voice boomed.

"No need to bark like that, we're not deaf," Clark told him.

"It's… it's for the machine guns," he stammered pitifully.

"Do you think they'll fire without your order?" Clark asked ironically. "They'd be too afraid of hitting your fat."

Being careful to keep their hostage between them and the firing line of the ship's guns, they headed quickly toward the helicopter. Clark rushed to the commands while Taylor, with a few well-placed kicks, forced the dictator to climb into the hold. He closed the armored hatch, activated the magnetic locks and joined his partner.

"Okay, Rudy, let's go!"

The helicopter shot up and headed for the Anza Desert. Clark turned on the viewer and shined a beam in front of the copter so they could see the Retrotimeship sitting invisible on the ground. After flying over the Salton Sea, whose blue water glimmered weakly in the fading sunlight, they were again over dry land. The screen soon showed the bulk of the Retrotimeship, unseen by the naked eye.

"Speed up, Clark. The Triangle is following us."

"No worries that it'll shoot, Commander. The guns wouldn't dare fire with their venerable master with us."

He typed on the keyboard linked to the Retrotimeship and the big ramp opened up. The oval helicopter came straight down and "floated" onto the carriage that showed up on the screen. Then the carriage slid up the metal ramp and stopped in the hold. The big hatch closed automatically.

The precious hostage, threatened by the disintegrators, entered the rear hold whose doors closed right away. He banged on the steel walls, shouted, ranted and pleaded. His barely audible voice was heard like a whisper by the two officers.

"Let me out! You will be free! I'll shower you with gold!"

Taylor walked up to the door and shouted back, "A little more patience and you'll get out!"

A minute later and the invisible Retrotimeship shot into the purple desert sky as the triangular ship was circling over the area. Its pilots were flabbergasted, wondering how the kidnappers could have just vanished right under their noses. The RT2 was staying only 50 yards over the flying triangle and flying at the same speed. Rudy Clark pressed a button and the hatch of the rear hold opened.

Marli Hyoky, cried out in terror when he felt the metal floor opening under his feet. He dropped like a stone and crashed onto the spaceship.

The RT2 sped off, accelerating through the atmospheric layers to come out into the darkness of outer space where its gravito-magnetic rockets were turned off. At the controls of the time travel mechanism Mark Taylor made a quick mental calculation while working the electronic keyboard.

"We're here in 1378 of the Age of Vrish-Ju, the Messenger of Good. If Avshton was accurate, then Kariven and his friends came into the Past around 2,200 years ago, or 822 years before Vrish-Ju."

He entered the numbers and flipped a switch.

"I hope Tradition wasn't wrong about the dates."

A quiet rumbling vibrated the Retrotimeship. The star-studded space around them turned gray, an opaque gray, with fleeting areas of light, then in a split second the stars were back.

"We should be there," Taylor said, leaving the gravito-magnetic controls to his co-pilot.

The RT2 tilted and headed for Earth to straightened out later and fly horizontally after penetrating the atmospheric layers. It came farther down and on the horizon the pilots saw the west coast of France. Clark was as nervous as his chief when they set course for Paris or rather the area where the city would be later, much later. At reduced speed they came down and stopped over the future valley of Chevreuse, almost exactly where they would find a future Guyancourt.

"There!" Mark Taylor's eyes opened wide as he pointed at an oblong shape in a clearing. "The... the RT1 of Harrington and Streiler!"

Indeed, the tarnished metal rocketship was sitting there, the brother of their own ship but a very worn-out brother, corroded by bad weather. A few miles to the south, in the middle of a wide clearing in the forest, stood a group of wooden and stone houses lined with streets and two big squares.

Seeing that Clark was about to land, Taylor stopped him. "No, it's too late *now*. Just to be sure let's try to send a message without landing."

"RT2 calling RT1. RT2 calling RT1."

A few minutes later the speaker crackled and a trembling, stuttering voice answered, "RT1 to RT2... Lord almighty! Kariven here!"

"Good God," Clark murmured with tears in his eyes. "Kariven! Rudy Clark here with Commander Taylor! I don't see you. Is your viewer broken?"

"For 17 years, Rudy," the anthropologist's voice trembled, weak and old, broken but gentle. "Only the radio works thanks to an emergency generator that we feed with a little badly refined fuel—very badly. My God," he sighed, "We lost all hope a long time ago. And here you are, Rudy, and good old Taylor... Old? Certainly not as old as I am, of course. You can't see me, Rudy, but you can tell how much I've changed by the sound of my voice. 49 years we've been here, free but prisoners of the Past."

"49 years!" Commander Taylor whispered. "And... the others, Kariven?"

"The others?" Kariven's quaky voice stammered. "There's only three of us now. Angelvin, Doniatchka and me. The others died a long time ago. Yuln... seven years ago, killed in an explosion of a boiler being built for our Celtic friends."

"You came here... how long ago exactly? Think carefully, Kariven," Clark was almost begging.

"I've counted the days, Rudy, and I don't need to think about it. We got here 49 years, seven months and 13 days ago, around ten at night... with a fog from hell."

There was a bitter little laugh and he added, as if to himself, "Bad weather, Rudy, like you've never seen in New York or Frisco, truly!"

But Rudy was no longer listening. He had launched the Retrotimeship into the sky and stopped when it was in outer space. Taylor swiftly changed the numbers on the keyboard using the ones that... old man Kariven had just given and a few minutes later the ship was coming back down to Earth, an Earth 49 years, seven months and 13 days younger. Flying over the same area they quickly spotted the shiny ship, radiant in the first rays of the rising sun that was slowly dissipating the morning fog. The RT2 landed silently around 50 yards from its twin brother and the pilots ran down the metal stairs... just when Kariven, Dormoy, Angelvin and their charming wives were stepping down theirs, followed by the engineer Leconte.

"Clark! Taylor!" they shouted in surprise.

One minute later they were hugging one another, giving slaps on the back and friendly pokes in the ribs.

Stupefied, Doniatchka grabbed Commander Taylor by the shoulders. "But... you're crying, Mark. And Rudy, too. But we've only been gone a few days."

"Did you already lose all hope of finding us?" Kariven asked.

Taylor quickly wiped away his tears, embarrassed, and forced himself to smile while speaking in a hoarse voice. "Don't accuse us of being too sensitive, kids. Pack your bags and climb into the RT2 right away. We're heading back to the Present... or to the Future as it were."

"But... we can't abandon the RT1," Kariven said. "Harrington and Streiler, who are resting at the moment, will get it fixed soon enough."

Clark shook his head, "Forget it, Kariven. The RT1 can't be fixed... *here*. You'll never get it up and running."

"Never?" Yuln repeated, probing the minds of the two pilots. All of a sudden she turned pale, shivered and grabbed her husband's arm. "Oh dear," she whispered, scared by the thoughts she had just picked up. "Mark and Rudy are right. Let's not stay here one minute longer. Go wake up Kurt and Red."

While the anthropologist, baffled, went to wake up the two physicists, Dormoy, as troubled as his friends, realized that he had not introduced Leconte to the two officers.

Less than an hour later the castaways of Time, all of them dazed by the hasty departure that felt more like an escape, were together in the cockpit of the RT2. Staring out the concave window of the cockpit they watched sadly as the shiny form of the first Retrotimeship got farther away, abandoned temporarily.

The countryside got gradually farther away, this countryside where the slavery of the human race by a long line of tyrannical despots almost took place. Under the greenery of the forest the frightened Celts, clutching the handles of their big iron swords, crouched down in the high grass. They watched on fearfully as the fantastic "iron bird" soared off and disappeared forever with the demi-gods who would never come back to drag them out of their crude lives.

They would remain primitive for a long time, fighting among the provinces, waging wars, suffering sicknesses that they knew not how to treat. But they would follow the normal path of slow evolution to which they *had to* submit in order to give birth, later, to the race that would create the Retrotimeship and not the triangular spaceships of tyrants.

"Heading for 1961," Commander Taylor announced, activating the time travel mechanism.

"But Taylor," Harrington said, "can't our departure wait a few days?"

"No, Red. No, my friends. You didn't have time to start your work educating the Iron Age men. An admirable work at first but in the future centuries it would turn into rivers of blood and the slavery of all the people on Earth. In a few days you could start this vast project of accelerated evolution that is altruistic in your eyes but disastrous for future humanity, even though you were far from thinking of it. But by leaving now, by *escaping* now, it won't happen. It will never take place. Our escape will cancel the History of a civilization... that will be replaced by ours."

"And ours is really much better than what you were about to give birth to," Clark completed the thought, remembering the suffering endured by the people under the tyrant's yoke.

The words of Vrish-Ju, the Messenger of Good, cited by Dr. Avshton, came back to mind: *Time will deliver them one day.*

Clark shook his head, as if trying to chase away a bad memory, and a radiant smile grew on his face. Taylor had just left the time travel controls and it was up to him now to take control of the RT2 to pilot it back to Earth.

He sped up, straightened the ship in the atmospheric layers and descending lower and lower came out under the cloud cover. He gave a long sigh of relief on seeing the vast extent of Paris, divided by the wandering Seine, and in the middle of which the Eiffel Tower stood proudly.

Afterword

Prisoners of the Past was the last novel featuring Jean Kariven and his friends that Jimmy Guieu wrote. No doubt, the utopia-like Earth of the Earth-Polarian Alliance was too limited a subject to provide good materials for future novels. As mentioned in our introduction, Guieu developed the characters of William Blade and Ronny Baker to continue to explore space opera themes, while Gilles Novak eventually took over the exploration of *X-files*-type phenomena in today's world.

The indomitable Kariven, however, made a recent return under the pen of Frank Schildiner in a number of short stories published in our annual anthology *Tales of the Shadowmen*; these stories also feature elements from the Polarian-Denebian war. They are:

TOTS 5. *The Smoking Mirror*
TOTS 6. *Laurels for the Toff*
TOTS 7. *The Tiny Destroyer*
TOTS 8. *The Death Bird*
TOTS 12. *Ancient Space Lizards and Other Visitors*

Finally, in January 2011, our French sister imprint, Rivière Blanche, published a homage anthology to Jimmy Guieu entitled *Dimension Jimmy Guieu*, edited by Richard D. Nolane. In addition to a translation of *The Smoking Mirror*, it also featured a new Kariven story by French author Thomas Geha entitled *La Ballade de Yuln* [Yuln's Ballad]. The story, however, is not, strictly speaking, in the original continuity, sionce it takes place in 1982, in the rewritten & updated versions of the original novels republished in the 1990s.

Other Fleuve Noir Translations

Black Coat Press has published a fair sampling of Fleuve Noir novels in translation:

Marc Agapit: *Despair*, a screenplay faithfully adapted from an *Angoisse* novel by Jean-Marc & Randy Lofficier (ISBN 978-1-932983-06-7).

G.-J. Arnaud: *The Ice Company*, an award-winning *Anticipation* novel, the first in a long, popular series, translated by Jean-Marc & Randy Lofficier (ISBN 978-1-935558-31-6).

Richard Bessière: *The Gardens of the Apocalypse* (which also includes *The Seven Rings of Rhea*) two *Anticipation* novels translated by Brian Stableford (ISBN 978-1-935558-68-2), followed by *The Masters of Silence* (which also includes *They Came from the Dark*), two more *Anticipation* novels translated by Michael Shreve (ISBN 978-1-61227-297-9).

André Caroff: The ever-popular series of 18 *Madame Atomos* novels from the *Angoisse* imprint, collected in nine omnibus volumes, the first translated by Brian Stableford; the others by Michael Shreve (ISBNs: 1: 978-1-935558-41-5; 2: 978-1-61227-018-0; 3: 978-1-61227-030-2; 4: 978-1-61227-069-2; 5: 978-1-61227-087-6; 6: 978-1-61227-119-4; 7: 978-1-61227-157-6; 8: 978-1-61227-223-8; 9: 978-1-61227-259-7).

P.-J. Hérault: *The Clone Rebellion*, an *Anticipation* novel translated by Michael Shreve (ISBN 978-1-61227-385-3).

Gérard Klein: *The Mote in Time's Eye*, an *Anticipation* novel translated by C.J. Richards (ISBN 978-1-935558-48-4).

Maurice Limat: *Mephista*, the translation by Michael Shreve of three *Angoisse* novels starring private eye Teddy Verano and the eponymous female incarnation of evil (ISBN 978-1-61227-434-8).

Kurt Steiner (pseudonym of André Ruellan): *Ortog* (which also includes *Ortog and the Darkness*), two *Anticipation* novels translated by Brian Stableford (ISBN 978-1-935558-28-6).

Pierre Pelot: *The Child Who Walked on the Sky* (which also includes *What if Butterflies Cheat?*), two *Anticipation* novels translated by Michael Shreve (ISBN 978-1-61227-107-1).

For the record, one should also mention Pierre Barbet, whose Fleuve Noir novels *The Napoleons of Eridanus, The Emperor of Eridanus, Games Psyborgs Play, Baphomet's Meteor, The Enchanted Planet, The Joan Of Arc Replay* and *Stellar Crusade* were translated and published by DAW Books.